TWO DOORS, NO MAP

WALDLUST SERIES
BOOK TWO

Two DOORS, NO MAP

TED MINKINOW

TWO DOORS, NO MAP
WALDLUST SERIES #2

Cover and Interior Design by We Got You Covered Book Design
WWW.WEGOTYOUCOVEREDBOOKDESIGN.COM

ISBN: 978-1-7362342-9-7

FOR NIKKI

ONE

THE BEST IDS are the ones you percolate over several decades—a dodgy doctor signs a birth certificate, and when that paper celebrates its eighteenth birthday, you apply for your passport. That's how I got my American documents, and how I've held the citizenship of many countries. But I'm getting ahead of myself...best to start with the exciting stuff.

Fifteen minutes of shuffling uphill from the train station through the May sludge of snow and ice, and I stood at the doors of the US Forces Commissary in Wiesbaden, Germany. That's where I work... bagging groceries and hauling them to customers' cars. For tips. It was forty-five minutes before opening, so Captain Tickles, the commissary officer, activated the switch that let me in. He checked his watch as I walked past.

I said, "Good morning, sir."

Rumor says that Tickles has been passed over for promotion to major so many times that he's the oldest captain in the history of the U.S. Army. People also say the only reason the brass allows him to stick around is that his sister is married to a Senator. So, Captain Tickles isn't likely to be leaving Wiesbaden anytime soon. Of course, the

Senator might retire or lose the next election. If either of those happens, I suspect Tickles would disappear within days.

It's the little things that give us hope.

Tickles said, "Only forty-three minutes early, soldier."

You'd be surprised how many Americans over here covet the bagging jobs. Teens to retirees. It's an easy gig, a way to legally remain in Germany, and the tips are enough to get by on. I don't need the money, but the anonymous existence flying legally under the radar of both the U.S. and German governments? Priceless. I offered up the only answer Captain Tickles expected to hear.

"I will focus, sir."

Whatever that means.

I show up for work three-quarters of an hour early and Tickles acts like I've deserted my post under enemy fire.

"See that you do, soldier," and then, "Carry on."

My dismissal. I headed over to the baggers' area and mumbled something under my breath about Captain Tickles as I shed my heavy coat and hung it on the peg. Grumbling tends to impede a guy's eyesight and I didn't notice Sister Christian until she already had me in her morning hug.

Not sensing Sister Christian would be like walking past Marylyn Monroe and failing to notice how she fought to keep her white dress from blowing up around her ears as she stood over the air shaft. Yes, Sister Christian is *that* hot...and probably also that old. Nobody except Pops knows her real age—not that she's ever provided a fake one or that any of us have asked the oafish question. Three things everyone *does* know about Sister Christian: she's smokin' to the eyes, warm to the touch, and she hides it all under her loose-fitting hippy clothes.

Not wanting to profane the rituals of the bagger gang, I responded to Sister Christian's chaste good morning hug, and she didn't seem to mind the extra squeeze. Well, at least not at first.

The two of us even had a moment last winter. It happened in my kitchen, after she and the rest of the gang found out about my secret. No, not the pornographic snaps of a Hungarian warrior woman that show up on my smartphone. I'm talking about my other secret. The *big* one.

She'd said something about how her life might have gone differently had I met her years before. Back then, I thought she meant a happier life. Now? I'm not so sure. I mean, most chicks say their life would be better if they *hadn't* met me. Technically, I was of legal age and available in the 80's. I'm still available, but I also look like any other nineteen-year-old. If I could age myself in super-fast most motion? I might do that for Sister Christian. But I can't…it doesn't work like that.

That particular encounter put a damper on that night and thinking about it still makes me grind my teeth. A bad night for me turned into a worse next day for Sister Christian and my other bagger gang friends. They ended up suspended in a medieval painting of hell.

Long story, and obviously they got better.

Back again to the good-morning-hug. As Sister Christian fulcrumed her body free of me, I caught sight of Captain Tickles interrogating his next victim. Bonnie Prince McDonald. His real name is Vince, but we thought it needed jazzing up because it doesn't sound sufficiently Scottish. As I recall, the real Bonnie Prince wasn't Scottish either, but hey, it's still a cool handle.

Captain Tickles was glancing at his watch and the Bonnie Prince was looking at his own wrist where a watch *should* be. Heck, the Prince couldn't see Big Ben if he was tied to its minute hand because he's a bit eyesight challenged. None of us know why he refuses to acquire glasses.

I mean, his eyesight is *so* bad the Bonnie Prince tried to load the general's wife's groceries into the engine compartment. The gang did give him style points for managing to cram all eight bags and two cartons of soft drinks into a space the rest of us bagging pros couldn't fit a napkin into, but the lecture he gave the woman about cleaning the junk out of her trunk?

Epic.

Captain Tickles ended his pontifications when spied potential infiltrators outside—students walking through the parking lot toward Wiesbaden High School—and he ran out the door to confront them in a military manner. The Bonnie Prince walked over to our usual corner, hung his jacket over another bagger's head, and sat down on the fire extinguisher.

We encountered Captain Tickles only one more time that day, so the remaining baggers got through the doors with no hassles…which meant this was one job where it didn't pay to be early. David Smith—Watanabe—was the next member our bagger clique to show up, and Jesus walked through the door as Pops initiated the preflight systems check of his conveyor belt.

Not the walk-on-water Jesus, but Jesus Rodriquez. J-Rod often spoke with a Latino-gangsta, East LA accent. I mean, he didn't speak Spanish at all, unless you consider ordering a burrito at the food center a marker for fluency. J-Rod thinks the fake accent gets him better tips. As far as his real voice, it sounds more like West Texas twang than a boy from the hood. He also speaks fluent German because his mom is one. I've met her once…one of the sweetest ladies I've ever run across in my two thousand years.

David Smith is two generations removed from his Korean roots, and when he asked us to call him Watanabe—The Last Samurai actor—everyone pointed out that Samurais were Japanese, not Korean. We brushed him off until that night I alluded to already…when something bad happened because of my big secret. Bottom line? Dave "Watanabe" Smith stood with me that night like a true ninja.

4

As we talked our small talk and waited for our workday to begin, I glimpsed Super Rumble waiting outside. I mean, it was hard to miss her because she stood so close to the doors that the fog from her breath vaguely reminded me of that city in Spain where they set the bulls free once a year.

Here's another secret for those of you who've never worked in customer service or hospitality. We assign regular customers with nicknames. Super Rumble shows up first thing every morning, and then again near closing time. And, when I say every morning and evening, I mean it literally.

She wore the same neon-pink stretch athletic pants she wore the day before. I remembered them because I recalled thinking about how they looked on the verge of total system failure as I rolled her bags of groceries before quitting time. Not a lovely thought, and I managed to tear my eyes away from Super Rumble's fashion choices before the image permanently burned itself into my optic nerves…or before the shapely, powder-white left cheek left strategically exposed hypnotized me into becoming the next of her nightly conquests.

I heard the door swish open and checked my watch. Still three minutes before the hour, so heads would roll if Tickles found out someone started the attack before Zero-Hour. But when I looked up, I saw it was the Captain who'd opened the doors…and it wasn't Tennille I saw walking beside him.

She looked more like Dorothy the Dinosaur's sister than a famous rock star. Her *big, big* sister. It wasn't so much the way she was dressed—a tent of a Marylin Manson t-shirt over gray cotton gym pants—as it was her bulk. I'm a guy who adores most women who make any effort at all to look feminine. Not this chick.

Her arms would have made her the Vegas-betting-odds-favorite for the world arm-wrestling championships, and if she ever decided to sell her body hair to rug makers in Tehran? Well, bagging groceries would be entirely unnecessary in her life.

But I'm wasting too much time on her good features.

Up top, our new colleague sported a face that could command abstinence out of an all-male colony of sex-starved gorillas. The girl was square-faced, greasy-haired, and had colossal shoulders that were only slightly broader than her waist.

As Captain Tickles navigated Big Bertha past us, Vince the Bonnie Prince McDonald said something about one of us guys needing to go back to the men's room to check our wipe. He had a point because I picked up the odor of rotten eggs as Tickles paraded her past.

"Hey homie," J-Rod said to me, "I think that big chick squeak one out when she go by."

He waved a hand in front of his face in case I didn't understand. Even Sister Christian wore a slacked-jawed look of surprise until she caught me glancing her way and she reset her face to that serene, tolerant smile thing she did when she didn't want us guys to know something flummoxed her as much as it did us.

"Be nice, guys," Sister Christian said. "I'm sure she's a wonderful person."

Why do women always mention nice personalities or cute smiles or some other pointless baloney when they catch a guy looking in horror at a woolly mammoth? They shame you for *your* honest thoughts0pp[-=, and yet they readily join in the criticism of a woman they think more beautiful than themselves…or better dressed.

J-Rod said, "I be nice," and added in a low voice, "Or da bitch shank me."

Customers came shuffling in and we took up our positions. That meant J-Rod, Sister Christian, and I didn't move, and Watanabe and the Bonnie Prince stepped up to Pop's conveyer belt. Both would pack the groceries and load the wire cart, and then one of the two would roll with the customer while another of us would stand up to help pack.

It would go on like that all day. The bagger staff was one short since Sarah Arias—the hottest female ever to put all the cold stuff in the same plastic bag, as well as the world's heaviest chain-smoker—quit. Turns out she was my guardian angel and had to resign. For real. I saw Sarah Arias in my mind and then looked over to Bertha Behemoth four lines away.

From one extreme to the next.

Bertha caught me glancing at her and held the stare long enough to make me suspect she was trying to tell me something. Like maybe, if I kept looking at her, she'd hammer my face to cream. I don't know how long I remained standing there slack-jawed when J-Rod elbowed me in the back.

"Hey homie," he said. "Go ahead and ask her out so we get back to work, man."

I swallowed a mouthful of vomit and returned my focus to Pop's belt. My momentary inattention to duty caused the groceries to pile up at the bagger end, and the old guy paused his scanning to take a pointed look at the disorganized mess that was already supposed to be on the wire cart. Pops resumed his beeping thing and the goods piled up even more.

In my peripheral vision, I saw Bertha launch her own run behind a young mother holding a toddler's hand. As luck would have it, J-Rod loaded my last bag, and I followed a soldier and his wife out the door at about the same time.

We halted at a dingy blue sedan that would have cost three times the soldier's annual salary when it was new. Fifteen years on the Autobahn had taken its toll and to the point I hoped the soldier and his wife rotated back to the USA before the next annual inspection.

I arranged the bags as the guy handed them to me. Most customers stand back and let me do the lifting, but this guy chatted amiably while we worked.

Everything made it into the trunk OK, and when I turned to say goodbye, he slipped a ten into my hand. Most customers tip five, max, but a soldier? They tend toward insanely generous…even though they can least afford extravagance.

I thanked him and felt more than a little guilty, though I wouldn't humiliate him by handing it back. Despite a budget so tight that the soldier and his family likely ate instant noodles several meals a week, he'd honored my effort.

Charitable actions make me smile, and I did as I watched the couple drive away. The happy glow was interrupted by a wheezing voice from behind.

She said, "Vampire."

TWO

AT FIRST, I thought someone had double-parked their yak along the sidewalk, but as my eyes focused, I changed my mind. Yaks don't come as large as the person who stood beside me. The new bagger. And, despite the close proximity, her features seemed ill-defined. I mean, to describe Bertha as unattractive would be doing her a great kindness, and I suspected the frantic squeaking that erupted in my mind was my cowardly libido fleeing for cover.

Think about an artist rendering a portrait in charcoal…in this case, a Neanderthal throwback sporting the head of a warthog. Now, intentionally smear the charcoal face, and you'll end up with the indistinct features I saw.

I whispered my response.

"Vampire?"

My communications skills were stuck in a season of understated overstatement. She'd said *vampire*, all right, and I understood what the word meant. Given my condition, who wouldn't? My one-word idiot's sentence didn't seem to faze Miss Jurassic. Perhaps she'd heard of me. She decided to give me another chance to practice my arsenal of witty repertoire and continued.

"I'm in trouble."

Uh-oh.

I did that thing all guys do when some chick walks up and lays that monumental line on them: I frantically cycled through the mental rolodex of the women I'd recently encountered. Once I managed to get a rope around my runaway heart, I zeroed in on the salient fact.

I'd never been *THAT* drunk.

I said, "What do you mean?"

Yes, I understood English. No, I didn't know why this wrecking ball of a human would want to let me in on her secret.

"Not here," she said, and she began pushing her wire cart back to the commissary.

She paused for a second and glanced back at me.

I'm supposed to follow.

I considered doing the European soccer player thing...you know collapsing onto the pavement to roll around gripping my hamstrings, but to what end? If Captain Tickles saw me like that, he'd suspect a chemical attack and inject my heart with two vials of atropine from an official, US Army combat auto-injector.

So, I caught up with her.

Something about the woman did ring a bell. I'd heard that sort of wheezy speech before, and not too long ago. It took a few paces of bouncing the metal cart over the asphalt before the mental light illuminated.

"Mestephos?"

The woman stopped so abruptly that even my vampire reflexes couldn't keep me from running my cart into her monumental backside. I worried for a second about how much Captain Tickles would dock my pay if I bent the stainless steel, but that was trivial compared to who I suspected stood within an arm's reach.

"Don't use my name," she/he said. "*Ever.*"

The woman in front of me was no lady.

Why do these things always happen on a Friday? I mean, I live for Friday night beers with the bagger gang, and I crave lounging around my flat in my underwear on Saturdays and Sundays. The previous disaster this behemoth got me involved in ruined an entire weekend.

"What the hell?"

Mestephos said, "Exactly."

And why wouldn't he? He was a demon, after all.

The relationship between Mestephos and me followed that love/hate routine so typical of romance novels these days. He'd love to eat the living flesh off my screaming body, and I hated him. Normal stuff. The last time we'd crossed paths he'd taken a few bites out of my soft parts and was on his way to eating my leg like an ear of corn before my bagger friends managed to distract him.

Once I regained my footing, I'd ripped his face off.

Later, he'd drawn me into some alternate dimension that coexists with our day-to-day earth. The portal for that vacation spot sat at the side-entrance to the cathedral in Aachen, and his alternate version of that place was a huge dark space that engulfed me in a cocktail of dread comprised of equal parts depression, confusion, and the helpless sense that you'll never escape the place.

Think IKEA, and you understand the context.

I've not returned to that cathedral since, and for more reasons than the bit about it being an entrance to the depths of hell. No need to go into my indiscretions that included damaging a thousand-year-old artifact and robbing the grave of a legendary German hero because you can read about it on the internet...check the news sites and then move on to those run by conspiracy theorists. I suspected somebody might recognize me or my bagger friends, so I've steered clear of Aachen and made sure they drank enough on Friday nights to take the glow off Saturday morning tours.

It was naïve to think I could close the book on that serious act of buffoonery. If I've learned one lesson over the last two thousand years, it's that the past always returns for another bite. And there stood Exhibit A. No Face dressed in drag.

Mestephos. No Face. Different names for the same demon. I'd redubbed him No Face after tearing off his face. Full disclosure: No Face did allow me passage back to the human dimension after I put a crowbar in the spokes of a huge bad-guy plan. He also helped me in another, more personal way, that resulted in saving the lives of some German police.

It's a long story.

Lest you think that dealing with demons is all butterflies and bumblebees, everything comes with a price...a tab that will always dwarf whatever small benefit you gained from the deal. And there stood No Face in the Wiesbaden Commissary parking lot. Time to pay the piper.

"OK," I said. "What do you prefer I call you?"

No Face responded in an instant, which told me this wasn't an off-the-cuff decision. A new name to go with his new job, and he'd put some planning behind it. A demon with an agenda. Who'd have thought?

"Donna," he said.

"Donna?"

"Yes," he wheezed. "Goes well with my eyes."

Uh, right.

I didn't ask because I didn't want to know. I glanced behind us and saw we were blocking traffic.

"Get going," I said, and I quickly rolled my cart to the side.

No Face followed with his, and we made it to the sidewalk and then back into the building without further conversation. I had nothing to say anyway, because my brain was doing the run-at-full-speed-and-arrive-nowhere routine. I'd shown up at the commissary expecting the normal Friday drudgery and found the physical incarnation of my metaphorical personal demon instead. In case anyone's wondering, I've had time to think about and therefore perfect that last line.

No Face returned to his bagging group, I returned to mine.

Watanabe said, "Meet the new girl?"

I looked hard into his face to detect any trace of a smile. If my Korean buddy was suggesting anything about Donna—No Face—and me, then he was about to get a chance to use some of his fake ninja skills. I responded to Watanabe in a tone I hoped would cut out further exploration down this path.

"No."

Like I said, it was my season of understated overstatement.

"I see you rappin' with her, homie," said J-Rod. "Gonna ask her out?"

J-Rod, on the other hand, knew I wouldn't do anything physical and he didn't care a bit about my guy-feelings. And, if his smile grew any broader, it would reach that size your mom always warned about…the grotesque face that would become permanent.

I was thinking of a good comeback to J-Rod when Sister Christian said, "Her name is Donna."

"As in Madonna?" said J-Rod. "She be like a virgin touched never, dude."

Sister Christian never laughed at a joke told at someone else's expense. *My* expense, in this example. That doesn't mean anyone else had that problem.

"Why you not laughing, homie," J-Rod said. "Don't mean to dis your babe or nothing."

More guffaws and this time Sister Christian *did* join in. Evidently, that rule about not seeing humor at another's expense didn't apply when that *other* happened to be me. It's always best to quit responding in these sorts of situations.

Bonnie Prince McDonald left his empty cart in front of the lady's restroom door, and he sat down in a chair already occupied by Watanabe.

He said, "Sorry, ma'am."

Watanabe pushed the Prince off him and stood up.

"There," he said, "it's all yours."

The Prince waited a moment and said under his breath, "Bitch."

We'd seen him walk out with Super Rumble, so nobody thought he was referring to Watanabe. We'd all been there…sometimes twice a day. The lady usually bought enough to feed an expedition to Everest…or maybe one to her bedroom, Sherpas and all. It took forever to bag the groceries, and super-human effort to balance them through the parking lot and then load them into a car that couldn't comfortably seat the tooth fairy. For that gargantuan bagger expertise, she always tipped five cents per bag, nothing on drink cartons. The five cents capped out at ten bags. More than that, you still got half a buck.

At first Sister Christian volunteered for the Super Rumble runs, but the rest of us decided it wasn't fair. Now we rotate. Why she always chose our line out of the several available? Dark karma, I guess.

The Bonnie Prince sat there grumbling and Sister Christian took her place in the batter's box. J-Rod should have been on deck—helping Sister Christian bag—but he'd run off to the men's room to pay the rent on his morning coffee. Sister Christian motioned me over and I began putting the stuff in bags.

She leaned in close and whispered, "You didn't laugh."

"Didn't what?"

"Donna," she said. "You didn't laugh at J-Rod's joke."

I stopped with a can of tomatoes half in the bag.

"If you're implying that I have the hots for her."

Sister Christian smiled and spoke in her placating tone.

"Of course not," she said. "I just thought it was sweet of you. You know, not making fun of another person just because you found her unattractive."

"I found her what?"

A brontosaurus in a negligee would look better than that demon.

Another smile from Sister Christian.

"I just wanted to say I thought it was darling the way you stood up for Donna."

"Wait a minute," I said. "Not joining in the humor is not the same as..."

"Stop," she said. "I just wanted congratulate you."

"For what?"

"For growing up."

No need to insult me.

I'd done nothing of the sort. I didn't laugh because I knew Donna wasn't a Donna at all. And No Face needing a favor? That scared the dickens out of me. But if Sister Christian mistook distraction for gallantry, who was I to argue?

I probed the depths of her gratitude by attempting a congratulatory hug.

No dice.

We did the bagger routine until just before quitting time. Customer traffic on Fridays usually comes on strong just after work and then slowly peters to a trickle an hour before closing. No Face waddled over in that bagger's time between times.

My back was turned, so I didn't notice him standing behind me...at least not until Prince McDonald accused me of floating an air biscuit. I detected it too, and I turned to rebound an accusation back at the Prince…the smeller's the feller. But there stood No Face, like a block of stinky granite some demented sculptor had abandoned.

He used that fake female-orangutan voice when he said, "I will depart with you."

J-Rod looked on the verge of saying something, so before he could I whispered, "If you enjoy eating with teeth, you should consider keeping your mouth shut."

J-Rod swallowed hard.

Just what in the heck did No Face mean? Depart to where? Surely, he didn't think I was taking him home with me. Not in a thousand years. No way. No how.

He said, "To your home."

Sister Christian was standing several feet away doing the typical chick thing—which means she was pretending not to listen as she soaked in everything we said. I saw her eyebrows raise a bit when she heard No Face invite himself to my place, and she gave up pretending and walked over to participate.

"Donna," Sister Christian said, "If you need somewhere to stay for a few nights while you get situated here, you're more than welcome at my place."

Why do women always use ten meaningless words for every one they need? All she had to say is, "You can stay at my place." I'm ashamed to admit I thought about letting it happen that way. But only for a second or two.

Of course, I didn't want one of the sexiest baggers alive to take a demon home with her. I bet you're wondering if I'd allow her to take a vampire home.

My fantasies are made of such things.

But a demon? No way.

I said, "It's OK."

Crap! What have I done?

You'd have thought someone muted the soundtrack. Everything went quiet. Even Pops paused the scanning to turn his head in our direction. Typical grocery store noise resumed with his next beep, and it was only my friends who stood silent. Funny thing, my own words shocked me as much as they did anyone else.

You know how you sometimes go with your gut feeling? Well, I didn't, and as soon as the words left my traitorous lips, I felt like asking Watanabe for one of his fake-ninja kicks.

To my balls.

The pain of two crushed eggs would be a joy compared to the notion that I'd just invited the most grotesque cross-dresser in the history of the universe to move in with me.

Except for Watanabe—who'd graduated from Harvard business school two summers ago and was taking time off before joining the grind—we'd all known each other for a few years, though we'd solidified into a clique the previous year. In that time, I'd invited the gang to my flat only once. More accurately, I'd *never* invited them to my flat, but they showed up once when Sarah Arias texted them all to meet up at my place.

The gang ended up suspended in a demon-rendered painting depicting the tortures of hell, and I came away within a stolen bag of bones after almost being consumed alive by No Face.

Yeah, the night could have gone better.

And it all started at my place in Bad Homburg. Since then, we'd resumed our Beer Fridays in Wiesbaden, and nobody ever mentioned meeting at my place again.

I didn't expect gratitude from No Face, the word isn't in the demon lexicon, so I wasn't disappointed when he snorted like a bull rhino gulping for air. He turned to complete what might have been his first day ever spent serving the clock. And as he walked away, I noticed a huge bulge in his back pocket.

One day on the job and his wad of tips dwarfed mine.

"Well, homie," J-Rod said. "At least she have a huge set of lungs."

Was J-Rod trying to make me feel better about my decision? Gosh did I hate him at that moment.

"Her chest give Super Rumble a run for her money."

Sister Christian didn't say a word as we performed the daily closing ritual. I think she might have been thinking of ways to retract her earlier statement. You know, the bit congratulating me for my maturity. Did she really think I intended to bump uglies with the ultimate big ugly?

I glanced over at No Face and saw him waxing the floor with one of those huge, military-grade, electric stainless-steel buffers. The thing weighed a ton, but No Face had no problem moving it around and getting the floor to shine with a sheen I'd never seen. Double impressive, when you consider he'd not plugged it in.

Captain Tickles returned from the command bunker—what he called his office—to gather the entire bagging corps for his typical, incongruous end-of-day speech. That's the one where he praised our courage in facing nearly insurmountable odds. One of the guys had rolled his full cart over another bagger's foot during the noon rush, and the dude went to the hospital for X-Rays. I think that's why the Captain added a new twist by extolling us to remember the wounded and do our best on Saturday to prove worthy of their sacrifice.

Were those tears I saw glistening in his eyes?

We did the hoorah shout and Captain Tickles dismissed us. The things I'm willing to do for tips.

Sister Christian said, "Coming tonight?"

Two words, many potential meanings. I decided to play stupid. Mostly because I'm a natural.

"Why wouldn't I?"

Sister Christian gave a hard look over my shoulder. I turned to see No Face picking up the shelving in aisle one so that he could buff underneath. That's what you get when a demon tries to act human. Two tons of canned goods in the air and a shiny floor.

"Oh," I said. "Donna."

"Yes, Donna," Sister Christian said. "Aren't you two going to be busy tonight?"

No clue why Sister Christian sounded miffed. Did everyone *really* think I was putting the moves on No Face? I promised myself I'd conduct an audit of my last few months to discover what I'd done to completely obliterate my reputation.

"Busy?" I said, as I saw No Face make it to aisle three.

Watanabe came to my rescue. Kind of reminded me of how he'd returned to certain death in a plywood tunnel a few months ago to stand beside me and fight the demons.

He said, "We can meet you in Bad Homburg."

Of course they could. That would solve everything. I thought about the five of us—six, now that No Face would tag along—sitting down to a few brews at one of my favorite pubs. My bagger friends. No Face.

Actually, that would solve nothing.

I'd just end up getting my friends involved in yet another, sure to be deadly, supernatural shenanigan.

I said, "I don't think..."

Sister Christian broke in with, "See you in two hours."

"Where?" said J-Rod.

He'd dropped his Latino gangsta shtick, and I tried to think of a way to fend off my friends and excuse myself from our Friday night routine. But the more I worked out the possibilities, the more I knew I'd end up looking like I wanted private time with Donna/No Face. The old two's company, three's a crowd cliché.

My pride's taken horrendous beatings over the past two thousand years, but I didn't think I could recover from them believing I wanted to find out if No Face's bra snapped in the front or in the back.

"Same café as last time."

"We'll find it," J-Rod said. "Two hours."

"Make it an hour," I said, and handed each of them a one-hundred Euro note.

We'd all gotten over my I'm-just-a-poor-bagger-like-you routine after they discovered I'd amassed somewhat of a fortune in two thousand years. They just didn't know how much because I'm careful not to flash my cash. Except for my flat, I have no other expenses, and I keep it that way to avoid attracting attention.

I needed some time alone with No Face to discover what this was all about. At the same time, I didn't see how I could ever face the crew again if they thought I'd spent the night doing Jamaica in the moonlight with the transvestite Buffer Queen over on aisle ten.

It would take each of them a while to meet at Bad Homburg. Getting home, freshening up, and then catching public transportation would take at least two hours…walking, waiting on the bus, bus ride to the Wiesbaden train station, train ride to Frankfurt, train ride to Bad Homburg.

A taxi would cut that by three-quarters. But thanks to the EU, you can only afford the exorbitant taxi rates if can also afford a car. Five hundred Euros to provide each transportation that allowed us to meet up earlier. A pittance when pride is involved.

Everyone put on their jackets and we walked as a group to the door. I smelled that rotten egg odor in trail, and I knew without looking that

No Face was back there. I didn't get the normal good-night hug from Sister Christian, but the rest of the guys acted normal as we did the see-you-later thing.

Had Sister Christian convinced herself that I was romantically inclined toward Donna? If you add up *all* the guys that ever lived? I doubted *that* level of desperation wouldn't show up in any of them... from cave drawings to present.

Donna/No Face and I separated from the gang at the parking lot and we headed down the hill. Morning slush had turned to evening ice, and I thought if I were lucky, I'd slip and break my neck before anyone might see me with her/him.

But I didn't slip, and it wouldn't have ended my shame anyhow. Broken necks don't kill vampires. Almost nothing does. I'd started the day looking forward to Beer Friday, and I'd ended the evening going home with a foul supernatural entity who'd attempted to munch down on my flesh on two occasions...and who was, at that moment, dressed in drag.

Some days it doesn't pay to get out of bed.

No way I'd squire that hunk of wasted gravity into a taxi. Public transportation all the way, and perhaps I could lose No Face in the process. No such luck, as it turned out. I even had to buy his ticket. Can you imagine a demon wearing fake human skin standing in the typical spitting spring rain and trying to figure out a German ticket machine? He'd think he'd gone to hell.

It surprised me that people didn't give us a wide birth. I predicted I'd see the Germans finally meeting their match as they tried to race around No Face for that final open chair. But no. Everything was normal on the crowded train. No Face even looked slightly intimidated by the German experience until some off-duty laborer stood up to offer his seat.

And, when this guy flirted with No Face? You can bet I thanked heaven that I'd skipped lunch. An equally-sickening ingredient for the trip was the way No Face radiated an ungodly, demon odor that enveloped the car with the suffocating stench of a malfunctioning sewer clogged by a million rotting disposable diapers.

If every challenge also represents an opportunity, I thought scanning faces for reactions to the repulsive attack on the interior environment might provide entertainment for the twenty-minute ride. Yeah, I can be perverse sometimes.

But once again, no dice.

Nobody seemed to notice…no reactions at all. They *had* to notice. Why those people worked so hard to *pretend* they weren't nosy and thereby to ruin what little fun the situation offered? You tell me.

Donna/No Face sat down next to some German grandma and the old lady kept nudging the demon toward the aisle. The old bat wanted her half, by gosh, and her half she was going to have. No Face ended up with one enormous butt cheek in the chair and the other one hanging out in the aisle…touching the floor.

We made it to Frankfurt like that and I decided I'd seen enough. Rather than switching trains and running the chance of repeating the same disgusting visuals, I navigated No Face out of the station and hailed a cab.

The driver spoke good English, and he insisted Donna/No Face sit up front with him. To each his own, I guess. I helped No Face shoehorn into a space that was never designed to house Moby Dick.

Once we got moving, the driver actually asked me if No Face was my friggin' sister. My adamant denial seemed to please him, because he spent the entire twenty-minute drive to Bad Homburg explaining every bit of local history he could shake out of his obviously-dented brain.

No Face wheezed and grunted at all the right times. I think he might have thrown out a few belches too, but I couldn't tell for sure because everything that comes out of his demon mouth—and his size 30X demon butt, I assumed—smelled the same. We pulled up to the Victorian house that held my flat. I got out before No Face opened his door, and it looked for a wild moment as if the driver intended to whisk Donna away from all of *this*.

No such luck, so I opened his door, and the most eligible bachelorette in Germany stepped out. The shock absorbers screamed in relief, and I had to jump back to avoid getting clocked in the chin as the car, now free of its enormous load, bounced into the air.

The ride cost fifty euros. That's about sixty-five bucks. For twenty minutes. No wonder the governments in Europe were failing. I'd seen it all before. A little different each time…sometimes the rich robbed the poor and sometimes the poor robbed the rich. It always ended the same. War.

With that happy thought echoing in my mind, I walked toward the back door. That's the one Herr Doktor allows the tenants to use. He and the Frau usually hang out on the ground floor to monitor everything that went on around their own little Third Reich. I mean, you never can tell when an unauthorized vehicle might pull into the parking lot, so they remain ever vigilant.

Thing is, they spend more time trying to determine what I'm up to than they do breathing. Germans are process-oriented people. We weren't like that two thousand years ago, but trust me, our descendants' gene pool ventured far enough down the detour to the point they could put a piece of coal between their butt cheeks and squeeze out a diamond. Survival of the fittest?

Back to my landlord and his maybe-but-I'm-not-sure wife. I didn't see them outside, so I assumed they'd moved indoors for the evening. The usual strong odor of stale nicotine hit me when I walked through the entryway and I stopped for a second to see if it camouflaged secondhand smoke of the fresher kind. Like maybe a landlord ambush.

I stood for a moment of indecision…not sure whether No Face and his unflushed toilet cologne was what I detected or if it was Herr Doktor's breath that made the stairway smell like the entryway to the only head on a World War II aircraft carrier. It turned out to be Herr Doktor, because I found him standing on the first landing… pretending to polish an electrical outlet that had been dead longer than Abraham Lincoln.

And where you saw the doctor…

I caught a glimpse of Frau Nosey halfway up the next landing as she swept the carpet with a hand broom. The faker. Stereotypes claim Germans are the most fastidious people in Europe. That one's a safe bet, unless your horse happens to be Frau CampGuard.

But then, maybe she isn't *really* German…maybe she started life in another country, volunteered for the SS during the occupation, and fled to Germany ahead of the advancing Red Army. Why do I think that? Well, in addition to a personality that could add a greater sense of hopelessness to a torture chamber, when I moved into my flat it looked like Genghis Khan and his horde had beaten a hasty retreat out of it a few moments before. And they'd left their dead behind, because I cleaned up more dust motes and bug bodies than you'd expect to find upon opening some Pharaoh's lost tomb in Egypt.

Herr Doktor's mouth fell open when his eye caught sight of me exhorting Donna/No Face up the stairs. I suppose a bridle would have helped, but Henry Ford had convinced me to sell all my horse gear. We stopped on the first landing beside Herr Doktor and I said hello. The old goat only had eyes for Donna/No Face because he grabbed her/his hand, then looked at me and said,

"And who have you brought down the stairs."

I didn't bother correcting him on his English and I almost said, "None of your business." But I ended up saying nothing at all because Donna/No Face stepped forward and took Herr Doktor's outstretched hand. Not a good idea for Herr Doktor, but I decided to allow this to progress to wherever it might go.

No Face wheezed, "Donna."

If I could remove memories from my mind with a magic wand, then I would have immediately dismissed what came next.

Herr Doktor popped up into that rigid, Hessian pose you see on the film noirs...the thing the tuxedoed leading man does before he pulls the damsel onto the waltz floor. My landlord then bowed and planted a perfunctory smooch in the center of Donna/No Face's outstretched paw.

I stood in shock as Donna/No Face threw out a few lines in wheezy German and Herr Doktor grinned and babbled back at her.

Well, not her at all. *Him*. And not a real him, either. A demon. I didn't even try to figure out the deal with older German dudes. I mean, Donna/No Face garnered more date night requests in one hour than I'd managed in three months...and only if I counted offers from chicks who wanted to spend the kind evening with me that comes with a fee afterward. Seemed the word was out that King Kong had fallen off the building and everyone wanted a shot at his widow.

Frau NoseHairs trundled down the stairs to exchange a few, crisp German sentences with Donna/No Face. It sounded like that fake-friendly thing women do with each other when one thinks the other might be impressing her man. Really? And Herr Doktor was working it. Charm oozed out of him like the black stuff from a rotten tomato. And boy was Frau Rhino getting pissed. If you forced me to choose between the Frau and Donna/No Face? I'd kill you and leave.

I interrupted the clown show with, "Gotta go."

And we did. Because if I didn't get away from this looney sight in the next few seconds, I ran a serious risk of ripping out my own eyeballs for the sheer relief it would bring. Donna/No Face turned to plod up the stairs toward my flat, and it concerned me that he seemed familiar with where I lived. That left me alone with Herr Doktor and Frau Terror.

Maybe-wife gave me that scathing kind of look that says, "You did this on purpose," and then she waddled down the stairs to clean the animal bones out of her lair. Herr Doktor didn't say anything until after we both heard the downstairs door open and then slam shut. Fun in store for him in Doktorville. I almost felt sorry for the old gaffer.

Almost.

Because Herr Doktor leaned close and whispered, "Your new girlfriend impresses me."

"Huh?"

"Mein compliments," Herr Doktor said, and he turned to walk down the stairs to face whatever hell Frau SaggyKnees was cooking up for him.

Served him right for trying to snake another guy's date.

Uh, date?

I smacked my own head. Hard.

No Face waited for me by my door, and I unlocked it and led him inside. Karl, the incontinent ghost dog, had heard the commotion outside and ran at us in joyous anticipation of a new person to love on. He launched himself into the air at No Face, and halfway through his love-trajectory, Karl must have gotten a good look—or smell—at the demon.

Poor little guy did that doggie back-pedaling thing in the air and ended up flying through No Face's leg. He hit the floor and decomposed into a rotting dog carcass on the spot. It would be at least an hour before I again saw the grinning idiot's look on his panting face.

I led No Face to the living room, and I saw Helmet standing beside the computer. Yeah, right, as if I didn't just catch him surfing the net. He's my other ghost-roommate—a WW2 German soldier who claims he can't speak or move things. The dead German glanced at No Face and then took a pointed look at me. It appeared he wanted to say something.

I said, "I don't like this either."

And then to No Face I said, "What are you doing here?"

THREE

"I AM TO be punished," he said.

I waited for more, but when nothing came, I said, "Why should I care?"

And why should I? He'd tried to eat me and kill my friends. Putting it that way, I wondered how he'd convinced me to help him get this far.

No Face said, "You should not."

Understatement of the year.

If some demon cop planned on an extra-excruciating session for old No Face, I'd be willing to turn state's evidence. Sing like a canary. No Face's next sentence interrupted happy visions of a grinning me reaching for the lever that would send the blade whooshing toward his neck.

"Except for one thing."

Every sob story has that *one thing*, doesn't it? And it's usually the one thing that ends up getting innocent people hurt. Or maybe killed. Helmet and I exchanged glances. We'd been roommates for a while now, and we had that ability of friends to communicate by eye contact. And if I read his face right, he was advising me to stop asking questions…to give the demon the bum's rush and stop whatever might come next before it started.

"And that one thing?"

"Sarah Arias," he said, and he spit the name of my guardian angel out of his mouth like you'd spit out a fly that flew in while you yawned.

Sarah Arias. My chain-smoking heavenly babe. She of the loose-fitting sweaters and butt-hugging jeans. I thought we'd had a moment or two on the flight to Israel last winter. The L-word might have teased its way into my mind a few times back then, but since I'd had time to reconsider, I'd decided it I must have been out of my mind. A vampire and his hot guardian angel.

Never going to happen.

Despite that, the sound of her name leaking out of his filthy mouth made me want to put my fist through his face.

So, I did.

I've always found impulse-control a challenge.

No Face flew backward, and I got a fleeting glimpse of his skull and eyes obscured beneath the human façade. That's how I remembered him. Ugly and faceless…though I think even he would have to admit he remained ugly with the fake face in place.

The demon-initiated reentry phase when he hit the far wall. Due to a lack of retrorockets to slow his descent, he fell hard to the floor. My hand felt like I'd put it through a shredder, but so what? I'd upheld the honor of Sarah Arias. Exactly how knocking the block off a demon upheld honor? No clue at all, but that lack didn't make the hard contact with his meaty flesh any less satisfying. I could weave the dozen broken bones in my hand back together within seconds.

The house shook when No Face landed, and I had a vague notion of Herr Doktor below, shaking his head and sighing something about Americans having all the luck. I didn't know what No Face would do after he regained his feet, and I knew that one of us might end up dead if this got out of hand. Fair odds said it wouldn't be the supernatural being.

With a voice sounding so strained I'm make sure to check under him when he stood up, No Face said, "Enough, vampire."

Karl's little indiscretions disappeared in an hour, it would take a steam shovel and a dumpster to clean up after No Face.

He said, "We waste time."

I concentrated on my left hand and felt cells growing, knitting themselves and falling into place. Waste time, he had said. Sarah Arias he had said. Was she in trouble? It smelled like con brewing, and I decided to give No Face one minute to explain before I tossed him out of the third story window. Maybe Herr Doktor would take him in. For a price.

I said, "Talk," and he did.

No Face described how he'd returned to his masters after failing the Aachen Cathedral assignment. The boss was furious because that failure cost him his quota for souls or mayhem or some other profit-center, business objective. And when the boss got mad? Things needed to happen. I asked which boss he meant, and No Face blinked his Donna eyes at my audacity.

"I dare not say."

That pretty much told me all I needed to know. Not the boss, but *THE BOSS*. Seems The Boss didn't bring No Face in on the entire plan. I guess it wouldn't be hell if they didn't have their own version of Captain Tickles. Turns out The Boss wasn't going to allow the Arabs to destroy the bones belonging to the Jewish Patriarch.

Which Arabs and which Patriarch? Not ultra-important. Suffice it to say, No Face used individual initiative that ended up screwing the pooch. His job was to get his demon paws on the bones because The Boss intended on distributing bits of them to worship cells on every continent.

No Face was vague as to the reason for that, though I assumed it had something to do with bolstering the morale of The Boss's acolytes. Maybe the bones would provide a supernatural jolt to spice things up? Evidently, this Patriarch caused The Boss a lot of grief way back when. Based on my brief glimpses of what Sarah Arias could do, I suspected anything they did with those bones might be akin to nothing more than making mean faces behind a more powerful entity's back.

What I do know is that this Patriarch guy supposedly interpreted dreams that provided timely warnings to save the known world from starvation. He'd also convinced a hot Egyptian chick to have his babies. Normal stuff for a superhero. Me? I can't even get Karl to crap outside.

Donna/No Face explained how The Boss went to great lengths in displaying his displeasure at the cavalier attitude with which No Face conducted the endgame. The top dog saw no humor losing the Patriarch's bones to the opposition…especially after four thousand years of planning, scheming, and even brooding as to how he would get his claws on them.

"In comparison to the way The Boss beat me," he said, "you hit like a girl."

Like a girl?

Demons must not understand irony. I mean, he had the audacity to say I hit like a girl…dressed the way he was? But I got the point. Not of the hit, I think No Face just said that stuff to hide the fact that I'd jacked him good. The specific point I got was the point of No Face's story. He screwed up and The Boss was mad.

But if he really meant the top boss, the story didn't make sense. Not completely. I dug for details.

"How'd you get away?"

And how *did* he make it out of wherever in one piece. Rumor has it that boss number one is everywhere.

No Face said, "I didn't."

The story made me uncomfortable, and that was *before* this latest twist in the plot...his somehow escaping the retribution of *The Boss*. But, not really escaping because he said he hadn't. Bile rose to my throat as I thought The Boss might be waiting outside the door for the right moment to crash our party.

"Wait a minute," I said. "If you didn't get away, then what are you doing here?"

"In transit."

"To where?"

No Face looked at me like I'd just asked him if the sky were up or down. It was the same how-could-you-ask-me-something-so-stupid look my dear wife Nellie used to give me, and it's also the same look I usually get when I ask a chick for a second date. Here's a clue for all the ladies...guy's never intentionally say stupid things. We can't help it. It's in our DNA. But I was talking to a demon, not a chick, so when he said he was in transit...

I said, "You're in transit to Hell."

FOUR

NO FACE SHOOK his head and said, "Sheol."

"I thought they were pretty much the same place."

Wrong thing to say. I endured a fifteen-minute lecture, from a wheezy-voiced, fart-smelling, supernatural transvestite on the difference between Sheol and Hell. According to No Face, Sheol—the place where all the dead, whether righteous or not go—existed. Hell did not.

"Wait a minute," I said. "If all souls go to Sheol, then what's Helmet doing here?"

I pointed at Helmet as if there were another ghost in the house. Well, there was Karl, but nobody ever counted that little idiot. No Face gazed at Helmet for a moment, and I saw my dead buddy draw back. Interesting, because I'd never seen Helmet afraid. I mean, if you're already dead it's probably no sweat to act brave all the time.

"Not uncommon," said No Face. "The dead can be summoned from Sheol."

Again, interesting, though I'd never summoned Helmet, and I certainly would have sent Karl packing if I knew the address of the place. Tthough I'd probably need an EU passport for the little git in order to export him anywhere. Even Sheol.

Summoning was No Face's vague explanation regarding Helmet's presence. Given that Helmet caught my eye and gave his head a barely-perceptible shake, I didn't pursue the subject.

I said, "And hell doesn't exist?"

"Not at all."

No Face sounded like he worked for Sheol's Travel Bureau when he went on about the various spots in Sheol that a human might end up. Some of the sections seemed kind of cool...like a resort. Other places? Not so cool. Places of pain, blight, and desolation. In other words, when the unrighteous of the world died, it sounded like they ended up in New Jersey.

"So, if hell doesn't exist, where do you and all your pals hang out?"

"Heaven," No Face said, and quickly added, "But we try to avoid it." He leaned in closer and whispered, "The place smells awful."

He did that wave-your-hand-in-front-of-your-nose thing to emphasize just how awful heaven smelled.

It sounded too pat for me. Righteous, unrighteous. Who would judge, and what were the standards? And this business about hell not existing? It was just the kind of misdirection I'd expect out of a demon. First distribute the word that a person needs to be righteous, next tell them they can never be good enough, and finally tell them it doesn't matter anyway because this hell thing? Doesn't exist.

Yes, as much like crap as the notion that *THE BOSS* and his demons capered around in heaven. I didn't pursue it because, what good could ever come from a theological discussion between a demon and a vampire who knows nothing of theology?

And, in the process of all that BS, No Face burned up the available time before the gang would begin arriving at Café Aus Zeit. No big deal. Each of them knew how to order beer and No Face and I could get there in less than a five-minute walk. I didn't care so much about heaven, hell—or the lack of either—or that Sheol place. I did care about Sarah Arias.

"If you didn't get away," I said, "how are you here and not in Sheol?"

He gave me the stupid look again.

"As I said, I am on my way," and he added in a tone dripping with condescension, "Obviously."

"How much time do you have before The Boss starts looking for you?"

At first No Face looked like he didn't understand my question.

"Time?" he said. "It means nothing." A pause, and then, "The Boss will not look for me."

Great.

I couldn't give a rat's tiny, left butt-cheek what happened to No Face. He'd mentioned Sarah Arias, and then gone on to tell me what went down on his side of the Aachen operation—interesting—as well as a 101 on the afterlife—total baloney.

"And Sarah Arias?"

"The Boss doesn't need to look for me because he's always seeing me."

Instead of answering my question about Sarah Arias, No Face answered the question I'd asked before…and I kind of couldn't blame him. We'd all had bosses like that at one time or another—the type you thought could be everywhere at once when you hoped to see them nowhere. No Face turned to leave the living room.

"Where are you going?"

"Your violence ruined my hair."

And he claimed it didn't hurt.

"Hold on," I said. "You haven't said anything about Sarah Arias."

"I have, vampire," No Face responded. "And perhaps I came to the wrong human for help."

"Have not," I said, and I thought about it for a second and added, "and have."

Now it was No Face's turn to look confused.

"What are you saying?"

"That you haven't answered my question and that you did come to the wrong human for help."

No Face thought about it, and then nodded in agreement.

"If you are the wrong human," he said, "then I am lost, and your white demon stays with me."

White Demon.

Probably meant Sarah Arias by that and not a metaphor describing that part of my body that often did my thinking for me. It didn't matter, because I was getting tired of No Face and his crap. You can't get a straight answer from a demon and expecting any truth at all from No Face would be like expecting Karl to beg to be let outside to do his doggie business.

As they say in Alabama, "Ain't gonna happen."

I checked my watch again and saw we'd be the last ones arriving. Then it hit me, and I almost smacked my head. What was I thinking? Of course I wouldn't bring Donna/No Face along for Beer Friday. This whole thing turned out to be a mass of unintelligible spaghetti. All I got from her/him was the National Geographic vignette on Sheol and then the doubletalk about white demons and helping humans. No doubt she/he visited me for a reason, and no doubt she/he wouldn't tell me. If I've learned anything at all in my prior dealings with No Face, it's that I'm far better off when he's not around.

I said, "Get out."

That put a smile on the Donna version of No Face, and she/he said, "Fool."

"That would be me. Now get out before I end up having to replace the window."

"And the white demon?"

"Yeah, I get it," I said, "You are in trouble at work and she spends time with you. Big deal."

Donna/No Face smiled again.

"Then after tonight we shall meet again in many thousands of years."

"I'll be sure to leave the light on for you."

"So too with your white demon. She'll be with me. Your Sarah Arias."

No clue what he meant or how it applied to me or to Sarah Arias. But I'd seen Sarah Arias under pressure. She could take care of herself. I mean, it wouldn't be great advertising if the guardian angel website had to remove photos of the staff because they couldn't guard themselves.

"Right," I said. "Get moving."

No Face said, "Because The Boss sees everything."

"We've already been through that."

"And he sees me here."

Uh-oh. Stop the presses.

Call me paranoid, but I thought No Face was finally getting to the meat of the reason for his contacting me.

"Let me get this straight," I said, "You're saying you've pissed off your boss, that he's sentenced you to some nasty sector in Sheol, and that you've intentionally brought his attention down on me?"

A naughty-looking nod from No Face.

"Why?"

"The white demon," No Face said. "The Boss needs to remove her assistance."

Of course. Why didn't I see that for myself?

What the heck was he talking about?

"The Boss says I must submit to punishment."

"You've said."

"The boss doesn't care when I am released."

Just goes to prove that if you search hard enough, you can find something to like about everyone. Even *THE BOSS*.

"You will bring me out."

"Come again," I said, "because for a second I thought you said I'd go into Sheol and break you out of jail."

"I did," said No Face. "And you will."

I could picture myself opening some tarnished, cobweb-encrusted wooden door with gargoyles and ancient runes carved into it—and don't forget the giant, iron latch and the screeching hinges. Actually, no I couldn't imagine anything of the sort. What I did see in my mind was me roundly kicking my own butt for even considering so stupid a scenario.

"Because," said No Face, "While we spoke, The Boss captured the white demon."

What?

"He's placed his mark on you," No Face said, "so that no demon—white or black—can assist."

Can The Boss do that sort of thing? I thought The Boss's competition—Sarah Arias's side—pretty much ruled things. What about that cliché that promises good always triumphing over evil?

"And if she and I remain," No Face said, "we return with damage."

I felt confident the word insane fit better than damage, but it appeared PC had found its way into hell. Probably started there, come to think of it.

"So, by letting you come here I ended up putting a beacon on my guardian angel?"

No Face nodded.

The dawn might come late, but it arrives, nonetheless. Case in point: No Face's game finally dawned on me. He was in trouble, but he never intended for me to hide him or to duke it out with whoever came to arrest him. He'd go to demon jail, no way to avoid it. Nobody got a retrial in hell, and no court existed for appellate purposes.

No Face had bored me with twenty minutes of modern history—the Aachen operation—and that heaven/Hell/Sheol travelogue to allow sufficient time for some demon civil servant to mark me as—as what? No Face's champion? His ticket to early parole?

It didn't matter to The Boss how long someone remained in Sheol's less architecturally improved side, he only cared that the victim obeyed and showed up. They'd probably get a promotion if they could organize themselves free. It made a sick sort of sense. The Boss won either way.

If No Face broke out, then he demonstrated potential for increased trust. If No Face remained for eons, then he'd return even more warped and dangerous than when he went in. So, No Face comes out more valuable to the black team whether he returns early or percolates for ages. A win-win situation if I ever saw one. For everyone but me.

And Sarah Arias.

"You're telling me they already have her?" I said, and I felt my temper buzzing.

Whether what happens when a vampire's anger meter moves off zero is good or bad depends on your point of view. If you're looking for a merciless killing machine controlled by a bloodlust so strong it could consume a whole convent without stopping for confession? Then you'd consider a rise in temper good. Otherwise? Bad.

My outrage fed strength into all the right muscles, and I parted my lips to make room for my extending teeth. I saw Donna/No Face's expression change from a knowing smirk to a wide-eyed apprehension. Good. Maybe I couldn't kill a supernatural being, but I sure could rough him up ahead of his appointment with the jailor.

"Calm yourself, vampire," he said. "The white demon was going to pay for her part anyway."

"How can that be," I said, "She doesn't work for The Boss."

"True enough," said No Face. "But she broke many rules when she provided assistance."

So, there it was. Of the major players in the Aachen debacle, three of us—No Face, Sarah Arias, and me—would now face the music.

The two culprits sharing the heaviest load of guilt for Aachen: Soyla—the Hungarian warrior-woman vampire—and Sparky—my childhood friend and adulthood pimple on my butt? They both got away. Perhaps the logic in that miscarriage of justice read something like: why go after someone who'd just end up enjoying it?

Isn't that the way it goes after all failed operations? The search for the guilty and the punishment of the innocent. *THE BOSS* had somehow gotten Sarah Arias's protection revoked, No Face claimed all the supernatural heavyweights worked at the same place. And if Sarah Arias lost her protection, was there any chance my pink vampire skin *wasn't* thrown in with the deal?

Of course not.

That left us—Sarah Arias and me—open for manipulation. Pawns, and at the whim of the vilest bastard in the universe. And if he's reading this, I hope he knows I mean vile bastard in a kind, respectful way.

I considered Sarah Arias and the "L" word that hovered between us. Truth? I couldn't pinpoint any time she'd ever stepped in to save me... from any freakin' thing.

Well, maybe my fight with Bernard, the Prime of The Seven and the most powerful vampire—and human—ever. But the more I thought about that, the more certain I became that Bernard never intended to kill me in the first place. Maybe that says more about how poorly I pay attention to the world around me than it does about how well Sarah

Arias does her job.

All that aside, could I live with myself knowing I'd not done all I could to help Sarah Arias? No Face could be lying, but it didn't smell like a lie. More importantly, I couldn't use that demons-always-lie line as an excuse for inaction. Not with myself, anyway.

I said, "What would I do? Follow you?"

No Face laughed.

"Of course not," he said. "You cannot follow me."

Perfect. Not having a guide would make my job so much easier.

"Then how do I find you?"

No Face didn't miss a beat with his answer.

"You find me, vampire."

Uh, right.

I didn't want to admit it to myself, but I *did* know where to start. Only a couple hours away by train. The Aachen Cathedral. I'd avoided that place like a prostate exam. Someone might recognize me if I showed up there. Perhaps No Face could lend me his Donna disguise.

"OK," I said. "When do you leave?"

No Face stood up and said, "Not tonight, vampire," as he headed out the living room door.

"Where are you going?"

"To the powder room," he said. "I've never been invited to a human party and I think I should freshen up before we leave."

Sticking my finger into the 220-volt power socket would have shocked me less.

"Nobody invited you anywhere," I said, but I didn't think No Face couldn't hear me over the portable hair dryer.

I sat paralyzed by sick amazement.

I think a future archeologist would have found my bones in that position ten thousand years in the future if a cracked voice with a wisp of a German accent hadn't said, "Don't do it, Gaius."

After two years of sharing both my flat and my soft porn texts from Soyla, Helmet had finally spoken.

FIVE

I HAD A demon in the bathroom touching up his makeup for an evening out with me, and a mute ghost babbling away—for him, anyway—in my living room. What next? Karl potty-trained? Speaking of Karl, I glanced around for the dead mop of love and saw the grey hint of a transparent furry face under the sofa. He'd gotten over his latest decomposing trick and crawled unnoticed back into the living to hide where he could monitor things without exposing himself.

"Helmet," I said, and then stopped.

What could I say after a couple of years' worth of not speaking with him? Oh, I'd spoken *to* him all right. Just never *with* him. And when I finally had my chance? I'm the one who went mute.

He said, "I never said I couldn't talk."

"True enough," I said. "But that's because you never said anything at all."

"Ridiculous," he said. "I have spoken to you many times."

"OK," I said, "my mistake. I mistook your silence for," I thought for a second, "silence."

"Brilliant observation," Helmet said. "You see why I prefer speaking with Karl."

The little idiot heard his name and responded with a series of sneezes. That's all, though. Somehow, he fought the overwhelming urge to crawl out from under the sofa and jump into Helmet's lap. Demons dressed as grotesque-looking women can extinguish those kinds of fires.

Helmet had finally spoken. Great. But I needed to get over the shock and concentrate on some other important issues at hand. For instance, I needed to find my way to the place all souls end up after they die. And, since No Face said I couldn't follow him, I needed to get there with no guide. I also suspected that not being dead might end up a disadvantage for me.

I replayed that thought in my mind and wondered how many wrong turns it took in my life to end up thinking that kind of thought. On the other hand, the part about me not being dead might change.

Because, if I made it past the first five feet of Deadville without No Face's big brother and his equally ugly demon wife impaling me on a telephone pole and serving me at the family barbeque, I needed to find my way to the supermax prison that housed the creation's wickedest beings in a state of eternal torture. Then, I'd need to defeat whatever outlandish security hell could muster.

Oh wait, I forgot, there is no hell.

After all of that, I needed to break my guardian angel out of her cell—and don't forget Ms. Hairy Hairdryer who was primping in my bathroom. If I sprung Sarah Arias, then I'd need to find my way out while some demon posse unleashed the hounds of hell to track us down. It sounded almost as terrifying as an evening stroll in Detroit.

One other thing to consider, no matter what the potential emotional reward I found in liberating Sarah Arias...that act would be huge enough to qualify me for a lifetime achievement award. The negative kind. It would ensure I ended up on *THE BOSS's* radar.

Forever.

Some people claim the intelligence of humans has advanced over the years. Not true. Scientific knowledge, maybe. Intelligence? No.

I could search for decades for someone with an IQ in the same solar system as da Vinci and I'd come up short. Anyone asking how that had to do with a demon partnership proves my point. What point? If you consider the human race a collective, we're getting more stupid as each second passes.

I remember the days when nobody trusted a demon, and bargains were entered with full certainty of the dreadful consequences. Today, most people don't even acknowledge that demons exist. I've heard pseudo-intellectual morons wax on about the concept of evil as a manmade value judgment, and thus either nonexistent or fluid or varying in definition.

They should schedule a date with Donna.

Helmet said, "Don't trust the demon."

Wasn't I just talking about that? At least a thousand questions for Helmet were queuing up in my mind—"what happens after you die" would kick off the tsunami. But that would need to wait. If I embarked on the incredibly asinine mission I was contemplating, I'd likely find out for myself. Why waste time when so many other pressing matters demanded immediate focus?

I said, "I don't trust the demon."

I saw the type of mental battle raging in Helmet that you see with people who want to say something but the consequences of speaking that nugget holds them back. It's that soul-searching internal conflict you experience when you see someone bend over and unintentionally expose half their butt crack.

"Avoid Sheol at all costs," he said and added in a calm, apologetic tone that sounded more like a sad sort of surrender than it did advice,

"Your angel is gone."

Nice to know that Helmet felt comfortable with my butt crack.

He sat down at the computer, gazed out the window at the promenade below, and began moving the computer mouse back and forth in a distracted way. He wasn't even looking at the screen.

Ah, did I say he moved the mouse back and forth in a distracted way?

By creating a sentence using words you'd never hear anyone actually say, like distracted, I'd almost missed the key aspect of the scene in front of me. Helmet moving the mouse.

"You. Lying. Nazi. Bastard."

That got Helmet out of his reverie.

Reverie?

OK, two useless words, though fancy words impress the chicks. Etymological effects on love life aside, I'd just seen Helmet move a physical object. No Face had Helmet frazzled to the point he'd abandoned his two major lies. He could speak. He could move things.

I'd remember that next time Karl dropped a transparent load of cold gravy on the floor.

As the band Styx put it, "the jig is up, the news is out."

Helmet looked down at his hand on the mouse and then back at me.

"Grow up," he said. "You didn't *believe* it, did you?"

He had me there, and I wondered why it was so important to me to prove something that both of us already knew.

"I caught, you though," I said. "Let's not either of us forget that."

Helmet didn't skip a beat.

"Small victory," he said, "small man."

Helmet hadn't spoken a word in the two years I'd known him, and I was already getting sick of his voice. But I wouldn't let things stand like that. And I had a witty comeback on the tip of my tongue when the obvious hit me in the face with the force of Dolly Parton offering up a first go for her lucky newborn. Maybe no living human could help me out. But Helmet could.

"How do I look?"

I'd almost forgotten about No Face, and there he stood in full Donna glory.

The reveal.

Impeccable timing.

Helmet would clam up again in front of the demon, so the important conversation would need to wait.

No Face had asked me how he looked.

"As hideous as the first day you rebelled in heaven."

And that was the kind version. I still don't know where he got that rouge he'd slathered over that indistinct, wrecking ball of a thing he used for a face. And he'd changed out of the gym pants into a sunflower-yellow tank top with an orange pencil skirt that barely dipped below the spot where, I assumed, he stowed his hairy boulders.

"What?" Donna/No Face said. "Does the skirt make me look fat?"

Was I really having this conversation? And where had he found the skirt? I suspected that somewhere a policeman was busy writing up a theft report from a circus. And a tank top? Was this demon so confident in my elastic standards for women that he'd been presumptive enough to bring along an overnight bag?

I said, "Do you look fat? Only in comparison to a brontosaurus."

That seemed to mollify Donna/No Face because he did a long exhale that would have sent sewer rats scurrying for fresh air.

He said, "Thank you, vampire," and then, "Shall we go?"

I said, "Maybe we shouldn't."

I struggled to come up with a reason. Believe me when I say I had an endless list of points why I didn't want No Face anywhere close to my friends, but when Donna/No Face put on female clothes it seemed he'd also donned a chick's attitude. I needed to select my words with great care, or I'd find myself in the humiliating position of trying to comfort a blubbering demon.

I looked over to Helmet. Perhaps he could pass the subliminal message that would get me out of this mess. No help there. Helmet must have departed the living room just after Donna/No Face returned. Karl was still hanging in there under the sofa. I thought I could see the little grey nose hiding a few inches out of sight, but on closer look I realized the little coward had executed his nuclear protocol and decomposed under there. Nice to have roommates you can count on.

"Shouldn't what?" said Donna/No Face. "Do you just want to have a drink here?"

Uh, no.

"Let's go," I said. "But if you harm my friends in any way…"

Donna/No Face interrupted me.

"Don't worry, vampire," he said. "Tonight, I sample human fun."

Hope he wasn't counting on a goodnight kiss.

Donna/No Face followed me out the door and pounded his way down the stairs.

We passed by Herr Doktor cooing something in German through his locked front door. Evidently Frau WunderBootie thought Herr Doktor needed some instruction regarding how to act when the American upstairs brought his next exotic date around. I almost felt sorry for the old buzzard.

It took him less than a second to burst that fragile balloon that held my sympathy, because Herr Doktor whispered to Donna/No Face, "Don't forget to send a friend request."

I stopped and stared at Donna/No Face in disbelief as Herr Doktor added, "I'm easy to remember."

And then he said his Facebook handle. Something that sounded like

Horst Lieberschnitzel. Easy to remember? We didn't need fifty letters to make a single word when I was a kid. Back then, we only needed a syllable. Two if you aimed for eloquence. It also helped to have a war club handy in case you used the wrong inflection.

I attempted to push Donna/No Face out the door, when I noticed Herr Doktor had snuck up behind us. He lept forward to assist in freeing the pins that secured the stationary half of the two-door entryway. That gentlemanly doubling of the space provided Donna/ No Face just enough room to seep outside. I didn't remember needing to do that when we arrived and wondered for a second if Donna/No Face had gotten fatter in the thirty minutes we were in my flat. Maybe she'd eaten some of the furniture or dirty laundry or something.

Herr Doktor caught my eye after he reinstalled the pin that locked the second door. He checked to make sure Donna/No Face wasn't looking and then he gave a wide grin and two thumbs up. What was with it with this guy? I returned a slack-jawed look of amazement. A feral growl erupted from the dark behind us and we both turned to see the Frau watching us from their apartment door. More fun in store for him.

Donna/No Face and I made it through the little parking lot and to the sidewalk that led uphill toward the shopping area and Café Aus Zeit. We didn't speak as we walked. Based on how the conversation went upstairs in my flat, No Face must have been feeling confident I'd show up in Sheol to attempt the jailbreak thing. And, once you have things the way you want them, it's foolish to keep running your mouth. The best that could happen is that you keep what you already have. The options go down from there.

My mouth didn't move either. And, not at all because I'd ended up getting what I wanted. Obviously, I did not. I didn't say anything to Donna/No Face during the brief walk because I didn't want anyone we passed on the sidewalk or anyone in the cars going by on the street to think Donna/No Face and I were a couple.

Despite the sure and permanent stain on my reputation, I might have had a few things to say while we walked through the chilly evening had I known just how close that trip to hell loomed ahead.

SIX

GIVEN THE LATE-SPRING, snowy sludge on the ground, the tables sat empty outside Café Aus Zeit. Same for the other little restaurants up and down the walking street all German towns tend to have now.

I never like the empty tables thing because my mind tends to fill them, and the chairs, with the hundreds of people I've cared about over the past two thousand years. Each person sits in a one of those snow or ice-frosted chairs, their hands folded expectantly atop one of the lonely tables. It happens more than it used to. Guess I'm be getting old and, sure, I understand it's just my imagination. But that doesn't make it any less heartbreaking, less sweet, or less real.

So, I didn't look to my right or my left as I went through the door. One of the owners was delivering a tray of food to a table full of old biddies when he saw me walk in. He smiled and waved his free hand. When the guy caught sight of Donna/No Face's amorphous shape pushing its way through the door behind me, the poor man's face changed from a calm, friendly expression to one of abject shock.

The owner also hit the old biddies' table at full walking speed, and whatever he had on the tray ended up all over his customers. I think Germans had passed a law against spilling things several decades before, so the surprised outrage I saw on the women was almost worth having to walk through the door with that hairy blimp of a demon in tow.

My buddy the waiter issued a bushel of embarrassed apologies, and the crash of plates brought all employees on deck to assist in sorting out the disaster. Café Aus Zeit has a lower level with three tables and an upper level where the bar and kitchen are located. The upper deck holds six tables. I didn't see my friends downstairs, so I climbed up.

Of course, Donna/No Face followed, and I caught sight of the bagger gang sitting in the far corner. Sister Christian waved, and Watanabe and J-Rod came over to help me pull Donna/No Face through the opening to the second floor. It took our combined effort, and the demon finally came free like a cork shooting out of a bottle of champagne. Rotten, soured champagne.

It took my vampire-assisted speed and strength to ensure Donna/No Face didn't end up falling on top of my two friends and suffocating them. We lined up three chairs, set them several feet apart from each other, and Donna/No Face distributed her/his bottom evenly among them.

J-Rod, Watanabe, and I also pulled up chairs and Friday Beer Night began. I have to give it to Donna/No Face, the demon remained in character for as long as he remained with us. But then, how hard is it to pull off the loud-mouthed-beer-swilling-gross-person-who-eats-every-morsel-of-food-ordered-for-the-table routine? He also erupted with some belches that would require that the owners repaint the walls.

A night out with the humans seemed to delight Donna/No Face. He put away one beer after another, and we had to watch him closely every time he emptied his mug, because his hands tended to wander towards other people's glasses. I kind of handled the situation by pushing the Bonnie Prince's stein toward Donna/No Face whenever I saw the demon had an empty glass. Cold hearted, yes. But where beer is concerned, every man is an island.

It didn't seem to matter at all to the Bonnie Prince, but I guess that's mostly because he didn't know what was happening. Like I said, I did feel a bit guilty, especially when I saw him take a sip out of the table-candle and then complain loudly about the warm beer they served in the place.

Even Sister Christian looked like she'd had enough after thirty minutes of Donna/No Face. Halfway through her first glass of wine she announced she needed to go to the ladies' room. I think she wanted just a couple minutes' peace from Donna/No Face's rapid-fire questions. "How do you put on pantyhose?" Or, "What is the purpose of soap?" Or, the lowest of the low, "How can you tell if a guy really likes you or he's just after what he can get?" Sister Christian gave me a look that was cold enough to refreeze an Antarctic glacier.

Really? Did Donna/No Face think putting on a girl-clothes made him a chick? And, I don't know how well mirrors work down in Sheol, but all he'd need to do is take a good look into one to see he had nothing to worry about when it came to guys lusting over him. Besides, if he really was looking for intellect over libido, why'd he paint himself into that pencil skirt?

So, Sister Christian excused herself to take a squirt, and horror of horrors, Donna/No Face followed. I wondered how both of them would fit in the one-seat water closet, but I stopped short for fear I'd create the mental image of Donna/No Face hiking up that skirt.

The dudes kept quiet, and I caught them taking furtive glances between Donna/No Face and me, their disappointment in my taste in females shining on their faces. Even J-Rod forsook the opportunity to rib me over my new girlfriend. I guess he thought he might catch whatever degenerative babe-judgment disease infected me and wanted as little contact as possible. OK, so I got it. I had cooties.

Sister Christian returned to the table. Solo, and I listened with sick fascination for the sound of a toilet exploding down the hall. If Donna/No Face lingered this long in the john, then it could only mean a bombing mission—not just a tinkle. I wasn't sure I wanted to remain within the blast radius.

My brain kept doing the mental countdown most guys do when they're waiting for something to happen.

Five-Four-Three-Two-One-Zero!

But nothing happened as my mind reached zero. No explosion from the ladies' toilet…no environmental catastrophe. Sister Christian caught me glancing down the hall for Donna/No Face.

She said, "Miss her?"

"What?"

"Your date, dude." J-Rod had finally spoken, and he'd dropped the Latino-gangsta accent.

"She's not my…" I began but Sister Christian cut through me.

"She?" said Sister Christian. "I didn't think we still lied to each."

Oh? Had we stopped?

Sister Christian needed to remember she was the only chick in our group and thus could afford to always tell the truth without fear of repercussions. The dudes on the other hand? I thought Sister Christian was more than old enough to know the only way to tell if a guy was lying was if his lips were moving.

That old saying brought a smile, and Sister Christian said, "What's so funny?"

"Nothing," I said, and it came out sounding guilty…even to myself.

"By the way," she said, "He's gone."

"He?"

It's best to keep answers brief when a chick starts unraveling your story. That way you end up with less to defend when the whole thing collapses.

"Yes," she said, and added, "If distinctions in sex applies to demons."

The guys moved in unison as they sat up straight in their chairs. I'm not sure if the word demon woke them up or if the movement was an automatic reaction to a totally hot, and somewhat mature, chick throwing out the word sex. Bottom line is that she knew about No Face. I didn't respond.

She said, "Don't even try to look innocent. I suspected it earlier today. When you told Donna that she could stay at your place."

Now the tongue-lashing would start, and I guess I kind of deserved it. What kind of a friend invites a demon to a members-only Friday night get-together? On the other hand, at least everyone knew I wasn't putting the moves on an ungodly beast like Donna/No Face. I mean, it made me sick to think they ever doubted me. I took solace in the knowledge Sister Christian suspected Donna/No Face from almost the beginning, and it was probably because she understood that I maintain high standards.

Then she said, "Oh, you're pig enough to hit on any incarnation of female."

I never knew solace could evaporate with such speed.

"But invite her to stay with you?"

Sister Christian shook her head.

"You would have just rented a room. More anonymous after you had what you wanted."

I looked down at the butter knife and wondered how long it would take to saw through my wrists.

I said, "Wait a minute."

That's when they all broke out laughing...everyone at the table except me. After a while, though, I couldn't help but join in. I wasn't sure what we were laughing at. My discomfort at squiring a butt-ugly mastodon in drag into the café like the two of us were making an evening of it? The shock on my face upon realizing the entire bagger gang outsmarted me? Something else? Nothing?

I suspected none of the above, and I didn't care that it sounded more like a gallows-laugh than anything else. It just felt good. The Bonnie Prince reached over to slap me on the shoulder and gave the back of my head a solid whack. That kept things going a bit longer.

The Germans in the place looked at us like we were crazy, and I was sure they knew we were Americans. Folks all over the world can spot one American in a thousand people, so the German customers at Café Aus Zeit probably wrote it off as, "the way things are done with crazy Americans." Someday "the ways things are done" will be added to the German national anthem. I didn't care about the smug looks or the shaking of the heads at the tables around us. The gang was laughing.

It went on for another minute or so and I still heard a snort or two as everyone took a sip of their drinks.

The yuckfest ended completely when Sister Christian said, "Gare, what are you doing with that demon?"

Tricky question.

A few months ago, events on a particularly awful evening exposed my big secret to the bagger gang. Bad enough news to win a Nobel Prize for bad news. It got worse. The very next day, my friends ended up suspended in a horrific painting depicting the tortures of hell. Medieval sort of art you find in just about any museum. Humans and demons. Done a thousand times, except the human subjects were my friends. It all ended well enough when I'd ransomed my friends with a bag of dry, old human bones.

I'd never probed any of them to ascertain how much of the ordeal they remembered. Not everything, it seemed. They did recall my secret, though. Lucky me. Oh, and also the bit about demons. Lucky them.

And how to answer Sister Christian's question? What, indeed, was I doing with a demon?

I said, "It's another *thing*".

Lame, but I thought the gang would understand. Sister Christian closed her eyes and shook her head, and the boys made the transition from ha-ha to game faces in less than a moment.

Watanabe said, "What kind of trouble are we in?"

If Sister Christian represented the wisest and most humane of the group, David Smith—aka Watanabe—filled the most educated role. Nobody knew when he'd take his place in the business world. I mean, graduating first in your class with an MBA from Harvard opens a lot of doors. We just understood it would eventually happen.

He was lucky he hadn't ended up dead before. You'd think a rerun of that possibility dampen his enthusiasm for demon involvement. It didn't seem to. Well, I wouldn't draw him, or any of the rest of my friends, into another dangerous situation.

I said, "We?"

J-Rod piped in with, "Yes, we."

He'd also returned to fight that night when anyone else with even a trace of self-preservation DNA would have run screaming. Heck, *I* would have run...if two demons weren't holding me down while another noshed on my leg. No, all my friends supported me that night. Courageous, yes. But it ended up nearly killing all of us. Like I already said, I couldn't let that happen again.

"Not we," I said. "Me. The question is: what kind of trouble am *I* in."

J-Rod flinched like I'd used a whip instead of words. They all did. I hated to disappoint my friends, but I could deal with hurt feelings. There's nothing I can do with dead bodies. Vampires are neither wizards nor faith healers.

"We'll save *that* discussion for later," she said. "Let's start with Gare explaining why he brought the demon along."

Donna/No Face. That reminded me. Where was he?

The door to the ladies' room down the hall remained closed. No telling the last time No Face used a crapper, if ever, so I imagined him in there, plunger in hand, frantically trying to get rid of the evidence before the next chick walked in.

"Where?" I said, using the question to delay what I knew was coming.

"Like I said," Sister Christian said, "he's gone." A pause. "At least I think it was a he."

I nodded.

Watanabe said, "What happened?"

Sister Christian said, "Remember our discussion at the commissary?"

Discussion? What discussion?

The Bonnie Prince said, "The rotten eggs smell?"

A rare benefit to demon stink. Allows the sight-impaired to hate them, too.

"Yes," said Sister Christian. "We said we'd keep an eye on Donna."

They all nodded.

"When I got a good look at her in the ladies' room, I knew she wasn't human."

J-Rod asked her why.

"Her face," Sister Christian said. "It looked like a copy."

No argument from me on that one.

"That made me certain. So, I decided to handle things before I used the bathroom."

Me? I consider *using* the bathroom as handling things. Sister Christian had all of us leaning forward in our chairs.

"So, I told Donna to leave."

J-Rod said, "And?"

"And Donna told me she had to go. I thought she meant go as in she had to go to the bathroom." A pause. "But that's not what she meant."

Sister Christian took a sip of her wine.

I wasn't sure what she was about to say about Donna/No Face's departure, and it didn't surprise me when she said, "And she disappeared. No poof, no noise of any kind…vanished in front of my face while we were talking."

J-Rod resurrected his Latino accent with, "Good thing she didn't poof, Sister C. You end up with covered in Donna stuff." After a moment's thought he added, "Too bad for her."

That seemed to surprise Sister Christian and she said, "Too bad what?"

"Too bad she miss a chance to show Gare her moneymaker."

That got us all laughing again, though Sister Christian looked like she was faking it. Chicks are good at that. I pretty much faked it too, because my mind was on No Face. He'd said he had to go, and then he'd disappeared.

It had started.

I needed to find the portal to Sheol and then I needed to find my way to the demon prison.

I caught Sister Christian staring at me while she continued the fake laugh thing. Yeah, her mouth smiled, but her eyes showed concern. She knew it too. Sister Christian understood that whatever brought the demon back among us couldn't end up well. For anyone. Especially me. She waited for the boys to settle and for the others in the restaurant to quit gawking and return to their schnitzels.

Then, she said, "Tell us."

So, I did…leaving out most of the important parts. Like Helmet, for instance. Despite his hesitancy at saying anything at all about Sheol, I still thought he would play an important role in my mission planning. The other baggers knew nothing of Helmet, or Karl for that matter. They couldn't see either of them, though I think Sister Christian sensed them that one time she visited my flat.

Of course, everyone remembered No Face and our battle at the Bad Homburg train station. And nobody seemed surprised when I did the reveal on Donna—told them she was No Face clothed in human-looking skin.

"You know all that," said J-Rod, "and still you ask her out, man?"

Right.

I. HAD. NOT. ASKED. DONNA. OUT.

At least *you* believe me. Right?

He'd invited himself along. A final fling before reporting to demon prison. To experience the human condition. But then, I couldn't allow my pride to send us down the rabbit hole of distraction. Whether I'd asked Donna on a date or not—I hadn't, BTW—wasn't what was important at the moment.

Sarah Arias, I told them, she was the reason I considered the crazy mission. She'd come through for me, so I owed her the same. I admit I felt thankful nobody asked exactly *how* Sarah Arias had come through for me. No good answer came to mind for that one...and that little fact should have concerned me. To my credit, I think it did gnaw at my mind for adult consideration. But put a dude's ego and libido on one side of the scale and his common sense on the other. Do I need to say which overloaded plate would clatter to the floor?

So, why consider going ahead with a rescue mission to hell? I mean, why would I commit myself to a suicidal path after a split second of consideration?

Because that's how I roll.

And...Sarah Arias.

The *L* word kept snaking its way into my mind, though I told myself the *L* stood for lust and not love. That's the safe-space, happy place in a guy's mind when he realizes he's thinking too much about a chick without first mentally removing her clothes. Speaking of clothes, the way Sarah Arias's jeans clung to her butt? Yeah, another rabbit hole.

But I'd never fallen in *love* with her. Had I? Best to steer mentally clear of that deadly bomb until the explosives rot away. Besides, I hadn't been in love for more than a century—since my dear wife Nellie died of old age.

How could I ever trust love again? Not after that. Trust me, it's the one who lives that pays the price. My argumentative mind pointed to Sarah Arias as a different story. Whereas even the hottest chick would age, Sarah Arias was eternal. Just like me.

Almost.

It all came down to one thing, and the logical side of my brain put its hands around the throat of my feelings side and squeezed until it confessed. I was willing to risk the entire package—me—not so much to rescue Sarah Arias but for the opportunity to see her again.

I wanted the chance for another plane flight or train ride where she pretended to be my wife and laid her golden head on my chest. I also wanted to hug her goodbye. One more time. Even if I knew it would be the last time I'd feel her body against mine, I still wanted that moment. Wanted it enough to risk everything.

Crap. She'd put the whammy on me all right, and I never saw it coming. Who does?

Everyone drained their glasses and I signaled for another round. My waiter buddy brought one extra beer. I guess he thought my date might be facing some challenges in the crapper. No worries, I'd have an extra liter to myself.

The Bonnie Prince grabbed the candle and said, "Jeez, Gare. What does a man need to do to get a cold beer in this place?"

Watanabe took the candle out of the Bonnie Prince's hand and replaced it with the proper glass.

Then he said, "Don't trust him."

No kidding. That's what Helmet said.

"Care to suggest another option?"

"Try common sense," said Sister Christian. "You're not even sure they *have* Sarah Arias, are you?"

Maybe, but something told me No Face played that part of the story straight down the middle. I didn't know why The Boss decided to kidnap her, or how he managed to get it authorized through Sarah Arias's folks. I also had no clue what anyone expected to gain from holding her.

One thing I did know. I'd only get the answers if I made it into Sheol, to the prison, and into Sarah Arias's cell. It's how demons work. You don't know everything until the end…when turning back is out of the question.

I said, "They've got her."

When Sister Christian didn't argue, I knew she agreed with me on that much. And if it took sacrificing Sarah Arias to keep me safe? Sister Christian would go there in a millisecond. Not the kind of help I needed just then, but certainly heartwarming that someone on the earth put my interests first. It made me want to reach across the table and give her a big hug. Think about it, the opportunity to legally do that doesn't grow on trees.

"And I'm going to get her back."

"Dude," said J-Rod, "They gonna to bust a cap in you for sure."

Thanks for the encouragement.

He had a point. On the other hand, with any luck at all I wouldn't be able to find the portal.

Watanabe said, "What's our part?"

The rest of the gang nodded, and I heard a couple of yeahs.

"No way," I said. "And don't try to guilt me into changing my mind."

"Really?" said J-Rod. "So how about we're a team and all that?"

"OK," I said, "I quit."

The Bonnie Prince said, "Quit what?"

"Quit the team," I said. "You've treated me like an outsider anyway for the past months."

I wanted someone to protest. Nobody did.

"So, I'm not on your team," I said, "And you're not on mine."

Easy as that. They'd whine and moan, try to talk me into including them in something they needed to avoid.

"Just like that," said Sister Christian. "Off the team?"

"Just like that," I agreed, and I picked up my beer mug to take another sip.

"I'm not going to tell you that you owe us anything," she said. "And you can't convince us we owe you either."

I took a deep sip to avoid speaking before I discovered where this was going. Chicks are tricky. Older chicks can be hot, sexy and *extra* tricky.

"Exactly," I said.

Sounded like a safe enough answer. It also made it sound like I understood the thread of Sister Christian's logic. Believe me when I say that I did not. She leaned in closer.

"That's what friendship is about, isn't it?" She looked around the table. "None of us are here for gain, and all of us owes the other only one thing."

"One thing?"

I looked at the guys and saw they followed this bull about as well as I did. Vince the Bonnie Prince McDonald sat with his mouth open,

Watanabe was playing with the water ring left by his glass. I glanced at J-Rod. He had his eyes caged on Sister Christian's sweater. At least one of us had his priorities straight.

"One thing," Sister Christian repeated. "Love."

I think all four of us guys must have grimaced in unison, because Sister Christian burst out laughing. And though I didn't want to admit it, I thought I understood what she meant. We didn't hang out with each other because we got something of monetary value. We did it because we wanted to. Because we enjoyed each other. And, OK, we did it because we *loved* each other.

Belch.

"Thanks for the philosophy lesson, Sister Freud," I said. "Still doesn't mean I'm letting any of you come along."

Sister Christian stopped laughing and sat up straight.

"Silly boy," she said.

Yeah, right. Sister Christian knows full well how old I am, and still she went into that I'm-an-older-more-experienced-woman-thing with me.

I wondered if she'd get around to paddling my bare...

Easy big guy.

I needed to get a grip and I needed to get out of the cafe. If bringing No Face along was stupid, coming at all was complete idiocy. What was it that obscured my better judgment to the point that just showing up was doing the completely incoherent thing?

Well, there was the demon, of course. Try thinking straight when a rotten-egg-smelling creature of hell shows up in women's clothes at your door. And then move to Helmet. Can't talk, can he? Can't lift his finger to move anything in the physical world, can he? Well, I'd found out the truth, all right. And after I did, I felt a bit like I'd been cheated on.

So yes, I guess I had a thing or two on my mind when we walked out the door and headed for Café Aus Zeit. And now there was Sister Christian calling me a silly boy.

"Stop it," she said, and I didn't think she was talking to the waiter who'd just showed up to carry away the empties.

"Stop what?"

Sister Christian formed her words in her mind first, and then said, "Stop giving us the aloof and lonely vampire thing. Stop patronizing us by saying what we can and cannot do. Stop trying to be a hero in search of victims to rescue."

Sister Christian paused to take in air. She'd said all three sentences in one breath. Impressive lungs.

"And most of all," Sister Christian said. She inhaled again and exhaled in what sounded like frustration with a snort of laughter at the tail.

"Most of all," she repeated, "Stop undressing me with your eyes."

Busted.

She started laughing again—we all did—so I didn't think she minded.

I waited for things to settle down before I said, "We're still at an impasse."

Sister Christian shook her head.

"Not at all. Do you think any of us are crazy enough to follow you into the afterlife?"

"Well…"

"Because you'd have to be about the dumbest person on earth to even consider it."

"Uh, thanks?"

Sister Christian gave a single nod and said, "We want to help, all right," and then, "Tell us what we can do."

Once she put it that way, how could I resist? Problem was, I didn't have a plan.

"I will," I said while I reached into my pocket and pulled out two, one-hundred Euro bills.

I threw them on the table and was surprised when Watanabe protested.

He said, "My treat."

Gangsta J-Rod said, "I help pay too."

"Get out of here," I said. "I've told you I've got enough money to go for a long time."

"I know, homie," said J-Rod. "But I don't want you to show up in Sheol saying I make you pay for your last meal."

How considerate.

"OK," I said. "I'll call you or text you later tonight."

They looked back at me in various shades of dubious. Sister Christian hurried around the table to give me a goodbye hug—the motherly kind. She also gave me that contemplative look mother's use when they're searching for the lie in the words their son just spoke.

"Promise," I said, though I wasn't certain I meant it.

J-Rod's parting words kept cycling through my mind as I did the fast-walk home. He didn't want me to show up in Sheol having paid for my last meal. I suppose could have taken the sentence several different ways, though all of them were bad.

I'd show up in Sheol all right, I sensed as much the way a Geiger counter sees radiation. Whether or not I'd get there having eaten my last meal? I put the key into the tenants' access door while hoping many more meals lay in my future.

SEVEN

"SHE HAS LEFTEN you."

Well, good evening, Herr Doktor.

I didn't see the old coot because he sat in the darkness with his back against his flat's door. I looked down toward the voice and spied a dozen cigarette butts surrounding the old guy...which meant he'd been exiled out there for the past five minutes. Just kidding. No doubt Frau Rootelboomsen hadn't let him back in since Herr Doktor begged Donna/No Face to friend him on Facebook.

And, it was Donna/No Face he was referring to when he said that *she'd* left me.

He said, "I knew you would make a mess."

I'd never heard that much English out of him, and I kind of felt sorry for the old cheapskate. Typical encounter with a demon. Put the forbidden fruit within your grasp and then dash away your hopes. But Donna/No Face? Herr Doktor needed a complete overhaul of his guy machine. But then, I've heard that humans carry Neanderthal genes, so Herr Doktor wouldn't be the first guy blinded by hormones.

"Yes," I said. "Too much sexy woman for me to handle."

Herr Doktor thought about that one for a second, and he lit another cigarette and exhaled before responding.

"She needs a good German man."

Yes, she does.

I didn't want my mind concocting scenes of Herr Doktor and Donna/No Face, so I changed the subject and said, "You need a bed for the night?"

I wanted to kick myself as soon as the words left my lips. The last thing I needed was a lovesick Herr Doktor coughing up his lungs in my guest room.

Another toke on his cigarette and Herr Doktor said, "Nein."

Not "No thanks," or "I appreciate your kind thoughts, but I need to serve my penance down here," or anything else. Just no. Served him right if I found his stiff body in the same position in the morning. And when Frau MaybeHisWife saw all those cigarettes on the carpet? Might be worth setting up a webcam to catch those fireworks.

I'd only mounted the first step when I heard Herr Doktor say, "I letted her already in your flat."

I froze.

He let who? Where?

With no hope of closing the deal with a true beauty like Donna/No Face, he'd lost all inspiration for careful English diction and proper sentence structure. On the bright side, Herr Doktor tended to get his sentences and meanings inverted, so it was too early to panic.

"Say again?"

"Your Schwester."

My sister?

In case I haven't mentioned it, I'm an only child.

Perfect time to panic.

"Uh, thanks?"

No need to waste time questioning him further because Herr freakin'

Doktor had let *someone* into my flat. A big no-no in the USA. Germans? They tended to do things as they saw fit. I ran up the stairs and approached the door.

I caught a faint, caustic aroma, and I wasn't sure whether it came from my apartment or Herr Doktor had floated one after I left—maybe even when I was standing there talking to him. Couldn't be another vampire, though. Not a strong enough odor.

Stink.

That's the reason vampires don't hold those big meetings in some castle high in the mountains above an Eastern European village. We can't stand the smell of each other. And it's more than that. If we're close for more than ten minutes the odor incapacitates us. Longer, and we're dead. That would be the dead kind of dead. For good.

Two exceptions exist. First, all those infected by the same vampire. In my case, there's Sparky and Rolf. The three of us killed a Roman soldier named Balus and ate his heart. It was a heat of battle kind of thing. The other exception? The Seven.

The Seven were likely the first to be infected with the vampire thing. None of us know for certain, though I think it's a safe bet. And that condition comes with several benefits. Like repair of cellular damage to the point we could sit on a nuclear explosion and still find a way to knit ourselves back together. I'm stronger than a heard of bulls during mating season. There are other amazing things I can do that you cannot. Take all those extraordinary capabilities and multiply them. That's The Seven.

They rule the vampire world. Not with laws or courts, but with arbitrary brutality. Rule number one? Don't do anything to threaten The Seven. Everything else springs from that. And only the opinion of The Seven matters, so no need to worry over the legal expenses and delays associated with appeals. Once they decide, it's final.

Any of The Seven can take out several vampires. And the debilitating odor aspect of our condition prevents us from ganging up and mounting a threat to them. We can't smell them coming because they're somehow exempt. One other thing about The Seven: they're all pygmies from some long-ago cannibal tribe.

Yeah. I know.

I'd encountered one of the little bastards for the first time a few months ago, during the grave-robbing thing Sparky manipulated me into. Bernard, and he waffled between helping me and wanting to rip my head off…the same reaction I get from most women.

Bernard was no help at all, but he did let me keep breathing, so I consider the encounter a net plus. He'd also said something about The Seven keeping an eye on me…that they'd predicted my powers would grow to the point I could end up a challenge. Not good news for the home team, because The Seven tended to make challenges disappear.

Herr Doktor had said he let my sister into my flat, so I knew one thing for sure. It couldn't be The Seven because they were all dudes. Tiny, sure enough, but powerful beyond description. I wasn't picking up the debilitating odor thing, so Herr Doktor hadn't let in a vampire.

Karl rushed to greet me with his customary cold shower of ghost love. It never soaked, but only because ghost pee has no physical substance. No so bad? If you could see what else erupted out of the dog's body, you'd hate the routine as much as I do.

I reached down to shoo the little idiot away and realized that in all the confusion of Karl's baptismal greeting, I'd forgotten about the woman inside my flat. No sweat, because the blade at my throat provided a convenient memory aid.

Knives don't bother me, except when pointed at one of two places. The second most important is my throat. Yes, I can grow everything back, but only a fool—or Sparky, but I'm being redundant—would willingly allow getting his parts hacked off or his jugular sliced.

The woman put her free hand on my spinal cord and applied the right amount of pressure cause the knife to slice through the top layer of skin, and I felt blood running down my neck. She stopped short of anything that'd be fatal on an average human. Even so, I did my best garden-statue imitation.

Her breathing brushed against the back of my neck. I saw something move out of the corner of my eye and caught sight of Helmet standing there with his arms crossed. He'd managed a reasonably fierce look, and I couldn't think of a better time for him to exhibit the full range of his recently revealed moving-things-in-the-physical-world skills.

But…unless I had things wrong, the crusty look was pointed at *me*.

Something strange was happening, and only two of the three of us present knew what it was. I felt warm lips on my neck and then a slight kissy-sucking sensation.

I didn't think hickies could be fatal—at least not until her husband showed up—so I said, "I'll give you just fifteen minutes to stop that."

I heard a kitten-voiced feminine laugh and the knife banged to the floor. I said a quick prayer before I turned around because if it were Donna/No Face that had just sexed me up, then I'd need to retrieve that knife so that I could cut my own throat.

It wasn't.

I wouldn't call the gorgeous hunk of dangerous woman standing in front of me *naked*, though I'm confident my departed wife Nellie would have argued that leather hot pants, midriff t-shirts, gold bracelet earrings don't count as clothing.

I said, "Soyla."

It shocked even me that I could say anything at all. I'd seen Soyla *less* dressed plenty of times—almost daily. But those were golden nuggets she'd sexted me on the smartphone. I'd never been this close because of the vampire repulsion thing.

I took a shallow sniff and it returned nothing more than the vague notion of a poorly-wiped bottom. Good enough for me.

I dove in.

We rolled around for a while. Her laughing, me trying to come to my senses, but not really wanting to. This woman possessed all the craziness of a normal chick and had the skills of a highly-trained, supernaturally-powerful, medieval Hungarian assassin. She'd been stalking me for nearly a thousand years, though maybe it was my penance for not discouraging her in any way more forceful than the occasional defriend/re-friend thing on social media.

I knew that if I spent one careless night with her? She'd own me. Bras drying in my shower and me off to the convenience store to pick up an emergency supply of hygiene products.

I don't remember stripping down to my boxers, but that's when good sense finally took over.

And…I will forever hate myself for it.

I figured that if I didn't stop things in the next thirty seconds, we'd be there all night. And after that? I'd never get rid of her. Especially if I couldn't use the fatal odor thing as an excuse.

Of course, there was also the thing with Sarah Arias.

She and I had snuggled a bit. Truth is, if I thought about why I'd decided to traipse through the gates of hell to rescue her? I'd probably come up with only one reason. Guilt. Because, that snuggling thing? Probably what landed her in demon jail. Wanting to see her again played no part at all in the decision. If I kept telling myself that, I thought I might begin to believe it.

Soyla ran a hand over my chest and lightly rubbed in all the right places.

Sarah who?

Alarm bells erupted in my head, and I knew that if I didn't find a way to silence them, I'd end up doing something stupid…like pushing Soyla's sweaty body off of me and then standing to take a long, calming, put-my-libido-engine-in-reverse look out the window.

I'd reached the point where I would either get on with *it* or stop.

Getting on with it might offer a final fling on this side of life's curtain, but stop represented the better choice. For some inexplicable reason, I didn't want to disappoint Sarah Arias.

I needed to get my focus back in the game…to force my brain out of the alternate command post and back into my bigger head. So I did what I always do to control myself when faced with similar situations: I tried to think of something dreadful, deflating. My mind found its way to a quaint café in Paris and Herr Doktor leaning over a tiny, round table to smooch Donna/No Face.

It worked.

My lust faded away like a waning sea breeze sure to make any mainsail go limp. After that, I walked to the bathroom and grabbed my only towel, and returned to the sitting room. and I tossed it to her.

"Get dressed."

She said, "I am."

Right, if you counted hot pants short and sheer enough to cause a Victoria's Secret model to blush and an almost shirt.

"Then get more dressed."

Soyla gave me a pouty look and took the towel. She fiddled it around to cover where she could, and I promised myself I'd never wash it again.

She said, "Not happy with Soyla?" and then took a pointed glance at the front of my boxer shorts.

"Not in the least."

Usually, I'm not so good at lying in such a compact way.

But she'd nearly gotten me killed in Aachen...and, while I was on Aachen, she'd set me up as the patsy for that grave-robbing operation. I needed to keep that in mind—the primary one—because my eyes kept returning to those two shapely items that urged me to forget this potential rescue mission stuff and go for round two of the wrestling match.

She stood, and when I followed her into the living room, I noticed that she'd placed jeans and a more substantial t-shirt on the sofa. I sensed Helmet gliding behind me, and I stopped to whisper something to him...but forgot what I was going to say when he smacked me hard in the back of my head.

OK, so I had one vote against my decision to disengage.

Karl also appeared smitten with Soyla. I could tell by the way he jumped up on the sofa and rolled on his back over her jeans. Soyla chuckled and brushed the little guy aside.

I intended on looking the other way as Soyla shimmied into her additional clothing, but what the heck. I mean, she'd dropped the towel to the floor before performing the ritual, so I needed to watch and make sure she didn't hurt herself.

Don't worry if that last sentence makes no sense at all to you because it *still* doesn't to me, either. I even considered doing the considerate host thing and offering to help her, but she seemed to know what she was doing.

I said, "How did you know?"

She knew I meant how did she know we'd be able to inhabit the same room and not suffer the incapacitating effects of the vampire repulsion.

"Bernard told me."

Bernard was that cannibal pygmy dude I'd mentioned earlier—one of The Seven. Not just one of them, but their Prime—the leader. He'd helped plan the Aachen mission and had driven me to starting point.

I would have appreciated some *additional* assistance once things got going and therefore dangerous, but he ended up disappearing until after the smoke cleared.

"He interviewed you after Aachen?"

She laughed.

"Oh, yes," she said. "In more ways than one."

I didn't want to think about the five-foot-tall cannibal with the six-foot beauty in front of me, but who can help it? Soyla smiled, and I could see she knew what I was thinking.

"Not like that," she said. "Got any beer?"

"What? Uh…yeah, I'll get you one."

Helmet didn't follow me into the kitchen. Neither did Karl. Who could blame them? I retrieved two bottles and brought them back to the living room.

Soyla sat on the couch with Karl in her lap and Helmet on the cushion next to her. She was saying something about the snaps we'd grown accustomed to receiving from her, though she changed the subject when I walked in. I kind of hoped she wasn't telling Helmet that she was going to take us off her sexting distro list. I handed her a beer, and she took a long sip of my own.

"You were saying."

"Oh," said Soyla, and she laughed. "I promised your friend a sneak-peek at my new portfolio."

Way to go, Helmet!

"Great," I said, "but I meant Bernard."

"Oh him."

Another sip.

"He did come around a few months ago. Accused me of complicity in a very public robbery."

I responded with mock outrage, "He didn't!"

Soyla smiled.

"He did," she said. "But we talked for a while and he didn't seem too mad about the Aachen thing."

Interesting.

I thought The Seven might just clear the deck after that debacle. Anyone foolish enough to risk public exposure of the vampire world always ended up in same stewing kettle they used for cooking European explorers. My theft of the bones belonging to the most iconic figure in German history still made the lesser pages of print news and offered up millions of links to conspiracies theories on the internet. If that wasn't public exposure, then I didn't understand the concept.

"Mostly," Soyla said, "Bernard talked about you."

"What?"

That didn't sound good. Getting on The Seven's agenda is sufficient grounds for cancellation of your life insurance policy. Soyla nodded once and took another sip from her beer. She stood and walked around the room—stopping to pick something up for closer inspection or to look out on the dark street below. She swept past me and ran her hand across my shoulders. Before I could react, she bent and planted a kiss on my lips.

I'd *like* to say I sat there stone-faced while she nibbled at my lips, so I'd better not say anything at all.

"Yes," she said, and then, "My poor little Gaius."

I pushed her away.

"Why poor?"

"They're deciding your fate now. And from what Bernard tells me, you don't have other supporters in The Seven."

Other?

I needed problems with The Seven like I needed a mission to hell. But I'd always found didn't-need and not-going-to-get to be different animals. I pulled Soyla onto my lap and let her run the tips of her teeth across my neck. A sacrifice on my part, but one I was willing to pay for the sake of clarity in communications. I mean, a guy can miss a lot of words and whole meanings of sentences if he's listening from two feet away.

"Tiny Bernard likes you," she said. "The others?"

Soyla gave me the throat-cut gesture that translates well into any language.

"And why do they want to," I repeated her gesture?

"Power," she said, and added, "Why else?"

"Power?"

She let her hand wander toward the place that might get the wrestling match going again. I stopped her.

"Power," she repeated, and then in a pouty voice, "But no evidence of it here."

Ouch.

"They think my Gaius is becoming a threat."

Bernard had mentioned something like that when he'd swooped in on me before the Aachen mission. He also assured me that I was centuries short of being a threat. If the rest of the little bastards thought it best to off me?

"Bernard likes you."

That was probably because I'm the only one in the past five centuries to endure his boring crap without either falling into a coma or attempting suicide. He droned on and on and on and on in my flat while we planned the attack, and then afterward during the hour and a half trip to Aachen. And that retired South African racist cop he employed as a driver? Well, I understood why Bernard would want to hang on to *anyone* showing the remotest interest in him.

I said, "So why are you here?"

Soyla never did anything for free. And even though our tussle on the floor might be Nirvana-level compensation for every female alive today or yet to come, I didn't think it would suffice for Soyla. She preferred cash...or large bank wires to her account.

Soyla turned up the pouty Hungarian accent when she said, "What a horrible question. I'm here for you, my love."

Right.

I said, "You're here for me," paused for her nod, then added, "And?"

She took a moment to pull up the tail of my t-shirt and plant one of her sucking kisses on my chest.

"And I'm spying for The Seven."

For the third time in less than five minutes I pushed her away.

"You mean spying for Bernard, right?"

Soyla laughed.

"Of course not, my love."

She gazed back down at my chest and the hungry look in her eyes reminded me I wasn't dealing with a wildflowers-in-a-basin and stuffed-animals-on-the-bed kind of chick. No. More like one of the Gabor sisters as played by Hannibal Lector.

Pure sex. Pure danger. Well, I'd witnessed the danger, perhaps the sex part was wishful thinking.

"Then who are you working for?" and I added, "No games, Soyla."

Put *No games* on one side of the scale, *Soyla* on the other, and what do you have?

An oxymoron.

And how can we do this without melting?

"But my love," she said. "No games at all."

She reached a hand down my shirt and rubbed and then she curled her body against mine. The top of her head touched my chin, and though I could still detect a trace of rot, but her hair smelled like the clean hair of a woman who spent a fortune taking care of herself. We remained like that long enough for me to start liking the way her body fit perfectly into mine.

She interrupted those thoughts with, "The rest of The Seven."

"Who?"

I'd lost the thread of our conversation.

I said, "What about The Seven?"

Soyla sat up and looked into my eyes.

"My love," she said…

I also wondered how it would be to hear that coming from those beautiful lips every day for the rest of my life.

"You asked me who I serve."

Had I? Oh yeah.

"I did."

"Well," she said, "I work the rest of The Seven, not Bernard."

I got it…or, I thought I did anyway, because I said, "And what do you do for them? Uh…In addition to spying on me?"

She laughed as if I'd asked a stupid question, and then laid her head back down onto my chest and pulled herself closer.

"Silly Gaius," she said. "I'm to provide them the evidence to change Bernard's mind."

I rested my cheek on the top of her head so that her expensive hair scent could mask the trace of rotten eggs baking off of her.

"Change Bernard's mind? About what?"

"Why, you, my love," she said, and she resumed stroking my chest. "Because if I can provide them sufficient evidence to force Bernard to remove his protection, then the rest will be allowed to kill you."

Sometimes relationships work better when one or the other just keeps their mouth shut.

EIGHT

I PUSHED SOYLA back and held her shoulders so that I could look her in the face.

"Let me get this straight," I said, "You are here to dig up something on me that will end up getting me killed?"

She smiled and tried to press herself back onto my chest.

"Yes, my love."

"And you see no problem with showing up half-dressed in my place?"

Come to think of it, I was sure *I* had no problem with her showing up half dressed in my place. But that was beside the point.

"Drinking *my* beer, and spooning with me like this on the sofa?"

She paused for a second and then said, "I'm off the clock." Another pause, and then, "But I do admit this is a tiny bit awkward, my love."

Tiny bit awkward?

I stood up and Soyla nearly fell to the floor. Helmet rushed to stand beside her, and he glared at me like I'd fondled his sister. Come to think of it, the way he drooled over her snaps and that smitten look in his eye as he sat down beside her in the spot I'd just vacated? My bet was that Helmet didn't think of Soyla as a sister.

Great.

First a demon in drag, then a Hungarian warrior-woman assassin acting cute with me, and now a lovesick ghost with a case of the green-eyed monster. What more could I ask for on the night I planned on heading into hell and rescuing my hot, nicotine-addicted guardian angel from Satan's penalty box? Karl provided the answer. I caught sight of him dragging his bony doggie butt across my floor—right next to the transparent, steaming gift pile he'd just deposited in the center of the room.

Icing on the cake.

But hey, a 2000-year-old dude should be able to unpack just about anything. Soyla's plan to spy on me and then sell me by the pound to The Seven? That would be the first thing I would sort out.

"Get out of here, Soyla."

Helmet snapped up in outrage, and detected his hand moving to his belt…to the spot where I'm certain his pistol hung during the hightide days of the Third Reich.

I said, "Save it for later, Pilgrim, because Pocahontas is heading out the door."

Soyla did exactly what I expected her to do. She didn't move.

I said, "See you later," and then, "here's your hat, what's your hurry?"

"Stop, my love," she said. "You know Soyla wouldn't sell you out."

Ah, right. Wouldn't *think* she'd do it? Four months prior…she'd done *exactly* that. Soyla wouldn't sell me? Maybe not until she had the price she wanted. Speaking of price…

"You still owe me."

Karl returned to sniffing around her feet, so she picked him up and set him in her lap. Neat trick to pick up something made up of nothing, but vampires can do it. Also, Karl had to want to be held. Never a problem with Karl.

She said, "Owe you for what?"

"For taking out two very bad people who gave you money and who were going to look you up for what probably would have ended up a huge refund."

She ran a hand through Karl's ghost fur as she thought about what I'd said.

"Thank you."

Thank you. That was it. No apology, no explanation. Nothing else. Soyla to the core. And, as I thought it over, I only half wanted her to leave. I still didn't know what happened to the vampire odor that kept us apart for a thousand years and I did want to hear more of what Bernard had said about me. I also kind of hoped she'd wear that half-naked thing maybe just one more time. The memory might offer me something to keep my mind busy while the demons peeled off my skin and shoved it up my nether regions.

"Uh, you're welcome," I said. And then, "Tell me how you can be here like this."

Soyla looked at me like I'd lost my marbles.

"Your sweet landlord let me in."

Right. I think she was talking about that snake Herr Doktor, so...red herring. I refocused.

"I mean, what happened to the stink?"

Soyla appeared scandalized.

"Did Soyla's scent offend my love?"

I thought long and hard before I answered. Truth was, all those times she got to within a hundred yards of me I felt like diving face-first into an open Paris sewer to get relief from her odor. Somehow, I didn't think she would accept that answer.

"Not so much," I said. "I was always worried my own pungency might cause harm to you."

I saw her run that one through her mind—put it through that filter some chicks use to detect if an insult's been thrown their way.

My answer passed inspection because she said, "Then I should thank you once more."

And it reminded me why I hadn't been in a serious relationship since Nellie died. I mean, as if we both didn't know the truth. But here we were, the man pretending to be the ogre and the woman pretending to agree.

She said, "Bernard explained it to me."

Soyla told me that The Seven had been watching me and they'd somehow concluded my vampire powers were growing to the point I'd end up being a threat to them. That synched with what Bernard told me earlier. The Seven tends to treat future threats the same way they do current ones. My mind replayed the visual of Soyla dragging a finger across her throat.

And the odor thing? A Centuria is composed of one or more vampires created by eating the same infected heart. The repulsive odor doesn't apply to them; thus, I can't detect Sparky or Rolf when they're nearby. Those in different Centuria, they smell so bad I can't *keep* myself from detecting them. And the nearer they approach, the more caustic—and dangerous—the stench becomes.

There's no way to adequately describe it. The closest would be what I experienced on the battlefield at Gettysburg…when the bodies and amputated limbs rotted where they laid. Nothing today would come close…other than a few locations near Omaha.

And now Soyla emitted only the faintest aroma. I suspected even that might soon disappear.

I said, "And you can't detect me?"

Soyla took one of my hands in both of hers and squeezed. I felt power

in her grip, and it sobered me to the damsel thing she'd been playing...
well, the role she'd been playing *after* she held a knife to my throat.

Best to remember how I'd seen her dispatch whole squads of veteran
soldiers. More than once. Her personal record—at least as observed
by me—was eleven guys dead in less than ten seconds. She kept the
twelfth alive long enough to drink his blood. Trust me when I say that
guy didn't die easy. That man's screams echoed in my mind as I looked
down on that seemingly helpless kitten arrayed on my sofa.

"Not a bit," she said, and then added, "Just like The Seven."

And there it was. Bernard told both Soyla and me something about
an increase in my powers. I'd never heard of such a thing happening
in the vampire world, but who was I to say it wasn't possible? I mean,
take The Seven. Nobody could detect them.

"Yes," I said, "Just like The Seven."

It's not unheard of for animals to change as they age, to drop the
camouflage of their youth in favor of vivid patterns that assist in
mating rituals. Was the odor a sort of camouflage? Kind of made
sense. If so, then I could expect to undergo other changes...like maybe
not only dropping my scent but also the ability to detect the scent of
others...like maybe an increase in physical capabilities. And that's
what concerned The Seven.

"Soyla," I said, "How old are you?"

She smiled, "Old enough for this to be consensual," and she ran her
tongue across the top of my knuckles.

"Right," I said, and I pulled my hand out of hers. "I need you to
focus for a second."

"Sounds exciting."

"Not that way," I said, and then, "How old are you in years?"

"Almost a thousand, my love."

I'd already known that, but I wanted to make sure. Me? I'd seen my two thousandth birthday, though I stopped counting at thirty. It's hard for me *not* to keep track because I was born in the first century of the calendar most people use these days.

"How many of us are older than me?"

She thought for a second and said, "Many, I think," and then, "but don't concern yourself, my love, those old fools don't interest me."

She took my hand again and put it over her heart. That's a G-rated way of saying where she placed it.

"I go for younger men."

Yeah, as in a barely legal two-thousand-year-old.

But she had a point. Not about me being young, but about there being several out there much older than me. That tended to eliminate age as the catalyst for the maturing process I was hypothesizing. Made a crazy kind of sense when you thought about it. I mean, how many times had Nellie assured me that age didn't equal maturity.

If it was really happening to me, then it had to be something other than age. And that's where I left it because I had no clue how to proceed from there. What I did know, is that I had a sexy, self-centered, tattletale of a self-serving spy sitting on my sofa.

"Younger men," I said. "Got it."

Soyla stood up and said, "Need to go now."

Perfect. I did want her to leave so I could get moving on that little trip I needed to take. At the same time, some part of me wanted Soyla to stick around a bit longer. Oh, and it's not the part of me that comes to *your* seedy mind. That part wants *any* female nearby. But don't accuse me of objectifying women…I swear the thing has a mind of its own. What I wanted was delve more into what Bernard had said.

Who was I kidding? No way to get anything bordering the truth from Soyla. It's fortunate for the world that nobody else thinks like she does. I mean, it would be easier to figure out what was running through an oyster's mind than to expect truth to flow from hers. She'd decided it was time to leave…and leave she would.

I'm not going to lie, the hug she gave me—a full-frontal bind—made my day worthwhile. I'm talking about an embrace where you feel every bone and bit of flesh from her neck to her knees. I even did the reach around thing I'd never dared attempt with Sister Christian or Sarah Arias. But good old Soyla seemed happy to let my hands explore. With such a monumental choice to make, I decided to give both cheeks a squeeze before I walked her to the entryway.

I opened the door and saw Herr Nosy Doktor sweeping one of the stairs outside my flat. I was tempted to recommend a broom instead of the rake he was holding but decided to just play along. Yeah, he wasn't out there snooping on the American renter and his visiting sister.

Soyla must have understood what the old geezer was up to, and she decided to give him a show. She wrapped both arms around me and hiked a leg, snaked it around my lower back, and pulled me in close. Then, she put a lip lock on me that would make a porn star blush. I played along. Not because I found the whole thing off-the-charts sexy and therefore enjoyed the explosive tingling reverberating through my body, but because I can play a role as good as the next guy.

We did the vertical mamba for a full minute before Soyla pulled back and went through a fake orgasm routine. Of course, uh, a guy like me doesn't know what a *fake* orgasm looks or sounds like, I just thought maybe that's what she had in mind to punk Herr Doktor.

The scene ended with her pulling away and blowing me a kiss.

"Goodbye, dear brother," she said, and down the stairs she went.

Neither Herr Doktor nor I moved until several moments after we heard the exterior door open and close. He was still raking/sweeping the stair, but sometime during Soyla's goodbye ritual, the rake head had fallen off. Overpressure, perhaps.

Have to hand it to him, though. He stayed in character and continued moving the stick as if a straw broom sat on the other end. I turned to walk back into my apartment but decided to give old Herr Doktor a poke. Just for fun.

"It's the way Americans say goodbye to their sisters," I said. "The way things are done."

I'd made it halfway through the door before Herr Doktor found his voice.

"Does meine Fraulein Donna kissen like that?"

I stopped dead still.

After the show Soyla just put on and the beating he took from Frau Schutzstaffel downstairs, Herr Doktor *still* fixated on Donna/No Face. Had his mind substituted himself for me and No Face for Soyla during the scene? Sickening to unimaginable proportions. I feared the mental image of No Face wrapping a boil-laden, harry leg around Herr Doktor and locking his fake human lips over the old goat might haunt me forever if I didn't sprint to my kitchen and immediately lobotomize myself.

But I played it cool.

"Better," I said, and I heard him exhale. "I have to admit," and I paused long enough for his drool to pool on the floor, "Donna kisses like a demon."

I heard him moan as I shut the door behind me.

And if my surreal basket weren't already full, I saw Helmet waiting in the entryway. He wore a crisp Nazi uniform, complete with the black leather strap over one shoulder holding up the pistol belt around his waist. He even had his officer's saber neatly scabbarded at his side, and I could see the butt of a sidearm peeking out of the holster.

He said, "I demand satisfaction."

Uh, what?

"Soyla just left," I said. "You can talk to her about it if she comes back."

I didn't realize I'd been slapped until I found myself wondering why I was looking at the wall beside me. Hadn't I just been speaking to Helmet? I turned my head back toward him and saw he held a pair of leather gloves in one hand.

The braying jackass!

"To the death," he said.

NINE

SLAPS MY FACE *and challenges me to a duel.*

And I'm the idiot who spent endless hours over many months concocting schemes to prove Helmet could both speak and move physical objects.

I said, "To the death?"

Helmet stood at attention and clicked his heels.

"To the death."

"And how is that a threat to you?"

I could see the wheels turning in that love-sick ghost-brain of his. I could also see Helmet struggling for a dignified response.

The best he could come up with was, "You insensitive boor."

Not bad, but off topic.

"Could this have something to do with Soyla?"

"You did not treat her like a gentleman."

I wanted to respond in the vein of "That's because she *isn't* a gentleman," but I could see my soft-core sexual encounter with Soyla hurt his feelings. As if I didn't have enough to worry about for one day.

"Well," I said. "Maybe it had something to do with the way she was dressed when I walked in. Half-naked."

Helmet flinched. I poured it on.

"And it's difficult to remember one's manners with a knife blade sitting against one's throat."

That brought a smile to his face.

He said, "I guess I can't blame you."

"Now you're talking." After a moment's thought, I added, "Next time Soyla gets undressed in our place, make sure you get some pictures."

"I did."

Nice. With my luck he probably snapped her with the knife to my throat and me with a stupid look of fear on my face. But he wouldn't be a true friend if he didn't use my vulnerable moments like a rolled-up newspaper to spank my ego.

"So, no duel?"

Helmet considered. Of course, he didn't want a duel. I mean, even he could see that slapping me in the face was a childish move.

In a tone that sounded like a formal pronouncement of parole, he said, "No duel."

Self-important jerk.

I reached out my hand to shake his. I know, sounds weird, but that kind of thing is imprinted in every guy's DNA. Dog's sniff butts. But shake hands with a ghost? Idiotic.

I started to say something about going back into the living room to plan my mission to Sheol, but another hand across my face slapped the words back into my throat. This time, he hit the other cheek.

My face hurt in stereo. I looked up at Helmet. He'd resumed the stiff, Prussian version of attention.

Guys don't like complexity, and I subscribe to a simple rule regarding getting punched in the face. The first time you hit I may pause to find out why. The second time, I don't stop for conversation but go directly into the ripping-your-parts-from-your-body phase. But...I considered

Helmet a friend.

"What was that for? I thought you said no duel."

Helmet relaxed his military bearing and shot me a smile.

"For fun."

All great times come to an end, and I muttered my way out of the entryway and into the kitchen. Would it surprise anyone if I said I needed a beer? I grabbed one and sat down at the kitchen table. A portion of one wall is made of glass that includes a glass door. It leads to a deck situated over Herr Doktor's breakfast room.

I took a long sip and gazed at the Victorian house next door. Bad Homburg used to be the place where the princes of Europe came for their summer fun. Most of the huge houses lining the street I live on were boutique hotels in those days. Each floor of my four-story building held a single suite. My flat was one of those suites, and rumor had it that it was the favorite vacation holdup for the Prince of Wales. I wondered if Herr Doktor and Frau FoulBottom were as entertaining back then.

None of those historical nuggets mattered, but I allowed my brain to splash in a pond of useless knowledge to calm myself ahead of the more difficult thinking ahead. Procrastination is the common word for it, though the only thing on my short list of daily chores was to plan a trip to hell.

Helmet floated into the kitchen and sat down in the other chair. I was mildly-torqued with him for the adolescent slapping antic, so I kept gazing out the windows and pretended I didn't notice him. I can do adolescent with the best of them.

Helmet said, "Don't even think it."

I knew he meant the Sarah Arias rescue mission.

"I don't see any choice."

"A choice always exists."

Easy for him to say. He already knew what lay on the other side of the great curtain that separates life from beyond life. But as I thought about it, who did I know more qualified to give advice in this situation? Helmet said to give it up…to not even consider heading through the looking glass in search of my precious Alice.

"A choice. Really?" I drained my beer in a long gulp. "What exactly would an honorable, face-slapping German soldier would do in this situation."

I thought about what I'd just said, and it didn't sound precise enough. I'd been a soldier many times over in the past two thousand years, but I guess the argument could well be made that I began as a German soldier. I looked Helmet squarely in his eyes.

"You see, I know a bit about German honor and German soldiering. It might be a bit dated compared to your experience so maybe things changed over the years."

I thought that might get under Helmet's skin and was surprised when his expression didn't change.

"Soldiering gets you killed," he said. "I'm speaking to you as a man."

He considered his next words for a second before he spoke them.

"As a friend."

Almost sufficiently heartwarming to make me forget about the stinging on my cheeks.

As we sat there looking at each other and I almost forgot that Helmet wasn't a real man at all, but rather the imprint of a man who lived and died in one of the most troubling eras humanity limped through.

Maybe I was selling Helmet short. I didn't know what he was for sure, but I couldn't with any measure of truth or fairness call him anything less than a man.

So, I'd checked off my sensitivity box for the evening, and I needed to consider more important things. Mr. Don't Do It sitting across from me didn't look like he'd help. Good thing I wasn't expecting anything.

I thought I'd sit there for a couple of hours and plan things through. Nothing came to mind though, and I found myself looking out across Herr Doktor's little parking lot and into the window of the second story apartment on the other side.

A Turkish family lived there. At least I thought Turkish. I also thought Herr Doktor owned that property too, because I'd seen him futzing around over there the same way he noses around here. As far as the Turkish family? I'd encountered a man, woman, and child enough times that I waved hello when we occasionally crossed paths. Nothing more than that.

I fell into the voyeur thing instead of planning my big mission. What was there to plan? I mean, who knows where to find the gates to Sheol?

From what No Face says, people are dying to get in there.

I chuckled at my joke and held up a hand against the concern on Helmet's face.

"Just told myself a joke I've never heard before."

I let Helmet chew on that one while I returned to staring into the window across the way. Gates of hell? I felt confident I knew where it would all start. The Aachen Cathedral. That's where No Face waited for me the night I robbed the grave. At the time, I thought that he was the one who created the portal into the alternate dimension.

I hoped No Face hadn't, because that might make a temporal thing and I needed it to be there. If No Face wasn't lying about the demonic prison thing, then I couldn't expect him to hold any doors open for me while he sat in a jail cell.

Let's assume I made it through the portal without No Face's help. What then? If paths existed, which one would lead me to Sarah Arias? I'd already spent my few minutes in that alternate universe inside a mockup of the cathedral. One big room. That was the limit of what I saw.

I thought about that big room as I stared into the window across the street. My view of the alternate dimension came from the inside of a cage constructed of demonic fire. The little Turkish kid walk past the window across the street, and my mental vision of that room in hell poofed away as the real world begged for attention. The little guy stood in the bright light for a moment, and then disappeared into whatever lay beyond what I could see. My mind went back to the cathedral.

I saw myself in the hellfire cage…No Face and his crowd on the other side bars. Try as I might, I couldn't pick additional details from the memory because, at the time, my bloodlust demanded I focus on the food at hand…which meant the other humans.

It irritated me that the ghost just sat and stared at me. I mean, if he wasn't going to help, then at least he could remove those doleful eyes of his to somewhere beyond my sight.

I said, "Don't you have somebody's grandmother to chain?"

He raised his eyebrows.

"You know, isn't that how you interrogated them?"

Helmet appeared insulted, but not enough budge him from his seat. I was losing my touch. Only one thing to do when you get knocked off your horse. Mount back up and hold on tighter. I dug deep into my vast repertoire of offensiveness and cued up a couple of doozies when the obvious hit me.

That black wooden door.

The one inside the giant room in hell where I'd encountered No Face and his two human partners. That door led to somewhere. Might not sound brilliant at first blush but work with me for a second. I had thought the door would lead back to our world…No Face even said so when he sent some of my enemies through it.

Uh…it didn't. Lead to our world, that is.

No other doors in that room that I could remember, but in my defense,

I was busy at the time. You know, dealing with things. Something about the notion of no other doors bothered me.

Not quite right.

I entered the space through the portal…not the black door.

"Two doors," I said.

This time Helmet did speak.

"What are you talking about?"

"Two doors in Sheol," I said. "One opens from our world to the waiting room, the next leads to the dance floor."

He seemed to know what I meant, because he said, "Yes."

Sometimes I can't shut Helmet up.

"Two way," I said, meaning I thought the doors could be transited in both directions.

Helmet didn't respond. No matter, I was speaking to myself… working through puzzle. I looked back out the kitchen window and focused my eyes on nothing as my mind labored to figure out what that meant.

Helmet interrupted my thoughts with, "Not supposed to be".

I almost fell backward out of my seat. He'd waited for me to reach that mental spot where the real-world fades and the mind's eye takes over. And then boom. His loud, grating, voice.

I said, "You did that on purpose."

"Stop being a pansy."

Right.

He'd said, "Not supposed to be."

I'd used the Aachen Cathedral portal to enter Demonville and then return from it. Twice. Helmet said the door only worked one way. No. Had to be wrong.

"Helmet," I said, "the first door into the waiting room is always two-way, right?"

Helmet just stared at me, so I took his lack of an audible response as agreement.

"So, you're talking about the second door," I said. "That's the one that's not *supposed* to be two-way.

Again, silence.

Based on my limited experience, it made sense. Like I said, I went in and out of the main door twice, and I counted myself lucky that I didn't follow the others through the black wooden door in the back. What others am I talking about?

Again, it's a long story, but trust me when I say things didn't work out well for them once they transited the door. But…if whatever got them on the other side could have passed back through the door to me? Vampire soufflé, though rest assured that their second bite wouldn't have tasted as good as the first.

Helmet said the black wooden door was one way. No, he said *supposed* to be one way. He didn't specify the black wooden door, but that's the door he meant…not the entryway, but rather, the back door.

Supposed to be one way.

My mind tends to repeat itself when it can't grab onto something solid. So, the black wooden door was one-way—from the portal area to something beyond. *Supposed* to be one way. Interesting. But…and it hit me.

I said, "How did you do it?"

Helmet raised his eyebrows and his lips thinned to the point they nearly disappeared. It looked like he wanted to tell me, but something kept him silent. Better sense? I doubted it. I mean, hadn't he gotten himself captured and executed during the big war?

So, why wouldn't he tell me? What could he possibly have to lose? Call me insensitive for pointing it out a second time, but the guy was already dead. What more could they do to him?

I didn't know, though I could see the topic intimidated Helmet. And it frightened him enough that he'd rather hold back than throw me a helpful bone. That bothered me. Because, from what I've seen of Helmet since I first met him, whatever it was he feared should have sent me into fits of abject terror. Why? Well, if I made it through the first door and found my way past the second? I'd get to meet Helmet's boogeymen.

Something made Helmet run the other way…and somehow, he'd escaped it. How could I be certain? Duh, who was sitting at the table with me? If Sheol was all rainbows and flower petals, why did Helmet leave?

I could have spent a week worrying about what I would encounter if I made it through both doors, and it would be time wasted. I would see whatever I saw, so I needed to concern myself with how to find my way to the demon prison, not the sights along the way. Maybe that much wouldn't prove too much for Helmet.

I said, "Can you draw a map?"

Helmet did his twisted face routine again, only this time he came quickly to a decision.

"No."

I wish he'd come out with a straight answer instead of forcing me to extract meaning out of sentences crammed with flowery prose. It was on the tip of my tongue to tell him as much, when Helmet faded away until he disappeared.

Show-off.

Most of the time he walks from room to room like a normal person. Put him under a little stress, and he pulls everything out of his ghost's bag of tricks. Reminded me of Karl.

I spent a few more hours in silent contemplation. That's a fancy way of saying I started out promising myself I'd get down to some serious planning and ended up doing hours' worth of that free association thing guys tend to do when there's no woman around to keep them on track.

I looked at the snow outside and thought about the coming summer. And what does summer mean? It means football season is less than three months away. Football season means fourteen exciting weeks that culminate with the Bama Crimson Tide raising a trophy.

Football also means hot dogs. Hot dogs need buns. Cheerleaders have nice buns. So does Sarah Arias. Football also means television. Television means blimps for those high-altitude shots. High altitude shots are nice; therefore, blimps are nice. Sarah Arias has nice blimps.

That's but a glimpse of how the planning session went for me.

All neural pathways led to Sarah Arias. And in my book, that made all the thinking worthwhile. I ended up with nothing beyond the mental images of Sarah Arias's buns and blimps. Didn't matter, because I *would* go after her...transit those two doors, and even if I didn't have a map to get me to her.

Two doors. No map.

Sounded like a good title for my autobiography. Or maybe I could choose "An Idiot Vampire Travels to a Violent Death Followed by Eternal Torture in Hell." That one grows on you after you say it a few times. I knew I had my head in the wrong place if I was thinking about anything other than the buns, blimps, or the task ahead. I pulled an emergency, focus-changing-beer out of the fridge. Medicinal purposes for a combat situation.

I checked my watch and returned the beer to its ready state in the fridge. It would need to wait. Shower time. That was, if I planned on heading out to the commissary in Wiesbaden for my bagging gig. I didn't know if any chance existed that I'd return from my mission, but if I did, I wanted to keep my job. Bagging, rolling, and loading. Where else could I find that kind of instant gratification or a greater sense of accomplishment?

Only one answer to that. Nowhere. So, I did my morning ritual and hopped the train to work.

TEN

I **ARRIVED EARLY** enough to observe Captain Tickles go through his General Patton routine. He checked each of our IDs as we swung through the door and whispered the daily password to each bagger. Handy, should the strategic situation in the store change and we'd need to verify whether the people we worked with each friggin' day were, according to Captain Tickles, "friend or foe." It's nice to plan ahead so one of your bagger buddies doesn't accidentally shoot you as you're returning from enemy lines. Have I mention that Captain Tickles is a moron? Maybe…but just in case I haven't: Captain Tickles is a moron.

It was Sister Christian's turn to roll first, so I helped bag as the first customer made it through Pop's line. It was payday, so both the loads and the tips would be heavier than on other days. It gave us time to speak.

As she separated the cold stuff from the rotisserie chicken, Sister Christian said, "Did you think about it?"

"It?"

I could tell by the way she looked at me that she was trying to decide whether I was just playing stupid or if I were really that dense. That's an easy one. I'm really that dense.

"Your mission," she said as she loaded a full bag onto the wire cart.

"Mission?"

The sudden voice behind made me launch a can of peas across the floor.

"Easy son," Captain Tickles said. "You've got to remember to pull the pin before you toss one of those things."

Captain Tickles picked up another can and gave Sister Christian and me a short course on grenade operations and safety. He even made us pantomime the motions of pulling the pin, counting to three, and tossing the thing into an enemy bunker. I thought he might move on after the lesson, but Sister Christian's word—mission—hadn't slipped his mind.

He said, "Non-standard."

"Pardon me, sir?"

"The order for a long-range patrol did not come through me. Did you receive proper authentication with the communication?"

Proper what?

The road led to two possible answers, and I needed to pick the one most likely to get Captain Tickles interested in a different bagger team.

"Yes sir," I said. "Stamped for my eyes only."

That impressed him.

"A FYEO mission," he said. "And in my command."

FYEO means "For Your Eyes Only," and I could see how happy it made him that higher headquarters was finally tapping his battalion for the important stuff. Do people like Tickles really exist? The answer can be found embedded in another question: Do vampires really exist?

He repeated, "Eyes only."

Pride laced with a tinge of disappointment. From what I knew about information security classification in the military, eyes only meant that only the person—or people—listed as authorized to view the communication could legally read it. Captain Tickles would obey the mandate without question—and it would eat him alive to do so. He'd want to be in on everything, from tactical planning to personal equipment inspections before heading out.

It didn't matter to him at all that we were standing in an American facility located in an allied country that had not seen a hint of war for the last seventy years. He'd never consider that I was a bagger in a grocery store and not a member of Delta Force.

"Sorry sir," I said. "But according to communications security regulations, I'm going to respectfully ask you allow us our privacy."

"No problem, soldier," he said. "I understand completely."

I could see the battle raging inside his head. He wanted to stick around for the opportunity to finally employ his planning skills, but at the same time, his military DNA wired him to obey orders. And he'd consider a security violation—acquiring information he was not authorized to see—a form of treason. Programming won out.

With one arm around me and the other around Sister Christian, he said, "Happy hunting."

He gave us both a quick squeeze and headed off to check where he'd situate the gun emplacements if the bad guys attacked.

With Captain Tickles receding out of earshot, Sister Christian said, "Still not know what I'm talking about?"

OK, maybe I had been a little dense. Well, maybe more than a little. "Don't rub it in."

"I won't. Just be ready at lunch to tell us how we're going to help."

Yeah, that's what I needed. If breaking Sarah Arias out of jail didn't prove challenging enough, I might get the bonus of needing to rescue my friends from yet another form of horror. Lucky me. I watched Sister Christian roll out the door. Pops relaxed at the scanner.

Payday or not, morning traffic usually proved light. Things would pick up around eleven…the time early risers started their lunch breaks. I turned to find my way back to the bagger bullpen and felt a strong hand on my arm. Pops.

He said, "Don't get her hurt."

Four words from Pops are like a two-hour sermon in a tent revival. The old guy hadn't been involved in the escapade to Aachen, and as far as I knew, he knew nothing about it. I'd taken a few days off, unheard of for a bagger, to fly to Israel with Sarah Arias. Somehow my guardian angel had arranged it with commissary management. Maybe she'd passed along an eye's only order from her boss to Captain Tickles.

The rest of my friends didn't miss so much as a day of work. That's how quickly it all went down. Unless one of the gang spilled the beans to Pops or they spoke when maybe they shouldn't have, Pops *couldn't* know. I didn't think any of my friends had let me down. So, not only would Pops not know a thing about Aachen, he'd also have no clue about my vampire condition.

Still though, I thought I saw more understanding than I expected when I looked him in the eyes. I could have said something along the lines of "what do you mean" or something equally trite, but I had the feeling he'd see through it…that he had a valid reason for thinking I could get Sister Christian injured. Maybe even get her killed.

And he'd be right.

I broke eye contact and said, "I'll try not to."

The grip on my arm tightened.

"Try is crap."

He had a point. But I wasn't about to promise anything I couldn't deliver. If I couldn't stop Sister Christian and the gang from getting involved, then the odds were ten to one that one or more of them would get hurt. I didn't want to think of the "D" word, but how could I not when I felt death creeping nearer each time the second hand passed twelve. Death was out there all right, circling ever closer like a shark inspecting its prey before taking a bite.

I locked my eyes on the fading gray ones that belonged to Pops. If I couldn't give him any promises about what may or may not happen to Sister Christian and the others, at least I could offer him the truth.

"It all depends on them," I said, and I could see he didn't like that answer. "Best way for you to help," I said, "is to do whatever you can to keep them clear."

We stared at each other for a few seconds, and the way Pops was looking at me made me feel sick. I'd always liked the rusty old nail of a codger and felt terrible about disappointing him. I didn't know Pops' opinion of me, and if I'd thought about it at all I'd think he probably saw me as a dropout loser on the path to nowhere.

Only the truth can be the truth and, as much as I wanted to, I couldn't make guarantees about anyone's safety. Not even my own. So, truth was all I had to offer Pops and if it made him think less of me? So be it.

Pops grunted and turned his back to prepare for a customer who'd just arrived. Gosh but how I love conversations that are laced with concern and fatherly advice. J-Rod was on deck, so he came up to help me load. Sister Christian returned from her run and she lined her cart up behind the others.

J-Rod worked the first couple of bags without saying anything, but as he leaned over to retrieve a large ham that came trundling down the belt he whispered, "When do we go?"

Maybe I should have just called in sick or gone AWOL, because that question seemed tops on everyone's mind. He hadn't used his fake Latino gangsta accent, which meant he was serious. I suspected J-Rod, the Bonnie Prince, Watanabe, and Sister Christian had spoken with each other after they left Café Aus Zeit the previous night.

I looked back at the three sitting in the bullpen. Watanabe, the Prince, and Sister Christian. All watched J-Rod and me with interest. They'd decided I needed their help alright and help me they'd decided to do.

Could they help? I didn't think so. I mean, I absolutely did not intend to let them follow me through the portal. Would they be stupid enough to try? I looked at J-Rod, who seemed engrossed in packing all the meat products together while really hanging on what I'd say next. I took another glance over at the three expectant faces in the bullpen.

Yes, they'd be that stupid.

And if I didn't bring them in on this mission by assigning each a safe, but apparently important role, then they'd make things up as they went along. If that happened, I'd be sure to have four tag-alongs in Sheol.

Nothing came to mind, though.

Except...

I said, "What do you suggest?"

I caught sight of Pops momentarily stiffen, and then go back to scanning. Like it or not, he'd need to understand the necessity of bringing the bagger gang in if I wanted any chance at of keeping them out. Convoluted, but it made sense to me.

J-Rod had an answer ready.

"We help you get in," he said. "And then we're there to cover your exit."

I didn't want to agree to anything without thinking it through, though J-Rod's suggestion sounded good at face value. Getting me to the door and then back away from it meant they didn't intend on going *through* the door.

"Sounds doable," I said, and added, "but give me some time to think about it and we'll discuss it at lunch."

If J-Rod heard what I said he didn't act like he understood, because he turned to the bullpen and gave the three sitting there a big thumbs up. They grinned back at us like J-Rod had just announced we had the winning numbers and would be splitting that week's Lotto.

I returned their grin, even though I didn't feel like smiling at all. The deal went down too quickly. Somehow it morphed from "I'll think about it" and "let's discuss it" all the way to "I agree."

At our designated lunch hour, the five of us walked down the hill to the Wiesbaden Post Exchange. After we cleared the security gate, we walked across the sidewalk and into the food court. Everyone scattered to buy whatever suited them and we gathered with bags in hand at one of the long tables in the center of the room. We took our lunch late, though a couple dozen diners still sat at the tables around us.

I waited for the conversation to start, but my friends were kind enough to let us work through our meals before Watanabe finally spoke.

"What do you think about J-Rod's recommendation?"

I put down the chicken leg and said, "I'm not so sure…"

"Me either," Watanabe said. "I think you need more out of us than that."

More out of them? I didn't want them anywhere near the portal. I looked at the others and they'd put their sodas, burgers, sporks, whatever, down.

"That's not what I meant."

What I meant was more like *stay home and watch Netflix* or something like that. But four against one? And when that one was me trying to talk my way out of a sticky situation? It would be easier to empty the ocean one thimble at a time.

J-Rod said, "What *did* you mean."

He'd not used his Latino accent all day, and that concerned me.

"Just that I don't see a good reason for exposing you."

I think they exhaled in unison, because the noise I heard sounded like a giant bellows blowing disappointment. I had the wild urge to put my hands over the last bits of chicken so communal spit wouldn't fly onto it.

Sister Christian said, "We're already exposed."

The Bonnie Prince chimed in with, "Damn straight."

He picked up the drink sitting beside his paper cup—my iced tea, as it turned out—took a long swig through the straw, and declared, "Crap soda has gone flat."

If I didn't know anything else about how the rest of my day would go, at least I knew one thing I knew for certain: I'd taken my last sip of iced tea. Other than that? The bagger gang and I needed to work some things out. The Bonnie Prince put down my drink and said,

"Who was Donna?"

Since he already knew Donna was a demon in drag, I guessed he was trying to make a point.

"All of you know who she was," I said. And then, "I mean, *he* was."

"Right," said the Bonnie Prince. "And is this the first time we've brushed wings with a demon?"

He said it kind of loud and I looked around to see if other diners sitting nearby were listening. And yes, two, ancient German war-brides had stopped speaking among themselves and were staring at our table. That's one thing you have to love about the culture. They never bother with the pointless courtesy of pretending they're not listening.

I leaned forward and lowered my voice. I considered coding my response with Pig Latin, but couldn't remember how to obfuscate the word no.

So, I said, "No," and added, "Think you can keep your voice down?"

I jerked my head toward the table next to us.

"The ErmansGay are isteninglay."

The Bonnie Prince looked at me like I just stood up and my butt had fallen off.

Watanabe said, "Pig Latin."

"Oh," said the Bonnie Prince. He looked at me and said, "You can isskay my…"

I held up a hand and said, "I get it."

But the Pig Latin worked because I noticed the two old ladiess sitting next to us had given up on deciphering the crazy Americans and returned to their own conversation.

That put the Bonnie Prince back on his original point.

He said, "First time with the demon?" and I knew he wouldn't give up until he heard an answer from me.

I said, "No, not the first time."

They'd beaten me. The bagger gang. I understood I'd lost as soon as the Prince forced those words out of me. "No, not the first time." The gang had spoken among themselves all right, and more than I'd anticipated. The Bonnie Prince made their best argument right out of the starting blocks and I understood the race was lost before the echo of the starting gun faded.

Yeah, it wasn't the first time they'd encountered a demon. Nothing gave me reason to believe they remembered their short prison stint in the torture painting. But those memories would only represent a pinch more spice in the recipe they'd all tasted…back when they stood beside me to fight off No Face and his horde.

If demon lore doesn't exceed vampire stories in popularity, then it's nipping at the heels. The vampire stuff mostly comes from us vampires. But demon knowledge? Not a clue. I suspect most of it comes from either direct contact or from second, third, or fourth-hand accounts of somebody who experienced that direct contact.

One big difference exists between what humanity thinks about demons and vampires. Everyone knows vampires are fiction. Right?

Demons, though? Whether they will admit it or not, I suspect almost everyone believes demons exist. Consequently, the things written about demons carry authority. And a main pillar of demonology?

The Prince knew because he said, "Yes, not the first time for us and demons."

He picked up my tea and took another sip. OK with me, because the rest was all his.

"It means," the Prince said, "that demons are *not* going to leave us alone."

I could see the logic but thought it didn't apply this time. Yes, the bagger crew battled No Face and crowd in the construction tunnel, and yes, they'd bagged groceries and had beers the day before with the fake-trans version of No Face. But in both cases, it was me the demon kept coming back to and not them. The sole reason they'd encountered the demon? Me. No Face and his bosses wanted something out of *me*. Not them.

I considered explaining all that to my friends, but knew I'd come off sounding like an arrogant jackass. I could just hear J-Rod, "Oh, so you think it's all about you." On the other hand, was J-Rod's interpretation far enough off base to get picked off by the pitcher?

Maybe not.

I mean, I *was* assuming the rescue mission was all about me. Probably because of the thing I had for Sarah Arias. Well, definitely that. Plus my guilt for begging her into giving me help she wasn't authorized to provide. Maybe that jumble of personal feeling caused me to ignore something important about demons.

They're are as evil as politicians. And the two, demons and politicians, pretty much share the same philosophy when it comes to the souls belonging to others. Sure, there might be a fat cat contributor that gets heaps of attention, but once the voting curtain closes, one person becomes equal in importance to everyone else. At least it's supposed to be that way, but who knows these days? I guess it's how the software counts the votes.

Rabbit hole.

Did No Face's fat cat—me—garner his extra attention to gain a larger prize—my friends? I didn't know, and the thought made those red beans and rice I'd put into my stomach want to explode in both directions at once.

Did I *think* it was all about me? Well...yes. Was it? Maybe. But also, maybe not. As I thought it through, employing my affection for Sarah Arias as a tool to feed my self-centered ego would clear the road for the demons to go after not only me, but also my friends.

And what about Aachen? No Face claimed his performance landed him in prison. It sounded reasonable, so I didn't dig deeper. After all, he'd lost the important bones and let me get away. More accurately, he'd *helped* me get away.

Go directly to jail, right?

Maybe.

But he'd also made another mistake that I hadn't considered. Yes, he'd bungled the heist his master stewed over for four thousand years, and it was easy for me to assume the boss would frown on the sorry a performance. Sarah Arias kidnapped in retribution and No Face off to the Marquis de Sade's torture hotel. No parole. But I'd missed another aspect of No Face's fumble that was so obvious, I felt like slapping my forehead...vampire hard.

The deal. No Face made the exchange. My friends out of the painting for the bones I'd stolen. Worthless bones. House rules must be obeyed. I'd gotten one over on the proprietor, and The Boss wouldn't care whether I did it intentionally or not. If the rest of the natural and supernatural world heard about it? No telling how many would think they could cheat on their own unholy contracts. Bad for business, worse for reputation.

And who else could spill the beans on the failure? I'd taken out the two witnesses straight away. Neither Sparky nor Soyla would know what went down once I crossed the portal because they'd conducted their business through human intermediaries. So, no leaks possible from them. Then, there was my guardian angel. In the criminal world, she'd be considered a loose end.

Somehow, they'd put Sarah Arias on ice in the demon prison. That left No Face and me. He was already in jail. Me? Wasn't I planning to do something sufficiently stupid that I'd soon be within The Boss's grasp?

Assume I was right.

That scenario would account for most of the people and the supernatural beings who could testify to that bad bit of business.

But not all of them.

Consider my good friends from the commissary. That's the kind of press that got Job in so much trouble. Why would the dark team come after my friends?

Two reasons. First, to eliminate the last bit of evidence of a deal gone sour. You know, negative press that proved that demons could be had by amateurs. The second reason?

Because they could.

Going after people was the core competence of demons. Their sweet spot. Hadn't Watanabe just said the demons would continue until they destroyed all of us? An understatement if I ever heard one, because I suspected that demons could do far worse than destroy a person.

Did they need to hear that from me? They wanted to help me all right, and I loved them for it. If courage means moving forward despite your fears, then these guys defined the word. Oh, I could sense fear beneath the calm faces—vampires can do that.

Could I lie to them? Try to convince them to go home and leave me alone? Tell them that if they wised up and turned their backs on me and the supernatural mud that I'd pushed them into, that No Face and his clan would forget about them and they'd never need to fear a demon encounter again?

You bet I could lie to them.

Watanabe had said the demons would keep coming after them. Now was the time to make them believe that was wrong. If I could do that, they'd live another day. If not, my friends would find themselves much deeper in this, and we could all forget guarantees regarding life or death from the moment they left the table we sat at until...

Until what?

My mind had an answer for that one.

Until hell devours the last of us.

Watanabe said the demons would keep coming after them, and my friends wanted an answer from me.

I said, "You're right."

ELEVEN

NOT ACCURATE TO say you could have heard a pin drop. Oh, the bagger gang sat in shocked silence all right, but those two German biddies chattered loud enough to drown out a whole squad of brown shirts out for night of busting commie heads after putting down a few liters at the local beer tent.

I'd thought it through over my three-piece meal of extra-spicy chicken—complete with biscuit and red beans and rice. Thanks to the Bonnie Prince, no iced tea to wash it down. Best to keep an eye on them right up to the moment I stepped through the portal. After that, I thought No Face's boss would sort me out before mopping up my friends. At least I hoped it would go that way.

"We're right?" said J-Rod. And then in his gangsta voice he added, "Yeah, homie, straight up."

He continued with, "So, when we ice some undead…"

The Bonnie Prince looked at J-Rod like he'd just farted aloud during a wedding prayer.

"You can't kill the undead," he said. "You bind them and then throw them into a lake of fire."

J-Rod didn't miss a beat, "Where you find a lake of fire around here, homie?"

We all waited for an answer, including the Bonnie Prince. Because, instead of offering directions to the nearest lake of fire, he picked up my tea and took another sip. One promising idea out the door.

Watanabe said, "We don't kill them."

"Then how you off them, bro?"

Watanabe smiled.

"We outthink them," he said. "Work something up so we get Gare where he needs to go."

J-Rod didn't look convinced. I wasn't either, and what was worse, I thought I might need to leave the rest of my biscuit on the plate, because it now tasted like powder, and no way I'd consider drinking any more of my tea with Vince the Prince's spit all over my straw and his backwash in the cup.

Sister Christian broke into the conversation.

"Outthinking them isn't good enough," she said. "Unless I'm wrong, these things keep coming forever."

She had a point. Hadn't I just witnessed a four-thousand-year grudge almost come to fruition several months prior? And if my logic wasn't flawed, that grudge did not go away when Sarah Arias took those bones to wherever she left them in the hills of Israel. How did I know that? Well, where was Sarah Arias? Where was No Face? And why were we involved at all?

I smelled a setup.

J-Rod said, "So what we do?"

Sister Christian said, "We trust Gare."

What?

First time those three words, spoken in that order, ever passed the lips of a woman. Especially one with so many reasons to demand untrustworthiness of me. I think it shocked the boys too, because they stared at Sister Christian like she'd suggested a round of strip poker. The Bonnie Prince missed his mouth with the straw and landed it in his right eye. No loss there.

Watanabe wasn't ready to buy into trusting me so easily, and he said, "Trust Gare for what?"

Sister Christian said, "Just trust him."

She might as well have said, "Lunch is concluded." As we walked up the hill toward the commissary, none of the guys mentioned the idiocy of trusting me. That didn't mean those thoughts weren't banging inside their heads. Wouldn't blame them a bit.

For the rest of the day, rolling groceries seemed a more an ominous chore than a mindless outdoor activity. Each trip I completed brought me one step closer to hell. And by the way the rest of the gang dragged their feet, I think they felt the same way. One thing happened on the positive side.

A retired sergeant led one of the other bagger cliques. Sister Christian convinced him to exchange their free day—tomorrow—with ours—the following Wednesday. I suspected she agreed to a date with the old warrior to close the deal, but I didn't ask. None of us did, and nobody celebrated the small victory. I mean, who cares about a library book that's due next week when you have an appointment with the hangman that night?

Just trust Gare.

Sister Christian's words kept bouncing through my brain. *Just trust Gare.* The emotional weight of her pronouncement grew each second. By the time we helped close the store, I struggled to take a breath, and I wondered if that was how a panic attack felt. I'd faced death before and I'd been wounded to the point my comrades left me for dead. But in all my long years I never experienced a level of angst so all-encompassing that it enveloped me like a crushing fog in a horror novel.

We decided to meet up at eleven p.m. at the Frankfurt train station. From there, we'd take a rental van to Aachen. Then the fun would begin. Sister Christian volunteered to rent the vehicle, so she'd leave the commissary and take the train directly to the Frankfurt Airport. She'd put the vehicle on her credit card and lease it for one month.

Watanabe suggested a month because authorities would think it less suspicious if a month-long rental showed up overnight in a parking lot somewhere other than Frankfurt. I'm not sure I followed the logic, but Watanabe represented the entire membership of the Harvard Club among us baggers. We agreed with his van proposal for no other reason than that. You don't squander that kind of brainpower.

The roundtrip to the Frankfurt Airport and back to Wiesbaden would take Sister Christian less than two hours—most would be tending to the draconian paperwork necessary to rent a vehicle in Germany. The boys would chill at their places. I suspected Watanabe wanted to make sure he'd laundered his ninja suit and I hoped the Bonnie Prince would spend the time closing a deal for new glasses at a one-hour optical shop. J-Rod? He'd down some brews. Me? Important business that needed tending to.

We said our temporary goodbyes and I headed down the hill to catch the train for Frankfurt. From there I'd take the S5 toward Bad Homburg, though I planned on getting off one stop early. I waited downstairs at Gate 104, hopped the S5, got off at Oberursel and took the U3—streetcar—to the An Der Waldlust stop.

Wald is German for forest, and what waits at the Waldlust stop. I crossed the main road in front of the Frankfurt International School. The buildings were deserted—it being Saturday—but even the vast sports field was dark. Perfect. It wouldn't take more than a few steps to get into the forest.

I've already mentioned vampire superhuman night vision, so you'll not be surprised to hear how my visual acuity increased as I left the streetlights and stepped into the trees. I could see things as well as in daylight, though in shades of green. The inventor of night vision goggles was one of us.

I walked several hundred yards into the woods, and I paused to gather my bearings. At least a dozen creatures waited within a three-hundred-foot radius—an approximation of my limit for most animals. Human blood? I can detect that much further away.

I don't like the taste of blood, though I'd be lying if I said I didn't enjoy the hunt. It's in our DNA. A man's DNA, that is. Dial 911 and report me to the PC police if you want. I don't care, and mere denials—no matter how heartfelt—don't change nature. Men hunt. They kill. They eat.

Say you're a vegetarian? That's cool. It's easy for me to sense vegetarians because their blood smells thinner and less vibrant than that of other humans...plastic-like, and in disharmony with the environment.

Sound like self-justification? Well, maybe it is...but still, I've never understood why hunters force themselves to graze like the animals that provide food for the rest of creation.

None of that in the wild. Animals follow the path that nature demands...they're the true ecologists. I try not to think too much when I'm hunting when people aren't my prey. Instead of human reasoning, I close my eyes to listen to the full range of my senses. It didn't take long for me to pick up the scent. Two of them, and I detected no stress in their movement.

Perfect, they didn't suspect what was waiting for them. I sensed them moving nearer in a random way. Stopping for a moment here and there...occasionally backtracking, but always moving forward. Toward me.

Heartbeats tell stories, and they said one was older than the other. I thought they were both males, which was rare for this sort of animal. Perhaps the lack of a female was the reason they weren't fighting. None of that mattered, though, because they carried everything I wanted in their veins.

Not deer, the compact, high volume of blood told me that much. A deer might hold as much blood, but it would be spread across a longer, leaner body. Only one animal fit the model: a wild boar. I consider myself lucky each time I encounter one. No animal, not even a bull elephant, can come close to matching my power. Even so, wild boars make fierce competitors. The meal you pay for always tastes sweeter than one that comes free.

Adrenaline supercharged my muscles, and I felt my heart switch into its calm, sure, hunter's rhythm. No need for nervousness, I'd done this thousands of times over the years. One of those two boars was dead from the moment I detected the pair.

My teeth grew in anticipation. They are the only part of my body over which I have no control—I know what you're thinking but work with me here—and the only outward appearance that marks me as a vampire. Long and sharp. Ready to serve my need for survival.

Animal blood does well in a pinch. Better than that really, because it can keep me going for two months, sometimes three. Eventually, it always came down to humans. Would I take a life to prolong my own? I can answer that question with another.

Am I still here after two thousand years?

The boars became fainter to my senses, a sure sign they'd passed tangent to me and were receding. Time for action. My pursuit began in an all-out sprint. No need to worry about stealth because they couldn't outrun me...not this close and not while the scent of their blood guided me.

When I heard grunting up ahead, I let out a roar in anticipation of the fight, of the kill. My challenge communicated to their most primal level, and they turned to fight. They were waiting for me in a small clearing.

I'm certain it was the older of the two that marshaled the pair to the uphill position. When I locked eyes with him, I saw a warrior. The younger one appeared the stronger of the two. Instinct would guide him the same way instinct drove me.

No telling whether their teeth gleamed in the night because I was on night vision…like I said, everything came to me in shades of green. I could have counted the bristly hairs on their wide faces and the battle scars on the old warrior's hide. No time for that, because I needed to keep the engagement moving. I allowed them little opportunity to plan their defense as I growled in delight and raced directly at the two of them.

The younger one lowered his head in anticipation of my attack and made ready his two magnificent weapons. He aimed to rip my legs or, if fortune smiled upon him, slice through my viscera and spill my guts onto the ground. The older of the two sensed death speeding for him and he decided to charge me head on. A courageous, last-ditch move from an experienced warrior.

His bravery earned my pardon. I didn't pause as I gave the older one a strong kick to the head. I heard bone strain but not crack as the force of my blow sent the boar flying in the direction opposite his charge. My mind saw a football—pigskin—sailing through imaginary goal posts set up in the forest, but I wouldn't laugh. The boar's courage earned that much from me, as did that of his comrade who waited patiently to repulse my attack.

I'd stunned the older one enough to remove him from the fight, so it all came down to the younger boar and me. He lunged for my knees when I got within striking range and I dodged to one side and parried with my foot. Two large teeth flashed past the meaty part of my leg and I slid to a stop and whirled, prepared to face or to give chase.

The young boar didn't disappoint. He regained his balance and came on in a graceful rush. I jumped in the instant before he'd have ripped through me and landed so that I could bring the full force of my elbow onto his spine.

Perhaps I could have also stunned the younger one. Disabled him temporarily or held him fast in my grip while I fed on only as much I needed to keep the bloodlust at bay for the next few days. After that, I could have let nature decide whether the creature recovered or dragged himself deeper in the woods to die.

But, for that boar and on that night, *I* usurped the role of nature and decided with a thumb pointing down. He would die. I could claim I didn't have time for the necessary care to immobilize and then take only enough before releasing him…that my friends would soon gather in Frankfurt and my guardian angel awaited rescue in hell. I could claim that, and nobody would be any the wiser. But even if all the time in the world existed from that moment to infinity, if I'd met neither my friends nor Sarah Arias… I'd have taken his life.

Who am I to judge the creatures of the earth, and who am I to decide which humans will become my food? I am Gaius Teutoberg, Prince of the Forest, slayer of the Roman Legion. And I have lived for two thousand years. I make no excuses and offer no apologies. I take what I deem worthy of taking.

I brought my elbow down as instinct drove the young boar to turn his head to face me. One of his two white razors ripped through my flesh as I delivered the killing blow. I yelled as much in triumph as in pain and I heard an exhilarated laugh. It sounded like neither mirth nor a lunatic's cackle, but more like the joy of a man in synch with the world around him. And it came from my own mouth.

The young boar departed life without a whimper. No movement at all as my blow snapped that precious nerve center that commanded of his muscles. I turned the carcass on its back to expose the jugular as something rustled the plants behind me.

The older boar stood three arm's lengths away. Watching. We locked eyes for a moment and I felt a calm sort of serenity as the hunter's message passed between us. We understood each other. Two old warriors, both victorious, and the battle had ended. No need for further killing.

I bent over the young boar and drank my fill. Life that left the beast flowed into me. Did I feel any different? Would I tell you that warm ambrosia flooded my body with a narcotic effect? No. Never. It was about the hunt, the battle, the kill, the victory. It had always been that way and would remain the same until some greater warrior rewarded me the favor of an honorable death.

I stood and left my prey where he lay in the same manner we left Varus and Caesar's precious Seventeenth Legion…to feed the scavengers. Not an insult, but rather an acknowledgment of a battle well fought and a desire to not disturb the brave. The old boar watched me walk away.

And.

My arm hurt like all get-out. Vampires might recover at lightening-speed, but, just like you, we're prisoners of our human nervous systems. Oh, I could repair everything, even regrow a head, should the need arise. But the process hurts. Try this experiment. Take the crowbar out of your car and ram the sharp end into the flesh below your shoulder. Feel good?

In addition to the pain, I also needed hide the wound from other passengers on the streetcar. I pulled off my jacket, sweater, and undershirt and did what I could to wipe the blood off my face—the boar's—and my arm—mine.

My best day as a housekeeper leaves my place looking like the Japanese army decamped moments before the Banzai charge. Despite that, I managed to wipe away most of the telltale signs of injury and death as I walked to the U3 stop. I decided to take the streetcar into Bad Homburg rather than the opposite direction to the platform at the Oberursel train station. It would extend my trip by twenty minutes, but I'd run into less people.

I waited alone at the stop and stood far enough down the track that I knew a couple of trolley cars would separate me from the driver. The forethought paid off when I stepped into an empty car and rode the thing through several stops and into the edge of Bad Homburg. I did the Aufsteigen thing—that's what Germans call getting off the train— and took the longer route home.

I was tempted to do my faster-than-a-speeding-bullet sprint but decided it safer to pretend to be a guy out for a brisk jog. I could be sure that many sets of German eyes would watch as I ran past their flats… even if I didn't see them. Come to think of it, I could be certain of being watched *especially* if I didn't see them. Today's Germans. A two-word sentence that could fill volumes.

Herr Doktor and Frau AlwaysOnMyAss didn't show their faces as I came through the exterior door and made my way into my flat. Karl greeted me like I'd just escaped a thousand-year kidnapping. Nothing special, because the little idiot acts the same way when I take two minutes downstairs to check my mail.

Ghostly paws scratched at my leg, though I couldn't feel them. I waited for a moment and Karl's typical greeting erupted from the body-part the long-dead dog spent half his conscious time polishing. I *did* feel that.

The little guy must have smelled the blood on my arm because he pirouetted a couple of times and then dropped a load on the hardwood floor. Beyond perfection. I'd only have twenty minutes or so to admire it before it disappeared into that great poopie pile in the sky. No chance Helmet would do the right thing and clean it up.

And speaking of Helmet, he was waiting for me at the computer desk in the living room. When I sat down on the sofa, Karl jumped in my lap too and licked at the blood. I mean, the dog isn't a dog at all but rather, he's the lingering spirit of a four-legged moron who last decorated a floor with solid substance more than a hundred years ago.

Tangible results or not, Karl kept at it. I gave up trying to shoo him, and I let him lick away with his wide, happy eyes and ineffective dog tongue. One thing I've learned about Karl, nothing, not even death, can stand between that brainless git and his unadulterated joy.

Helmet and I stared at each other for a few moments before I said, "Anything new from Soyla?"

Our typical man-greeting.

On the surface it meant I wanted to know if the Hungarian Warrior-Woman had updated her portfolio, and underneath, it was our way of saying hello. Of course, I'd never turn down a look-see if she'd indeed sexted some new snaps.

"No," Helmet said, and I didn't hear the normal disappointment I'd expect from his having to cycle through photos he'd already memorized down to the last ingrown hair bump.

OK. The stuff I just said about our typical man-greeting? Truth is, I normally just wanted to know if we received something new from Soyla. The rest of it was garbage to make my life sound deeper and more literary. But that night, it was different.

It wasn't every day I came home intending to strike out for the gate to hell so that I could face whatever ungodly creatures opposed me on my way to rescuing my guardian angel. Good thing too, because if it happened every night like that, then I'd need to keep my laundry in a travel-ready condition.

Getting back on track, that night was different and we both knew it. Up until the day before I'd thought Helmet couldn't speak—some ghost rule or something. But he'd finally come out of the aural closet and now I worried he'd return. I didn't want that to happen. Not that night, as I considered placing my own bacon into the proverbial fire.

Helmet knew what I wanted without me having to ask for it. But by gosh, it appeared he'd make me—no, force me—to ask for his help. To be fair, he'd already said he wouldn't get involved; that I shouldn't consider risking myself. Not for Sarah Arias or any other pot of gold lying at the end of a rainbow that arced in shades of black across what remained of my life.

Yeah, I note that to be fair to Helmet. On the other hand, the fair comes to town only once a year and it had already been. I needed information.

Helmet sat back in the chair and I decided not to ask after all, not to force *my friend* to give me the information about Sheol that I needed. If I were to go and not return, I wouldn't want to leave Helmet drowning either in a sea of fear—for revealing something he thought dangerous to himself—or guilt—for not helping me when he could have. So, I said nothing…even when Helmet finally looked like he was ready to talk.

"What?"

OK, so I said at least one word more.

"You know *what*," Helmet said. "I know you want to ask questions."

He leaned forward.

"So, ask them."

Bingo.

It looked like Helmet might come through after all. And, in the nick of time because I'd need to leave within the next half hour to keep my date with the gang for our meet-up in Frankfurt.

"How do I get there?"

Helmet made a tsk-tsk noise and shook his head.

"Always brute force," he said. "Losing at American checkers when you should be thinking about German chess."

I didn't think the Germans invented chess, but I decided to hold onto the challenge flag for the possibility of a more critical call that might come later in the game. No point in making Helmet mad when I needed him to open up.

"And your point?"

"That you're asking the wrong questions," he said. "And also, that when no question can be the right question...you should just listen."

I thought about it and decided to let him have it his way. This time. Anything he gave represented more than I had, and if his story turned out a bust for me, I would walk out the door with no less information than I had when I'd walked in.

"OK," I said. "Let's hear it."

And Helmet told me a story.

TWELVE

IT BEGAN IN the weeks prior to his execution…the waning months of the war, and during the last-gasp German offensive in the Western Theater known today as the Battle of the Bulge. Helmet's commanders—of course Helmet wasn't his name in life, but he assured me it would do fine in death—ordered him and several others to dress in captured Allied uniforms and infiltrate enemy lines.

They received little training the spy craft because by then the Allies rolled in from the west and the Russians pounded the remnant German armies in the east. Every day brought endless processions of Allied bombers with load upon load of screaming death. All day. All night.

Helmet paused, and he pawed at the front pocket of his uniform like he was reaching for a pack of cigarettes. A blank look crossed his face as he seemed to forget where he was. What he was…and that the pocket he reached for offered up its last cigarette many decades before. His face morphed from confusion to a look of such profound sadness that I felt ashamed of the times I'd allowed hours, days, and years go by in casual disregard for the beauty of my life.

"You said something about training."

Helmet looked at me and blinked as if he'd forgotten I was there. He nodded.

"My family died in Dresden," he said. "In the fire or the rubble or afterward."

"Sorry," I said, and Helmet waved away the word like he was swatting a gnat.

He had a story to tell, and he cared not one iota for anyone's sympathy. Not even mine.

"An army friend told me about my parents and my sister," he said. "We were both from Dresden and he'd deserted for a few days to check on his own people." A single grunt of a laugh from Helmet and he said, "My comrade made it home and back before anyone realized he'd left." Another derisive snort and, "The grand army of the thousand-year Reich," a pause, "And we couldn't even take proper attendance."

I thought about a level of disorganization so foreign to German DNA that it must have seemed like a deadly, virulent virus.

"The allies used special bombs to create a storm of fire," he said. "It swept through the city."

I remembered the firebombing of Dresden. The news didn't hit me as anything out of the ordinary at the time. I was a foot soldier in the American army...one of the millions heading east for the German heartland...my homeland. The Air Force bombed every day until hearing about it became routine. And, back then, that's what Dresden sounded like to me. Just another day.

But it wasn't.

"They went after civilians," Helmet said, "and by doing so they thought they could break our iron will to fight."

Helmet's hand once again moved toward his empty pocket, though this time he stopped it halfway.

"But how could they break something already melted away in the furnaces of death?"

I didn't say anything. What *could* I say? Tell him I was one of the Joes fighting my way to the Rhine? Or maybe I could recount how my rifle and my blade sent hundreds of my descendants to their deaths?

"They gave us no training," he said. "Because we had nobody left to provide it."

It made sense. German civilians fell at rates nearly equal to the soldiers because the Allies had made the entire country the front line of battle. After the war, I found out that the bombing even claimed some of the top bureaucrats of the Nazi machine. And if *they* couldn't protect themselves and their wives and children, how could anyone else hope to be saved?

Hitler, limping and shaking from the failed July assassination attempt, attempted a final counteroffensive to push the Allies out of Europe. Enter Helmet, who was in Germany recovering from wounds received on the eastern front. His grandfather had immigrated to Texas after the First World War and was moderately successful as a cotton farmer.

According to Helmet, the old guy loved his new country—I could relate—but sent all three of his sons back to Germany for proper University schooling and engineering degrees. Two returned home—one to a job in Pennsylvania and the other to an architect firm in New York.

Helmet's father met the Frauline of his dreams in the Gasthauses ringing the old university in Dresden. They married, and less than a year later Helmet's older brother was born. The couple decided to remain in Germany to raise their family. Helmet's grandfather sent sufficient American dollars for the young couple to comfortably weather the depression and subsequent hyperinflation of the late 1920's and early 1930's.

But money always tends to carry stipulations, and for Helmet's parents, the condition came in the form of the two boys—Helmet and his older brother. The old man decreed they'd spend their summers in

Texas. Take it or leave it. Helmet's parents took it.

That was how he acquired a Texan's version of English perfect in tempo and diction, yet ultimately flawed by immersion in his native German culture. Flawed English or not, Helmet's language skills made him a shoo-in for the ad hoc unit of spies to be infiltrated ahead of the offensive.

Once in place, the new spies were to cause as much havoc as possible with the aim to disrupt Allied logistics and communications in the critical first hours of the German offensive.

Helmet said, "I saw such disorganization among the Americans that it felt like I was back with my unit in Russia."

He didn't specify how, but Helmet made it through the Allied lines. I have to hand it to him, from the antics he described, he did manage to raise more than his share of confusion among the allies in the days before he got himself captured. For example, he switched the directions road signs pointed, and witnessed entire infantry battalions take the road that led to German ambushes rather than the safety of Allied lines. Helmet claimed he slashed enough tires to raise Firestone's quarterly profits, and he even set a few light explosive charges here and there, though he didn't know whether any of them went off.

The German infiltrators also mounted a psy-ops—psychological operations—campaign when they discovered that American units proved fertile ground for rumors. The first days after the giant German Tiger tanks came rumbling in for the attack left the Allies in disarray and on the verge of collapse. Helmet would fall in with groups of American soldiers and fill them full of scripted baloney. Those nuggets served to destroy morale.

Helmet said he just needed to plant the seed and stand back as the American soldiers watered it and fed it into a forest of misdirection. "General Patton has been wounded and it looks like he's not going to make it," or "the krauts collapsed our front lines and are pouring in," or "German paratroopers are behind our lines." Anything to spread suspicion, hate, and discontent inside enemy lines. Helmet said he also went so far as describing the combat deaths of fictional friends in gruesome detail.

But under the protection of their air force and with fresh troops rushed to the battlefront, the Allies first slowed the German attack and then ground it to a halt. Oh, the Germans nearly succeeded, and at one point, the Allied lines bulged like a festering sore. Hence the name Battle of the Bulge. But the Allied lines never broke, leaving Helmet and the guys like him behind to fend for themselves.

The enemy already wise to the infiltrators—they'd discovered some of the less linguistically talented fellows early on in the battle. The failure of the German offensive and subsequent reorganization of the American units gave the military police time to search for the spies.

There were a couple days of constant questions as American soldiers challenged every face they didn't recognize to prove their American-ness. Helmet learned the answers by listening to how other guys responded. It almost always involved sports or holidays, and none of that tripped up Helmet. He sealed his fate in a mess tent.

English is a Germanic language so many of the words sound the same, and those words that nearly-the-same words represented Helmet's Sword of Damocles. The intense stress Helmet must have felt served to heighten the odds of a slip-up.

"Pass the pfeffer," Helmet had said.

Not pass the pepper or just pointing and grunting. Pass the pfeffer. Courtesy can kill.

"One second I had a plate full of SPAM, the next I felt hands dragging me off the bench."

The American stockade already held a few of Helmet's associates, and each received a trial in front of a military tribunal that condemned each to death. Helmet said his sentence didn't worry him as much as the manner in which it would be carried out. He understood that dead was dead, and he'd never expected to survive the mission anyway.

I wanted to ask him if the whole operation was his version of suicide. I mean, his mother, father and sister were already dead, and his brother had died years before as a Stuka pilot in the Battle of Britain. He'd seen everyone and everything he'd loved either bombed into dust or obliterated by Allied bullets. I suspected he raised his hand when they asked for volunteers…more to go out in a blaze of glory than to serve the Fatherland. I was curious, but some questions are so unseemly they're best left unspoken.

"I wanted to be shot," he said. "Hanging was for criminals, shooting for soldiers."

Uh, spooky.

I kind of got it—why he wanted to be shot instead of hanged— but really couldn't see how it would make much difference. I've experienced both in my time, and I can testify that neither method of dead feels better than the other. But Helmet wanted to be shot so I let the conversation move on without comment.

I did find it interesting, but at the same time, none of Helmet's story helped prepare me for my own looming mission behind enemy lines. I needed to nudge Helmet in that direction, because time was getting short.

I've already described how I'd found a video playing on my computer one evening…Helmet's execution by firing squad. I remember marveling at the way Helmet marched with the firing squad like he was a part of the unit, and how he stood at rigid attention until the volley of bullets ended his life.

The alive and breathing version of Helmet who I saw march so upright and stand so courageously was feeling fortunate he was about to be shot, not hanged. On the surface? Pretty sick, though I understood. Family? All killed. Hometown? Burned to the ground. Country? In ruins. Nothing to live for.

I did have one question that gnawed at me and I decided to go ahead and ask before we moved on to more important matters.

"How is it you ended up in a German uniform?"

Helmet knew what I meant. I wasn't asking why he joined the German army but rather how he was in a German uniform when they marched him into the pit and ended his life. Because if I'd heard right, he'd inserted himself behind Allied lines wearing an American uniform.

"One of the guards," he said. "A guy from near where I spent my summers in Texas."

Helmet went on to tell me about how shocked the American guards were at the perfect English spoken by Helmet and the others of his spy group. He even managed to strike up a friendship with a kid from his grandfather's area of the world.

"He'd heard of my grandfather," said Helmet, and I marveled at how mischievous that rotten spirit called Fate could be at times. "And he brought me the uniform from captured materiel," he said. "We promised to link up at my grandfather's place after the war," Helmet added, "but we both knew how things stood with me."

Two young men who would have been friends under other circumstances.

"I asked him to be on the firing squad," Helmet said. "And he promised he would."

I let that bombshell settle between us. It made a samurai's notion of sense, but still, I couldn't imagine firing a bullet into the body of a friend. Well, Sparky maybe…and it wouldn't kill him anyway.

"I was looking at him as they blindfolded me. And one moment I was standing there waiting and the next," he paused, "nothing."

I took advantage of the perfect opening that last sentence provided.

"And then you found yourself here?"

Helmet looked at me as if I were crazy.

"Of course not," he said. "After I was shot I…"

He broke off in mid-sentence.

"You what?" I said, and I tried to use my only-casually-interested voice.

Helmet saw through it.

"You're interrogating me."

Not really…but…yes.

I said, "Interrogation seems too harsh."

Helmet responded by folding his arms in front of his chest and clamping his mouth shut. Maybe that's a little dramatic because ghosts don't really have physical mouths to clamp. Bottom line, it looked like I'd be leaving with nothing more than my limited knowledge of the demon portal in Aachen. Well, there was also my insatiable sex drive. Even though it seldom comes in handy, I take it with me wherever I go.

"Come on," I said. "You're dead, what more can they do to you?"

Helmet thought for a second before and his answer came out sounding unvarnished and direct.

"They can force me back."

Yikes.

"How?"

"Do you think if I knew how they could bring a person back I'd be sitting here talking to you right now?"

I didn't know the answer to that one because I wasn't following the logic. I took a stab anyway.

"Where would you be?"

Helmet didn't skip a beat when he said, "I'd be back there trying to get out, wouldn't I?" And then he added the obligatory "Dummer Esel."

Ouch. he'd just called me a dumb ass, or something like that, but I could have been wrong, so I took it as an archaic honorific.

"Thank you," I said, and felt a measure of satisfaction when Helmet rolled his eyes.

I needed to get something straight about the reason for his hesitance.

"You think if you give me information about hell..."

Helmet interrupted with, "Sheol."

Gesundheit, I almost said, but Helmet tended to the formal side of things and if he took my childish humor as the insults I intended them to be, the dialogue would cease.

"OK, Sheol," I said. "You think if you gave me information about Sheol, then they'd punish you?"

I took his silence as agreement.

"But you somehow escaped."

Helmet nodded.

"And they haven't come for you thus far?"

He seemed to have expected that question.

"I don't know that," he said. "Not for sure."

At first, I thought he had a good point, though I changed my mind in less than a second.

"Wait a minute," I said. "If they did know where you are, and they don't come for you," I paused to let it sink in, "What makes you think they'll come for you at all?"

Helmet thought about that for a second and said, "True enough. But what if they haven't come for me because they don't know I'm here?"

Was he for real? Time was running short and I really didn't need this sophomoric baloney. I felt my anger rising and worked hard to swallow it back down before saying anything stupid.

"Helmet, if they don't know you're here," I said in my most patient Gaius Teutoberg voice, "Then how are they going to know you helped me?"

I could have sworn I saw the tumblers in his head click. One by one. Lock free, safe open. Time to have a look at the treasure.

Except...I'd led Helmet down a path that didn't ring true to me. The demons didn't know? Well, what about Donna and her quick stop to freshen makeup and shoehorn into a pencil skirt. The two of them—Helmet and Donna/No Face—locked eyes for a moment, and I thought I saw something there between them. Maybe it should have concerned me that Helmet accepted my baloney about the demons not knowing, but with everything else queued up on my dance card for the Disco Worry, I let it slide.

And, in doing so, like always, I missed the belle of the ball.

THIRTEEN

HELMET SPUTTERED WHILE seeking an appropriate response, and I ended up feeling sorry for the wispy fellow. Being dead can be hard on a guy, and if that weren't enough, he'd logged only one day's worth of speaking and had already mired himself in the quicksand of his own words. You would be safe in assuming I knew exactly how the poor guy felt.

"No matter," said Helmet, and he looked as if he wouldn't say anything else.

I'd nearly given up when he did speak again.

"No matter because I could provide a map and photographs and you'd still fail."

I considered thanking him for his confidence in me, but I decided on flipping him off.

Helmet said, "You are childish."

It was on the tip of my tongue to say something like "I know you are but what am I?", but Helmet saved us both from that epic putdown by picking his story back up.

"After they shot me," he said, "I didn't wake up as much as I became conscious of myself."

This chick I dated a few times back in the 60s used to say the same thing. What a load of crap. That relationship didn't end well because she left me for some ninety-year-old skinny dude from India with a scraggly white beard. Father Time in a turban. Maybe that old backstabbing snake of a swami would have understood what Helmet was trying to say.

"I had no sense of sight," he said, "though I don't think I can call anything I have a sense."

"Got it," I said. "No sight, fake senses."

Helmet looked with raw longing at the beer I'd opened.

"No senses," he said.

My conversation-off-the-road warning bells rang in my head and Helmet continued.

"One thing I like about living here," he said.

"Living here?" It cost me every bit of self-control to not roll that line up on a Q-Tip and stick it in his ear. Hello, the guy didn't live anywhere. He just existed.

Logic like that could earn me my own turban.

I said, "What do you like about *being* here?"

I wondered if Helmet caught the substitution of his word living with my word being. The subtle difference didn't seem to register because, rather than take offense, he just answered my question.

"I like the smoke," he said.

"Say what?"

"Smoke," he repeated, and then added as more of an afterthought, "And Karl, of course." A pause, and then, "The photos on the phone make things pleasant, too."

Uh, he left someone out of the reasons to like being in the place *THAT I PAY FOR* every month. OK. I understood the attraction to Soyla and kind of understood the thing he had for Karl. I'd even accept my own unworthiness. Hypothetical unworthiness, that is. But smoke?

He said, "The man downstairs and his maid."

Maid? Two years here and he still thought Frau UberBelly was Herr Doktor's maid? If word like that got out, she'd come up here and either kill him again or maybe deport him to one of the camps.

I don't know how I kept myself from bursting out laughing and breaking into a Lord of the Dance routine. Maybe my intended trip through the gates of hell was holding me back. Still though, *maid*?

"What about them?"

"The smoke," Helmet repeated, and he sounded a irritated by my dullness.

"They continually burn their cigarettes," he said, and the wolfish look on his face changed to wistful. "It's been forever since my last cigarette," he said. "But here?" he pointed a finger at the floor, and I took it to mean Herr Doktor's apartment below us. "Here a cigarette always burns. And I can feel that glorious smoke as it wafts through me."

Lovely.

Helmet was fond of my place because he liked Karl and craved the forest fire's worth of stinky, second-hand cigarette smoke generated by the two numbskulls downstairs. If I had any feelings at all they would have been hurt. Did I have a friend or a nicotine fiend haunting my flat?

I said, "If we could get back to the topic at hand…"

Helmet didn't seem to like my brusqueness. Good, because I didn't like getting left out of the lineup of the top attractions to be found in my flat. We'd both need to get over it.

He said, "Don't take the train."

"The train?"

Helmet nodded.

"Yes," he said. "Avoid the train."

A lot of things don't make sense to me. Take making a bed. Aren't I going to get back in it sometime in the future? Besides, what if The Seven or No Face and his crowd happen to off me? Worse, what if I woke up in a strange place after a hard night's drinking and saw a naked Super Rumble beside me and I tore my own heart out of my ribcage and crushed it with the last vestiges of my waning strength? Do I really care if Herr Doktor finds my bed unmade and shakes his head at my shoddy housekeeping standards? No, making a bed doesn't make sense.

Something else that doesn't make sense? Helmet's "don't take the train" advice. How could I *not* take the train? Was he suggesting I spring for a taxi to Frankfurt?

"I *have* to take the train."

Helmet pursed his lips and said in what sounded like forced patience, "If you already know about the train, then what did you expect from me?"

Earth calling the otherworld, come in please.

I ride the Deutsche Bahn to Wiesbaden…like every freakin' day.

"Helmet," I said, "I can assure you that not only do I already know about the train, but I also intend to take it."

He stood up and said, "Then we have nothing further to discuss."

Wait a second.

We had plenty more to discuss. I admit I found his life and his death stories touching, but as they say back in the USA: That ain't gonna to feed the bear. I needed more. Like perhaps *anything useful*. Yeah, that would have been a good start.

I could see that wasn't going to happen because Helmet began his fading away routine, and I marveled at His Butt-Holiness's knack for mining insults out of benign statements. And if he followed his regular pattern, he wouldn't reappear for another couple of hours.

Perfect.

The one person I knew who'd actually been to Sheol and somehow escaped decided to offer no help at all. Well with any luck, I wouldn't run into his ugly mug again after they ate me alive down there.

I sensed sneezing below and looked down to see Karl doing one of those twenty stupid performances he did when he got excited. And yes, there came that other thing that always erupted too. Perfect. I stooped down to pet the little fur bag. What the heck…I picked him up and hugged him as much as his non-physical body would allow.

"You be a good boy."

A waste of breath, and I felt a pang of sadness at Karl's panting grin and how he wagged his tail so hard that it shook his body. I returned him to the floor and was halfway out the door when I turned back to the idiot ghost dog.

"You take care of Helmet," I said. "And you tell him I said goodbye."

I closed the door behind me and headed for the Bad Homburg station. Contrary to the incongruous—and useless—advice I'd just received, I had a train to catch.

It must have been a cuddle night for Herr Doktor and Frau NoseyNose, because for the second time in a single night I detected no trace of them as I passed by their door on. I did my best to keep my mind running in neutral. No way I wanted to wrestle with a toxic mind-cleanup to exorcize visions of Herr Doktor's and the *Maid's* nasty frolicking.

A quick glance at my smartphone, and I saw that if I could make the eight-minute walk in six minutes, I could catch the next S5 to Frankfurt. Otherwise, I'd need to wait at the platform for thirty additional minutes. I picked up my pace. Obviously, my friends wouldn't leave for Aachen without me. That would be like the funeral starting without the guest of honor.

German workers are exacting, but not tireless. From my point of view—two thousand years, so send me note at ImaVampire@ youaredefinitelywrong.com if you think I'm mistaken—European socialism has done nothing for the working people. Far from it. But what it *has* managed to do is slow progress to the point everyone's waiting on something. Except rich people with enough money to hire the clock so that it works for them.

Now that's what I call equality.

What am rambling on about? Nothing, other than the damnable construction tunnel was still the only way to get to the departure platforms at the Bad Homburg station. That plywood tunnel reminded me of how my pal No Face noshed on my left leg. Come to think of it, exactly why was I considering risking my life to spring him from demon jail?

The answer came in less than the couple of seconds it took to traverse the plywood tunnel and climb the stairs to Platform 3.

Sarah Arias.

The train had arrived, and I activated the mechanism to open the door. In moments, I heard that clicking of hydraulic pressure that ensured all the doors were closed for departure. I scanned the car and saw only one other passenger. A hot chick.

Understatement. A five-alarm fire of a sexy grade-A babe. I chuckled under my breath and made my way to sit in the seat facing hers. No need for cheesy pickup lines because I already knew this gorgeous brunette.

"Hi Soyla."

I couldn't stop myself from gawking. She'd planned it that way because, even with her athletic frame, it would have taken several hours to wiggle into those leather pants. I'm certain the leather bra presented less of a challenge, though I'm certain it overstressed the engineering limits. Soyla didn't waste time with a shirt over the bra, and twin visual cues told me she found the early spring evening with its snowy slush and dropping temperature every bit as frigid as I did.

Sometimes a guy has to cheer for cold weather.

I considered doing the gentlemanly thing and offering to warm those parts, but I restrained myself.

She said, "Hello, my love."

"How did you know I'd be here?"

She moved from her seat to mine, picked up my arm and ducked under. Use your imagination as to where she put my hand once she snuggled against my chest. I will say I was happy to see she also had conservation of heat on her mind. Going green does come with perks.

She looked at me with those big dark eyes and said, "But my love, fate intertwined our souls."

I thought about that for a second and she added, "I can search my heart and there I see you."

She can see me in her heart? I couldn't even begin to imagine how terrifying life would be for a heck-of-a-lot of guys if chicks had *that* skill.

"Right," I said. And then, "No they aren't, and no you can't."

I meant intertwined souls and voyeuristic hearts. She sat in pouting silence through the first stop at Oberursel. Nobody got on, nobody got off. Hydraulic noise. Doors locked. The train resumed, and Soyla finally spoke.

"Maybe not," she said. "But it could be like that, my love."

The crazy chick alarm began beating in the back of my mind.

"Soyla," I said, and my voice sounded weary to my own ears.

She sat up and said, "OK," and then, "it was that electric thing in your flat."

Uh-oh.

"What electric thing?"

Soyla looked at me as if I'd just claimed an alien abduction.

"The one the cute little men gave me, of course."

Cute little men.

I assumed she meant the little guys from the African jungle and not little green men from Mars. The Seven. Perhaps The Six might fit better, because if what Soyla said earlier about Bernard standing between my execution and me were true, then the remaining murderous little ankle-biters had hired her to build a case against me to change Bernard's mind.

And now Soyla was telling me she planted a listening device in my apartment. I ran through my conversation with Helmet and it still didn't make sense. Her being on the train. Helmet *did* mention a train, but all he said was not to board it.

And for her to be waiting on me like this? She'd had to have either gotten on one stop north at Friedrichsdorf or been riding the circuit for several hours in hopes we'd somehow chance upon each other. That would leave too much to luck because there was more than one S5 running back and forth on the line.

The most likely scenario was the first one. She'd boarded at Friedrichsdorf and would have disembarked at Bad Homburg and waited for me had she not seen me standing at the platform. That made the possibility highly likely that one or more of The Seven had set up a headquarters for their anti-Gaius operation in Friedrichsdorf.

The little bastards.

I considered hopping off the train in Oberursel and catching the opposite S5 to pay some pygmies a visit. Bernard told me about my growing strength and Soyla confirmed it with her story about the tiff I'd caused among the miniature wrecking crew. It tempted me to head on up to whatever hotel room said pygmy or pygmies hid inside and give this new, deadly power a test flight.

But, I've found that when I combine anger with arrogance I've always ended up with a double portion of stupidity. Take my word for it, it's one of the surest recipes in Gaius's Cookbook of Life Experiences. I'd let the boys from Botswana—or wherever—stew in hotel beer. Perhaps I'd consider other options for handling them if I made it out of hell in one piece. Still, Soyla on this train made no sense given the nature of my conversation with Helmet.

Unless it wasn't a listening device. Something else?

"So, you planted a bug in my flat?"

"Of course not," Soyla said, "I hate spiders, my love."

Yeah, right. I didn't buy the coy act. Soyla's tech knowledge ran rings around mine. She knew what I meant by the term *bug*, and was therefore stalling. Heck, not even stalling, but using that wonderful misdirection of hers to throw me head-over-butt off the track. Next, she'd be putting my hand back on her breast. I prepared for that horrible possibility by promising to play along.

"Right," I said. "You know what I'm talking about."

Soyla gave the you-just-caught-me smile and sat up straighter.

Next, she'd be putting my hand on her breast.

"I didn't put anything in your flat."

I didn't believe her. Not at first. And I made sure to move my hand to a more obvious location near her breast. Just in case.

"I changed the battery in your smartphone."

Bingo.

If she'd changed out the battery in my phone, then I could assume six of The Seven already knew my travel itinerary for the evening. I'd gone over everything with the bagger crew and we'd confirmed with text messages.

They knew I'd be on the S5 and they knew the approximate timing. If Soyla missed me in Bad Homburg, then she'd catch a car to Frankfurt. I suspected they pre-positioned transportation there to get Soyla to Aachen…in case she couldn't convince me to let her tag along in the larger vehicle they would know Sister Christian intended to lease.

It all fit. But not perfectly.

"They know about tonight?"

"Of course, my love."

I thought about the implications. Ambush. That's where all roads led. My grave-robbing escapade in Aachen stirred up more than local attention. The whole civilized world was tracking one conspiracy theory after another. That kind of fame represented the worst nightmare for The Seven.

Bernard had involved himself. Even decided to help...if my definition of help included exposing my life to a decrepit racist speed freak who blew air out of both ends when he laughed at inappropriate times. And now, according to Soyla, he still supported me against the better judgment of the other six piggies.

I meant to say, pygmies.

I didn't think it would break Bernard's heart if I turned up dead. On the other hand, he'd need to find another idiot able to sleep with his eyes open while he waxed on about nothing in a droning Oxford accent. They were waiting for me in Aachen, all right. So why send Soyla? Wouldn't her chance presence on the S5 tip me off to something stinky in the state of Denmark?

"They don't know, do they?"

"Know what, my love."

"That you've told me."

Soyla snuggled in closer again. In addition to raising the hopes of my right hand, it confirmed my line of thought. Playing one side against the other. Vintage Soyla.

"They pay well," she said, and she raised an eyebrow in a perfect caricature of the greedy temptress. "But I think my Gaius might pay better."

So, there it was. Soyla offering loyalty for hire. But Soyla and loyalty fit as well in the same sentence as honest and politician. She'd snooped around the edges of my wealth before. I lived simply. No need to highlight myself in a world where a simple background check could unravel my best false ID. But simple life and simple means are two different things.

It's rumored that The Seven owns banks, casinos, and hotels. I do too. I'm also the majority shareholder in an airline whose name everyone recognizes. Been that way—not the airline, but the other investments—for more than three centuries. Putting a little away each year for more than two thousand years can build a nest egg.

I moved my operations out of Europe after Napoleon ravaged the place, and I rightly predicted the fledgling country across the Atlantic as the best place to secure my wealth. There, nobody raised an eye as immigrants amassed quick fortunes. A good decision at the time, although I'm concerned that the government now has the people swimming in so much debt that they may raid bank deposits behind the mask of taxation "to make things fairer." Read: steal your money to buy me votes. Seen it all before.

I might get back to the topic of my finances later but suffice it to say the lady with the Hungarian accent sitting next to me wanted a cut. Most likely, she wanted a double portion...one from The Seven *and* one from me. It would take more than one hand on one breast to get that out of me.

Both hands, both breasts? I was all ears.

I said, "So, they don't know."

She shook her head and I believed her. It's the walk like a duck, talk like a duck, look like a duck cliché. Soyla was walking, talking, and looking like...Soyla, and that gave me an odd sort of comfort.

"No, my love."

"And they're waiting in Aachen?"

"Yes," she said, and this time she didn't add "my love" at the end of the sentence.

Then came the pivotal question.

"How much?"

I figured it best we either close the deal or not before I linked up with the bagger crew. No doubt a portion of The Seven waited for me in Aachen. I could either tell Soyla to pound sand and try to talk my friends out of accompanying me to Aachen, or I could cut a deal.

Talking my friends out of it didn't seem too promising an option. They already knew they would face demons, so in comparison, how scary would a couple of pygmies sound? Even if I could convince them of the real danger, it would prove to them that I needed their help more than ever.

If I closed the deal with Soyla? Then we'd need to take her along with us. I didn't know that for sure, but logic told me she'd insist. Whatever we came up with, it needed to be quick, because the we'd resumed moving after the Frankfurt Messe stop, and the main train station came next.

She said, "Don't be vulgar."

I snorted a laugh.

"Rich," I said, "Coming from you."

I saw anger flash in her eyes and prepared myself to encounter the train-derailing, psycho-assassin version of Soyla. BTW, if you're a lady reading this, you can be certain that I don't consider you in that same category that I've put Soyla in. So, if we ever cross paths, please—and I'm begging you with tears in my eyes—don't hold it against me. As for Soyla? I caught sight of her teeth extending.

Calling all cars. Body of stupid fool found gutted on the S5. Murderess at large. Approach with extreme caution and be prepared to just listen instead of attempting to solve things.

Imagine that in a German accent.

But I saw her swallow it down. Eyes cleared, and teeth returned to normal. Just like that. Chicks can do that kind of thing. Scary.

"We have three minutes," she said. "Interested, or not?"

"Interested."

She snuggled deeper into my chest. I brought my hand around her shoulders, though she swatted it away when it roamed.

"No time for that," she said. And then, "We will discuss the terms later. Until then," she said, "I'm not letting you out of my sight."

How can eight words invoke such terror?

The train halted at the downstairs platform and we found our way to the escalator. Earlier in the day, I'd inked a deal with the devil. My help for No Face in exchange for the opportunity to spring Sarah Arias. I'd bet my mortal soul like a stack of chips on crooked roulette wheel run by a seedy casino...and that horror paled in comparison to the huge mistake I was certain I made by hiring Soyla.

FOURTEEN

SHE'D GRABBED MY hand sometime between getting off the train and our riding to the top of the stairs, and we walked like that past the closed food stands and out the door by the hamburger joint. My friends were waiting, and I could see that Sister Christian had the van parked in the spaces reserved for taxis.

Everyone greeted us…uh, with the exception of Sister Christian. She did the look-up-and-down evaluation ritual chicks do when another enters their territory. Soyla understood what was happening even though she pretended not to notice, and even I could see through her unconcerned grin and the fake way she demurred as she waited for introductions. I half expected the two women to sniff butts.

The guys didn't disappoint me either. Somebody needed to reiterate to J-Rod and Watanabe that old adage regarding how slack jaws catch flies. At least Soyla was a hit with them. I stepped in before the two women arched their backs and hissed at each other.

"Sister Christian," I said, "This is my old friend Soyla."

By mentioning Sister Christian's name first, I hoped I'd mollified her. I didn't think it worked, because she returned the automatic smile chicks use when they want everyone to know they aren't smiling. It makes sense to the guys anyway.

Sister Christian reached out her hand and said, "How old?"

Passive-aggressive female vibes…the missing ingredient for the awful night. Soyla looked at Sister Christian's outstretched hand like it had snot on it.

She tapped it with her own hand and said, "Let's just say older than you look and leave it at that, darling," and she put an arm around me and nipped my earlobe.

Thanks for calming things, Soyla.

Watanabe and J-Rod both moaned, and the Bonnie Prince looked on the verge of an OD from pheromones flying around us like swarms of gnats.

I said, "Yes, well," and then thought better of saying more.

In a rare display of judgment, instead allowing my mouth to make things worse, I introduced Soyla to the rest of the gang. Each of the guys responded with a caveman grunt. Obviously, Sister Christian suspected Soyla was one of *my* people and I sensed that it concerned her. The guys? Judging by the pools of drool at their feet, I don't think they would've cared if Soyla were a shape-shifting black widow spider.

Yeah, they'd feel comfortable enough sharing a ride with six-foot-tall hunk of lean warrior-woman dressed in nothing but skin-tight leather pants and a skimpy leather bra on the verge of mechanical failure. I mean, who wouldn't?

Sister Christian? Different story, because something told me she didn't appreciate the "older than you look" comment. That made me concerned they'd exchange jabs until open warfare broke out. If that happened, I'd need to jump in fast. I'd also need to keep in mind the ease with which Soyla separated an arm from its rightful owner a few months ago.

Sister Christian said, "What is her part?"

"Whatever she wants."

Uh, I didn't say that. J-Rod did.

Not sure how my response would have played because I had no clue what role Soyla filled. At least Sister Christian shifted the stink-eye from me to J-Rod and, of course, he crumbled faster than the French army.

"I mean," he said, and none of us got the benefit of knowing what J-Rod meant because he stopped in mid-sentence under Sister Christian's toxic scowl.

With J-Rod sorted, Sister Christian returned full attention to Soyla, and I could literally see her struggling against instinct to bring the femi-conflict under control.

I think Soyla understood that Sister Christian wanted to get on with a truce and she helped things along by turning to me and saying, "Gaius, darling. Is *this* woman your lover?"

Awkward.

That seemed to snap the guys back to the moment, meaning they closed their mouths. Funny thing is that everyone looked at me for a response.

Really?

Even Sister Christian seemed interested in what I'd say. I mean, she *knew* the truth. Why didn't she sound off with it?

One thing I've learned over the years is that when a question has an obvious answer and a woman doesn't step in to provide it, she maybe doesn't want the obvious answer revealed to the rest of the crowd.

Say you have lunch with a chick and return to work. If someone asks, "What did Sally eat for lunch?" You can bet Sally knows what she ate for lunch. So, if Sally doesn't answer, it's probably best not to say, "She had the lumberjack's cut of prime rib and the bottomless garlic mashed potatoes while guzzling the fireman's boot of beer. Impressive how she put it away and then chased it all down with a double-portion of eight-layer chocolate nirvana."

You'd run the risk that Sally might inexplicably consider that honest response offensive…even though you intended it as a supreme compliment.

Here's the corrected version. "Just the same old bird food for her." If you feel safe enough for a little embellishment you can add, "and I don't see how she can stand that plain vinegar." Now you can bet Sally will ask you later if you were implying she was a pig by lying about lunch, but you could consider the accusation her way of thanking you.

Sister Christian knew that she and I weren't lovers. You can bet I did too. But she didn't step up to set that straight with Soyla. Confusing, yes. And like I said, everyone waited for an answer.

From me.

"Depends," I said.

"Whatchu mean depends, homie?" said J-Rod the Latino gangsta. "Did you lay in on Sister C or not, man."

"Well," I said, and I glanced over to Sister Christian for some help. She stood there looking as interested in what I'd say next as anyone else. "It depends on whether you mean now, or before."

Soyla laughed with such derisiveness that it even pissed me off. She saw right through the lie and was about to embarrass Sister Christian.

"Stop this, my love," Soyla said. "You've never made love to, to *this*." She pointed at Sister Christian.

Hard to argue with it when I thought about it. Heck I'd never even given serious consideration to making love to Sister Christian…that is, if you only counted the things I'd considered in the last five minutes. So Soyla would win the little battle just like Soyla always won everything.

But then, maybe I'd declared a victor before the clock ran out, because Sister Christian threw a whopper of a Hail Mary Pass when she said,

"Of course we've done the raunchy. Many times."

Through the disorienting haze of pure confusion, I understood she meant she'd done the raunchy with me. Now, I'm not sure what doing the raunchy means, but I thought if I had one guess, I'd nail the correct answer.

Soyla spoke in a not-so-confident tone when she said, "You have not."

Had to agree with Soyla on that one, but I knew enough to keep my mouth shut.

Sister Christian detected weakness and attacked it with, "I can prove it."

She'd backed herself in a corner because everyone froze in place to make sure they didn't miss a syllable of the proof Sister Christian had on the way.

"OK," she said. "OK."

I could see by Soyla's taunting grin. Hesitance had turned the tide of this completely freakin' Close Encounters of the Third Kind, alien fight they were engaged in.

Sister Christian understood she was back on the defensive and that she'd better come up with the proof she promised...and do it immediately.

"Gare has three testicles."

I have WHAT?

You'd have thought someone hit the mute button on Soyla. I mean she cut off a laugh she'd begun like tap water.

Sister Christian looked at me and said, "Sorry for letting out your secret Gare."

Yeah, I was sorry too. I mean this was such a closely held secret that not even *I* knew I had three testicles. And I'd been hanging out with *two* of them for two millennia.

THREE FRIGGIN' BALLS?

Why couldn't she have said I had teddy-bear tattoo or that I wore pink toenail polish and an orange polka-dotted shower cap to bed… either would have been far less humiliating.

But it did shut Soyla up.

"Hey homie," said J-Rod, "bet you do it up right when you power it with three huevos, man," and he gave me a high five.

"Well," I said, but didn't get any further because Watanabe interrupted.

"It's called polyorchidism."

Freakin' Harvard know-it-all.

I said, "Well, thank you Dr. Ninja. You've put a name to my affliction. Now maybe I can join a support group or something."

Soyla said, "Is this true?" and I think she regretted the question because she realized she'd admitted to Sister Christian that *she'd* never done the raunchy with me.

At least I suppose that's why she went ahead and added, "of course I knew that."

Soyla looked at Sister Christian and said, "I just wanted to know if it were true that Gaius showed all three to you."

Why did I think I needed a portal when I was *already* in hell?

"Showed them?" said Sister Christian, "I've held all three of the cute litter furry things in my hand."

That's when the Bonnie Prince decided he couldn't keep his gob shut.

"So, having three testicles makes them all smaller than they'd be if there were only two?"

I opened my mouth to defend the honor of my imaginary third boulder, but I didn't get a chance to say anything because Sister Christian and Soyla spoke in near-unison.

"Much smaller."

Neither of them had ever seen my non-existent three balls or any other imaginary part of my body. You believe me...right? Now the bagger guys would not only believe the three-egg-theory, but they also that each of their own two exceeded the gross tonnage of my three. Which I didn't have, by the way. I mean, I do have two healthy nuts that power my machine of universal satisfaction quite well.

"Bet they runnin' overtime hot," said J-Rod. "That little engine got to work hard to keep Sister C smilin'."

I didn't know what to say. I mean, I was on my way to hell to slay demons, and after they ended up killing me, do you think anyone would remember me as the Demonslayer? No. When I didn't return, the bagger gang would be talking about Gare, the man with three field peas.

On the positive side, nobody in Sheol would know anything at all about Sister Christian's three-ball fairy tale. And that's why I couldn't wait to get there. Also on the positive side, that story was *so ludicrous* that the two women went from two hissing vipers to chuckling with each other. Perfect. I love sacrificing my pride for world harmony.

Where was that door to hell?

We climbed into the van. Oh, and the Bonnie Prince offered to drive. Shades of my previous trip to Aachen in the so-called backseat of an expensive European sports car with the legally blind, ex-white-supremacist-retired-South African-cop-speed-demon at the wheel returned like PTSD.

No thanks. I'd rather walk.

Sister Christian said she would handle the chauffeuring and she and Soyla took the two front seats. I put my three-balled butt in the seat behind the driver and the other knuckleheads claimed their spots in the cabin.

The women chatted up front as we made our way through the streets of Frankfurt to the Autobahn that would take us to Aachen. How do they do that? One second I'm worried they will claw each other's' eyes out, and the next they're acting like BFFs. Every guy should keep that in mind.

The guys kept their mouths shut, though I could have sworn I heard J-Rod whisper something about polyorchidism in the back row. I pretended not to hear so I wouldn't be forced to strangle him.

I thought the guys might not speak at all until J-Rod leaned over and said, "The chick Soyla."

"Yes?"

"You two really tight, homie? I mean, two beautiful babes in the car and they both your hides?"

Yes and no. Well, *no* more than *yes*. Soyla worked hard over the past thousand years to get me into the sack. Until yesterday, it couldn't happen for logistical reasons—vampire repellant stink. We almost overcame that a few times over the years, but I always knew Soyla only made effort to do the things that pleased Soyla. And for her, physical pleasure lagged the good feeling of a full bank account by more than double.

Sister Christian? If she'd ever given a hint of a green light, I'd have jumped. But her signal always shone bright red. Oh, there'd been the occasional flirty hug and sexy talk, but she'd given me the Heisman each time things almost got interesting.

I said, "Not my hides."

That pricked the Bonnie Prince's interest, and he said, "I call the one in the leather."

"Whatchu wanna be doing with her?" said J-Rod. "You don't see nothin' anyway. That Donna be OK for you, homie." J-Rod paused for a second and then, "But you steal her drink like you do everyone else's and that bitch bust a cap in you."

Watanabe piped in, "I'll tell you what I'd do with her."

"Eshay isway ittingsay inway ethay ontfray, uttheadsbay," I said.

She is sitting in the front, buttheads.

Pig Latin. I mean, a guy needed to use caution when speaking of Soyla because her logic-defying moods could change in less than a heartbeat. And yes, I did mean moods, as in plural, because Soyla possessed a skill for displaying multiples of those potentially deadly things at the same time.

Watanabe said, "Yeah, got it."

We sat in silence for a few kilometers. You might think we sat quietly for a few miles, but it's always kilometers on the Autobahn.

The Bonnie Prince broke that careful silence with, "Got a question for you Gare."

"Shoot."

"Those two...up front," he pointed to up where Sister Christian and Soyla still chatting away like they'd cheered on the same squad in high school.

"Yeah?"

"They *are* at least kind-of yours, aren't they?"

I thought about that.

"Maybe."

"And you're going after Sarah Arias," he said. "Right?"

"Maybe."

"She yours too?"

Even the bird-noises coming from up front stopped at *that* question. Chicks don't have ears; they have listening devices that the guys at the NSA can't match. And Vince the Bonnie Prince McDonald hit on the seminal question. What was Sarah Arias to me?

She did the bagger gig for a few months after the folks she worked for got wind that the forces of evil were brewing a plan to desecrate the bones of a Jewish patriarch. To say Sarah Arias was hot would be like calling the sun a frigid planet. I mean, Sarah Arias takes hotness to its ultimate level…even if you count her chain-smoking habit.

When I began the series of events that culminated in displays of utter buffoonery at the Aachen Cathedral, Sarah Arias outed herself as my guardian angel. The jury is still out regarding how much she helped during the operation, but what I do know is I fell in *like* with her as we flew the bones I'd stolen back to the place some bureaucrat in her chain of command decided they needed to be.

I considered the two women sitting up front. I liked Sister Christian and I also had this love/hate thing going with Soyla. As far as their bodies, I lusted after both. No big deal because I've been known to lust after anything wearing lipstick. Was what I felt for Sarah Arias different than what I felt for Sister Christian or for Soyla?

Yes, but did it matter? And this wasn't about the rescue in Sheol. That was a done deal. I couldn't *not* do that. What I meant was did anything I felt for Sarah Arias matter in the long run? Did I think a guardian angel would move into the little house surrounded by clichéd white picket fence and raise a family with a vampire? No, and maybe I'm OK with that. Those are, after all, the kinds of thoughts that terrify most guys anyway.

Was Sarah Arias also mine? I had to stifle a laugh. As if both Sister Christian and Soyla belonged to me. I thought I knew the answer to the Bonnie Prince's question, and it was no. No to Sarah Arias belonging to me. But also, no to the notion of *too*. On the other hand, yes. Kind of. I mean, Sister Christian and Soyla both belonged to my heart… each in their own way. So, I suppose enough room existed there for Sarah Arias. Maybe that's why it's a weakness in the heart that can kill a vampire.

I answered the Bonnie Prince's question with, "Can we quit jabbering and get down to a plan?"

OK, I didn't answer his question at all. But my lack of an answer seemed to relieve everyone.

Soyla turned around and said, "Two of them will be waiting."

When I confirmed, "The Seven?" Soyla nodded.

"Wait a second," said Watanabe. "Is it two or is it seven?"

Spoken like a Harvard math genius. I went through the short version of the long story about The Seven.

Afterward, J-Rod said, "Cannibal pygmies, homie. You got some loco friends."

And loco was as good a word as any when it came to The Seven. They'd been around at least four thousand years…twice my lifespan. All those years *had* to shake a few bolts loose in a guy's head. I mean, if their collective sanity was a dot on a scatter diagram, Hannibal Lector's would plot higher.

Mental health questions aside, I needed to get past the ambush.

Soyla said, "They'll expect you at the cathedral, my love." And then, "I don't know how they plan to capture you, but I do know that's where it's going to happen."

What? Capture?

And it dawned on me as she spoke. I'd not thought about the possibility of capture because I'd assumed they were just going to take me out. There was logic in capturing instead of killing.

The little guys would want it to go down quickly. I didn't know for sure, but I suspected the Germans didn't want to lose what dust of their national hero I'd left behind, so they'd upped the security at the Aachen Cathedral. No way The Seven would want a bloody, and potentially very public, super-human fight to get caught on a security camera. If that happened, then they could hardly condemn me for blowing the vampire secret when the murder video, starring three vampires, would score at least a hundred million online hits in its first hour. Maybe Bernard might not offer *them* the same parole he granted me.

Kidnapping? It made sense. They'd need to get me out of sight quickly, and they'd need to do it themselves. I don't know how far my new ability to withstand the scent of other vampires went, though I suspected The Seven wouldn't use hired vampire muscle for the same reason all of them, except Bernard, wanted to end my life. If word of my increased powers got out to the vampire community, then cracks in the iron-fisted rule of The Seven would soon ensue.

Yeah, it made a strange kind of sense to me—their reasons for seeing me as a threat and taking actions to eliminate it. For some reason Bernard had come down on my side. I didn't fool myself into thinking Bernard liked me. No, it had to be professional for him…something else up his toddler's-length sleeve.

And again, for some incomprehensible reason, The Seven trusted Soyla. I thought about that for a moment and decided it wasn't accurate. Better to say they'd hired Soyla. Trusted her? No. So would they expect so quick a double cross? Probably not. But then, Soyla hadn't really double-crossed them. Not yet. She'd only promised me she'd move off their payroll and onto mine.

She'd found me—no difficult feat as I'd not moved in several years— and I'm sure she'd let her two little masters know she was tailing me. Did she tell them she planned on coming to Aachen with me? If she had, then I could bet she was still playing on their team. I'd need to move cautiously once we set foot in Aachen. Yeah, Soyla bore close watching. And, judging how close to failure that overloaded leather bra appeared, I thought I could focus on the task.

I needed a plan to take on two of The Seven. No need to worry about other vampires…not unless Soyla did the double-double cross on everyone. What about non-vampires? I didn't think so. No, they'd not risk bloody pieces left behind for the Polizei to find.

And if they captured me? Perhaps they'd take me somewhere and kill me, but I didn't think so…not immediately. My guess was that they'd bring me to the pygmy version of a kangaroo court to try to make Bernard see their side of things. If they did, I'd be meat in the big black kettle.

Of course, there was always the possibility of a full-blown coup… that they didn't care about convincing Bernard.

Well, as Willie Nelson says, "If they take me back to Texas, they won't take me back alive." You bet I'd go down fighting. And if my vampire powers really *had* grown? I'd do my best to kill one—or both—of the little bastards.

Sister Christian pulled off the road into one of those middle-of-the-Autobahn gas stations and said, "If you need to use the restroom or want something to drink, now's the time. Next stop is Aachen."

They all piled out except Soyla. I needed to take my dog for a walk, but I decided it best to hang behind and keep an eye on her…make sure she didn't steal all the change out of the cup holders…the normal stuff. Normal, as in, warning a couple cannibal pygmies we'd arrive within the hour. People do that kind of thing all the time if you turn your back on them long enough.

Soyla sat in the front seat and grinned at me. Didn't say anything, just smiled. She knew I didn't trust her, and she was having fun with it.

I said, "Don't you have to use the potty?"

"Went before I left," she said. And then, "Couldn't I also betray you in the loo?"

Good point. I looked her up and down. No obvious place to hide a smartphone, and I didn't think she'd ever served time in a French island-prison.

I passed Sister Christian on the way into gas station. She was walking toward the van with a bottle of water for everyone in her arms.

I said, "Play nice with Soyla."

"No problem."

I did the necessary and joined the gang back inside the van, where Sister Christian handed me a bottle of water. The atmosphere felt less like a vehicle and more like the inside of a locker room before the big game because everyone sat in silence, waves of tension so thick they were nearly visible. Watanabe and J-Rod were peeling the stickers off their bottles and the Bonnie Prince was trying to plug his seatbelt into the air conditioning vent near his window.

Sister Christian said, "Everyone listen to me."

We did.

"Here's how I think we should do things."

Even Soyla seemed interested, and it was the first time I could remember her letting another woman get all the attention in a roomful of guys.

"The bag in the back," she said. "Jesus, could you please pass it up?"

J-Rod did, and Sister Christian tugged back the zipper of the oversized gym bag and pulled out two identical sweatshirts. She handed one to Watanabe and the other to me. Next, she gave each of us a balaclava, one of those knit hats that pull down over your face and leave only your eyes, nose, and mouth exposed. I looked down at mine and wondered whether Sister Christian had ever dated a terrorist.

"Put those on," she said.

We did, and I changed into the sweatshirt and Watanabe its twin. We put on the hats but stopped short of pulling them over our faces.

"Perfect," said Sister Christian.

She pulled out another sweatshirt and handed it to Soyla, who took a look at it and shook her head.

"The color clashes with my hair," she said.

I thought black pretty much went with everything, but I kept my mouth shut. This would be the part where Soyla exerted her female dominance.

"Put it on," said Sister Christian. "Or they'll be able to see it's you from a mile away."

I didn't know where all this was leading but I did know that Sister Christian had a point. There'd be no mistaking Soyla. She'd be the one in the too-tight pants and the too-small bra. The sweatshirt would serve to break up the sexy effect. Nobody who knows her ever expects Soyla to frump up. So as simple a disguise as it was, it might prove effective. At least for a while.

Soyla must have come to the same conclusion because she did an about-face and accepted the sweatshirt. She put it over her head. *OK*, I thought. *This is starting well enough.* But Soyla doesn't give up that easily, and nearly caused a stampede among the guys when she reached back under the sweatshirt and came out holding that leather bra.

That made me half wish Sister Christian had also brought along a pair of ugly pants for Soyla. I heard Watanabe take a loud breath and I think J-Rod bit a piece out of my headrest. You could be sure he'd need to pay for that at the rental car return. The Bonnie Prince missed the whole spectacle. Served him right for not investing in glasses.

I said, "Now what?"

According to Sister Christian, we'd drop Watanabe off early, he'd walk toward the Cathedral, and we'd wait near the church square in the van until Watanabe came into sight. This was the tricky part because if we were the only vehicle parked on the street, we'd be sure to draw attention.

Once things got going, J-Rod would stay behind to drive the getaway car in an emergency with the Bonnie Prince riding shotgun. We didn't really have a shotgun, so it was obvious to me that Sister Christian just wanted the Bonnie Prince out of harm's way.

"We're running a bait and switch," said Sister Christian. "You," she said to Watanabe, "need to move quickly and with confidence."

Watanabe scratched under the balaclava and said, "I can do quick." A pause. "But I don't know what you mean by confident."

"Act like Gare," she said. "You need to look like him. That's the bait."

Watanabe didn't fall in love at first sight with that idea, and I understood why. It would be one thing to tag along for support—they'd all seen how I can inflict damage on powerful supernatural beings. But exposing yourself to the potential first strike of someone more powerful than me, and with the bad guys thinking they needed to attack with sufficient strength to take *me* out? Not the same.

J-Rod said, "And the switch?"

"Gare," she said. "Watanabe will run toward the Aachen Cathedral once he's in the town square. And at the same time," she said, "Jesus will park near the café we ate at a few months ago." J-Rod nodded. "Then, Gare and I will get out of the van." She looked at me. "We'll walk toward the front of the café arm-in-arm like we're married."

Sister Christian's plan began to coagulate into something I thought just might work. The two pygmies would need to conceal themselves right up until the moment I appeared, and then expose themselves the least amount possible as they first took me down and then took me away.

How accurate would witness reports to the police be of two normal dudes mugging another guy in the dark of night? Even though we were in Germany where being nosey is considered the national duty, I suspected the descriptions would be sketchy…low light and all. Now substitute two normal-looking attackers for two kindergarteners. You get the point. Improved accuracy of eyewitnesses.

"Once Watanabe passes in a trot," Sister Christian said, "Gare will get ready for one of those super-speed sprints of his."

I got it. Good, but with one potentially devastating flaw.

I said, "Won't we all end up at the same place? I mean, you'll get me close to the portal. And if The Seven dudes are concentrating on Watanabe and not me," I said, "I *do* have a better chance of slipping through." I let that sink in for a second. "They'll eventually realize their mistake and turn their attention to me."

Truth? Once the cute little murdering dart-gun blowers realized Watanabe was just Watanabe, chances exceeded 99% that they'd take me down and halt the rescue operation before it started. First, I'd go down like an Iranian gunboat and then I'd be riding inside a garbage can to whatever destination they'd prepared. And the odds were equally high that they wouldn't do me the courtesy of washing out the can ahead of time.

The Bonnie Prince said, "Think."

His voice surprised me. Vince the Bonnie Prince McDonald was a cool enough guy. But his role in the gang usually stopped at that guy everyone made sure didn't hurt himself or anyone else. But nearly blind doesn't mean stupid.

I said, "Think what?"

"Vampire doesn't mean stupid," he said.

Uh, nice one, Vince.

Soyla cut across whatever response I had in mind. She spoke in her softest, most casual-sounding voice, and I wondered if the Bonnie Prince understood the danger he'd spoken himself into.

"Please explain that last comment."

The Bonnie Prince looked over to Sister Christian and said, "Sorry, Soyla. No insult intended. Not for you, anyway."

Wrong chick, but Soyla seemed mollified. Still, I hoped the Bonnie Prince would hold back on that level of transparency for the rest of what he had to say.

Sister Christian sensed the tension and broke in.

"Vince is right," she said. "If things go according to plan, then you'll have a few unmolested seconds to get through the portal."

Right. And here I was hoping someone *would* molest me. Like perhaps Sister Christian. My fake wife. Why do chicks always want to pretend to be married to me and then only in public? Is the honeymoon tradition dead?

I said, "And how can you guarantee that?"

"Because," said the Bonnie Prince, "Watanabe will sprint to the *other* side of the cathedral. Hello, we're talking the whole building between you and danger."

OK, so the sound of the obvious was deafening…well, not really. Everyone was quiet while they waited for my steam-driven brain to process what the Prince just said.

Duh.

Of course Watanabe wouldn't lead the two deadly gits toward me, and of course he'd use the other side of the cathedral to shield me. I needed to get my head in the game if I wanted to survive more than a second or two on the other side of the portal.

Sister Christian said, "Do you think the bad guys know where to find the portal?"

Ouch. I hadn't thought of that.

"I don't know," I said. A few seconds of thought and I added, "Probably not."

Aachen Cathedral? They had that much. But then, so did the rest of the world. Bernard would have told them everything about the mission. Sure, the full membership of The Seven would have requested the 411 and I'm certain Bernard obliged in intricate, coma-inducing detail. But I didn't think the little water bug actually *saw* me enter the cathedral.

That made the bagger gang's plan hinge on two things. First, the con. They'd need to convince The Seven that Watanabe was me. The second thing? The pygmies were blind as to portal location. We'd both confuse them and then use that confusion to lead them off the map. Smart and simple. A plan that raised my odds for going to hell. But hey, what are friends for?

That closed the strategy session and Sister Christian handed the keys to J-Rod. He started the engine and pulled back onto the Autobahn. Sister Christian and Soyla moved to the middle row of seats and Watanabe rode shotgun.

We'd driven for a few minutes when Soyla said, "What's my part?"

Sister Christian raised her eyebrows in that way that means, "What?"

Soyla held out the tail of her rather oversized and rather unflattering sweatshirt.

"Why this," she said.

"Oh that," said Sister Christian. "I needed you to cover up, sweetie."

I braced for hurricane Soyla. Soyla's response came in that same breathily smooth, dangerous tone she'd used with the Bonnie Prince. Ultra-frightening, but kind of sexy at the same time.

"Cover up?"

"Yes," said Sister Christian. "I needed the boys to concentrate. And how could they think of anything while your gorgeous boobs radiated into their brains."

Soyla thought about that for second. I leaned forward to intercept the blow I expected, and I hoped I could keep things from degenerating to the point I couldn't save the van. But Soyla smiled.

"Of course, darling," she said. "Those naughty boys."

Well, really it was naughty Soyla, but I decided to keep that one to myself. Soyla being Soyla had taken what Sister Christian said as a compliment. And I guess it was, in a back-handed way. We drove in silence until Soyla spoke up again.

"I see a flaw."

Sister Christian said, "Oh?"

"Yes," said Soyla. "Who would believe my Gaius would marry you?"

OK, so Soyla wasn't completely won over with Sister Christian's wardrobe enhancements. And if I were being honest, I kind of preferred the overstretched leather bra look too. Perhaps Sister Christian should have done the democratic thing and taken a vote before she drastically altered everyone's ocular environment. But Soyla's nasty comment? Vintage Soyla. The boys and I showed perfect judgment by keeping our mouths shut, and we were rewarded with a dose of Sister Christian's own version of the silky-dangerous voice.

"And who would Gare marry?"

I'm not a wizard at math, but I do understand basic set theory. I did a quick mental manipulation to organize all the females in the van into their own set.

"Why me, of course," said Soyla. "And," she added, "No woman's husband I've been with would ever hold his wife's arm in public."

Sister Christian didn't sound convinced when she said, "You?"

"Yes," said Soyla. "If you want to step out of this dreadful vehicle with us," she said, "you can play the part of Gare's mother."

"His mother?"

"Perfect, darling," said Soyla. "My Gaius looks like the kind of boy who would bring mommy along for protection."

Whoa now.

And women complain about testosterone? But I was still smarting from the three-ball talk, so I continued to keep my mouth shut.

They both turned to look at me. I'd have preferred jumping naked into a vat of boiling oil, but someone had forgotten to pack the vat.

"Don't look at *me*," I said. "You two decide."

Now you'd think my two thousand plus years would make me smart enough to understand I needed to make the decision. I mean, *they* were the ones trading catty barbs and I'd end up with both ready to claw out *MY* eyes.

"Fine," said Sister Christian. "She's the date, I'm your mother if that's the way you want it."

"Hang on," I said. "I don't recall saying I wanted it one way or the other."

The Bonnie Prince passed me a look that said, "Shut up before someone finds your weighted body washed up on shore."

Soyla turned to me and said, "Thank you, my love."

Thanks for what? I *didn't* say a thing and I made it clear to everyone that I *wouldn't* say a thing. And to add insult to Sister Christian's injury, Soyla wiggled her way back to my seat and sat down in my lap. Normally I wouldn't have minded, but the crusty look Sister Christian threw me? It made Soyla's weight feel more like Lady Liberty had just worked her way off the pedestal in New York and somehow plopped down. I should also add that Sister Christian's selfish attitude robbed me of the enjoyment I should have gotten from the experience.

With Soyla perched atop my lap and Sister Christian staring daggers at me, the last two kilometers took twice as long to cover as the first one hundred and fifty. I'd never been so thankful to see a city limits sign as I was when the Aachen marker went past my window. J-Rod drove for a couple more minutes, and we stopped to drop off Watanabe. He jumped out the passenger's door, slammed it, and banged the side of the van two times. We exchanged thumbs ups with him and he turned to head toward the Cathedral.

Game on. If all went well, within the next fifteen minutes I'd find myself safely in hell. And that sums up the low bar I'd set for my life's aspirations.

FIFTEEN

J-ROD STOPPED THE van by the café in a spot that offered good visual coverage of the cathedral square. We only needed to catch sight of Watanabe, and we knew which direction to look. It seemed fortune was with us because there were several other cars parked in the lot, so we could blend in.

It was dark, but my vampire sight provided a clear view past the tiny spaces the dim, environmentally friendly streetlights reached. No pygmies. As expected, though I knew the two little guys waited out there, monitoring the same cathedral square. Soyla told me that much. Somewhere close, but out of sight. Even though they didn't know the exact location of the portal, they'd know I would begin the journey to Sarah Arias somewhere near the cathedral.

Hence, they'd hunker down in a spot that didn't commit them to one side of the cathedral or the other. The Seven formerly held a key advantage over all other vampires, in that they weren't detectable by smell. After the acquisition of that same capability, I'd discovered the drawback. Maybe no other vampires could smell me...problem was that I couldn't smell other vampires either. I'd need to remember that if I made it back.

Fifteen minutes elapsed before I spotted Watanabe trotting into the square, his balaclava covering his face. Soyla, Sister Christian, and I eased out of the van, and pulled my balaclava down. Two lovers and their mother might look reasonable enough at first glance not to warrant a second. Of course, a dude escorting two hot chicks while wearing a terrorist hat might actually *demand* a second look.

As Soyla and I intertwined arms like the two lovers we were supposed to be, I lost confidence that the frumpy sweatshirt Soyla wore would do anything at all to disguise her. As for Sister Christian, I didn't worry because I didn't think they'd ever seen her. Soyla? Different story. *Everyone* knew Soyla, and I doubted only Helmet and I sat on the photo distro list.

Watanabe continued to trot, and we were committed. I could only hope our thin veneer of disguises fooled two of the cagiest beings ever to put bones through their noses. I kept my eyes on Watanabe as he approached the front of the cathedral and then cut hard in the direction opposite the portal. I'd begun to wonder if my two adversaries were really there when a little meteor sprinted past us and into the square toward Watanabe.

I can run fast enough to beat cars in the zero to sixty and quarter mile. And I can maintain it. But I'm comparing myself to automobiles when I'd need to use a jet fighter rocketing at the speed of sound for an accurate simile for the little guy. He flat out burned with speed, and I knew I'd better kick in my own afterburners if I had any hope of finding the portal without a fight.

I dropped the two-young-lovers act and headed for the opposite side of the cathedral. It would take no more than a few seconds to make it to the construction entrance and the portal. My brain works faster than my feet, and as I cut the air with my shoe soles, elbows, and butthole, the old warning chimes sounded for the millionth time in my long life.

I had seen one comet streaking past. I expected two. If this business of increased power wasn't just bunk, then the little guy chasing Watanabe seemed overly sure of his ability to take me on solo. But I'd already committed myself and in the blink of an eye, I found myself standing at the construction entrance for the cathedral.

Did German architects put construction entrances into the original blueprints? Most of the world thinks soccer is the German national sport. Just proves that most of the world can be wrong. Renovations. That's the thing all Germans live for. They don't count their lives in years like the rest of us, but rather they use numbers of renovations. It's a long way of saying I wasn't surprised to see the work wasn't completed.

I reached for the giant wooden door and found it unlocked, and saw the same black curtain obscuring the cathedral's main floor as was there before. I took a hesitant step into the ancient building.

If this didn't work, then Sarah Arias would be lost to the underworld because I had no clue where to find another portal. If so, I would keep trying to rescue Sarah Arias for as long as I breathed...maybe thousands of years. But then, no telling what an eon of torture would do to her...the state I'd find her in.

I didn't want to dash into the cathedral like Karl sprinting for visitor because I didn't think things worked that way. No good reason to come to that conclusion, I just thought it mattered. In truth, I hesitated because as long I stood on the threshold, hope remained that it *would* work. Once inside, if I didn't find myself through the portal? Hope would evaporate. No doubt desperation would move in to fill the void...and desperation tends to have a much longer shelf life.

So, in I went. Almost. I decided to step through the door, only I never made it. Not on that first attempt. And, where I expected to see a cathedral, instead there was an alternating view of cobblestones and those ineffective, environmentally friendly, German streetlights.

I'd just discovered vampire cannibal pygmy number two, and he was on me like Herr Doktor on a half-smoked cigarette left smoldering on the sidewalk.

Our roll halted in a dark, cobblestoned area between the cathedral and an adjacent building. Somehow, I ended up on top with the little, snarling dude. I almost laughed at cliché I saw beneath me. Vampire hissing, fangs exposed, the rest of his teeth filed to sharp points. I felt my own fangs extend in a millisecond and a preternatural growl erupted from my throat. That was new for me, but I'd ride the wave wherever it took me.

The little guy didn't even struggle. Just lay there hissing. It made me feel like a bit of the brute holding down the diminutive man with the almost cute-looking fangs. Then he brought his knees into my nut sack with the force of wrecking ball and I immediately possessed two important pieces of new information.

First, a good crack to the eggs doesn't result in immediate pain. My balls sat still for a second in shocked outrage. Oh, I knew the pain would come. And when it did, I'd get to play the role of Pompeii while excruciating pain starred as Vesuvius. The second thing? Cannibal pygmy vampires with superhuman strength are not cute, no matter how adorable their fangs.

The curtain rose on my pain. Nut-crushing doesn't feel good on its best day. This? I felt like I needed to die to get better. I puked out of reflex as I fell forward on Ballboy, and I think I got some in the little bastard's mouth because he gagged as he wiggled out from under me.

Vampires recover from injury at lightning speeds. That's not the same as recovery from the hurt. This special pain came in debilitating waves. My brain worked fine, though it flashed neon-red-framed images of the hairy, two-egg omelet that spilled in my underwear. It also detected Ballboy's next blow before it landed...a not-so-cute little foot aimed at my temple that I managed to duck under.

Ballboy couldn't stop the momentum of his missed kick, and when he ended up exposing a sliver of his back, my battle reflexes took command. Good thing too, because all I wanted to do was hold my aching groin while I lay sobbing in the fetal position. My fist crashed into Ballboy's ribcage.

Cracking ribs sounded like music. So was the cry of outraged pain. I didn't have time to hear the whole tune because wily little rascal pivoted, brought his other foot into my face and landed a clean blow that sent me sailing toward the cathedral. Throbbing balls and a face shattered like a stained-glass window.

I was down in the first round of this fight and there was no referee to give me a ten-count to recover. Ballboy grabbed his side in obvious pain. That last kick had cost him too, because he limped his way forward to complete my destruction. Good. I hoped my face broke so many of his bones that it would take a week before he could wear his little footie pajamas.

I took a submissive position and waited. My American friends call it playing possum and the doomsday-protocol ploy had worked for me many times in the past. But Ballboy approached with caution. Not good for the possum.

Want to hear more not good news? In addition to caution, he also displayed something long and sharp in his hand. If I wanted to be dramatic, I'd say it was gleaming in the moonlight, but my night vision was sufficient to see the syringe without the need for moonlight or the flaccid German streetlights.

I assumed Watanabe had cannibal number two engaged. Much as I loved the boy—in a manly way of course—I didn't think he'd delay the other prickly little bastard. The pain in my nuts had improved to the point where they felt like they were caught in a car door, so I had brain cycles to spare.

No matter how much caution the little guy exhibited, we both knew he'd eventually need to get close to use the syringe. My screaming had awakened a few dogs, and their subsequent barking woke up the rest. In a few moments the Polizei would show up. And, given it was the Aachen Cathedral, the site of the most culturally devastating theft in the history of the Germanic people, they'd show up in force. Ballboy crouched for the frontal attack.

And yes, he did fly. Even with my two-thousand-year lifetime loaded with rich and varied experiences, I can't concoct the proper words to do a flying cannibal pygmy rocket justice. I gaped in amazement while dropping the possum pose and throwing out a leg to counter the pygmy missile.

My move worked. I'd aimed for the torso and ended up clipping that flying pile of crap in his crotch. Do I need to report how exuberantly my mind did the happy dance? Even better, if I had a recording of the yell that erupted from behind that little set of filed teeth, I'd use it for mood music. I mean, if I'd *aimed* for his acorns, I would have missed. I'd forgotten my microscope.

The revenge party last less than a second because, as I leaped to my feet, another tiny foot connected with my chest. I think I heard my bruised balls scream a thank-you for being overlooked as I flew toward the church. I hit, rolled and managed to get to my feet and dodge the next attack—a dart blown my way from what looked like an oversized straw. Fiendish little Killer Two had entered the fight, appearing as the poster child for bigoted cannibal pygmy stereotypes. Though the dart gun didn't completely surprise me, I wondered what dark hole he'd hid the thing in to get it past customs.

I'm certain I didn't want to know, though maybe it was the lingering taste of that hiding place that threw his aim off, because projectile stuck in the wooden door within a couple inches of my right arm.

Were these two guys really *that* clueless? I mean, everything they did pushed me closer to the very spot I wanted to go. If I didn't know better...

She hit me square in my waist. Soyla. Or rather, her boot. The force slammed me hard against the door and I heard wood splintering. Why was everyone kicking? Were we people or freakin' donkeys? At least Soyla kept things above the belt, and once again my aching eggs offered their thanks. My gratitude ended there, because once again, I'd trusted a fellow vampire and they'd turned on me.

Her blow knocked the breath out of me. Well, truth is it also had me seeing stars, and if she'd hit me a little harder, those little blue cartoon birds would chirp merrily as they circled my addled brain. Yes, a girl hit me *that* hard. My eyes cleared, and I saw Soyla returning for another swipe at me. When I say *returning*, I mean through the sky.

Not the sky as in a bird or a plane or even an unguided murderous cannibal pygmy missile, but the sky as in a linebacker diving to block a punt. And I wasn't even holding a football.

Soyla wrapped herself around me, and the old cathedral door finally gave way from all the abuse it endured from the various people that kicked my butt. It offered me a perverse comfort knowing I'd hurt something besides my own pink body. Once the door started to cave, it gave up completely...no resistance as we fell backward.

Ever notice how people close their eyes before something painful happens? I'm no different than anyone else, because I closed mine as I fell backward...as if those two thin membranes of skin could cushion my body and somehow keep my head from cracking on the stone floor. Oh, and there was Soyla's weight to add to the pain equation.

You can be sure I'll edit that last sentence out of my memoirs...in case Soyla ever gets her hands on them.

With my eyes closed and Soyla-enhanced weight stuck to me like a monkey on my back, I hit the pavement. Only, it wasn't pavement I felt, but...

Spongy grass?

I looked up in time to see Soyla's lips descending on my mouth. She laid a kiss on me that could make nations go to war. I pride myself in putting the feelings of others ahead of my own, so to be nice, I responded.

I took a quick peek during the marathon lip lock and what I saw did not match the tiniest sliver of my expectations. A broad, rolling hill covered in wavy stalks of wild grass hued in shades of a green I'd not seen in nearly two thousand years. Yeah...no cold, stark German house of worship. But...perhaps I'm taking too much literary license and overstating things...German cathedrals are no longer considered places of worship. Bottom line? I expected the dank stone floor, not the Elysian Fields.

Soyla remained atop me doing her magic lip thing and I decided it prudent to continue playing along. All tiresome challenges do eventually come to an end, and the noise of Soyla lifting her lips sounded vaguely like a victorious toilet-plunger. It felt like she'd ravaged every cell in my body. I mean, one kiss and I felt dirty and used. Instinct said to give the girl another chance to be sure I wasn't exaggerating.

I heard someone nearby clear his throat, and both Soyla and I turned in the direction of the noise. A dude in a gray robe the citizens used to wear back in the days of Rome.

He said, "Sorry to interrupt."

Not sorry at all was the message I got from that grin on his face. But what the heck, I needed to stop anyway because kissing Soyla might lead to doing other things with Soyla. After that, no doubt I'd end up owned by Soyla and her nasty, ever-shifting moods and arbitrary lines of thought with no traceable logic. In other words, like the average married dude.

BTW, I knew the guy in the robe, and I'd prepared myself. Not specifically for *this* guy, but I thought I'd experience a shock or two. Think about it. Only a fool *wouldn't* expect an eye-opener to kick things off after passing through a portal to hell.

SIXTEEN

ALL RIGHT, MAYBE a bit dramatic. I didn't smell brimstone and I didn't see half-human red monsters with leathery wings capering about. And come to think of it, no fiery soul torturing.

Perhaps the word hell was an overstatement.

One moment I'd been kind of standing in an ancient, but German town square on a blustery German early-spring night. The next, I opened my eyes in a green rolling meadow with the world's sexiest female lunatic sucking the air out of me with a kiss that would compel an entire monastery of silent Buddhist monks to shout for joy.

So, what am I complaining about? Uh, who's complaining? It had worked. I'm not talking about Soyla's kiss, my raw, sexual heat makes that kind of thing work every time…or maybe my sex-starved desperation. Same thing.

I digress.

As far as *working*, I meant the portal and the bagger gang's strategy. Though, you'd need to ignore my throbbing walnuts to award the bagger gang a perfect score. Even so, I made it through the portal. So did Soyla. Granted, not part of the original plan, but she was there, so I'd need to adapt.

Oh, and the man who cleared his throat to interrupt the kiss? Balus. If I built my own hall of shame dedicated to people I wished I'd never met, Balus would be the statue in front of the building. Well, No Face could give Balus a strong challenge for that kind of top billing, but then non-human evil entities belonged in their own wing.

And who is Balus? Answer: The Roman soldier Rolf, Sparcius, and I killed two thousand years ago, causing the three of us became vampires. How do I still know his name? He introduced himself. After we killed him. True story. The battle continued around us and Sparky decided it would be chill to eat our slain enemy's heart. Only Balus wasn't quite slain, and eating the heart gave the three of us—Rolf, Sparky, and me—the condition we've suffered from since.

Last I'd seen, Balus was missing his head. Rolf severed it after we all sampled a piece of Balus's heart. Might sound like overkill to lop a dead guy's head off *after* you've cut out his heart. Not that time. We'd stabbed Balus about a dozen times and eaten his heart. Rather than die like a decent, honorable casualty, the dude started talking about us turning into immortal creatures.

It would be an understatement to say we three forest rubes nearly crapped our pants. So, Rolf beheaded him. End of story. Right? No. Balus kept blabbing, though we had to listen a little harder because the head landed several feet away.

In those days, the Romans considered the German Tribes as frenemies. Big mistake. We united to give the Romans a catastrophic defeat in that battle, and I took down my fair share of the enemy that day. I can still recall the jubilation I felt with each kill. Balus, though? He was one dude I regretted killing.

And it wasn't the battle wounds that did him in. Removing his heart, that's what did it. He told us so as he lay there authentically dying. And we would have had centuries under his mentorship had we not cleaned our plates. Turns out vampires can regrow everything—even heads. Everything that is, except a heart.

None of us knows if it's a cosmic rule or a chemical limitation of our condition. Heart out, vampire dead. For the three of us knuckleheads, it was our first bit of vampire-lore. Balus died after giving us the basics about our condition, though we lost much of what he said in the shock of disbelief and the confusion of battle.

I'd known him for only fifteen minutes. But oh, the monumental impact of those few ticks of the clock. And there he stood again, at the end of a long road that took me two thousand years to travel. Seeing him made something clear to me that I never, through all the years, considered.

"You committed suicide."

Balus smiled and said, "I fought a battle."

I understood, because I'd taken advantage of the same trick countless times over the years. Perhaps he'd been ready for a new identity and needed to close out the old one. Death offers a host of opportunities for a new life. If that makes sense. But he'd allowed us not only to take him down but also take out his heart. Vampire coup de grace. Looked like a suicide to me.

But what did it matter? I changed the subject.

"What language are we speaking?"

I detected no trace of an accent when he'd spoken and recalled speaking to him before. Latin. Not the hesitant and inaccurate priest and professor lingo I occasionally hear today, but the down and dirty workingman's version of a language that lived and breathed as much as any person. Latin, a language embalmed yet unburied.

Balus's chuckle sounded genuine enough.

"What language do you hear?"

Not much of an answer, but as I thought about it, I realized he'd hit the nail on the head. What language *did* I hear? I didn't know. I've spoken many languages and multiple dialects over the years. Thing is, I always knew which one I aimed for because each took conscious effort. Whatever tongue Balus and I communicated in rolled out of my mouth with no thought at all. Kind of blew away that thing my mother used warn me about engaging my brain before opening my mouth.

"I don't know."

True enough, though I felt that irksome inability to identify something I thought I *should* know. I was sure I'd heard it before. Not the language so much, but the tempo. That's what seemed familiar to me.

"Shall I introduce myself?"

Soyla, and sounding peeved. And why shouldn't she? I mean, she'd not been the center of attention for a whole *twenty freakin' seconds*.

Balus said, "You're Orsoyla Bokor," and he bowed and kissed her hand.

I was pretty sure that wasn't a custom in Rome, so it looked like my formerly dead Roman acquaintance was hitting on my date. You know how to change a chick from someone you wouldn't trust with a cockroach carcass into your most prized possession? Add another dude.

Soyla gave him the mechanical smile...the one some women use because they know it makes them. Like a practiced selfie-pose. It worked like that for Soyla. Only in addition to prettier it also made her look more predatory.

She said, "And you?"

Another bow from Balus. The guy was working it hard. I mean, had he missed the soul kiss Soyla had just laid on me? It made me wonder if he was the kind of dude who'd hit on the bride at her wedding reception.

I was beginning not to like him.

"Balus," he said, and he didn't offer any other name.

Come on, everyone who ever lived had more than one name. The self-centered twit. Who did he think he was? Liberace?

"Ah," she said, "the Roman centurion."

OK. So Soyla had heard of him. Enter green-eyed monster from stage left.

He said, "The same."

Soyla looked at me and said, "You never told me you knew Balus."

"You never asked."

Actually, I'd never had a real conversation with Soyla because there was that odor-repellant thing we couldn't get past for a thousand years. Consequently, we'd only been in the same room, train, or car for the sum total of about three hours. Not enough time for biographical chats.

"Bernard told me all about you," she said. "You're primary."

Whoa. Stop the presses. Primary? THE FIRST VAMPIRE?

"Yes," he said. "And how is Bernard?"

"The hell with Bernard," I said. "Did you just say you were primary?"

"I did."

Soyla wasn't surprised...and how did she know so much about Bernard? I thought she said she'd been hired by the bastards *opposed* to Bernard...that she'd only spoken briefly to Bernard. Primary? That made Balus the father of the entire vampire world.

"That must mean," I said, "You had incredible power."

Balus nodded.

"And yet...,"

Balus completed my sentence with, "And yet you killed me."

He did commit suicide.

He could have powdered Rolf, Sparky, and me, but instead, he let us not only take him down, but eat his heart.

"And The Seven?"

Balus said, "If you mean Bernard and the boys, then yes."

"They ate your heart?"

Soyla picked that moment to pull out the thin leather bra and somehow wiggle into it under her sweatshirt. Then she did the reveal... pulled off the old sweatshirt and threw it onto the grass. Something told me Balus would lose interest in our conversation.

I clicked my fingers in front of his nose and said, "Focus, dude."

"Yes," he said, "they sampled my heart. But they weren't as hungry as you and your friends."

So, we'd out-cannibaled a bunch of raw-dog cannibals. Lucky us. One of those elephant-in-the-room questions came to mind. How on earth did a big European find his way to an ostensibly lost pygmy cannibal tribe in Sub-Saharan Africa? I'm talking at least four thousand years ago. But the clock was ticking, and I really wasn't *that* interested. If I didn't get anything useful out of Balus soon, it would be time to knock the dust off our metaphorical sandals and get back on the road.

But to where? The bagger gang cooked up a great plan to get me to the portal and then through it. I guess they thought I'd be smart enough to formulate what to do after that. I wasn't. In summary. Their plan equaled great. Mine equaled nada.

"Sorry about that," I said meaning I was apologizing for ending Balus's life.

I wasn't sorry, at least not the way I made it sound. Balus was a Roman soldier, the guys we loved to hate. Half the time we wanted to be Romans ourselves and the rest of the time we wanted to kill them. But that was thousands of years ago.

Balus seemed to accept my apology because he showed his pearly whites and said, "You did me a great favor by speeding my transition from one state to the next."

Good for you, you date-stealing snake.

Soyla cut in with, "Balus made you?"

No, Soyla, my father and mother made me.

"Yes."

It was Soyla's turn to do the opened mouth, fish starving for oxygen thing.

"So that means," she said, "that you, Rolf, and Sparcius are as powerful as The Seven."

Not quite.

If I needed a reminder of the gap between The Seven's ability and mine, the throbbing pain in my crotch would serve as exhibit one.

"Maybe not," said Balus. He looked at me, "Do you?"

"Do I what?"

Now he was the one who sounded impatient. I mean, the guy had been here for thousands of years. What better appointment than talking to Soyla and me was penciled into his calendar?

"Do you have powers different from the rest?"

"If you mean other vampires," I said, "Nothing." Balus didn't respond so I added, "Unless you're talking about my stamina during…"

Soyla broke in, "Not true, my love."

Nobody likes it when someone contradicts them in front of others. On the other hand, I kind of liked the way Soyla called me "my love" in front of that horny old soldier. Of course, I needed to clear up her "not true" referred to my powers, that they were, indeed growing, and not to my sexual stamina. It didn't need growing. I mean, I didn't want that kind of baseless rumor getting out. Not even in Sheol.

"That's what I thought," said Balus. "And it's likely why you're here."

What? Hello. I wasn't in Sheol because of my growing powers, I was there to rescue a totally hot guardian angel. And I opened my mouth to say just that when better judgment overcame my instincts. Had I decided to think before speaking? Mom would have been proud.

True, my vampire-induced powers did seem different. I couldn't smell Soyla, and I had to assume that I also shed that classic block to others of my kind. The way I saw it, a new talent, not growing powers. Growing powers would mean I could take on The Seven. But that little dude kicked my butt before I escaped through the portal.

And I hoped the two little guys might someday forgive me. Talking about my balls, here, not the two pygmy cannibals. The Seven don't forgive. No, they maintain the grudge until they kill you and eat you. The two little cannibal guys in question would need to wait for another day, though, because they'd already tried, and I'd escaped.

Unless they did kill me.

A mind-blowing possibility. As I recalled the way things went down a few moments before, I didn't so much *step* through the portal as *fly* through it. And then I "woke up" in the happy green meadow. Hard as I tried, I couldn't put my finger on the moment I transitioned from the grayness of Germany to the brightness of where I stood. Of course, doing horizontal lip-calisthenics with Soyla can overload your memory circuits.

And was that her intention for the concentrated bout of tongue-wrestling? Confusion or manipulation? To get my motor running and addle my brain? But for what reason? The only way to tell for sure if Soyla is being dishonest is if she's speaking. But why would she feel the need to lie to me now? Didn't know. Maybe she wasn't lying at all…though I couldn't count it out.

Not at that moment, with the shock of Balus standing in front of me once more…and not with his claim of being primary. The first vampire. Because, if he were the only one among the three of us who was telling the truth, then it might be reasonable to assume I possessed…what? Power equal to each of The Seven? That would put me at number one on their hit list. Bernard's included. But if I believed what Soyla said, Bernard didn't want me dead, because according to her information, he'd vetoed my execution.

The pair of pygmies back in Aachen. They exhibited great caution... if you call a shot to the groin cautious. I had expected them to walk up to me like I was a mannequin, rip off my arms, and shove them in a place that would have made sitting a challenge. Scratching myself might have been easier but I could live without that kind of bonus if it meant keeping my arms connected to my shoulders.

None of that had happened. They knocked me down, but not out. I'd thought if the Watanabe misdirection didn't work then the mission would fail before it began, and the two pygmies would spirit me on my way to a trial. We didn't expect the two to split up, and I'd held Number One pretty much at bay until Number Two got there. Even then they didn't rush me like I'd expected, but rather they kept their distance.

Neither of them followed me through the portal. That bothered me. Either they couldn't make it through, were too smart to try, were concerned I presented a real challenge and didn't want to cut off their escape routes, or? Of course, there was another, less personally gratifying reason. Perhaps they couldn't continue the chase through the portal because I was dead and they were not.

"Gaius, my love."

I refocused my eyes and saw both were staring at me. I'd like to add they had concern in their eyes, but even I don't take *that* much liberty with the truth.

"Sorry," I said, and then to Balus, "You were saying?"

Soyla intervened, "Nothing important, my love."

Uh, Soyla, what's your game?

I remembered exactly what Balus had said...that my increased power vis-à-vis The Seven might be the reason I was in hell. I'd only asked her to repeat to stall for the time necessary to reboot my brain. So why did Soyla find the conversation uncomfortable? I could ask, but she'd only lie.

Another thing about the setup bothered me. How did Balus happen to be the first person I encountered in Sheol? I decided to subtly probe around the edges of that question.

"So why are you here?"

Subtle enough?

The soldier laughed.

"I like the frontal attack," he said. "So many hide their intentions in riddles rather than speak plainly."

"That's nice," I said. "You didn't answer my question."

Balus took in a deep breath and exhaled.

"Is this not the most beautiful place you've ever seen?"

I can recognize a rhetorical question as well as the next guy. I didn't respond.

"It's my job," he said. "Think of me as half guide and half gatekeeper."

Neither of the two answers provided much in the way of actionable intelligence. I mean, who couldn't figure out the guy standing at the gate might be the gatekeeper? And as far as the guide bit, it could mean many different things.

Would he guide me through Sheol to the place I'd find Sarah Arias? Was he the man in the meadow who could give a tour director-type history of every tree and blade of grass? Was he a spiritual guru? None of the above? Gatekeeper? Obvious. Guide? Not much to go on.

"Can you guide me to the demon prison?"

A sharper intake of breath and Balus's face flashed from a flaccid sort of serenity to stark terror. Only for a moment though, and I would have missed it if I weren't looking at him.

He said, "Not that kind of guide."

Well surprise, surprise.

"And what kind of guide are you?"

Balus didn't pause a microsecond.

"I tell you what you need to know."

"Perfect," I said. "Do you know the way to the demon prison?"

This time I anticipated a reaction and watched his face closely. Nothing.

"I do."

"Can you help me out with directions?"

Another quick answer.

"That's not something you need to know."

"Of course not," I said. "I just showed up in Sheol for a nature hike," I said. "Got any brochures?"

Balus didn't look amused, but I didn't care about my insult. I jumped through the looking glass for one reason and one reason only. To spring Sarah Arias. I couldn't help it if other folks put their own priorities into play. I'm accustomed to that much. Happens all the time when I let someone else involve me in their problems.

Soyla made a stab at helping me out when she said, "What do we need to know?"

I still didn't feel comfortable alone in hell with Soyla for a partner. And I wasn't sure which of us guys she was talking to.

"Not we," I said. And then, "You're going back."

Balus said, "She can't."

OK, I had to admit, that last statement represented something I needed to know. Score one for Balus.

"Why not? Can't she walk out the same way she walked in?"

"One-way portal," Balus said. "Doesn't go both ways."

Neither did my grandmother. I was pretty sure Balus had just lied to me.

"I've been through it both ways."

That didn't seem to bother Balus. He even nodded.

"I told you I'm the gatekeeper," he said. "If you want to traverse in both directions, you need a gate *operator*."

Great to know they've unionized hell. In my mind I saw two demons standing between a prone, tortured soul. "Can't pull out fingernails," one of them says, "I only do toenails."

"And when is he going to be along?"

Balus said, "You don't want to run into a gate operator."

Soyla said, "Why not?"

"Because they're *permanent employees*."

The way he said permanent employees made me shudder. No Face was able to open the portal in both directions. I'd seen him perform that trick twice. I never wondered where demons came from, though I guess I'd assumed they began life as humans and somehow devolved into the hideous monsters I'd encountered. Lazy thinking on my part. Especially when every indicator pointed to a different answer.

Much as I didn't want to, I recalled No Face dressed in drag. He said he wanted a nibble of the human experience. Not-so-hidden-meaning? He'd never *been* human. I kicked myself and wondered what other obvious and important indicators flew past me while I sat the café mindlessly swilling beer.

I said, "And what are you?"

"Me?" said Balus, "I'm a temporary hire."

Humans. Temporary hires. Demons. Permanent staff. That begged a whole new set of questions that had to do with the origin of the universe, of man, and of angels and demons. We could spend a few days mired in that, but I'd need to save it for another day because I had one more question before I set the topic aside.

"You say you're a temporary hire?"

Balus nodded.

"How long is your contract?"

He showed no outward sign of fear at the question.

Balus said, "Don't know."

"Been about two thousand years," I said. "You must have accrued maximum vacation by now."

A wistful look came over Balus's and he said, "Has it been that long?"

"It has."

Balus didn't respond with words, but rather just shook his head in a tired sort of disbelief. He'd proven nearly a bust as far as providing anything helpful for the rescue mission, but I had learned one thing. Sheol is a temporary place. I didn't know what came next, I just knew Balus expected that something else did.

It made me feel a little sorry for him. Emphasis on the word *little*. As the Primary, he had to have been the most powerful human that ever lived. Yet he'd allowed the three of us German tribal numbskulls to take him out in an insignificant battle that's lost to even the most exhaustive book on Roman military history. Why?

My guess is that he'd decided he'd lived long enough. He'd made The Seven and he'd made me. All born of the Primary. Nobody in the vampire world knew for sure what that meant, but the legend around vampire circles was that eating the Primary's heart elevated a normal human to a demigod. Just look at The Seven.

How many others had Balus created in his lifetime? I stopped myself from asking. Sure, that tidbit of data would come in handy…a list of vampires I needed to avoid. But Balus would think I wanted a list so that I could kill them. And that might end up not too far from the truth once I had time to reason things out. I've done worse in my life.

Soyla? The more names she gathered the more blackmail and

betrayal she could wreak. No, best leave things with The Seven and with me. Well, not just The Seven and not just me. Rolf and Sparky were also involved now. I'd need to warn them at the first opportunity.

After the mission.

Speaking of the mission, "Can you tell me which way I need to go?"

Balus said, "Don't know."

"Are you sure you're not only the gatekeeper? This guide thing seems like title inflation to me."

Balus laughed and said, "Just kidding."

We both got a chuckle out of that. Soyla stood there stone-faced. Chicks seldom appreciate childish guy humor.

Balus said, "Take the train."

"The train?" I said, and I felt the electric prickling of gooseflesh on my arms.

Hadn't Helmet warned me against the train? "Don't take the train," he'd said, and I'd thought he was warning me about Soyla on the S5 in Bad Homburg. Perhaps I'd misjudged.

"The train," Balus said in a tone indicating finality. "You want to find your angel? Take the train."

Who said anything about rescuing an angel? I did think about it a couple of times while we spoke, but I didn't remember any of that thinking coming out of my mouth. The needle on my paranoid meter moved into the red quadrant.

"Which way?"

I was asking if I board the train heading to the left as I approached the tracks or waited until one came from the other direction.

Balus crossed his arms over his chest and rubbed his chin. I didn't like the stress I saw on his face because I didn't see how a few thousand years loitering in a pleasant meadow could raise a guy's blood pressure. That goes double for already-dead dudes.

He said, "Only one direction."

OK, I could roll with a one-way train. Took away all possible error in the boarding decision. But then…

"Hold on a second," I said. "If the train only runs in one direction, then how does it get back to the start?"

No sooner than I'd asked the question then I realized how stupid it was. Circular track. I'd need to get my head into the game if I expected to survive long enough to even board the thing. I felt my face turning my favorite shade of buffoon-red.

Balus said, "Don't know."

Was he pulling my leg? How could he not know? Two thousand years in Sheol and he didn't know how the train reset? "Don't take *the* train," Helmet had said. "Take *the* train." That was Balus. Both talked about *the* train. Not *a* train. Take *a* train would imply more than one. Take *the* train meant the opposite. One train in Sheol. Perhaps the place never bought into the European style of public transportation.

"OK," I said. "I'll just hop on the first train."

Balus nodded.

"And how do I know when I've reached my destination?"

The answer formed in my brain just ahead of Balus's reply.

"Only one stop," he said, "Your destination."

Of course. One and only one train, and it goes in a single direction, starts from nowhere and stops at the one place which happens to be my destination.

Check.

I said, "Gotcha."

I didn't know what Sheol or hell—or whatever to call where we stood—did to a human soul. Balus gave me a good idea that it could turn a mind into an omelet. A gatekeeper who didn't know how to open the door and who moonlighted as a guide who couldn't find his way out of a one-holed outhouse.

"Any other words of wisdom for us? I have a train to catch."

Soyla spoke up with, *"We* have a train to catch."

Even in hell, a guy can't be right when there's a woman nearby to correct him. Made me wonder if earth-bound relationships are dress rehearsals for eternal punishment.

Balus stood quietly for a few moments, and I got the sense of a man who knew he had forgotten something important and was trying hard to remember.

I said, "Well I have one more thing."

Balus looked relieved...like perhaps the extra moment might dislodge something in his mind.

Balus said, "What?"

"Am I dead?"

A simple question. So why did it feel like every nerve in my body wanted to shake apart as I stood waiting for an answer. Balus thought for a second and snorted something that sounded like laughter. Dude was the strongest human alive for several thousand years. He'd fought his way through hundreds—if not thousands—of battles and rubbed elbows with the first kings on earth...and here he stood in the cliché, rolling green meadow you'd expect to see as the backdrop in a cheesy movie where the two lovers run to embrace.

Once more, I felt sorry for the guy.

"Are you dead?" he said. "Gaius of the Teutoberg Forest, you are no different from always."

Right. So maybe I didn't need to worry as much about feeling sorry for the guy. What kind of baloney answer was that? No different from always? Did that mean I was still alive or was Balus making a primeval-beatnik comment about souls and immortality and other crap that transcends physical boundaries? Whatever it meant to Balus, it meant nothing at all to me.

I said, "You've been helpful."

Not.

The dude *bowed—actually bowed—*in acknowledgment. Here's a tip if you ever find yourself in hell. They don't get sarcasm. Don't waste your best material there because it will fall on numb ears. I did have one more question for old Balus but hesitated to ask. It's the once bitten, twice shy thing.

"What language are we speaking?"

I kept hearing those familiar notes and tempo, but still, I couldn't place it. It wasn't Latin or the old Germanic we spoke before anyone recorded our history...or English or anything else I remembered in between. We could have been using one of the many dead languages I'd brushed wings with over the years, but I didn't think so. It sounded too familiar. Old, but also up to date.

Balus said, "The true language."

Intuition told me to give up and walk away. I'd not gained anything from the meeting other than the opportunity to catch up with... With what? Did I consider Balus and old friend? Nope, though I'd thought about him at least one time each day for two thousand years.

So, I got to touch base with Balus, and I'd received some advice on transportation. On the other side of the coin, I hadn't lost anything either. I gave it another try.

"One language," I said. "Do you mean the language of angels or something like that?"

Balus smiled and nodded. Bingo.

"Angels, yes," he said, and then he added something that floored me. "And everything else here."

Angels? Everything else? I'd only been fishing when I used the term angels because I'd heard that language-of-angels malarkey on a

YouTube channel this hot chick I was dating liked to watch...one of those spiritual channels. Something about speaking in tongues. The preacher would get up and rattle off some undecipherable monkey-talk and then ask for money. The babe said the man spoke in the language of angels.

Now here it was again. The language of angels. Hadn't thought about that chick in a few years. Nice girl. Said she wanted to wait for marriage. Done that once and I have to admit it worked out great for me...up to the point Nellie died.

"Gaius, my love."

Nellie?

No, Soyla. It was no wonder that two millennia here left Balus loopy...it was getting to me after two minutes.

"Just a second," I said, and the three of us stood there in awkward silence while I tried to engage my brain.

When Soyla said, "We should get going," her voice made the gossamer line of thought vanish from my brain.

"Just give me another second, will you?"

I'd been staring at the grass between my feet, trying to divine what it was about Balus's response—angels, but also everything else—that bothered me. I had my finger on it but lost it when Soyla babbled. When I looked up to bark at Soyla, I saw what made her anxious to depart.

Clouds were forming. Not overhead, but off in the distance. I'd seen plenty of storms brewing in my long life, but this one was a sight to behold. I wasn't sure how long it would take for the storm to get from where it was to us, but what I did know was I didn't want to be here when it arrived.

Black, purple, and red. Clouds that reached from high in the atmosphere and that extended all the way to the ground. I was going to ask Balus what we should do about the storm when I saw the second reason Soyla wanted to move on.

My old acquaintance didn't look so well. In fact, you might say he was decomposing in front of our eyes. The gray robe he'd been wearing went from perfect and seamless to faded, ripped in dozens of places, and mottled with that green ooze that leaks the gasses formed when bodies rot.

I said, "Balus?"

His skin had shriveled to a thin covering for his skull, and his eyes looked like rotten grapes in huge sockets. He reached for me with black hands that belonged on an Egyptian mummy in the Louvre. Balus grasped my shoulders with two hands that felt more like the wet branches of a bush than something that was once a human.

"Go," he said, and now his voice sounded—and his breath smelled— like it came from the mouth of Death himself.

I stood my ground. Balus had been a soldier of Rome, and I'd engaged him in combat to protect my land and my people. He deserved the honor of my witness to his misery.

"Can I help?"

He shook his blackened head.

"No hope for me," and then in a croak, "Don't come back here."

"Will you die?"

His skin now looked like scales on a rotting fish...or dead rattlesnake. In the corner of my eye, I detected Soyla backing away.

Perhaps she'd need a cuddle later.

"Never," Balus said, and it came out like the high-pitched croak of a bat. "I've spoken too much."

Spoken too much? A repeating loop of "I don't know?" Too much? No use in asking Balus to explain, because based on the way he was putrefying, he'd do well to answer in single syllables. With great effort

Balus twisted his head toward the storm.

"Go," he said. "It will trap you here."

That got my attention. Soyla and I would leave, and we'd make haste in doing so because we could both make super-human time across the ground. But then, our speed depended on what lay between where we stood and where we were going. And who knows what to expect in hell? The tourism bureau should publish brochures. I turned to leave but Balus held me back with his skeleton's hands.

It would have been easy to break his grip, set my sneakers to chopping and to leave Balus and his whacky storm far behind. I didn't, though, at least not right away. I sensed Balus had something more to say, and was surprised when he managed an entire sentence.

"Don't take the train."

SEVENTEEN

DON'T TAKE THE *what?*

Balus released my shoulders and crossed his arms over his chest. It appeared he'd stand there in the approaching storm. Me? No, and as much as it pains me to admit, I didn't worry about him. If he didn't know the way things worked after eighty generations in the same spot? Then he deserved whatever he got.

I expected Soyla to pull me away and plead with me to leave. Didn't happen that way. It took a few minutes for me to catch up with her. Good thing for me that meadow extended for about twenty miles because if she'd hit the woods before we rejoined, I'd still be looking for her.

Or maybe not, as things turned out later.

We sprinted side-by-side, and I realized I had more gears available to me, meaning I could have left her in the dust. Interesting. I'd had the opportunity to do combat with Soyla in the near-past, and I'd thought she and I were equal…far ahead of most vampires and far behind The Seven…but equal in terms of power. Perhaps I needed to reassess.

We ran until we'd reached the end of the meadow, and I held out my arm to stop her. It took fifty yards for us to slow to a halt. I glanced back over my shoulder. The storm still loomed, but further behind. Wishful thinking, perhaps.

Soyla said, "Got to keep moving," and she had that wild-eyed look a predator gets when it discovers *it* has become the prey.

I agreed with her...in part.

"To where?"

Soyla understood what I meant, and she took some deep breaths. I'd never seen Soyla frightened before and I'd file that reaction to fear in the persistent part of my memory. Why? Because the knowledge might give me an advantage if circumstances forced me to kill her. Also, I liked the way her heaving breaths stressed that leather bra.

When she could speak, Soyla said, "You're right, my love."

A check of the storm's progress suggested we had time, that it hadn't gotten any closer in the past few moments. And if I were to guess, it looked like It was concentrating its power over the spot we'd just vacated...over rotting Balus. Multi-colored clouds swirled around massive flashes of lightning, and I could see sod thrown into the air in huge clumps.

I focused my vampire sight on one of those green clods that the storm dislodged, and it looked like it was wriggling. Soyla spoke, and I held up my hand for silence. Wriggling all right, I was certain. But not green clods of earth. I felt a vomit rise to my mouth.

Bodies. But not dead bodies. Bodies that were still, in some measure, alive. The storm pulled them out of the ground, carried them high into the air, and then hurled them back down. Rinse and repeat. Over and over. I think I watched the cycle for ten minutes, and I felt Soyla slip her hand into mine and we both stood in horrified silence.

We couldn't hear their screams...there was no need to because we could see them. And that made the sight so much more terrifying. Earlier, I'd said that I saw no tortured souls? As I stood watching the suffering for those thousands caught in the storm, I felt ashamed that I could be so blithe.

We'd seen a purple, black, and red storm approaching, and now we knew the reason for the strange colors. Clouds made black by the sheer volume of humans borne aloft, purple from the decay of fatal bruises. Do I need to explain the red?

I sat down in the grass, secure in the unfortunate knowledge that more horrors waited for us. Like perhaps a train up ahead. But then, I never expected hell would be a one-trick pony.

Soyla followed my lead and sat down with her back against mine. Good. We could keep watch in both directions. She laid her head on my shoulder. Uh, maybe she didn't care about sentry duty. I turned to look at her saw she had her eyes closed.

We sat that way for a long while, me facing the storm and Soyla facing the forest.

She broke the silence with, "What have we done?"

Good question with no good answer. What *had* we done? I volunteered myself for the rescue mission, and for some reason, Soyla decided to tag along. Why? Nothing popped into my mind, but if she'd done it for the wrong reasons, then she'd deserve any suffering that came her way.

But then, so would I.

I watched the storm first wane and then disappear altogether. I didn't doubt it would return. Why wouldn't a place with a train that always came from the same direction not have a storm that did the same thing?

I was about to wake Soyla to get us moving when she spoke.

"The language," she said. "You asked Balus about the language."

I had. And I thought his response was the first piece of real information he'd offered. Sure, he mentioned the train, but I already knew about that from Helmet. He'd told me to avoid it, and Balus ended up giving me the same advice. Disturbing, but not new information.

But the language...that's where Balus passed some *real* INTEL, and maybe under the jailor's nose.

"I did."

She said, "I know what we were speaking," and then, "Hebrew."

"Are you sure?"

"Positive," said Soyla. "I took a life as a Jewess in Budapest."

Jewish Soyla. How rich. I bet her scams didn't find as much success. But Hebrew made sense when I thought about it. I didn't speak the language, but I'd lived in or near Mainz, Germany every couple of hundred years.

At one time, Mainz was the center of the Ashkenazi, and I could be wrong, but I think most of today's Jews are Ashkenazi. And boy did they like to speak in their version of German mixed with Hebrew. I could understand some of the words. It was from the scholars that I'd heard the same tempos and tones that sounded so familiar as I spoke to Balus. Hebrew, the language of angels.

That's what Balus had said. Well, not *specifically* Hebrew, but the language of angels. Obvious, once Soyla put a name to it. But still...I still missed something. Can you blame me? What with Balus decomposing and with an ungodly storm blowing in. I closed my eyes and replayed the scene.

Balus stood there with his parts looking shiny...compared to what would happen in a few seconds. I asked him, and he'd said we spoke the language of angels. He also added something else. I could hear it in my mind...the language of angels, and then in what appeared an unimportant afterthought, he'd said, "And everything else here."

That was it.

Angels and everything *else* here. Perhaps Balus's "I don't knows" were his way of putting whatever watched us at ease. And something *did* monitor us. Something that kept its presence hidden. I'd like to say I felt it, but I didn't. I just knew something watched.

Balus at the gate waiting for us. If whoever watched knew anything at all about my history, then it would not have allowed that to happen. I don't know how much it cost Balus to come forward and meet me at the portal. Whatever the price, he would pay the tab on that bill for a long time.

He'd adhered to the party line by providing no information at all… at first. I suspected the watcher wanted us to board the train, so Balus followed the script. My question about the language offered Balus an opportunity to step away from the party line, and he took it.

Would he have found a way to slip us additional information had I not asked about the language? I don't know, but I suspect so. Why else would he be there like a giant deus ex machina? Maybe calling him a machine of God is taking things a bit far, but Balus found out I was coming through, and I suspect he volunteered for gate duty.

The conversation distilled into two nuggets…One recommended action— "Don't take the train"—and the other provided context— "the language of angels…*and everything else here.*" If I looked at it that way, I might solve the uneasy feeling that kept scratching at the back of my brain.

"Gaius?" Soyla said. "Do you know how to get us out of here?"

The bagger gang did a great job getting me to the portal, but I'd done zilch in planning for what to do next. The term rescue mission carries the implication of going in and getting back out. Otherwise, no rescue. I didn't intend on a one-way deal…a suicide slightly more spectacular than weary surrender Balus made to Sparky, Rolf and me. What could be cooler than walking into the afterlife while you were still alive? Soyla had asked me if I knew how to get us out of here.

"No."

Soyla thought about that, and I must admit I liked the feel of her warm body leaning against my back…one of the more stellar benefits of my new ability to withstand proximity to other vampires. It wouldn't take much for me to get used to having her around. I mean, sitting up against me on what might loosely be called our first date, she emitted a clean, flowery scent. She'd even washed her hair. A glimpse of the girl that hid beneath the sometimes psycho, always deadly and never trustworthy self-centered Hungarian warrior woman façade?

"I thought so, my love."

At least my poor organizational skills didn't disappoint her. That was cool.

I said, "Do you?"

"Do I what, my love?"

"Do you know how to get us out of here?"

Soyla's laugh came back before the sound of the question mark faded, and it got me chuckling too. I rolled onto my side and laid down in the grass. Soyla fell beside me and we did the nervous hysterical laughing thing.

When we'd gained a measure of control, she rolled to put her head on my shoulder, and I wiggled my arm under her and then pulled her close. She arched her back and hovered her face over mine.

She said, "Do you think we're safe?"

Uh…no.

I suspected Soyla wasn't as helplessly dependent as she was acting, though I liked holding her in my arms on the soft grass…and with no living world around us to interfere. She wanted to know if I thought we were safe. In Soyla talk, it meant she wanted to know if *she* was safe. Well, there *is* that saying about zebras and stripes.

I said, "Not one bit."

Soyla smiled and put her head back down on my chest.

"I agree, my love."

Nice, though the question was about the easiest I'd ever been asked. Safe? In hell? Come on. Perhaps she was probing the borders of my honesty…trying to discover if I'd lie as easily to her as she planned on doing herself.

Oh Soyla, what a mess.

I could spend a lifetime lying in grass with her and wonder why I'd ever wasted time doing anything else. Another bit of 411? My balls no longer throbbed. They did tingle though. I mean, did you understand anything about what I just said about the situation in the grass? I could almost see the footprints left by my brain as it marched from my skull to that alternate location where it does its best work. Kind of like my own self-contained Camp David.

"Is she worth this to you?"

I didn't know what she was talking about. Do all chicks ruin perfectly good moments with their incessant questions and meaningless jabber… use their tongues like pins to pop happy balloons?

I heard an irritable edge in my voice when I said, "Is who worth this?"

Soyla blew out an exasperated breath and said, "Sarah Arias."

Sarah who?

I thought about it, but only for a second. Of course Soyla meant Sarah Arias when she said, "I she worth this to you." How could I miss that one? Well, I know how I missed it, and don't expect an apology from me for being a guy and acting in a way that comes natural to us. On the other hand, why do babes always want to smack you in the face with another chick's name when you've got a good thing going?

I sat up.

"Yeah," I said. "Sarah Arias is worth it to me."

The irritability found its way into Soyla, and she sat up, too.

"Fine," she said. "We better get moving."

Her voice had come in the sound of air leaking from my happy balloon, and I said, "If that's the way you want it."

It's the way things had to be. What was I thinking? Well, I knew what I was thinking, but I promised myself to guard against thinking that way again...at least for the duration of the rescue mission. But hey, notice how this dude's sex drive overcame the perils of hell? Sweet! And with no small sense of pride for that accomplishment I got to my feet and pulled Soyla to hers. We both made a show of brushing imaginary grass off ourselves.

When Soyla said, "Which way?" she left out the fake "my love.."

Which way.

Forest in front of us, clear meadow behind us. But clear only because the giant storm of tortured, falling bodies dissipated to reset at whatever point in hell it considered home plate. When I looked back toward where we'd come through the portal and I didn't see Balus.

"The forest."

And yes, the forest represented the logical choice. At least for me. I was born in the forest and learned to fight there with my tribe. We'd met the Roman legions in battle there and devoured them to the last man. If any advantage for me existed in this dimension, I'd find it among the trees.

"OK," said Soyla. "You lead."

I bowed and grabbed her hand, and I intended on kissing it. Parody only though, because I knew my comment about Sarah Arias had her miffed. But Soyla had left her sense of humor in the grass because, when she realized what I intended to do, she jerked her hand away and gave me a sharp punch in the nose.

Tears flooding my eyes indicated she'd broken it...that, and the blood pooling on the ground. But, describing how a chick bloodied my nose would prove embarrassing, so I'll leave that part out. I wiped the tears and looked at Soyla with my best mask of outrage.

She stood there smiling one of those chick smiles that tells you that they don't think whatever you did was funny, and that they're happy you got whatever they dished out to you in response. Of course, I did owe Soyla a debt of gratitude for reminding me how quickly she can bite. I'd be wary not to let it happen twice.

OK, maybe not more than half a dozen times.

Smiling Soyla said, "Don't you think we should get on the road to finding Juliet?"

EIGHTEEN

HILARIOUS.

"Just give me a second to repair the damage."

If I thought that reference to the broken nose might make Soyla feel a bit of shame for her actions, I was once again wrong.

"Of course, my love."

Note to self: *My love* doesn't mean squat.

We took our first, wary steps into the forest. I didn't know whether to expect an attack of demon banshees or for the ground to swallow us and belch while it digested. None of that happened, but the lack of nothing happening didn't soothe our jagged nerves or calm my heart. It felt like a gorilla beating its way out of flimsy wooden cage.

I saw everything I expected to see in a forest: hardwood trees and pines, some healthy, some fallen and rotting to return nourishment to the soil. Moss hung here and there, and so did the occasional vine. Brambles that clung to us along the way came off with little challenge. Rather than reassure me, the familiarity stirred additional tension into my already overstressed nerves. I think I'd have felt better if a gruesome, supernatural horror had come screaming down upon us.

After an hour of silent progress, I held up my hand, and Soyla said,

"What?"

When I put my finger over my lips in an emphatic shushing sign, Soyla tilted her head and rolled her eyes to the sky. OK, so she didn't like taking orders. She'd need to get over it because I'd detected the first abnormality.

Smoke. I couldn't see it, but I could smell it. Traces. And as I thought about it, I'd been tracking it for the past quarter hour.

Forest fire? Maybe, but I didn't think so. Forest fires emit a thick, bitter, panicked odor. This was more the scent of a campfire or perhaps a chimney. I

Intentional, not accidental.

If my assumptions regarding the smoke proved true, then it meant Soyla and I would encounter other beings—the word humans might prove a poor assumption.

Soyla spoke with greater insistence when she repeated, "What?"

At least she whispered. Good for her, because she needed to take the situation seriously. I leaned in close.

"Smoke."

Soyla rolled her eyes again, and said, "We're in hell."

I shook my head.

"Not that kind of smoke. Fire."

Soyla said, "Brilliant. First smoke and now there's fire."

I kind of got her point, though I already had a butt full of her pouting about Sarah Arias. Yeah, I thought rescuing Sarah Arias was worth a trip into hell. I mean, I was there, wasn't I? Let that fact speak for itself. And I'd never invited Soyla, though maybe she worried I'd find a good time and she tagged along to make me miserable.

"People," I said, but only because I couldn't think of a better word.

"People?"

What was she, a woman or a parrot? Yes, people. Well, maybe not people, but who wanted to get into a thirty-minute discussion with a grump? The most reasonable answer to that question would be any dude who wanted to get laid.

Since I didn't see that sort of activity in my immediate future I said, "Shut up and listen."

She understood I'd only been so abrupt out of immediate concern for the both of us. I could tell that because I saw her fangs extend and I had to move my arm at lightening-speed to parry that blow she'd aimed at my face. *Of course* that knife got into her hand by accident.

I grabbed both of her arms and pulled her close. Not for hanky-panky but to make sure I smothered any attempt she might make at kicking me. I'd suffered enough nut-trauma for one day. Fortunately for both of us she didn't struggle.

"Quiet," I said, and for once in her long life, she obeyed. "Can you smell it?"

Soyla lifted her face to the air and I got a quick glimpse of the Hungarian warrior who'd slain so many when the Crusaders came calling around Budapest. Pure predator.

"I think so," she said. "Cooking."

Bingo. That's what I detected. Cooking. I was thankful that it didn't smell like meat...more like a vegetable stew. If it were meat, I didn't even want to think about what we might find boiling in the pot.

I said, "Approach or avoid?"

Soyla might look like a supermodel, but I knew better. She'd employed those hot looks and her skills with the blade to increase the population in this place. Overall, a dangerous package stuffed into tight leather pants and a leather bra screaming for relief. No chance I'd lower my guard.

She said, "Approach."

Why avoid a bloodletting when there's blood to be let? Soyla's motto. Right. Neither of us possessed a significant weapon, but that didn't matter. Our bodies were our weapons.

"OK," I said. "But let's find out what we're up against before we attack."

Soyla grinned. "Of course, my love."

Of course, my butt. That smile told me she'd say whatever I wanted to hear and do whatever she wanted to do. At least one of us was regaining their balance.

We shifted into hunter mode and crept through the forest as we followed the scent. Each step brought me not only closer to the source of the smoke but also excavated long-buried memories of my childhood. Of my father and my mother.

I became the forest, and it was me. Without needing to look my feet, I found places where they would stir no noise from broken branches or crackling leaves. Soyla maintained a position twenty yards to my left, and when I glanced at her I saw the lithe confidence of a mighty python slithering through home territory deep in the Amazon jungle.

My fangs extended, and I could see Soyla's were also prepared to rip and to feed. But we wouldn't feed in hell, and I hoped Soyla had already seen to that necessity before she followed me through the portal. Adrenaline filled my veins. My muscles ached for action and I worked hard to restrain a howl of impatience. I wanted to kill something, and my instincts told me to hurry over that next hill, make haste through the next ravine.

Just a little further. Just until I reached the smoke.

An amoeba with a cold could have tracked that smoke, because whoever tended the fire and cooked the beef stew did so with no apparent concern for what they might attract. If anything, the cavalier manner they cooked a meal could only mean one of two things. Where smoke met fire, we'd find either a fool...or a trap.

I didn't care which.

I halted at the edge of a tiny clearing, and I saw that Soyla had maintained her combat distance.

Good.

If anyone—or thing—came for Soyla, I could flank them. She'd do the same for me. At least I hoped she would.

In the distance, I could see five, maybe six tents arranged in a circle. Canvas, and weather-worn to the point I didn't know where the white ended, and the dingy yellow began. I couldn't see the fire, though the smoke told me it sat somewhere in the middle.

I'd seen tents like these before, back during the war…the Civil War as the Yankees called it and the War Between the States as was the popular term for those of us who fought on the southern side. Round, nearly head-height, and rising in the middle like a teepee. Not the pup tents common soldiers were issued, but the larger variety reserved for senior officers. And the circular placement? Atypical. Back in the war we organized tents in rows by units. Terrain permitting, we built our campsites to mirror our battle formations.

The scene said permanence, like whoever pitched the tents did so a long while back. The smoke told me they were still around. Another aspect of the scene didn't play true with what I remembered of that war: They'd posted no sentries.

"Who goes there?"

Correction.

They'd posted at least one sentry. Soyla and I both did the smart thing and kept our mouths shut. The voice came from the camp and not the woods behind us, so that meant nobody tracked us here and we couldn't know if they'd seen us or merely suspected our presence. And even if they'd caught sight of one of us, favorable odds existed they hadn't seen us both.

"Two of 'em," said a different voice. And then "Your turn to check."

The voice came in the same tone and cadence Balus, Soyla, and I'd used back at the portal. Hebrew. And impossible as it seems, the voice sounded American and it sounded southern. Tennessee.

No, not Tennessee but Northern Alabama.

I'd fought with the boys from Alabama and I can tell you if the south had a few more of those guys everything might have turned out differently.

"'Taint my turn a'tall," came a third voice. "And nobody needs to check," he said. "We know who they are."

Maine Yankee for sure. I'd spent the better part of two years as bartender in Bangor. Those folks spoke their own version of English. Rather pleasant, once you got used to it. But what had he said? That they knew who we were. Impossible.

"We gonna play this right or we just whistling Dixie?"

A fourth voice. New York, if I had my accents right, and I'd bet a month's worth of J-Rod's tips that I did. I wondered what he meant by "playing this right?" No clue. A new sound came from the middle of the tents. Somewhat musical in nature but nothing I'd call real music. The hesitant and mildly grating sound of someone attempting to whistle through dry lips.

Dixie.

He made it through the first two famous lines of the song before others joined in. Not all at once, but in ones and twos. "Look away, look away, look away, Dixieland." My mind matched the words to the tune, and by the time they started the second stanza I thought I heard around ten distinct voices.

They whistled their way through half the first line of the second stanza when some of the voices began sputtering into laughter. The one with orders of magnitude more talent for whistling than the rest kept going.

"Away, away, away down south in Dixie. Away, away, away down S—O—U—T—H"—he held his melodious rendering of that high note—"in Dix—EEE." The other guys alternated between laughing and cheering and not the protests you'd expect out of enemies. Sounded more like a group of old college chums out for a weekend of camping. And drinking, of course.

"Looks like we gonna whistle Dixie," said Mr. New York in a burlesque attempt at a southern accent.

That got the guys laughing again.

"Mr. Gaius and Miss Orsoyla."

Yet another new voice. Couldn't place the accent. Perhaps Kentucky?

"Stew's about ready," he said. "Please join us."

Soyla and I locked eyes across the distance and both of us raised our eyebrows.

Should we?

If they knew our names, then it stood to reason they weren't bluffing about knowing we stood there peeking through the trees. Duh. We nodded in unison and stepped into the clearing.

Rather than walk over to me and enter the circle side-by-side, Soyla kept her distance. Good girl. If he'd ever *really* marched into hell for a heavenly cause, then Don Quixote might have done well to trade Sancho for Soyla. Despite her many irritating deadly quirks, the woman was a professional when it came to the art of defense. And killing. Plus, I'd bet my now-happy testicles that Soyla was a sight better to look at than the chubby little sidekick whose hair probably never smelled as clean and sweet as hers did.

She entered the circle from the side opposite of the one I used. I saw about a dozen men sitting around the campfire I'd expected. They only glanced at me, but Soyla? They stood up and welcomed her with hoots and cheers. A mind must make quick and important decisions when you walk into a potentially dangerous situation. My first impression? Relax.

The camp reminded me of every camp I'd experienced during my stint in the southern army, and the guys looked just as I'd expect. I didn't think these dudes were the kinds of guys who do the weekend reenactments, either. Instinct told me I was looking at the real deal… men who fought, and most certainly died, in that long-ago conflict.

But as I took a moment to look closer, I saw the Civil War boys weren't the only ones. I saw a guy dressed in a French uniform from the Napoleonic period and another wearing the white flowing robes of a soldier of Suleiman the Magnificent. If you don't know, he's the dude who smacked the Crusaders in the Holy Land. The only other uniform that stood in stark contrast to the Civil War group was a guy dressed in a no-kidding, World War Two Nazi infantry officer's tunic. And that uniform served to remind me that no matter how cordial the campground seemed, I was in hell. I'd do well to keep that in mind.

The Frenchman made it to Soyla first—who else but a Frenchman could manage such a thing among ten rowdy soldiers? He reached for her hand in the dainty, effeminate way French officers use to seduce their mothers.

"If you please, Mademoiselle," he said, and he led her to one of the two camp chairs that sat near the fire.

Mademoiselle? Yeah right. Captain Frog was taking great liberties with the truth. Madame Death would be more like it. And no, it wasn't jealousy talking. Why would I be jealous of the way she beamed at Captain Frog and the fake blush of hers when he kissed her hand? And why should I care when Soyla promised to never wash Frog's kiss off the top of her hand for the rest of her life. Hah. The idiot had smooched the same hand she used to wipe her butt. She'd be scrubbing it again.

Trust me.

Ok. So maybe Soyla was just ingratiating herself with the boys to allow me a few free moments to scan the place and to get a sense of the people. But she could have done it without acting so bubbly. And without telling Captain Frog, "We're just old friends," when the dude asked about her situation with me.

If I didn't know that the guy was already dead, I would have ripped his arms off and shoved his own hands into that smooth mouth of his. Maybe that'd make him forget about what he'd just tasted on Soyla.

So, he liked kissing hands? I could offer him something darker, hairier and more humid to smooch.

"Don't mind him," said the guy with the Alabama accent. "Likes to talk about his female conquests but we all know he died a virgin."

"Really? How do you know that?"

Bama laughed and said, "Ain't no secrets 'mongst us here, brother."

"No secrets? Does that mean you can read minds?"

Another laugh from Bama, and I glanced over at Soyla. She sat on the camp stool like a princess holding court. Only Bama was paying me any attention. The rest of the guys? Hook, line, and sinker under Soyla's spell.

And why didn't someone give her something to cover that awful leather bra of hers. Couldn't they see the thing was close to failure from the load? And *what* had Soyla been *thinking* with that wardrobe selection? Has the word decency been banished from the English language?

"No," said Bama. "Nothing like that." He spit a dark stream of tobacco juice to one side and said, "We just know if folks is OK or not when they show up here."

"OK or not?"

"Yessir," he said. "The good ones we invite in for a spell."

"And the bad ones?"

"We make them git," Bama said. "Ain't no doing nothing for them sorts. They done made their choice and they got to stay with it."

"Just make them git," I said. "Because you know they're not OK."

"Not just know they're OK or not," Bama said, "But we know everything about what they done in life. Comes to us just like that," and he snapped his fingers.

Perfect. I was talking to a guy who could pull up mental YouTubes of every time I'd ever picked my nose in private...or in public, come to think of it. Despite the off-the-charts disgusting scene of Soyla running her sex machine at full speed and the obvious effects it had on her ten drooling admirers, something about what Bama said made one of the tumblers in my brain click into place.

"OK and not OK, you say," and this time I said it as a statement, not a question.

He nodded.

"How can you tell?"

"Well," said Bama, "some is easy just by looking. Take them monsters that never was real men."

He smiled and said, "We shoo them away quick-like."

Bama was talking about demons, and not in fearful terms at all. See a demon? The boys shoo it away.

Hee freakin' Haw.

"Just like that?" I said. "You can do that kind of thing?"

"Truth is," said Bama, "We can." He thought for a moment and added, "at least we can here."

At least he can here.

"And there are other places where it's more difficult to get rid of the monsters?"

"Oh hail yes," said Bama, and he still didn't look the least bit frightened. "This is our part of the woods. They got theirs out yonder where the train runs."

The shiver extended across my shoulders and down my back. Electricity pulse my spine as my brain fought to formulate my next question. A minute or two with Bama and I was beginning to connect the dots between what he said and the important pieces of the information that Balus passed to us.

I thought about how dearly Balus paid for his insubordination to the unseen entity watching at the portal, and it made me feel sick for whatever horror awaited Bama and the rest of the soldiers here for having the temerity to invite Soyla and me among them.

I said, "Are we going to get you into trouble?"

"Hail, no," said Bama. "Nothing's ever touched us here," he said. "And far as I know, nothing ever will."

"How can you be sure?"

Bama sent a stream of tobacco juice into the fire and when he spoke, he spoke with the unwavering certainty of a warrior.

"We made the right decisions when it counted."

No Alabama accent this time, but the calm, neutral sort of voice commonly used by educated people in our dimension on earth. If I were reading Bama correctly, then somehow Balus had made decisions in life that left him open to the whims of a malevolent entity. No Face's boss, perhaps? But for Bama and his buddies? No worries at all.

Opposite concepts existing, if I believed what Bama said about their being untouchable, in a cosmic and imperturbable balance. Concepts, heck. Understatement of the century. Not conflicting concepts, but rather two completely different worlds occupying the same territory, and apparently able to interact.

And everyone spoke the same language. That's what Balus had said. "Language of angels and everything else here." It's what got him into trouble. He'd already started the shrivel bit when he spit out his last piece of advice. "Don't take the train." Then the body-storm that revealed the unnatural horrors this place could gin up. Not promising real estate for a couples' resort.

"Y'all want to eat with us?" said Bama. "Getting dark, ya know."

Sure enough, the light was fading.

"Who are you?"

Sergeant New York broke into the conversation.

"Just some guys."

I looked around and saw he was right about that. A bunch of guys. Strange thing though, some were Yanks and some were Rebs. Except for Captain Frog, the German, and the Arab, all were Americans and all from the Civil War era. None of the boys seemed to care that they were enemies on my side of the portal. The jovial air of contentment in the place would be all but impossible to counterfeit. Comfortable and sweet. An iron stewpot hanging over the fire. How many times had I seen something similar during the Civil War?

Sergeant New York saw me looking at the pot and said, "Best we got here."

And the best they had smelled great to me. I'm like most guys when I say the best meal I've ever eaten is the one in front of me. Even so, the aroma wafting off the stewpot made my stomach gurgle.

I said, "Well the best you got looks great to me."

Bama smiled and said, "No meat though. Least not the way you're used to. We do have stuff what tastes jest like it. But we don't kill to get it."

"Hunting bad here?"

Bama and New York both chuckled.

"No hunting at all," they said. "No more need to shed blood."

It sounded like double-talk, and by the way they were looking at me, I got the feeling they knew about my vampire condition. No need to shed blood? If they waited a couple weeks they could get ringside seats to just how much blood *could* be shed here. If my bloodlust hit, they'd know it all right.

Bama said, "I know what you thinkin'."

"You do?"

"I do sho 'nuff," he said. "You thinkin' that it's the blood that keeps you going."

They did know.

"And it's not?"

Bama said, "Maybe."

"But not here," added Sergeant New York. "Never here."

Did such a place exist where I could spend my days sitting around the campground with fellow warriors at peace, and never again feel compelled to feed on another human? A place where you could throw guilt into the campfire like a knotted branch and watch it burn away to ashes? Could I live where everyone knew all there was to know about each other and nobody cared…where you could eat savory meals and cause no pain for another living creature?

If such a place did exist, then I could find only one word in my personal lexicon to describe it.

Heaven.

NINETEEN

HEAVEN?

Any possibility I'd stepped through a portal to hell and ended up in heaven?

Short answer: No.

I'd seen Balus shrivel, and if the weather in heaven included storms that rained tortured bodies instead of water, then the Travel Channel had it all wrong. I mean, what would be the point?

I repeated, "You said OK ones and not OK ones."

"That I did sho' 'nuff."

"Are you saying the good customers get treated one way here and the bad customers another?"

Soyla still held most of the other boys captive, though a few managed to wiggle out from under her spell to join us. Another couple of Bluecoats and Rebs along with the German and the Arab. It was the German who spoke.

"Good and bad are tags here," he said. "Not concepts as you're thinking of them."

I thought about what he said. The commonly held belief among those on earth who thought about heaven or hell was that good people go to heaven, bad people go to hell. I'd accepted that cliché at various points in my long life, though I'd not seriously considered either of the places since Nellie died.

I'm not proud of that admission, especially given the inconvenient truth that I'd met an authentic guardian angel. Hello. Would I be standing among these tents if I weren't on my way to rescue said gorgeous—and nicotine freak—angel from a demon prison in hell? As the television lawyers tend to say, the preponderance of the evidence indicated that I needed to pay more attention to the universe around me.

"And how am I thinking about them?" I said, referring to the concepts of good and bad.

The German returned a knowing smile, and I swore I saw a flash of good old Herr Doktor in the smugness.

"You labor to make the right decisions," he said. "Compare your actions to some moral code and then judge yourself as a good person or a bad one."

"And it doesn't work that way?"

I mean, everyone knows there are good people on earth and there are bad ones. If any sort of afterlife exists, then rewards go to the good people. It *has* to be that way.

"Not at'all," said the Maine Yankee. "Whose rulebook would we use?"

Good point, but I didn't see how the philosophical discussion would get me any closer to completing the mission.

I said, "Each of us has our own. What's good or bad depends on the point of view."

The boys had me out of my comfort zone, and I was flailing. Truth time: none of what I said was my original thought. Rather, I'd just quoted guests I'd seen on blabbing talk shows.

None of the campers responded...at least not at first. They did chuckle, but I have this thing about not counting ridicule as a proper response.

The German said, "You just keep thinking that, and see where it gets you."

He still wore his smile, but I saw no humor in it. And he dropped that minimalist happy mask when he said, "And you'll will not complain when we fail to extend hospitality should we meet again."

Fine. I didn't plan on an encore-tour to hell anyway. I promised myself I'd spend the first week when I made it back home to Bad Homburg one-starring this place on every travel site I could find. Not even Sarah Arias tried to get into my head this much. Good and bad? Get real.

Captain Frog managed to edge out the rest of the boys, and he halfway crouched in the air next to Soyla. Why did I care that he was obviously leaning in to get a good look inside that leather bra? I didn't…other than I didn't want him to take advantage of her. You know, pretend to show interest in whatever drivel she spouted while really burning up his brain cells with thoughts of how she'd look in her birthday suit.

I made sure to speak at sufficient volume for both Soyla and Captain Frog to hear when I said, "We've got to get moving."

They pretended not to though, and the ever-present green-eyed monster crawled up my spine. Not fair I know, especially when I'd risk everything to go after a woman—one *other* than Soyla. And when I thought about it, I'd made Soyla risk everything too. I could say she made her own decision to follow me…that for whatever twisted reason she thought following me benefited her most. That didn't change the bottom line. If I hadn't seen the need to find the gates to hell she wouldn't be here.

With Captain Frog.

I didn't know whether she was playing it up with the Frog as revenge for me hurting her feelings, but what I did know is that it wouldn't work…even if she casually laid her hand on his arm to make a point and insisted on staring unblinkingly into his beady French eyes. Those common irises couldn't make it through the first round with my baby blues. Soyla would know that for herself if she'd just break contact with the twit and have a glance over at me.

But she wouldn't.

Once more I thought, "We need to leave."

"Nah," said Bama.

Guess maybe I thought out loud.

"Y'all need to wait a spell and have some stew."

And Captain Frog needed a few more minutes to slither himself into the tiny chair so he could meld his body into Soyla's. She might as well take that skimpy bra of hers off and hand it to the guy. Maybe that would stop his leering at it like it was the Hope Diamond. I mean, how could Soyla strip herself any barer than had the Frenchman's horny mind?

"Soyla," I said, and this time I spoke loud enough that she couldn't ignore me.

If that didn't work, I'd need a crowbar to force them to break lock.

"Yes, my love."

Her response came with the impatient sound of an indulgent mother putting aside adult conversation to respond to an insistent and unruly child. Embarrassing, but at least she'd used the "my love" in front of Captain Frog. I decided to ignore the way they looked at each other and rolled their eyes in unison. We'd see how long she kept up the farce when I revealed the guy's secret about being a virgin.

On the other hand, I'd keep that nugget to myself. Soyla might see it as a challenge.

"We need to get going."

I was going to puke from seasickness if they rolled their eyes just one more time.

"Why, my love?"

Why indeed?

Because maybe I wanted to get her out from under the spell of Captain Frog before she lost what little clothes she had on. Where would that leave us for the rest of this mission? Once we left the warm light of the campfire, we'd be stumbling through an alien landscape in complete darkness.

Captain Frog said, "The stew is ready."

So what?

And did he really need to lay on that French accent as if he couldn't clearly speak the language every creature in this place seemed to know by heart? Soyla was smarter than that.

"And if y'all gonna take that train," said Bama, "you'll be 'preciative for the fortification."

Now there was a man's accent. I smiled and nodded.

No virgin there.

He spit another mouthful of tobacco.

Nope, no virgin.

The Arab retrieved tin plates from one of tents, and he passed them out. Captain Frog and Soyla finally pulled themselves away from each other and sat on one of the logs arranged around the campfire. The rest of us selected our own log, and the Arab remained standing.

Being completely sick of Soyla's act with Frenchy, I put the fire between them and me, hoping it would hide whatever moves Soyla allowed Captain Frog to make on her during the meal. I mean, how long would she allow the charade to continue?

Everyone waited to eat until all had been served. The Arab filled his plate last and sat down beside me. Bama stood and offered a prayer, and I made sure to wait until I heard spoons scraping. Once again, my mother would have been proud.

I'd never smelled such a divine aroma coming off a simple plate, and my stomach insisted I not wait. My brain said other things. I'd already committed myself to the notion of not feeding while in hell. At the time I meant blood. Doing the vampire thing on one of hell's creatures seemed utterly moronic and at least as suicidal as putting the barrel of a loaded shotgun into my mouth. Not in the deepest wisps of my cramped brain had I expected stew…or any other variety of edible food.

Sure, I wanted to dig in all right. The Arab ate with prim precision and I heard Bama snorting his meal down like he was eating out of a trough. Everywhere around the campfire I saw men concentrating on one of the two things men like best. Through the fire, I saw Captain Frog spending his concentration on that other thing.

Did the Arab fellow forget to give Soyla her own spoon? He must have, because Captain Frog was alternating between feeding himself with feeding Soyla. How disgusting was that? And what effect would the alien food have on her? I didn't want to scrap the mission because of food poisoning, and I wouldn't leave her behind.

Had nothing to do with Captain Frog. The game Soyla was playing with him would end the moment we put this campsite behind us. No matter what her reasons for tagging along, I felt responsible. And as I sat there with the spoon nearly to my lips a thought fell on me like a boulder hitting an ant. My mission wasn't to rescue one person in distress. Not at all. It morphed the moment Soyla followed me through the portal.

Not one. Two.

I put aside my worries over an angry stomach and took a bite. Sublime. I'd never put such flavor in my mouth in two thousand years of gobbling grub. No describing how good it tasted other than to say it put me into a restful equilibrium.

Strange, I know, and I'm the kind of guy who considers the Swedish Meatballs from Ikea as gourmet. This stew? Whole new level. If a restaurant served this, I'd buy a meal card.

Bama said, "Good, ain't it."

He'd been waiting for my reaction and I could see my look of rapture pleased him.

"What's in it?"

I moved my spoon through the thick both. What *was* in it? I thought they called it vegetable stew. So why couldn't I find a single identifiable vegetable?

"Nobody knows," said the German. "And with a taste like this," he added, "why would anyone care?"

Good point.

"Tastes different to each of us," said Bama. "We figured as much a while ago."

I gazed across the fire and saw Soyla hold out a plate for more. If she'd gotten her own plate in the first place instead of sharing with Frog, then perhaps she wouldn't need to look like such a chowhound and ask for more…long before anyone else completed a first serving.

We didn't sit like silent monks—the guys *did* speak to each other… every now and then. But the conversation ebbed and flowed in proportion to the amount of stew consumed. Why shouldn't it? Me? Once I had my fill, I sat brooding about what the German had said about decisions in one hand, good and bad in the other. Try though I might, I couldn't make decode what he meant.

Enough with the philosophy.

I bent over the fire to refill my plate. Perhaps I'd not had my fill, after all. The Arab had hung the ladle on a leather strap beside the fire. I almost dropped it as I reached to dip it into the pot. Not out of clumsiness but because of what I saw. I turned to Bama.

The old Reb held up his hand. And when I say old Reb or old German soldier or old Arab defender of Jerusalem, I don't mean old literally. The camper boys were all young, though combat tends to consume a person's youth. So, when I refer to Bama as the old Reb, I mean old in the sense of out of time. The Confederacy is a cause no more.

Now when I say the old Frenchman when referring to Captain Frog, I mean the guy looked out-of-place old and physically spent.

I mean, was Napoleon so desperate at the end that he hung recruiting posters in nursing homes? Enough about Captain Frog—who really *might* not look as old as I make him sound.

Back to me over the stewpot, Bama holding up a hand to stop my question.

"Never empties," he said. "Not once it's full."

He'd nailed my question. The reason I almost dropped the ladle was that when I looked down into the stewpot, I saw that, despite all the eating, the level of stew hadn't fallen.

"What do you mean by not once it's full."

The German provided the answer.

"We eat when we need to eat."

So?

Sergeant New York said, "The food shows up at breakfast, lunch, and supper."

I thought about that.

"Just shows up?"

Bama nodded and said, "Like manna from heaven."

That sent another of those electric shocks buzzing through my spine. Manna from heaven. I'd heard that one somewhere, and it didn't take long to remember. The Israelites. After they left slavery in Egypt. Forty years in the desert, and led by a white-bearded, crazy-haired dude who looked a lot like Charlton Heston.

That crowd ate something called manna. They gathered enough for a day and left the rest where it lay. Rinse and repeat. Day after day, month after month, year after year. For forty years. Not only perfect nourishment, but also reputed to taste better than anything before or since.

Manna from heaven.

Was that what Bama was calling the stew? Not specifically, because he'd used the word like. "Like manna from heaven," he'd said. And if I believed what the guys claimed, then the stew showed up the same way. Day after day, month after month, year after year.

Like manna from heaven.

I filled my plate, sat back down on the log beside the Arab, and I took a furtive glance across the fire. Soyla had found her own spoon and her own plate.

She and Captain Frog spoke quietly to each other. I hoped she was gathering intelligence rather than making small talk. My own time? It hadn't been wasted. Seems these guys knew that we intended to take the train. Hadn't Bama said that we'd be "' 'preciative for the fortification" once we got on the train?

Yes, I'd accumulated a lot of data.

My problem? All that data equaled no information, so I stuffed it all in my red mental clueless bag…the one with the question mark embroidered on the outside. It could sit in the dark place jammed beside the notion of Hebrew as "the language of angels and everything else here." Yeah, much data but no distillation into something that might help the rescue mission.

But that wasn't necessarily true. Not completely. I had the train. Helmet and Balus voted no, Bama said to eat first. One thing I'd figured out for sure? If you wanted to get to the demon prison, you needed to take the train.

To nobody in particular, I said, "Where do we catch the train?"

Bama, the Arab, and the German all exchanged looks. Sergeant New York let out a loud exhale and even Captain Frog levered his eyes off Soyla long enough to see who might answer my question. Silence. Until the Arab broke it.

"Walk until you find it."

Which way?

I almost asked the question, but I thought I already knew the answer. It didn't matter. We could walk north or south, find a fork in the road and go in either direction. Didn't matter because we'd end up at the tracks. The train wasn't the reason I'd stepped through the portal. Well, got launched through the portal by my balls, but that's not important to anyone except those two little fellows. I'd come for one reason only. To free Sarah Arias.

The locals already seemed to know that. I could assume every other person—or thing—we'd run into here would also be in on my secret. And the whole place was set up to help me. Right? Need a train? Walk in any direction and you'll find it waiting.

And it *would* be waiting. I knew that too. Normal considerations, like a train schedule, didn't matter. Not here, and not with Soyla and me needing a ride. Just walk until I found it.

"Thanks," I said. "We will."

"Fair 'nuff," said Bama. "I s'pose y'all will get going at first light?"

"No," I said, and I mimicked his southern drawl when I added, "I s'pose we'll get going now."

Instead of taking offense, Bama laughed, and it made me like the guy even more than I'd already grown to in the brief time since I'd run into him. Everyone else laughed too. Everyone except Soyla. Perhaps she didn't pick up the nuance of the Alabama accent. Her loss.

The Arab said, "But you cannot."

"Can't what?"

"Catch the train now," he said. "It will not be ready for you until the morning."

The others nodded. I looked as close as the fire allowed into each of the faces sitting near me because I wanted to see their reactions to talk of the train. I'd seen a glimpse of terror under Helmet's controlled, Prussian façade. Balus? Couldn't tell for sure because he was in the process of drying up after he'd given me a quick, "Don't take the train."

These guys, though. I couldn't detect a trace of anxiety regarding the train.

I said, "Really?"

The German nodded once and said, "Safest for you if you spend the night here. More comfortable, too."

"And we won't miss the train?"

Everyone shook their head. Interesting. I'd hoped our *need* would drive the train schedule, but evidently not. Soyla and I must wait until the morning. These guys didn't seem afraid to openly discuss the train nor did they try to discourage us as Helmet and Balus had done. Their simple advice: "Don't go tonight."

They seemed concerned about what could happen to us in the woods…in the darkness. Well, they could save it for the next cookout. As the cliché goes, Soyla and I had more than one trick up our sleeves. For example, our superhuman speed and strength. I'd gone toe-to-toe with some powerful entities and I'm still around to update my autobiography. We could also see in the dark better than most people can at high noon. And both of us knew how to fight.

I could spend two weeks doing nothing but listing the battles I'd fought in, and I'd still leave out many. Soyla? She'd started as a member of a sort of Magyar Praetorian Guard for Hungarian nobility. And it was just her first job. She'd had many since, and I've heard most of them involved assassination for pay. Only in the last thirty years or so—the internet age—had she shut down that operation and moved onto con-game shenanigans. Bottom line, we didn't worry about any big bad wolves lurking in the forest...we fed on those sorts. But then, neither of us ever hunted in a forest located in hell.

"OK," I said. "If you're saying you have room, we'll spend the night."

Captain Frog jumped up. I could see it coming. Not in his wildest dreams would I allow Soyla to set foot in his tent.

"Bama," I said, and I'd called him that so much in my brain that I'd forgotten it wasn't really his name.

Bama smiled. He didn't seem to mind.

"Any way Soyla and I can share one of the tents?"

"Sho 'nuff," said Bama. And then, "Reynard, I'll bunk with you."

Captain Frog appeared to dislike the idea. I think Captain Frog preferred sharing a tent with a scantily clad Hungarian warrior-woman. Who wouldn't? Glad you asked, because I'll tell you who wouldn't be sharing a tent with a scantily clad Hungarian warrior-woman. Captain Frog. Not Soyla, anyway. If a *different* scantily clad Hungarian warrior-woman happened his way? All his.

Soyla didn't protest when she left Captain Frog behind and followed me to Bama's tent.

C'est la Guerre, Froggy.

We said our goodnights to the boys, stepped into Bama's tent, and closed the flap.

It was similar to every other army tent I'd ever seen, except for the canvas flooring. That was a new one. His small number of possessions either hung on a leather strap stretched between two of the poles or sat inside a primitive-looking footlocker that Bama must have made himself.

There were two bedrolls neatly folded atop two cots. *That's right*, I thought. *Six tents, nearly a dozen guys.* Of course they shared. Soyla and I'd not just put Bama out for the night but also one of the other guys. Whichever of them made that sacrifice didn't seem to mind because nobody said anything. My money was on Sergeant New York. That would represent a perfect kind of symmetry. A Reb and a Yank.

Soyla didn't need to undress. Why would she when her outfit already put her a few square inches of thin material above the naked category.

I pointed to the cots and said, "Your choice."

Soyla pushed one of them until it touched the other. I was pretty sure she didn't have hanky-panky on her mind, but probably just wanted the comfort of another living human nearby. Nice as the boys, their stew, and this campground were, we'd seen some strange sights since stepping through the portal.

I didn't have hanky-panky at the forefront of my mind either. It sat back there on my mental bench ready to spring into the game should Soyla give it the slightest glimmer of a green light.

"Have a good time with the Frog?"

"Jealous, my love?" said Soyla, and when I shook my head she smiled.

Yeah, she knew better.

"Let's just say," I replied, "that we don't need that sort of thing to complicate our mission."

Sounded good, but even I didn't know what the heck I meant with that utterly meaningless drivel. Given the slightest sniff of willingness out of Soyla? *I* wouldn't care about complications.

I think Soyla had that all figured out because she said, "No complications," as she laid down on her cot and patted the one next to her.

I pulled off my jeans, kind-of folded them, and put them down beside the cot. Luckily for me, I hadn't gone commando and was wearing a clean set of Valentine-motif boxer shorts. Soyla giggled at the repeating pattern of naked cupids with little yellow wings and drawn bows. At least I hoped that's what made her laugh.

But, enough about that.

I took my place on the cot beside Soyla's and said, "Did you find out anything from your boyfriend?"

After I got comfortable, and gosh how that cot and bedroll felt as good to my body as the stew had been to my taste buds, I did something so subconsciously that I wondered which of my two potential command posts housed my brain. I reached over to Soyla's cot with my left hand and she interlaced her fingers into mine.

"He said everyone thinks he's a virgin."

"Correction," I said, "Everyone *knows* he's a virgin."

She obviously needed further clarification that I wasn't asking about Captain Frog's sex life when I asked if she'd gotten anything useful from him.

"And I meant, did you learn anything useful to our mission."

"Yes."

You know something? If Soyla put that Hungarian accent of hers into a pill, Viagra would have some *stiff* competition.

I said, "And?"

"They do not fear the train."

My impulse answer would have been something like congratulations on nothing or big whoopee. Probably something a bit subtler and a heck of a lot cuter. But, maybe she got more out of the train thing than I did.

"Why do you think that's important?"

Soyla thought for a moment. She brought my hand to her lips and kissed it. For the third time in a few hours, buzzing pulsed down my spine.

She said, "Because the train cannot harm them."

It matched my thinking. Perhaps these guys were management, on the kicking team and not the receiving team. Could be, but I didn't think so. It wasn't their collaboration with the powers here that put them beyond caring about the train, and Soyla had also picked up on it.

I said, "Any guesses as to why they aren't afraid of the train?"

Soyla didn't take long to respond.

"Two places in one."

"What do you mean?"

I thought it would be polite to bring her hand to my own lips and kiss it. I also made sure to speak so my breath didn't blow in her direction. The stew tasted great and all, but I wasn't sure about what it did for my breath. I hadn't brought a toothbrush—who thinks they'll need one of those in hell—and I hadn't expected to have Soyla tagging along.

Even if I'd known she'd come with me, I never expected to experience the sort of confused feelings regarding her. My hand in hers. Trading little hand kisses.

Time to slit my wrists.

Soyla answered my question with one of her own.

"What do you call this place, my love?"

Easy answer.

"Hell."

Silence for a second, and then she said, "And what about Mestephos, what did he call it?"

I knew she was talking about No Face because it was the same name Sarah Arias had used for him. And No Face didn't like people bandying it about because something about knowing a demon's name puts him at the disadvantage. Soyla wouldn't know I'd called him No Face.

Come to think of it, I couldn't remember ever using the name

Mestephos in front of Soyla. I scrubbed my memory all the way back past the spiders and to abandoned cobwebs. I couldn't put a finger on any opportunity for Soyla to glean the name Mestephos from me…or from Sarah Arias. And yes, that kicked off some warning bells. The casual way she brought my hand to her lips again indicated Soyla didn't think she'd made a mistake. I decided to let it ride.

"Sheol," I said. "He called it Sheol."

I was careful not to use Mestephos, No Face, or any other name for the demon…especially not Donna.

"Yes," said Soyla. "I heard Sheol plenty of times when I was a Jew."

Right.

I didn't remind Soyla that she never *was* a Jew. Yes, she played one for a few years, but I've heard that being Jewish isn't like joining a club you can resign from later. The non-Jewish world wouldn't allow it.

I said, "And what would you call this place?"

A pause, and then she said, "Right here in this camp?"

"Why not," I said. "Let's start small and work our way out."

"This camp, my love…the happy men, the food, the comfortable tents and beds."

"Yes. All that."

"My love, I would call this place heaven."

TWENTY

HEAVEN.

Soyla thought the place seemed like heaven. At least the campground. The word didn't hit me like a tidal wave, but rather, it engulfed me as I lay there on Bama's cot holding Soyla's hand. No, not all at once, but like the slow sinking of a canoe in the middle of the Pacific Ocean.

Heaven.

It made as much sense as it didn't. I know that sounds convoluted, but that was exactly how I felt.

Balus rotting followed by the immense storm raining bruised bodies. Screaming bodies, let's not forget. Definitely not heaven. The campground and the happy gathering of ex-soldiers? Opposite of opposites. Heaven. Doubly so, when I considered an endless supply of the most nourishing and pleasing food ever.

I'd recognized the tone and tempo of the language we spoke. The tongue everyone seemed able to use with no effort—or even training, in my case. Soyla had identified it as Hebrew and I had agreed. Balus called it the language of angels and everything else.

"Soyla?"

She took a while to respond and I thought she'd fallen asleep. But then she kissed my hand and said, "Yes my love."

"Do you believe in heaven?"

A longer pause, and then, "Why does it matter, my love?"

Good question.

Believing wouldn't make Heaven real if it didn't exist any more than not believing would make it disappear if it did. And what if heaven *did* exist? What then? Was I prepared to work my way through the labyrinth of potential ramifications? Nope. But then, two thousand years can close a person's mind.

One thing at a time though, and Sarah Arias waited somewhere down the train tracks for her knight in shining armor...who was holding hands with Soyla. If this really was Heaven, then things were as messed up here as they were on the other side of the veil.

Heaven.

If so, then someone on Sarah Arias's team would need to explain the tortured bodies raining from the sky.

No, I thought, *the place couldn't be heaven.*

Not with *that* happening. And back to Soyla's question. Why did it matter? It didn't. Not as long as a prison for demons existed and not as long as it held someone I cared about.

Vampires don't need much sleep, almost none. When I've needed to, I've gone weeks without closing my eyes. Yes, I do miss that exhausted feeling I used to get after a long day of loafing with my friends in the forest. The hot fire. The soft straw. A bear skin or two piled over me in the winter.

But when your body doesn't need sleep, it's impossible to fake the experience. Let me draw a picture. Since Balus infected me, I've spent more time studying the theory of relativity than I've spent asleep. And I'm no rocket scientist.

Even when we vampires do sleep, it's more a state of lessened alert.

Me? A cockroach running through the room next door sounds like Napoleon's Army on the march. That's the sensitivity of my hearing. You might also glean what I thought about Napoleon's army from my careful wording of the simile. That went double for Captain Frog.

Why the soliloquy? To put my shock at sunrise into context. I opened my eyes. Why is opening my eyes shocking? Because I didn't remember closing them. I also didn't remember Soyla rolling out of her cot and onto mine. On top of me. Made it a little hard to breathe, but it also felt good. Sometime during the night I'd thrown the bearskins on the floor. Soyla had replaced them with…Soyla.

A definite trade up.

Like I said, I hadn't remembered closing my eyes or nodding off to sleep. I thought back to the previous night. Soyla and I discussed Heaven, hell, and Sheol. Next thing I knew? Morning. Try as I might, I couldn't remember the point where I stopped listening to Soyla and began sawing logs.

Married dudes know what I mean. One moment you're logging points by pretending to pay close attention to every word your darling speaks, the next, you vaguely discern the deadly statement that you know will mire you in a trap. One woven with your own words.

"You aren't listening."

"Yes I am."

"OK then, what did I just say?"

Uh-oh.

"And does snoring help your concentration?"

"I wasn't snoring, just breathing heavy from excitement. I mean, that's an interesting story."

"What's so exciting about my sister's yeast infection?"

Another uh-oh, and the facade crumbles. Even if you've bought her that diamond bracelet and planted flowers in the yard all day, you've pissed away all that credit by doing what's natural for a guy to do: flee brutal boredom by falling asleep. If you're lucky, she's only angry at you. Even luckier would be her refusing to speak.

In my experience, that's too much to hope for.

Back to morning in the camp, I didn't even *need* to sleep. Yet, I'd committed that fatal sin with Soyla. I scrubbed my brain for any details it might still hold regarding the last thing I'd heard her say. Complete blank. Soyla's eyes fluttered open and she stared at me with open confusion on her face. I knew I needed to act and to do it quickly.

I said, "Too bad about your sister."

That only seemed to addle her more.

"My sister?"

"Yeah," I said. "That awful yeast infection."

Soyla laid there on top of me for a few moments more before rolling onto her own couch.

"Gaius, my love."

"Yeah?"

She'd added my love without using that fake happy voice women use right before they spring the trap.

"I do have a sister."

Going good so far.

"And I buried her a thousand years ago."

Busted, but I'd still use that sister with a yeast infection next time. It would hit for me eventually.

"I see," I said. "Well then..."

"Gaius," she said, and I was happy she interrupted me as I had no clue what I'd say next, "Did we sleep?"

"Well," I said, "You did." And then to pile it on a little higher, "I did guard duty."

"You did?"

"One of us had to."

She rolled out one of those fake smiles.

"Tell me something," she said. "Do you always snore on guard duty?"

"You slept too?" I said in a masterful attempt to change the subject.

"I did," she said. "Slept. Really slept."

Exactly what I'd been thinking before Soyla opened her eyes. Obviously, she felt it too. Rest. I've heard that if sharks stop swimming they suffocate. If that's true, then vampires and sharks have more in common than grumpy personalities.

"Felt great," I said. "It's been centuries."

A clear understatement, but Soyla got the point. Not centuries. Millennia. Rest. Calm, deep, uninterrupted sleep. I'd forgotten how precious sleep could be. And I halfway thought I'd be willing to spend eternity in this little camp of ex-soldiers just to experience that infinite blessing just one more time.

Soyla stood and stretched. You'll never know what can get a guy's engine running, and the cute way she yawned while she held her arms extended high over her head? I surprised her by putting my arms around her and planting a quick kiss on her lips.

At first, she just stood there like a mannequin posed in the morning-stretch position, though my lips were ready to go as long as it took to assist her in waking up. Soyla dropped her arms around me. She didn't use that sex-on-steroids overdone kiss like the previous day when I'd come home to find her standing half-naked in my apartment.

This kiss was gentle, and if I were any measure a poet, I'd find a way to weave in words such as fragile, exposed, and vulnerable. Truth might also make an appearance. I got a glimpse of little girl Soyla, before the martial training and her service to the Hungarian nobility. Before she became a vampire.

The kiss ended as abruptly as it began. Soyla pulled away. Truth? She shoved herself free and looked at me in terrified accusation…as if I'd been trying to suck out her soul or something.

I smiled and said, "Can't be Soyla all the time."

Her look morphed from fear to anger in a heartbeat and she moved with lightning speed. I easily blocked the punch she threw with her right fist. So easily, that it made me suspicious of what the pretty little left hand had in mind.

I barely dodged the knife. She'd aimed for my eyes and I felt the bow wave of air the tip sent past. Close call. Close enough that I felt the blood begin out of the bridge of my nose. *Really* close call.

I grabbed her left hand as her momentum carried the knife past my face. I stood there with both her hands trapped by both of mine. I expected the knee she aimed at my nuts, so it missed too. Was I crazy, or had we been sharing an honest kiss less than a minute prior?

I lowered her onto her cot and kept her still. That's a nicer way of saying I kept the dangerous parts of her immobilized. We remained that way until I saw the flash blink out of her eyes. I didn't know what had just happened and even less what to say. I only knew enough to keep my mouth shut. If I'd said anything at all while Soyla regained control of herself I ran the risk of her turning my balls into earrings.

"Let me go," she said, and in it I heard both resignation and warning.

"I think we're fine like we are."

"Let me go," she repeated, and this time she sounded truculent.

"I will," I said, "If you promise not to hurt me."

Soyla smiled and said, "I promise."

Not so easy.

"You promise what?"

She rolled her eyes and said, "I promise not to hurt you."

"Good."

When I released her, I did that jump-back thing you see on TV when a naturalist releases a healed rattlesnake into the wild. Soyla laid there and looked at me like I'd lost my mind. Better safe than sorry though.

I said, "What was that about?"

The flash of anger returned for a split second, and then she smiled.

She said, "You know."

Like heck I knew. But I saw all the warning signs of another seismic event, so I decided to play along.

I said, "I'm sorry."

For what, I didn't have an inkling of a clue. But that seemed to do the trick.

"Just don't ever do that again."

Right. Don't genuinely kiss her because she's a human being who might occasionally deserve tenderness?

"From now on," I said, "I promise to treat you like a warm hide to use for my perverted, sexual gratification...and nothing more than that."

Soyla said, "Thank you, my love," and crazy of crazies, I swear I saw a tear of gratitude in her eye.

It all proved to me that wherever you go—even hell or heaven—there you'll find yourself. Along with your baggage. Anyway, our touching love scene lasted no more than a minute. Once I determined it safe to concentrate on anything beyond keeping my genitals attached, I realized I heard talking outside the tent.

We didn't find a mirror in the tent and judging by the rustic hairstyles, I didn't think there'd be one in the camp. I ran my fingers through my hair and threw back the flap to walk into the morning light outside. When I closed it, I saw Soyla hadn't moved from the cot. Probably a good place for her to chill for a while.

I suppose mornings come in shades of gray wherever you are,

because what I saw outside the tent was no different from what I would have expected on my side. It's dark when I leave for work... and I like it that way.

It's a quiet time when what few people I run into display a common reverence for the hour by keeping their voices low. Bama and Captain Frog were adding kindling to the fire and the Arab stood stirring the stewpot. I grabbed a couple of dry branches for my contribution to the fire—it's a guy thing—and walked over to stand beside the other two.

Bama said, "Latrine's over there," and he pointed towards the trees off to my left.

"A building?"

Bama smiled and said, "Nah. We're talking nature's latrine."

Latrine. An army word if there ever was one. Not toilet, crapper, or one-eyed porcelain god. Latrine. Glad to know the word existed in Hebrew.

"I don't need to go just yet."

The Arab hung the ladle on the leather strap, turned to me and said, "Did you sleep well?"

"Like a baby," and I wondered if any of them understood how long it had been since I'd experienced that sort of rest.

Frog said, "Is Soyla awake?"

Yeah, that would be the first thing out of Captain Frog's mouth, but I found it hard to get annoyed on such a clear, cool morning. And the stew. It smelled as good as it did the night before.

"Yes," I said. "I think she might be a while."

Thing is, I knew nothing at all about Soyla's morning routine, but Captain Frog didn't need to know that. The amorous Frenchman needed to think that Soyla and I shared a tent *all* the time...no matter what she might have told him the previous evening.

"Should I see if she needs help?" Captain Frog said, and I actually felt sorry for the boy when I heard the hopefulness in his question.

"I think she's old enough to know what to do," I said. And then, "Did you serve with Napoleon?"

Captain Frog stood straighter and said, "But of course. The Emperor's personal guard."

I knew the question would make him happy. It would also serve to deflect his mind off Soyla.

"Killed at Waterloo?"

Captain Frog blinked at me as if he didn't understand the question. And maybe he didn't, because he didn't respond.

Sergeant New York said, "Died of old age in 1877."

I hadn't heard him join us at the fire. He laughed when he saw the shock on my face.

"I just thought…"

"You just thought," interrupted Bama, "that we's all ghosts killed in battle."

Everyone chuckled. Have I ever said how much I like being the butt of another guy's humor? And a whole crowd of dudes laughing at me adds to the enjoyment.

"Well," I said as I cracked my branches and threw them into the fire, "I guess I did."

"Natural 'nuff," said Bama. "In your shoes I'da probably thought the same."

"Me too," said the Arab.

"And me," said Captain Frog.

"Most of us boys," said Bama, "lived to be ripe. Though a few," he pointed at a tent with an open flap with the German and another Confederate soldier inside, "got their discharge papers while the bullets was a flyin'."

Interesting.

"Each of you woke up here?"

Bama handed me a plate. Looked like stew for breakfast. I didn't mind. I could eat it every day for all eternity.

"Nah," Bama said. "We all got together a few years back and commenced to coming out here for a spell every now and then."

"Ghosts can do that?"

Captain Frog stiffened again.

A deaf guy could have detected Captain Frog's outrage when he said, "We are not ghosts."

Right. And I'm not the idiot who decided to leave a perfectly good earth to go chasing guardian angels in hell.

My expression must have been doubtful, because Sergeant New York said, "No, really, we aren't ghosts."

The Yankee held his hand out to the Arab, who pulled that curvy-shaped dagger they all wear in the movies out of the scabbard. Sergeant New York took the dagger and opened a small cut on the top of his own hand.

I saw blood for a second before the wound healed itself. Faster than I could have done it.

"See?" said Bama. "Bleed same as you."

Right. And Karl can lay a load on the floor. Doesn't prove he's not a ghost. I thought about those little piles of disgusting incontinent dog droppings. Steaming yes, but also transparent in shades of white. And thankfully temporary. Sergeant New York's blood was red.

Big difference, and Bama could read it on my face.

"It's all us," he said. "Bodies, that is. We the same now as we was back then."

"Not quite," said Captain Frog. "We're alive all right, but not the same."

The Arab took my plate and filled it with stew. He picked up another and handed to someone behind me. I turned to see Soyla. She smiled and took the plate. The guys stood quietly for a second. I don't think anyone could have broken the spell Soyla cast over our little gathering.

She'd found a gray tunic to drape over her leather bra, though she hadn't bothered with the buttons. She still wore the tight leather pants that would have been enough for ten million views on YouTube. But it wasn't just her body that flummoxed us into silent reverence. She'd also fixed her hair and somehow adjusted her makeup. And all that without a mirror...and without makeup. Where do chicks learn the alchemy?

She said to Captain Frog, "You were saying?"

I have to give it to Frenchy. I saw him battle to regain his senses. He went from knocked to the canvas to back up and fighting well inside the mandatory ten-count.

"That we," he said, and he waved his hand in the air to indicate he meant the entire camp, "are humans."

Soyla smiled, and this time I saw calculating and cunning in the look. Great to see things getting back to normal.

"Of course you are."

Soyla left it at that. A few more questions for the guys came to my mind but I followed Soyla's lead and shut my trap. Except to insert stew. Once the food started flowing everyone else showed up. We pretty much ate in silence just as we had the night before. I noticed Captain Frog let Soyla sit by one of the other guys. I guess he made his best play the night before only to see Soyla end up walking into the tent with me. Rejection can be a nasty thing.

Uh, not that I would know.

Much.

Meal completed, I offered to help with the dishes. Bama said we didn't need to worry about it. "They'd be takin' care of." So Soyla and I stacked our plates in the place the Arab indicated, and everyone gathered to see us off.

Neither of us packed clothes so we left the group as empty-handed as we'd arrived. Except one of the soldiers said Soyla could keep the tunic.

Soyla demurred, but he said, "Another'll be waitin' in the tent."

I shook everyone's hand and Soyla gave each of the guys a hug. Captain Frog was smart enough to keep his hands away from Soyla's curvaceous, tight, warrior-woman caboose. Good for him. They could heal cuts? If he'd let that right hand wander south a few more inches, I'd have seen whether they could also regrow body parts.

Bama walked with Soyla and me for our first five minutes in the woods.

"Keep headin' any direction," he said, "Just be sure to pick one and stick with it."

I got it. Walk in straight lines and not in circles.

Easy enough.

"Bama," I said. "Anything in the woods I need to worry about?"

"Nah," said Bama. "Woods just gitcha from one spot to the next." A pause to consider, and he added, "And ain't nothin' there you can't handle."

Bama's made the woods sound like a kind of demilitarized zone where entities transitioned from one place to the next. And as far as Soyla and I had seen thus far, it meant one clearing after another. First, we stepped into the large meadow. Then the woods. After that, the campsite. We were in the woods again, so I thought it a safe assumption we'd find the tracks in a clearing.

"What about after we're out of the woods," I said, "Anything I should watch out for?"

Bama put out his arms to signal we should stop walking. He stood there for a second looking between Soyla and me.

"Gonna give it to ya straight," he said. "There is something that should scare you into turnin' round."

Perfect. I suspected we'd eventually get around to this, and there it was. "Giant demon in sector four" or something like that. Your life choices have landed you at rock bottom when you hope there's only *one* demon waiting for you up ahead.

"What's that?" I said. "Lay it on me."

Another stream of tobacco juice off the path and into the trees. Bama wiped his mouth with the side of his sleeve. I expected to see a brown splotch when he pulled his arm away, but the tunic remained as crisply gray as if it were laundered five minutes ago.

"Bama?"

"Y'all already know," Bama said.

"What do I already know?"

I said that...but I knew.

What did I already know? A word made up of five letters.

Train.

When I didn't say anything, Bama spit again and nodded.

He said, "Told ya so."

I said, "How far?" and I saw that Bama knew I meant how far to those unspoken five letters.

Bama pointed straight ahead.

"Less than five minutes," he said. "In the valley just ahead."

I looked in the direction of his finger and could see a gentle downward slope.

"Anything we need to worry about between here and there?"

"Nah," said Bama. "Like I said, woods just gitcha here to there."

Good. I held out a hand to do the goodbye ritual with Bama, and he surprised me with a hug.

He said, "You watch yourself, brother."

I'm not a guy prone to emotional goodbyes...you know, the touchy-feely sort who seem comfortable enough with their masculinity to put their arms around another man. Bama didn't suffer from the same sort of guy-reticence because that hug he gave me was a lung-crusher.

Bama seemed like a man's man to me, so I didn't worry about a reach-around squeeze. He repeated the goodbye ritual with Soyla, and she allowed it to happen. Watching him take Soyla in his arms made me wonder if he'd handled rattlesnakes back in his days on my side of the veil. Back in his living days.

That got me thinking more. Not the usual stream-of-consciousness I'm prone to, or about those two female adornments everything tends to remind me of.

Back in his living days.

As far as I could see, and if I believed what he said back in the camp, there was no back-in-his-living-days for Bama or any of the rest of the eternal campers. Not at all. No back in his—or their—living days because they were all alive when we found them in their camp. Same when we left.

I don't know why I expected to find hideous, brainless creatures—ghosts, demons, the undead tortured souls of mass-murderers, Notre Dame football fans—once I made it through the portal at the Aachen Cathedral. Maybe because I thought I was entering hell?

But the short time on this side of the mountain changed my mind. Not so much about hell, I'm still certain that place is nearly as bad as East St. Louis. What modified my thinking about where Soyla and I ended up? Everyone speaking the same language, and despite what a few of the good folks in Alabama think, that language ain't English. Not with a Southern drawl and not of the Seventeenth Century variety either.

Speaketh not thy language of dead Puritans but rather thou shalt speak the tongue of Miami. Hebrew. The language of angels and everything else here. One moment Soyla and I saw the battered bodies of screaming people falling like hailstones out of immense, beaten clouds, the next we come upon happy men camping in a forest so pastel that Monet could have planted the easel in one place for his entire career.

Soyla and I left Bama standing where he'd hugged us, and we began the slow descent to the valley. I'm not sure what passed for five minutes in Bama's camp, but I'd say we picked our way around the trees for half an hour. I guess time didn't matter when you sat around a campfire for all eternity to exchange war stories with your buddies.

The trees thinned in proportion with the drop of elevation, and we picked up visuals on the little station ten minutes before we reached it. I used my normal vision because my vampire condition didn't help. And no, I'm not going to claim our superior strength and powers didn't work this side of the veil. It worked fleeing the storm, so I suspected all would be there when we needed it. I didn't use enhanced sight capabilities because it doesn't see through solid objects. Take trees for instance. I'm a vampire, not Superman.

Little station might be an overstatement, but I can't think of a better way to describe what I saw. A single track, a raised concrete-looking platform, and a metal box that looked identical to ticket machines you see everywhere in Germany. And yes, when we made it to the platform, I saw that the metal box was indeed a ticket machine.

It didn't shock me to see the red DB logo of Deutsche Bahn. Plenty of places in Germany remind me of equal parts heaven and hell. Made it more convenient for me anyway, because my Bahn100 card—first class—sat tucked in my wallet.

Think of a library card that allows you to board every public conveyance in Germany for an entire year and you get the idea of a Bahn100 card. It costs $10,000 each year, and it's one of the few extravagances I allow myself. Soyla? We'd need to hit the ticket machine.

Good thing I'd also brought along a credit card. As I pulled it out of my wallet, I suspected I might just get to meet the people who came up with this whole credit card fad. But to do that I'd need to wait around for the next body-storm, and we were in a hurry. Maybe something to do on my next trip to hell.

The machine operated exactly like the DB ticket machines with one exception. The language. No row of national flags allowing the user to choose his favorite. The screen showed a series of symbols arranged in perfect lines. At first it all looked like Greek, but I knew better. The more I stared the more the lines came into focus until it all began making sense.

I touched the box that said one-way. And no, it wasn't pessimism, I bought the one-way ticket because no selection existed for a round trip. Three hundred freakin' Euros. Are you kidding me? Nearly four hundred dollars to take somebody I hadn't invited to somewhere I didn't want to go. I could get anywhere in Europe for much less than that...if I planned ahead. Three hundred Euros and *of course* Soyla didn't produce her own credit card.

I inserted my card when the screen said it was time to pay. It would have cost an additional six Euros to get assigned seating, but enough is enough. We could find a place in the dining car if the train was too crowded to score adjacent seats. One other thing: I didn't buy her the first-class ticket, so despite my Bahn100 card, *I* would need to sit in the cheap section too.

The machine went through the gyrations and spit out the paperwork. It even returned my credit card. The screen morphed from all business to "Have a pleasant journey."

Right. I considered giving it a pleasant view of my rear end. We'd hit the dining car first thing to grab a couple of beers and wash the bitter taste of three hundred Euros out of my mouth.

Soyla hadn't said a word during the ticket acquisition and didn't even say thanks when I handed her the boarding pass. Probably thought being on the clock with me also meant I'd cover all travel expenses.

The electronic sign over the platform said, "Train Arriving," and, sure enough, I caught sight of it sweeping down the broad, green valley. If I thought about it, I would have expected one of those old-fashioned steam engines puffing a labored path across the tracks. Not so. Evidently Deutsche Bahn extended more than its ticket machine service to hell, because the engine looked the same as those servicing the Frankfurt Main Station...sleek and whitish-silver with a red stripe and an aerodynamic nose coming down the track.

Germans call them the ICE trains. Don't know what ICE stands for, though I do know they can speed along at more than 185 MPH. I tried to look through the big front window for the driver—human or demon? But it sped past too quickly for anything more than the notion of something human-looking standing there. I saw the markings for the second-class dining car go by and took up a quick jog to chase it down. Soyla followed close behind. The train stopped, and the door opened.

If you don't wait for debarking passengers to clear the door before climbing the two stairs, you run the risk of causing a rip in the fabric of German society. I mean, the Chancellor might even dissolve the government and call for elections. That's how seriously Germans worship order. Just the kind of unholy fetish that would make DB the contractor of choice to run hell's transportation system.

But nobody got off the train. I don't know how long I would have idled with that stupid look on my face had Soyla not nudged me from behind. I took a hesitant step forward and felt the familiarity of the metal-grated first stair. Two more and I found myself in the train. Soyla came up behind. The door closed, and the train began moving.

We rounded the corner and found ourselves entering the dining car. As I kind of expected, it was full of people. Everyone stopped to stare at Soyla and me as we staked out a spot at one of the tables where you stand and lean against the hull.

Nothing like a grand entrance.

And that was indeed nothing like a grand entrance because as the train pulled around a sharp bend, the momentum threw me into the crowd standing at the next table. They fell around me like dominos, and I ended up sending two full beers to the floor.

The looks on offended passengers' faces said to eat-crap-and-die. As they reorganized themselves, I saw each glance disapprovingly at the mess on the floor. It offered me comfort that the ride started the same as most of my morning trips to work. Was this train going to Wiesbaden?

I expected Soyla to pretend like she didn't know me, but she surprised me by asking if I were OK when I returned to our table.

"Sure," I said, and I followed her eyes down to where she stared at my shirt.

Soaked in beer and a huge mustard smear where I'd landed on someone's bratwurst. Kind of embarrassing, and I did the quick look around to see if anyone else noticed my clown act. Everyone in the car stared at me.

"Cower in hell," I announced to faces that went from smug to scandalized surprise, "Gaius Teutoberg has arrived."

TWENTY-ONE

SOYLA HANDED ME a napkin.

"You might want to get rid of the curry sauce, my love."

Crap. It's always the curry sauce that gets you when you think all you need to worry about is the mustard. She pointed to my elbow and, sure enough, another big smear. Red, instead of yellow. Am I the only one impressed I made it onto to a train without a skull fracture?

I heard the door swing open and saw the conductor enter the dining car. Boarding, finding a table, and the humiliating stumble when we hit the first curve. I might as well have been wearing a t-shirt saying, "Caution, American Tourist."

After the curry sauce and mustard represented no more than a bad memory, I glanced around at the other passengers. They'd slipped back into the German habit of avoiding eye contact.

The better to stare at you from the corners of my eyes, my dears.

I was vaguely aware of the conductor and my need to fumble out my wallet and display that all-important Bahn 100 card. First class version, and I held it high in hopes the other passengers would see how I'd spent ten big ones to ride this train.

Tourist? Not me.

Nobody glanced my way as I held up the card and the conductor said, "Good."

You bet I'm good. As I heard him ask Soyla to show her ticket, I realized that someone on the train skipped their morning bath. Or, perhaps they'd eaten one schnitzel too many, because I detected the tang of rotten eggs in the air. I looked around for a likely person to blame but nobody seemed to wear that half-baked smile of the guiltily contented.

Great.

We had a phantom-pharter on board.

And, of course, they'd all blame the stumbling American. At least *two* people in the dining car would know the truth. The sulfur-smell came on stronger as the conductor reached across the table to return Soyla's ticket. I looked up to tell the guy "Nice rip," but the words caught in my throat. That's a literary way of saying the words dried up.

A demon. Of course. Sulfur smell. And wheezy voice, now that I paid attention. Oh, he wore a DB uniform all right…hat and everything. It even looked like he'd gotten it laundered and starched. A natty demon indeed.

I'd seen a few demons in the past year—No Face and his gang of six. Those took ugliness to a professional level, and you wouldn't find this guy in an A&F ad either. He was as skinny as No Face and crowd were huge. The demon stood average height for a human, and the features on his face appeared thrown on in random order.

What passed for a mouth hung on his forehead, just beneath the hat's polished brim. Then came a nose sharper than a straight razor and at least pointed in the correct direction. One eye sat so close to that nose that it looked like a giant, disgusting pimple begging for harvest. His other eye was situated on the side of his face, no more than an inch above a pointed chin that sprouted an authentic, giant pimple.

I'm talking a disgusting Vesuvius of red and white. I mean, a single, intemperate squeeze would bury a farming village.

As I gaped at him, I thought that somewhere in the universe, an ethereal designer took first place for revolting against tradition. Even so, he looked vaguely familiar, and I wondered if I'd ever dated his sister.

"Your ticket, Miss Bokor," Conductor said to Soyla. And then to me, "Welcome aboard."

Why do demons always sound like their forcing the words through a clogged strainer?

"Personal space," I said, and I did the shooing gesture at him.

He didn't seem to get the message and stood there next to me smiling out of that misplaced, forehead grill.

He said, "I hope you find your trip entertaining."

"Yeah." I replied. "You can start the show by backing up a few steps."

That didn't seem to offend Conductor because he said, "As you wish," and turned to move to the next table of riders.

Something on his lapel caught my eye…a little round pin. I looked closer. Not just any little round pin, but with the letters NSDAP enclosing a swastika. Perhaps nobody told Conductor that those kinds of symbols went out of style decades ago, and that wearing one on the job could prove career-limiting.

I wasn't in Germany anymore. Oh yes, there was the ICE train with the DB motif. All smoke and mirrors. For my benefit? I didn't think so. Helmet already knew about the train, as did Balus and all the boys in the camp. I do occasionally free my ego get from the restraining leash, but I'd need to allow it run to presidential proportions to believe that hell was created just to con me.

Conductor did his rounds in the dining car. People handed him paper tickets, or they flashed Bahn cards—the normal routine for an ICE-run anywhere in Germany. But Germany was not the place where train conductors walked around with swastika pins, mouths springing from foreheads, and with eyes placed wherever somebody tossed them. The other customers didn't seem to notice.

Strange.

Those other customers? They looked like regular people, and they acted like regular Germans. Not Conductor. And speaking of everyone else…where, exactly did all these people think they were going? They'd all boarded the train before me, and I wondered when and where they got on. I focused on one of the tables.

People chatted over bratwursts and beer. Typical scene on the DB. I thought about asking them their destination but what did it matter? My INTEL said the train went to one place. *My* destination. Obviously, these people were going to the same place.

I said to Soyla, "Want a drink?"

"No."

"Fine, I'm grabing a beer.

Why not? the tap seemed to work fine for everyone else. I turned to make my way to the bar and Soyla grabbed my arm.

"Don't do it."

I wouldn't pick Soyla as the girl most likely to join the Temperance Union, so she must have had more than the evils of alcohol on her mind.

"What's up?"

Soyla shrugged and said, "Don't you think you're taking this too lightly?"

Was I? We'd just made two meals out of the most delightful stew I'd ever put in my mouth. Thing was, I ate enough in those sittings that I still had that sleepy, full feeling. I didn't need the beer. Perhaps I should restate that to put the thought in proper context. I wanted a beer and beer seemed readily available.

"Maybe," I said. "But what's the harm?"

Soyla made a theatrical glance toward the Conductor.

"That's the problem," she said. "He's hideous, and nobody notices."

"Careful," I said. "You're talking loud enough for him to hear you. You'll hurt his feelings."

"He's got an eye where his mouth should be," she said. "And a mouth where nothing should be."

"Get used to it. Other guys tend to lose their luster after a girl's been with me."

Soyla blew out her breath and shook her head.

"Do you want to put something into your stomach that somebody like him," she pointed at Conductor, "brewed?"

Putting it that way, no. The opportunity for beer does tend to make a guy blind to trivial matters. But I wouldn't let Soyla know her logic changed my mind. Give them an inch, and all that.

"I'm not thirsty, anyway," I said, and I returned to my spot beside Soyla.

Almost beside her, because a confused-looking old man walked into the dining car and stood searching for a place to park himself. Soyla motioned him over and squeezed him into the small space between us. And when I say small space, I mean the very spot I stood in before I took a step in the direction of the bar. Now there were two of us in space made for one. That left the majority of me hanging out in the aisle.

"How are you doing, my love?"

Strange question because she knew exactly how I was. We'd been together the better part of twelve hours.

I opened my mouth to say something cheeky when the geezer grinned and said, "Fine, thank you."

Soyla needed to recalibrate the threshold for calling dudes "my love." And I'd remember to add another grain of salt each time she used that phrase for me. This guy looked like all the lead left his pencil many decades back.

Soyla said, "Can I get you something?"

"No, no," Geezer replied. "I'm only looking around."

And he did look around in a theatrical way, as if we didn't understand what looking around meant.

Soyla leaned toward me and mouthed, "That's so sweet."

That's such baloney.

Soyla combined friendly concern with sexual overtones to warm Geezer up for conversation. He claimed to own a tire store in Cleveland, but I pretty much thought he claimed that with every chick he wanted to romance out of their adult diapers. I'd keep an eye on Geezer.

Soyla said, "Impressive."

Not.

I stood elbow-to-elbow with five dozen sweating Germans while Geezer gave us the ins and outs of steel-belted versus the way they used to do things. After ten minutes of that crap, I considered swallowing my own tongue to end it all, though I perked up when Soyla turned the conversation to something useful.

"You said you were looking around, darling?"

Geezer smiled and nodded. What guy wouldn't smile if a hot babe like Soyla called him darling?

"I've never been on a train."

Not shocking because, I suppose, most Americans would say the same. Europeans? Trains are part of their daily lives.

"And now you have," said Soyla. Geezer nodded emphatically and Soyla continued with, "You on vacation?"

Good girl, Soyla.

Establish the relationship, act interested in harmless conversation, slip in the important question like a wolf dressed in sheep's clothing. It came out sounding simple enough, though Geezer seemed flummoxed.

His lips moved to form an answer several times, but nothing came out.

After he managed to gather his wits, Geezer said, "I don't think so."

I would have dived in with several more questions that popped up in my mind, but Soyla intervened with a hand on my arm. This was her show and she seemed to be doing well enough without my interference. We both kept quiet while Geezer traveled down mental pathways and tested one potential answer after another.

"No," he said. "Not a vacation." A long pause, and I got a sense of rumbling velocity transmitted to your feet when standing in a train. "Not a vacation," he repeated. "But a relocation?"

He was asking *us*? I was beginning to consider expanding my personal space by chucking old Geezer back through the door that brought him in. Either Soyla sensed my impatience, or maybe she always expects me to do something stupid, because she put her hand back on my arm and squeezed until I felt nails digging in. It hurt. In a sexy way.

"Relocation?" she said. "How exciting."

Right, but I did have to admit I saw Soyla's point. Leaving Cleveland for hell would represent a step up in anyone's book. Something told me she really didn't mean it though. Perhaps she meant to draw more out of old Geezer.

"Thing is," he said, "I don't remember telling anyone I wanted to relocate."

That statement made me forget about the cramped quarters at our table, though nothing could make me forget about the tufts of hair growing out of his ears like palm trees on a tiny desert island. The vacant look returned to the little guy, and I felt sorry for him. Hot chicks do the same thing to me, and if Soyla hadn't covered that scanty bra with the Rebel tunic, old Geezer might have popped a circuit breaker before he said anything at all.

"Of course you didn't, my love," said Soyla. And then, "What did they say to you."

Geezer smiled, and I guessed he knew the answer to that one. Funny how the instant a guy meets Soyla he'll do just about anything not to disappoint her.

"That I needed to move east," he said. "Told me I could no longer own a business in Cleveland and that I'd get a job in a factory or on a farm in the east. Allowed me one suitcase and ten minutes to pack."

Didn't make an iota of sense…so why did it sound familiar? Soyla seemed to understand, because she smiled at Geezer and nodded.

She said, "And you will."

He responded with, "Will what?"

"My love," Soyla said. "You will find a good job in the east."

"I will?"

It sounded more like pleading than a question…like Geezer wanted reassurance for something he knew in his heart couldn't be true. I could identify with the feeling because I'd felt the same way many times in the past. That it-can't-be-true sensation that usually came hand-in-hand with some sexy lady finally coming off her phone number. And yes, it almost always turned out illusory because the numbers led to the "this line is not in service or has been disconnected" chick.

Did I *really* put the word *almost* in front of *always*?

Anyway, Geezer looked at Soyla with equal parts gratitude and suspicion.

He said, "You think so?"

"Yes, my darling."

Relocating east. Lost his business because he couldn't own it anymore. Plenty of good work at the factories or on the farms. Like I said, vaguely familiar, and as I ran it through my mind, a smoky trace of answer began to resolve in my brain. I'd like to think I would have come to it even if it hadn't been shoved down my throat. Because, as I stood there contemplating what scant data Soyla managed to milk out of Geezer, everything changed. And it happened quickly.

The tables melted away…didn't just disappear all at once like you'd expect at a magic show. No, they fell in on themselves. I half-expected to see a puddle of molten metal when I glanced down at the floor, but when I say they melted away, I'm describing the way it appeared.

As I said, the tables collapsed and then disappeared, along with all the contents they'd held. And those tables, so packed with beer or wine, brats, giant pretzels, schnitzels, left nothing behind on the floor. No trace of broken glass and none of the beer.

Speaking of the floor, it changed from synthetic material to wood. Not sure when that happened, and my feet felt missed the transition. One moment, solid and shining. The next, long, splintered boards used on mid-twentieth-century freight cars.

I stared at the floor for a few moments in disbelief and when I looked up, I'd missed whatever happened to the rest of the car. And something *did* happen because what I saw would have stopped me in my tracks had I not been wedged where I stood by the bodies of my fellow passengers. No need to worry about stumbling onto someone's bratwurst anymore. No room existed.

And the car went dark. The windows had disappeared, and I saw the walls were made of the same splintered wood that formed the floor. Here and there bright beams of light knifed into the car. Vampires don't need to switch on night vision like a soldier switches on their goggles. For us, that extra capability is always there. I could see everything in monotone.

Above me, the ceiling looked a few feet taller. That did nothing to compensate for the several feet in length we'd lost in the change. Far less usable square feet pressed fellow travelers together.

For a panicked second, I couldn't breathe, but got myself under control. The same didn't apply for many of the others because the screams erupted immediately. Men and women. All of them terrified. Their eyes shone with the same fright I'd witnessed in animals I'd cornered...when knowledge buried deep in their DNA revealed what I was going to do.

Geezer said someone confiscated his business...that they'd exiled him from Cleveland. Sent him east with promises of jobs and resettlement. They permitted one suitcase. Put your life in a small leather box with a handle. Did that sound familiar to me?

You bet it did.

And if the train made it to the intended destination and someone rolled back the cargo door? I expected the greeting would include whips and machine guns. Men and women dressed in black uniforms. Vicious dogs to keep things moving. I'd expect to encounter the people who lent personification to the dictionary concept of evil. Men. Or maybe demons. Didn't matter which, because at the Nazi death camps, they were one and the same.

TWENTY-TWO

IF THE SCREAMING morphed into pandemonium, then the little wooden boxcar would become a deadly place. Well, for everyone *else*. On the other hand, as far as I knew, this crowd was already dead. I mean, how else could they be in hell?

Not quite right. Just like the soldiers in the camp, these were living, breathing people. From what I saw, they came with all the frailties, the desires, the hopes and the fears that make us human. Yeah, more accurate to say that they'd experienced one death on my side of the veil, and that they'd found themselves resurrected on this side…where they faced—and feared-- another death. Maybe more, body storms considered.

I scanned the car for Soyla but couldn't pick her out of the mass of flesh pressing in around me. I called out her name. She didn't answer. It didn't worry me…not at first. No way to pick my voice out of the screaming.

I'm ashamed to say that considered eliminating some of the noise. Kill one person after another until whoever remained exhibited sufficient sense to be more frightened of me than they were of the train. But that was my own rising stress talking, not my heart.

I hoped.

Heart or not, I'd need to keep tabs on myself. It wouldn't be the first time my instincts blotted out good sense.

Everyone's heard of tortured souls in hell. If you haven't, evacuate the phone booth. I'd never stopped to reason out how exactly *how* an entity—a soul with no solid mass—could even *feel* torture. If I threw a book at Helmet it would just go through him and knock a figurine or something equally valuable off the table behind him. I know because I'd tried it once. I also tried to set him on fire. He only yawned. It's a long story.

But one with a moral: there's no way to injure a ghost. Trust me. If you think you how I could get one over on Helmet, fire off an email to ImaVampire@YouAreDefinitelyWrong.com. No smacking Helmet, and I always assumed the same held true for souls. I mean, isn't ghost and soul two words for the same thing?

Again, I yelled again for Soyla. Nothing. I already mentioned how the wood walls dimmed the car. I'd have thought that blocking out the sun would cool the car down.

Wrong.

Perhaps it was heat outside baking over us like we were a giant casserole dish or maybe it was the hundreds of bodies stuffed into the car to the point no room existed to sneeze. Either way, the humidity shot up well beyond the pain threshold, and I don't remember when I first realized I felt sweat soaking my clothes. If the crowd didn't get fluids, they'd start dropping.

Not dead, though that is exactly what would happen on my side of the veil. Dehydrated, dead, and left to rot inside a crowded boxcar for however long the trip took. Over here? I suspected they'd dehydrate and die all right. Over and over and over. A continuous cycle until we arrived, and everyone moved on to a new torment.

I screamed for Soyla. Nothing, and I pushed through the crowd from front to back and from left to right. A few of the braver ones resisted and I thumped them out of my way with no more effort than swatting away a gnat.

No Soyla.

I stopped in one of the corners and carved out some space by shoving bodies. Relief, but only temporary because each time I heaved away a body, two more would flow in to replace it. Like scooping out wet sand between waves at the ocean.

I don't have claustrophobia. Never saw a reason to because, when all is said and done, I can't be smothered. But packed in with hot, screaming, frightened people? Dark curtains of panic closed in around me. I quit using my muscles and switched to my underworked mind.

I reminded myself of my near-immortality and of all the times I'd been left for dead on the battlefield, and I brought up visions of the dozen or so times I'd been executed…some of them so sadistic that I'd spent centuries in futile attempts to expunge them from my mind. But this felt worse. And I think I knew why.

Each of those times I'd faked my death it had been just me. Mostly. Yes, many others did fall around me at Gettysburg, and that burial detail put me into the trench beside hundreds more, but we all knew what we were doing and accepted the risks. We were in the army—blue or gray—and we'd marched into battle, not boarded a commuter train.

Geezer had said someone removed him from his business and forced him to pack. And in even his addled state, he'd smelled a rat. Maybe his brain might have already been gone—Alzheimer's or some other degenerative horror—and it served to make him more difficult for the bigger brainwashing.

The rest of the people? I didn't know for sure, but I suspected that dying in their first body created sufficient confusion for someone to rush them through the in-processing line. And unlike the young soldiers in the camp, these new bodies likely looked just like the old ones.

Promises offered and accepted at face value. Of course they needed to leave homes, businesses, and loved ones behind. Isn't that what death is all about? But they'd found themselves in one piece on the other side, and they did what most humans do best. They followed instructions from someone or something that seemed in charge.

And they ended up on the train heading east. Off to a new life and plentiful jobs. Oh, I'm sure they'd been told they'd need to work hard to earn their keep, but those kinds of warnings tend to season the con with the salt of truth. Deal's too good to be true? Probably is. Add a promise of some hardship to overcome? Where do I sign up?

A masterful sting. And once they had everyone herded into the train the pretenses proved unnecessary. Drop the curtain of civility and get ready to manipulate the next crowd.

Civilians, not soldiers, and the terror radiating off them threatened to make me lose all hope. No way I'd give in and let myself sink with the others. Not yet. Besides, I'd already left hope behind. Back in Aachen. I never expected to survive the mission.

Time for honesty?

I wanted to give Sarah Arias my best attempt. She deserved it, and if everything for me came to a halt? Two thousand years of life is more than enough for anyone. Hadn't Balus already set the precedent?

Somehow Soyla left the car. Good for her. She possessed the same capabilities as me, though what advantage did a vampire have in this place? I didn't know. That question made me think about the others in the boxcar and how they'd shed their old bodies on the human side for their bodies in hell. The big difference between them and me blinked through my mind.

Everyone else died to get here. Soyla and I had not. As far as I could tell, we'd not shed an old body for a new one at all. Even though I didn't know how that difference would play out, I thought the distinction important. The first time I entered the portal, several other people came across without dying and therefore in their original bodies.

None of them survived the trip. But…that was a different story, and I didn't need any flat tires on memory lane slowing me down. The bottom line was that, of the humans who came through the portal, only one made it back in one piece. Me.

The screaming lowered to a hypnotic level of continuous sobs and murmurs. I wished the heat would withdraw too. It didn't, and it overtook the desperation surrounding me to become what I hated most about my time in the boxcar.

Heat, with its invisible hands crushing air out my lungs and pulling liquid from my body. People panted—and yes, people *do* pant. Before they die. First a gasping rattle, then death.

I thought whoever designed this act would let the bodies rot…at least until we made it to our destination. After that? I suspected they would reanimate so they could experience the full measure of what awaited. In the meantime—while we remained on the train—they'd function to up the misery and hopelessness of the rest of us. It didn't take long in that oppressive heat for the stink to begin.

Many of the wretched creatures vomited. Others needed to relieve themselves. Both jobs. We organized enough to make one corner the latrine. Men used it. Women used it. Human waste piled up.

Soon we were walking in the filth. It stuck to our shoes and our clothes. Animals in undersized and forgotten cages couldn't die any dirtier than some of the people who took their final, miserable breaths in that boxcar.

One young man went insane. He beat his head against the splintered wall until he'd painted it red. I would have let it go on as long as he wanted, but he started screaming. That got some of the other people going. Voices combined in a screech that pounded in my ears. I pushed my way to the man did a quick twist of his neck. He fell limp in my arms, and I dragged him to the pile of bodies.

It went on like that for several days. One hour after next. Each minute its own decade of misery. Several times I reached the point that I couldn't remember why I'd ever boarded the train, but my mind would return to the image of Sarah Arias suffering in that demon prison at the end of the tracks.

End of the tracks. Destination. Demon prison.

That's what I'd been told to expect. A demon prison. I gazed around boxcar and I laughed aloud. Like a lunatic. No demons in route to this prison. Not one. That kept me laughing for more than an hour. What was the first law when dealing with demons? Never trust them. It was No Face who'd set me into motion.

Me laughing, everyone else silent. They'd seen my violence, and that had them cowering. None of them would attempt to twist my neck as I had done to Head Banger. They could only deal with it…and pray the death rattle found its way into my throat.

I was still laughing when train stopped. That got me going even more. I laughed so hard it gave me hiccups and I nearly puked. All else was silent. Inside the train and outside. Nothing. Not a sound. Not until I heard the metal click of a key turning in a lock outside and the sound of movement in the giant hasp.

The door slid open, and the instant flood of incandescent light smacked us blind. My insane laughing was the only sound in the night…until the dogs began barking and the men began yelling.

TWENTY–THREE

STUNNING LIGHT. CONFUSION. Disorienting noise. Men screaming "Raus!"

The others shuffled like zombies to the door. I was one of the last to touch ground.

When No Face first mentioned the demon prison, I expected something between a modern-style maximum security affair and a mountaintop castle. Once the train morphed into its true nature, I understood what I'd find at the end of the track. Anyone who wasn't raised in a penguin colony could have guessed.

What better location for the end of hope than the place that personified the end of humanity?

My feet hit the gravel beside the train, and I wondered if I'd arrived at the authentic Auschwitz or if they'd constructed a copy. It didn't matter, because anything that happened would be real enough. To some people. But I was curious.

Made sense that the place on earth where two million were murdered had its roots in hell. I glanced both ways down the tracks. When Soyla and I boarded the train, there'd been less than ten cars. Now I saw closer to thirty, each unloading an overstuffed cargo of the walking dead.

Speaking of the dead, camp workers in striped uniforms climbed into the boxcars to heave out those who'd succumbed to thirst, heat, or the filth…stiff, black, and bloated corpses. No sooner did they splatter to the gravel than they opened their eyes and stood to line up with the others.

Thousands of feces-encrusted wretches, but only a few guards to watch and organize. Black uniforms with death's head insignia. Jackboots. Machine guns. They paraded up and down the gravel pathway. Unconcerned. Some led creatures that resembled dogs. Sapped of both our strength and will by the torturous trip, the crowd offered blind compliance.

Sapped *our* strength? Not really. *Their* strength put it better, because all of mine remained. I considered ripping heads off the first pair of guards to stroll past…even moved in behind them. They sensed me and stopped walking. I didn't care. If they shot me, I'd still get them.

They turned to face me, and I scrubbed my attack plans. Not men in black uniforms. Demons. Both of them, and I assumed the same about the rest of the guards. In the past I've fought demons to some measure of a draw. But a couple dozen? Probably not. I could hit them in ones and twos and hope to keep the rest of them off balance long enough to escape.

Then what? How would I spring Sarah Arias? I'd suffered the worst journey a human could endure for a single reason. The destination. Even if I didn't have Sarah Arias holding me back, where would I go? I glanced around. The camp sat on a broad, muddy plain surrounded by razor-wire. Not much of a problem, but what would happen on the other side of the wire? Would I find help?

I suspected some measure of a town existed out there, because one existed back in the Poland of my side of the portal. Would I find comfort and support as an escapee? Probably not. On second thought, certainly not. I suspected the people in the town would summon the demon authorities. Could you blame them?

Yes.

I would always blame cowards intentionally blind to the systemized suffering of fellow humans.

But then, that's just me.

Wasn't their fault? Demons on both sides of the veil built the place, but those who lived around it—humans that went about their daily lives while ignoring the horror sitting like a cancerous sore on the face of all mankind? Yeah, maybe they didn't build the place, but they're the ones who could take credit for allowing it to remain open for business.

One of the black-uniformed demons poked me with his submachine gun and said, "Line up with the others."

I stepped back to the disembarking crowd. One positive bit of news I saw as I stood there: No children. None on the train either. I'd noticed that while Soyla and I stood at the dining car table...back when I stupidly thought beer was so important to me. Funny how priorities can alter in the blink of an eye. No children meant there'd be no mothers screaming and children wailing as the demon SS wedged them apart.

The camp didn't appear large enough to process the deaths of two thousand people per hour. If I remembered my history correctly, then concrete buildings waited for us at the end of the gravel path. People walked in; ashes were shoveled out.

Our group began moving down the path, and I could see long and flat buildings off in the distance to my left. Barracks. Small buildings stood between...administration and whatever. SS stood beside a table up ahead. People shuffled past, and a guy sitting at the table directed them to one of two lines.

The youngest and most robust got in line to the left of the path.

The oldest and weakest made up the line on the right. That one grew exponentially compared to the few people selected to stand with the healthier group. Every so often, the officer behind the table would stand and ask a person a question or two, though I never saw him change his mind once he directed a person to one of the lines.

The men in striped uniforms scurried like ants in and out of the vacant boxcars. They carried out the dead and removed any luggage left behind. I use the word uniform for lack of a better way to describe what I saw. Tattered pajamas would suit better. Slush and snow lined the edges of the pathway and mud was everywhere.

One important aspect of history was clearly missing. There were no yellow Stars of David to be seen. None sewn to the clothing of miserable people on the train and none on the striped uniforms. Evidently, the Jewish people were beyond the reach of hell's Auschwitz. Oh, and still, everyone there spoke Hebrew.

Along with the snow and icy mud came the biting cold. The striped uniforms appeared threadbare and frazzled...not much for blocking out the freezing, and the shirts bore a small triangle of one of three colors. Black, green, or red. Like I said, I expected to see the Star of David, but observed none of them.

Perhaps that symbol hadn't made it to hell. But the swastika had. I'd seen it on Conductor's pin and there it was on the armbands the guards wore. Jewish symbols hadn't made the transition, but those of Germany had. I was thinking about that when my turn came at the table.

I expected to walk past as the others had done, but as I approached with my head down, I heard a wheezy voice bark, "Stop."

I looked up to see—surprise, surprise—No Face standing behind the man arranging the lines. And it *was* a man and not a demon doing that most evil task. Behind him, my buddy No Face. He'd not taken the time to cover his skull and bare eye sockets the way he'd done with the Donna face.

He said, "Glad to see you here."

Right.

He'd lied to me about being a prisoner. Another huge surprise.

Not.

"And you too," I said. "This place suits you."

No Face wheezed a laugh. An Auschwitz-Birkenau—or whatever they called the place in hell—would suit a demon. If I hadn't ripped off his cheeks a few months ago they would have been rosy. I almost accused him of lying to me but ended up keeping it to myself. Accusing a demon of lying would be redundant.

He said, "It suits you too."

The man behind the table stood up and smiled. Definitely a human, and it surprised me that he seemed to be wielding the power.

He said, "Is this the one?"

No Face responded with, "He is."

The SS-officer held out a hand.

"I'm Doctor Mengele," he said. "And you are Gaius Teutoberg, my fellow countryman."

I looked at his hand and said, "If you continue to wave that rotten piece of meat in my direction, I will rip it from your arm and use it to wipe my butt."

No Face made to backhand me. Stupid move. Maybe the train depleted everyone else and maybe I stood there haggard and with human excrement caked to my knees, But I was still a vampire. I blocked the blow at his elbow. And I maybe it was to counteract the helpless frustration growing inside me that made me employ more force than necessary for that trivial task.

Cracking bones in sync with yell of pain that could have been heard over the crowd after an Alabama touchdown. That brought a genuine smile to my face. Two of the other demon-officers took a step toward me. Good. I was ready to rumble.

Dr. Mengele neither scampared away nor dropped the affable grin. He held up an arm and the two demons stopped.

"No need for this," he said over his shoulder. And then to me, "I understand your hesitance, but you will adjust well."

I saw No Face bent over his broken arm, and he looked at me with as much hate as two floating bulbs in lidless eye sockets could muster.

"I will kill you," he wheezed. "Mark that, vampire. You'll die screaming while I feed on your living flesh."

So, we're were back to that.

A new voice said, "You will not."

WHAT THE...

She said, "Not part of the deal."

No Face said, "You get paid when the vampire dies."

"Yes," she said. "But I get the bonus if I do it myself."

Dr. Mengele maintained his smile while he scanned my face for a reaction. Glad to see I had a talent for entertaining the troops. So, the vile little pimple of a man had authority here? I hoped it did nothing to relieve the stress of a sentence to eternal hell.

Back to the voice. I was shocked all right. But really, I should have expected as much.

On the plus side of the equation, at least I didn't need to worry about Soyla anymore. I'd found her.

TWENTY–FOUR

SOYLA IN A black uniform. Kind of. She'd changed the overstressed brown bra for a shiny black one, so the black leather pants matched. And she wore a hat. A black, military-style formal hat with polished leather brim. She'd jazzed it up with sequins and the diamond skull and bones insignia of the SS.

"Gaius, my love."

She looked fresh, like she'd spent the last few days of the train ride in a comfortable, first-class compartment. Complete with food, a hot shower, and even Wi-Fi, if they provided that in hell.

"You owe me four hundred bucks."

Dr. Mengele looked on with evident interest, No Face with an expression difficult to read—he had no face, after all, so let's call it a *pained expression*—and Soyla with two raised, perfectly-shaped eyebrows.

She didn't understand.

"For the ticket."

She pretended not to get the joke. A chick who didn't appreciate my humor? As if I needed additional proof the place was hell. I glanced at the new bra and thought it might be stretched tighter than the last one. Who designs these things? For the first time in my life, I wanted to get my hands around the neck that owned those hooters more than I want to get them around the hooters themselves.

I felt my teeth growing.

Dr. Mengele took a step closer and said, "How lovely."

"Give me a few more seconds," I said, "and I'll get lovelier."

He turned up the wattage on his smile. Was this guy crazy? Well yes, if even an iota of what I read about his life was true. "Was this guy suicidal?" better described the situation. He had to understand the danger he faced. But he just smiled. I must admit it would have been charming, if it weren't for the brown, irregular, fence-post teeth…and if we hadn't been standing in the spot where the universe received its enemas.

"Calm yourself, my love," said Soyla. "He can't be touched."

I didn't want to touch him, I planned on pulling off his arms first and his head next. After that I couldn't decide whether I should stuff them down his neck hole or stand there and watch his nerves twitch.

"What do you mean he can't be touched?"

"That if you injure him," Soyla said, "the force behind this place will give you to him."

Doctor Mengele said, "Think what great things we could do. I could discover what makes a man a vampire."

He spoke in a calm, conversational tone, as if he were talking about collaborating on a high school science experiment instead of peeling back my skin to see what made me tick.

"Thanks for the invitation," I said, "but I think I'll pass."

"Such a shame," Mengele said, "Perhaps you'll will change your mind."

"I'll be sure to let you know."

The SS doctor clicked his heels and performed a curt bow. He also pointed me to the line that held the people destined for slavery in the

German factories. Well, not really *German* factories, I thought about them as German out of habit. I mean, those folks ran the slave business in the history of my side. I didn't know who performed that function in hell, though judging by the heel-clicking Dr. Death standing in front of me, it looked like they'd hired some free agents from the original team.

No Face—arm dangling uselessly at his side—stepped forward before I moved away to follow my line.

He wheezed, "We'll see each other again," and added, "Soon."

I turned to Soyla.

"*He's* not untouchable," I said, and I used a tip of my forehead to point at No Face's arm.

Soyla said, "Not him."

Did I detect a note of disgust in her voice?

"Good," I said. And then to No Face, "Pencil in a two-hour block into your appointment calendar."

"For what?

"Because that's how long I plan to enjoy kicking your butt."

No Face snarled, but I noticed he didn't come any closer. I think he knew Mengele wouldn't allow the other demons to intervene if I decided to go all vampire again and break his other arm. Then I'd move to other, more painful and permanent renovations. No, Doctor Insane would relish the opportunity to see the vampire in action so that he could use his observations as an aid when sketching out ideas for his experiments. On me.

One of the other black-uniformed demons shoved me toward my line and I got moving. But only for a second. I had a question for Doctor Mengele.

"How do you like it?"

He looked at me with curiosity and said, "How do I like what?"

"The language," I said. "Sound familiar?"

He looked at me like a parent looks at a child who's just asked for a pail large enough to empty the ocean.

"Good German," he said. "Everyone here knows it."

"Uh-huh," I said. "Everyone *does* know it, but it's not German."

Mengele smiled like I was bringing him in on a knock-knock joke.

"Not German," he said, "what do you say it is?"

I flashed him a broad grin.

"Hebrew," I said. "The language of Moses."

The doctor went from serenely confident to yelling like a lunatic in less than a heartbeat. Just a figure of speech. I'm certain the doctor never *had* a heart. He meant to scream obscenities at me but evidently, he'd not picked up on that part of the lingo. I only heard babbling. Loud babbling sure enough, but babbling, nonetheless. Maybe the language of angels and everything else omitted the kinds of words the doctor required. Or maybe he needed to spend more time in the Torah.

Happy thoughts are important to good mental health. That goes double for trips to hell. Watching Doctor Scum implode sent yellow smiley faces whizzing through my brain. I think Mengele already knew the bit about Hebrew and not German. He just needed a reminder.

I took a spot in the line shuffling toward wherever we went next and took a final glance at the doctor. He'd grabbed a bayonet from one of the demon guards and was trying to hack out his own tongue. The demon fumbled to stop him while at the same time trying to avoid touching him too much. Seemed they'd gotten the memo about his special status. More smiley faces for my brain.

I caught a glimpse of Soyla, and all those imaginary little yellow winged happy faces fluttered to the ground. Soyla. She had me believing I'd hired her…that she was working for me. Sure, we'd not agreed on a price for her services, but she knew I could pay more than that faction of The Seven who wanted me dead. At least I thought I could.

My line moved at the pace of a box turtle and I kept my eyes on Soyla for as long as I could. She caught me, and I expected her to look away in shame. But she didn't, because we locked eyes until we couldn't see each other anymore. And I'd held hands with her all night in Bama's tent. Held hands, heck. She'd spent part on the night rolled atop me on my cot.

Women.

They act like they love you one minute and then happily condemn you to slave labor in a death camp the next. Happens all the time. Now she wanted to kill me with her own hands. Was that a marriage proposal?

My line marched toward the wooden barracks while the other line, those who looked like they wouldn't last five minutes as slaves, continued down the gravel path. The stripes took the suitcases from those in my line. Good thing I'd packed light—nothing—because I had a feeling everyone had seen the last of their stuff. The people in the other line carried their luggage down the gravel path.

Two of the stripes stood by the open door of an empty boxcar. They smiled and waved at the other line as the people walked past…they also mimed thumbs across their necks. Death ahead. Didn't slow the line, though. The doomed people put one foot in front of the other as they made their way toward what everyone had to know awaited them.

We marched to a wooden structure. Doors opened, and we were led into a large room with benches placed against the wall. Stripes moved among us and told us to undress for a disinfecting shower. A person would easier forget their own name than what undressing for a shower at Auschwitz meant.

The others in my group appeared as nervous as I felt. Good. I sat down on the nearest bench. A particularly large stripe with a green triangle sewn to his shirt ordered me to remove my clothes. We did the guy staring at each other thing for a few moments.

The man stood at least four inches taller than me and I estimated he carried fifty more pounds. All muscle. His arms looked big enough to be legs, his shoulders wide enough for a movie screen. He wore an armband that said Kapo. From my later research on the web, the green triangle meant habitual criminal and the Kapo armband indicated a kind of prison trustee. Someone allowed to beat other prisoners to death.

So yeah, we stared at each other long enough for him to determine he didn't scare me and for me to understand this guy wasn't smart enough to be afraid of me. When he spoke, his voice came out in a baritone growl.

"Get undressed," he said. "Now."

I gave him the finger just as two black-uniformed demon-guards walked through the door. The lumberjack turned to see what caught my attention, and when he returned to me, he spoke in a whisper.

"Please."

Shocking.

"Please?" I said because nothing better came to mind.

Lumberjack said, "You're the vampire," and it came out sounding like neither a question nor an accusation, but a statement of fact.

I nodded.

"Here for the angel."

Uh. Yes.

I'd fallen so completely into the mindset of the camp that I'd forgotten I sat in a reflection of the place on my earth, and that the clock on my side of the portal was set to several decades after 1943. If Mengele expected me, why not some of the inmates?

The trusted ones, anyway. Kapos like Lumberjack.

I said, "I'm not removing my clothes."

And I wouldn't. If they planned on gassing me, I'd go down wearing my own stuff. Mostly so that I could come back that way. After that, these guys would find out how I could turn up the intensity a notch or two. Even in hell.

Lumberjack gave me a long look. He'd dropped the fierceness act and replaced it with a look of calculation salted with fear.

"OK," he said. "It might cost me but suit yourself."

Lumberjack backhanded me. The cliché version would go something like a mighty blow that sent me sailing. But that would sound too much like Moby Dick, and that whale only destroyed a ship. Lumberjack? He'd destroyed me. Bottom line: Not prepared for that one.

I flew backward off the bench and hit the floor. I'll never know if my slide would have set a new record for distance because I crashed into the wall a few feet behind the bench. The blood began, and I remained on the ground long enough for my brain to reboot. Also, I needed to come up with a manly way to pick my butt up, so I could commence to tearing Lumberjack apart in style.

I heard a snort of that wheezy-sounding laughter from one of the demon guards and I heard his jackboots clicking as he walked away.

Lumberjack kept his distance—wise—as he leaned over and whispered, "Sorry about that."

"Not as much as you're going to be," I said, and I felt like backhanding myself for the inability to come up with a snappier response.

"Don't," said Lumberjack. "Or they'll come back."

I thought he meant the guards and I wondered why I should care. Maybe because anything that didn't lead to finding Sarah Arias also ultimately hindered that goal?

Nah. Lumberjack needed stomping.

But then, he did seem to know something about my mission.

"Leave your clothes on," he said, and I detected a note of conciliation in his voice.

Or maybe it was my imagination.

"Thought you said it would cost you," I said.

He looked at me still sprawled on the floor and smiled.

"Not anymore."

Well good for Lumberjack. He even helped me to my feet.

I said, "Thanks," and then punctuated my gratitude with a fist to his stomach that drove him head-over-heels into the same wall.

If jerk-tossing were an Olympic event I'm pretty sure I'd have taken the gold and left the silver for Lumberjack. I felt a little sorry for him when I saw him puke blood. He'd heal. Everyone seemed to in hell. The better to die a thousand deaths. It was my turn to help Lumberjack to his feet.

"We're even."

Lumberjack nodded, but I remained alert for another blow in case he decided he didn't like even.

"These showers are real," he said. "No need to worry."

Did I look worried?

"Good," I said. "Then what?"

"They take you to your block," he said, "your bunk."

I expected as much and nodded.

"And?"

Lumberjack looked around for eavesdroppers.

"Your block Kapo assigns a job," he said. "And then you work."

He said the word work as if he were spitting a razor blade and I saw fear creep across his face. And why not? I mean, what jobs could a soul expect in hell? I didn't think I wanted to stick around long enough to find out.

"Block Kapo?"

Lumberjack nodded and said, "Me."

Uh-oh.

Seemed I'd just punched out the guy who decided how I'd serve my time in hell. I like to get off on good footing with people who are important to me.

"You?"

"That's right," he said, "Me. And right now," he added, "you need to take a shower."

Lumberjack directed me into a larger room containing exposed plumbing and a dozen showerheads. A hundred or so of my newest closest friends crowded in with me. I don't ever do showers with dudes—ever—and I just needed to look around to reinforce that personal policy.

The guys were haggard, flabby, skinny, muscular, and weak. Most of all though, they were naked. Awkward. The cold water appeared without warning and ended the same way. We filed out of the room and the demon-guards watched as a half-dozen stripes threw powder on us. I didn't know whether fleas and lice found their way into hell, but I had the feeling I was going to find out.

Outside the shower they provided us the same striped uniforms the others wore, and we formed up into a marching mass and headed for the dark wooden buildings that quartered the slave labor. My uniform smelled of fear and lingering death, and it did nothing to insulate me against a cold so biting that it felt like acid on my skin. We halted between two of the buildings and Kapos came out screaming names. One-by-one the ranks thinned until I heard my name and followed Lumberjack away from the crowd. Looked like I'd be his only charge from the latest train.

He shoved me toward what I assumed would be my temporary home away from home and I decided to play along. Even stumbled to the ground a couple of times. An Academy Award-level performance. Lumberjack opened a door that reminded me of a barn door with a clever wooden mechanism, and we went inside.

I saw rows of wooden platforms, one above the next, where the slaves slept. I'd seen the old photos on the internet. But the pictures didn't convey the stark feeling of lost hope created by the Spartan building or the thought that so tiny a space housed so many. Lumberjack interrupted my journey down that mental road to despair.

He said, "We've got to get moving."

TWENTY-FIVE

"WE?" I SAID as if I didn't understand the meaning of the two-letter word.

Lumberjack kept his mouth shut for a while. Maybe he was updating preconceived notions regarding how smart two-thousand-year-old vampires really were.

"You want the angel, right?"

We'd already established that in the Turkish bathhouse. I didn't respond.

He said, "Have a plan?"

If I had a shekel for every time I'd been asked that, and then another for every time I'd had to say no…

I shook my head.

"Didn't think so,."

"Why?"

Lumberjack understood. He'd been a professional football player—of the American sort. The real kind. An All-Pro defensive lineman. The best of the best. I didn't ask which team he played for because I was certain it wasn't mine. Those knuckleheads haven't seen the playoffs for two decades, and Lumberjack said he played in the Super Bowl.

That made him a relatively recent addition to the camp. I wanted to ask how he landed here. I mean, he had a body that would embarrass Hercules and face that would make Adonis wear a mask. Basically, he was almost as good looking as me...not that I'm a good judge of men. So, what clipped him? I didn't need to ask because he told me.

He said, "Cheap lay."

"Say what?"

"Beautiful girl," he said. "But not my wife."

He explained how he'd bought a condo in the mountains for her—he could have bought the whole mountain with his signing bonus alone—and how they rendezvoused a couple of times a week. It didn't take long for the snakes to make their tongue-darting appearance, and for the when-are-you-going-to-leave-your-family-so-we-can-be-together-forever conversations to begin. The relationship survived for six months before a combination of guilt and weariness overtook him.

"I told her it had to end," Lumberjack said. "And she fell apart. My wife was in New York shopping with her friends, so I decided to hang out a while. Felt sorry for girl. And she seemed suicidal." He laughed. "We fell asleep on the couch together. I woke up here."

"Stroke from the stress?"

Lumberjack shook his head, "Lead from the gun."

Turns out the beautiful but fragile young chick *was* indeed suicidal. And how, she reasoned, could Lumberjack live without her?

"I think seeing my head explode cooled her to the idea," he said. "She used a shotgun on me, and I don't think she carried through with the suicide part."

A murder-suicide without the suicide is just a murder.

"And you ended up here because you did what guys are designed to do?"

You ladies needn't throw your ereaders against the wall for my last comment. First, it was a guys-only conversation, and don't attempt to claim chicks don't have their own version of the same. Second, you already know that I can be a pig.

Another shake of the head. Lumberjack walked over to the bunks and sat on the bottom platform. Not enough clearance for his head, so he sat bent over like the statue of that thinking dude. When he spoke, his voice trembled, and I saw tears welling in his eyes.

"It's not how you live your life that gets you here," he said. "Not what you do," he continued, and it sounded to me like he might have been talking to himself more than to me. "It's what you don't do. And I'm not talking physical doing either," he said.

Uh. OK. Whatever.

I'd heard it all before and for as long as I could remember. I never met the man Jesus, but I'd run into a few folks who had. Crazy people trying to love all over me. Always up in my personal space. Me? I'm much more comfortable when people know their boundaries… especially with dudes involved. Always yammering about accepting a gift and living forever.

I could give them a fresh opinion about immortality. On the other hand, so could the boys Soyla and I spent the night with…the soldiers in the camp. Those guys seemed happy. That made me think about my wife Nellie. She called herself a believer, and I saw the peace it brought her when I held her as she closed her eyes for the last time. But then again, that was after seventy years of holding her every night and waking up beside her every morning. Immortality can be a curse.

Nellie nearly had me, and I prayed to her God all night. One follower of The Way told me he saw Jesus raise a smelly old decomposing man three days after he croaked. Why not my Nellie? Yeah, I thought, why not. Like maybe because Nellie's God only cared about the limelight. Prayed all night for my love and she laid just as still, just as dead the next day. I've not considered praying since.

And now Lumberjack wanted to give me that same two-thousand-year-old line. The good news. At least I thought that's what he meant by "it's what you don't do" that condemns a person. Sure thing. Well, I'm good at not doing things.

Me in hell as a prisoner in the prototype of the vilest place in the world's history, an angel to rescue, a looney but infinitely sexy Hungarian warrior-woman vampire itching to rip out my beating heart in order to collect a bounty large enough to keep her in facials and designer handbags for the next two centuries, and now an ox of a man sitting in tears. Had I made a wrong turn somewhere down the wide road of doing nothing?

What next? A shaved head and a number tattoo? I didn't want to find out. I needed to get what I could out of Lumberjack before he broke down into a puddle of contrition and both of us ended up singing teary hymns and waving our hands. Still, my curiosity insisted on one final answer.

"The people," I said.

Lumberjack looked back with the blank stare of someone who'd forgotten another person sat beside him.

"What people?"

"The folks Mengele sent to the other line," I said. "The people who kept walking down the path."

Lumberjack said, "Them."

He gave me the short version of the story I expected to hear.

"The storms," he said. "The rain."

It all clicked in my mind. Of course. Hell would hardly be a place of torment if everyone stood around sobbing about the opportunities they'd miss. Emotional punishment only goes so far before things need to get physical.

The demons marched the other line to the special showers...the ones that spewed gas instead of water. They intimidated those unfortunate souls into stripping themselves naked. Humiliation. And then they crowded them into the concrete room and locked the doors. Twenty minutes of pure agony before death, the furnace, and black smoke carrying souls into sky.

Horrible enough, but things didn't stop there. Though I didn't want to think about what came next for those people, what I want and what I get are seldom one and the same. I'd seen the storm, seen the tortured bodies writhing in agony as they plummeted down from the sky. After that? I suspected they evaporated just like water and got to do it all over again. A continuous cycle of dying and death. Forever. Hell.

I said, "And these are the Jews from the Holocaust?"

"Jews?"

"Yes," I said. "We are all speaking Hebrew. Right?"

Lumberjack blinked. Seemed he'd remembered where we were, and he looked toward the door with that same surprised fear you would get when you realize you've nodded off for a second while driving. The door was still shut, and I heard him exhale in relief. He looked back at me.

"Jews?" he said. "Don't know about Hebrew, but I do know there aren't any Jews here."

"No Jews?" I said. "I just thought..."

"You thought," Lumberjack interrupted, "that since they did these things to the Jews before that it would all continue here."

I nodded.

"Well, it doesn't," he said. "Some of the people on that path are those who didn't step in to stop the thing while they lived on earth." Lumberjack let that sink in for a second before adding, "or the types of people who would have turned a blind eye, had they been alive during that period."

"They still exist?"

Lumberjack snorted in a derisive way.

Interesting, but not germane to the task at hand. I had the feeling I'd just spent the lion's share of what time might be available to get some actionable intelligence, and I hadn't learned a thing. But then, I seldom do. Perhaps I'd friend Lumberjack on Facebook if I had the hankering for more trivia after I left this place. What I needed to do was to find out how to make leaving-this-place happen.

"You asked if I had a plan," I said. "Do you?"

"No," Lumberjack said, and somehow his lack of a plan deflated me more than mine did.

OK, I need some work on the self-reliance thing. The word crestfallen appears here, because that's the expression Lumberjack saw on my face. I never thought I'd find an ally—kind of what Lumberjack seemed to represent—so why did I expect anyone to set me off down a yellow brick road?

Despite tears in his eyes, Lumberjack gave me the hint of a smile. Maybe I just imagined it. I mean, what could possibly make a guy happy in hell? As quickly as I saw that glimmer it disappeared.

I said, "What?"

Another trace of a smile and Lumberjack said, "You don't need one."

Uh oh.

"And why not?"

"Because there's nothing you can do to help."

Most people underestimate me that way because I come across as this incredibly handsome ne'er-do-well. It's my shtick. But sometimes I surprise them. That reputation must not have made it all the way to hell.

"Maybe you haven't heard of…"

Lumberjack interrupted.

"We all expected you," he said. "And I know. People talk here," he said. "So do the demons." Another of those rare smiles. "And you have one of those boys really angry."

"The one without the face?"

Lumberjack nodded. On second thought, perhaps my reputation made it to hell just fine. And that worried me. I'd pulled off a powerful demon's face as easily as a politician pulls off a prostitute's underwear. Despite that, Lumberjack thought I couldn't help Sarah Arias.

"Yes," said Lumberjack. "Him."

The guy actually held up his hand for a high-five. Guess he'd taken the down elevator before the jump-and-bump became popular. I smacked his hand with mine.

"So why the no confidence in me? I've made it through a lot of situations."

"Because," said Lumberjack, "she doesn't need your help."

"What?"

Lumberjack nodded as what he said sunk in.

"Then what am I doing here?"

A rhetorical question. Lumberjack answered anyway. And his answer left me feeling like a trap door had opened beneath my feet and a rope was about to snap my neck.

"You're here," said Lumberjack, "to help the demons."

TWENTY–SIX

IT SOUNDED CRAZY. Me in hell *not* to rescue Sarah Arias, but to help the demons. I gave Lumberjack the you're-pulling-my-leg laugh. Just a joke at my expense. When he didn't join in the chuckle, I felt puke rising in my throat. Of course I wasn't in hell to help the demons. Of freakin' course. But the more I tried to convince myself, the more Lumberjack's statement sunk in.

I didn't know why it sounded so true in my ears, and I couldn't think of a way I'd been hoodwinked. But I got the feeling that I had. I've already mentioned the first rule in dealing with demons. Expect nothing but lies. And I had. Hadn't I? Well, no. Would I have run headlong through the gates of hell with less than one day's consideration if I'd scented a lie? I didn't want to answer that one and would appreciate it if you didn't answer for me.

A lying demon? That made sense. Other things didn't make sense. Like why everyone on this side of the looking glass seemed to expect me. The good guys—the boys back in the camp—as well as the bad ones—the masters at Auschwitz. How had they known when I didn't even have a clue about Sarah Arias and her troubles until not so many hours ago? Pulling on that thread a bit more, what were good guys doing in hell, and why did all of us speak Hebrew like we'd all wandered the desert together for forty years?

And Soyla's involvement. That didn't add up either. Oh, I believed she'd signed a contract to whack me. I had put The Seven at odds with each other, and when there's a power struggle of that magnitude, people start disappearing. A war is hardly a war until the casualties start piling up. But did The Seven possess enough horsepower to wage war in hell?

Probably not. But on the other hand, I couldn't think of a better place to hide a body. I'd left a couple stiffs here myself during my last visit. But then, nobody *really* seemed to die in hell. At least not for good. Had the two I'd killed stood back up to board their own boxcar? Were they raining down and floating up as part of the macabre ecological system?

Maybe I should have thought about all of that before I stepped through the door. Well, not maybe. For sure. Even if I had engaged my brain instead of my libido and my pride, the immense coordination effort between The Seven, Soyla, and No Face would have made the scenario I now faced...

What? Impossible?

Lumberjack stared at me as my mind processed the possibilities. I could accept the notion that No Face lied to me. Him being a demon and everything. Truth was, I expected as much. It's why I wasn't surprised to see him in his black uniform at the train platform. Let's assume the various parties—The Seven, the demons, and Soyla— kicked off a baroque plan in minimal time to snuff me, and that they did get past the coordination challenges.

Still unlikely, if only because demons know how to drive a hard bargain, and the negotiations would have taken longer than it takes the EU Parliament to decide which country's beer to serve at the next office bash. But let's say everyone worked through it. Two things still didn't add up.

First, the rogue members of The Seven could have killed me whenever they wanted. It didn't make sense to go through all the paperwork and end up owing demons. If they feared potential retribution from Bernard, then killing me in hell would only serve to delay the reckoning. No, they could get the same outcome if they picked a spot on our side of earth.

The second thing that didn't make sense? Sarah Arias. My gut felt her nearby, and *that* part of No Face's story wasn't completely fabricated. Though, I couldn't convince myself that her presence lent any measure of credence to the rest of No Face's malarkey.

That thought gave rise to another possibility. If the demons wanted me dead, they'd have snuffed me as soon as I passed through the portal at the Aachen Cathedral. Hadn't I seen them do that sort of thing before? So, the demons didn't want me dead. Not yet...at least not until something they wanted to happen...happened. If I could believe anything Soyla spouted as we played cuddle bear, then the rogue factor of The Seven *did* want me dead. And as soon as possible.

The Seven wanted me dead, the demons wanted me dead. On the other hand, the demons let me live after I tiptoed into their domain... by my balls. Why? I thought the answer to that one would solve most—but perhaps not *all*—of the mystery. Lumberjack said I was there to help the demons, and as I finally took that moment to think about this crazy rescue mission, I thought Lumberjack just might have something.

Someone duped me all right. I didn't know how...or why, for that matter. Sure, there was the contract on my life, and though that might drive the actions of The Seven and Soyla, a contract on my life by itself wouldn't interest No Face's demon hierarchy.

Bottom line, I didn't know.

Crap.

Once again, me starring in the role village idiot. Worse, I'd signed up for the part. What started as my "march into hell for a heavenly cause" might just end up a "one-way dash into hell on a fool's errand." I couldn't find any holes in that line of logic, and believe me, I tried.

Why do I always need for the trap to spring before my brain wakes up? Lumberjack claimed I came to help the demons?

The only response I could muster for that accusation was, "Did not."

He shook his head like you do when a drunk friend says something asinine.

He said, "Why haven't they allowed the female vampire to touch you?"

Good question.

When I didn't answer, Lumberjack said, "And why do you think they've kept their hands off you?"

Another good one, and I guess I could have waited all day for him to ask an easy question, but it appeared none were on the way. So, I took a stab at an answer.

"Because they need me to do something."

"Touchdown," said Lumberjack. "Try for the extra point?"

I nodded and waited for his next question. Lumberjack said nothing. Looked like he wanted me to do this on my own. A teaching moment in hell.

"And they're going to kill me later?"

Lumberjack gave the signal for a missed kicked, and even I had to admit my statement sounded lame...and self-serving. I gave it another try.

"Because maybe it's not my life they want as much as me just being here."

Lumberjack said, "Bingo."

In a series of things not sounding good, *that* sounded the worst. Why? Because it opened the possibility that I'd have been more help to Sarah Arias if I'd not shown up…that my current position on the team roster was better filled by a vacancy.

I said, "Uh-oh."

Lumberjack just smiled one of those you-idiot smiles.

Uh-oh, right.

I said, "I've got to get out of here," and a panicked wave of desperation washed over me like a first sickie probing of diarrhea.

I heard an explosion outside followed by the chatter of small arms.

Lumberjack said, "Too late."

I sprinted toward the wooden door. Lumberjack made no move to follow me. Just another day in non-paradise for him, I guess.

I didn't know what to expect when my feet hit the mud. I ran with my head up, seeing well enough, but not processing that I saw. In case you can't relate, it's how people run who think they're running for their lives. I felt my teeth extending and raw vampire strength filling my veins with preternatural heat. I hit max velocity as I rounded the building and headed for railway platform.

I didn't have time to worry about whether that was the right direction because as soon as I cleared the corner, I ran headlong into one of those proverbial immovable objects. Something bright and evidently charged with electricity. Well, not evidently, but *certainly* charged with electricity, because the jolt I got when I collided sent me flying.

In my experience, manned flight without the aid of an aeronautical device never ends well. I splattered against the wall of the next barracks. Vampires heal quickly. Even so, the volcanic eruption of pain hinted that this landing was going to leave a mark.

My whole body tingled from the electrical shock…I mean, I buzzed from my brain to my balls to the soles of my feet. And if that weren't bad enough, searing heat erupted around my waist. I looked down and saw my pants had caught fire. Buzzing nuts represent a bad situation...I draw the line when buzzing nuts become burning nuts. Pretty sure every guy does. I rolled in the mud and smacked myself to beat out the fire. I'm not going to attempt to describe what that must have looked like.

Fire out and numb from the jolt, I looked up to get the number of that truck I'd just hit. The sight nearly made me forget about my sore nuts.

Almost.

The thing was bright all right. So much light, in fact, that I squinted to avoid burning my retinae. Sounds dramatic, but believe me when I say light like that—such perfection in pure white radiance while at the same time physical in raw power—does not exist on our side of the ethereal tracks.

It wasn't only light I saw but also the source. A woman dressed for battle. At first, I thought it was Soyla come to collect on her contract. That added fuel to the wildfire of terror my panic had become. But it wasn't Soyla all aglow in front of me. This woman had blonde hair flowing from beneath a golden, jewel-encrusted battle-helmet. She also wore a breastplate inscribed with ornate renderings of Hebrew verse—I could speak Hebrew in this land, so I thought I could likely also read it...but I had no plans for getting any closer to that woman to find out.

Around her waist I saw a thick leather belt that held an empty scabbard. It didn't take a rocket scientist to know the huge fiery sword she held in her hand lived there. In her other hand she rocked a burnished shield with the Greek symbols for alpha and omega etched on it...the letters shining like two fires. Her armor was positioned over a robe made of the whitest material I'd ever seen. It extended to her feet, where I saw leather sandals tied with simple thongs. Interesting, but I would have preferred a miniskirt.

I looked up to her face—OK, I admit I lingered few seconds at chest level to guess the weight of the gold it must have taken to form the breastplate—and saw a beautiful, radiant anger. When she spoke, her anger came out like thunder, and her green eyes flashed.

She said, "You fool."

"Nice to see you too, Sarah."

TWENTY-SEVEN

OK, NOT THE greeting from her I expected after I fought through The Seven to cross the portal into hell. Call me an optimistic sentimentalist, but I'd hoped for more. Like maybe a hint of freakin' gratitude. Of course, I was still new to Hebrew and perhaps there was a translation issue. I mean, "You fool" might be a colloquialism for "My hero."

Sarah Arias took two of the deep, clearing breaths the Lamaze folks recommend. So, she *was* excited to see me.

She said, "Idiot."

I think…maybe…NOT excited to see me.

And maybe it wasn't so reasonable to blame translation issues. Also, something told me she wasn't speaking in metaphors. The small arms fire that had closed my conversation with Lumberjack and brought me running from the barracks intensified. A few light explosions—in my experience, that meant grenades—and return fire coming from inside the camp.

Sarah Arias glanced in the direction of the fighting and then back to me.

"Stay close," she said and took off toward the battle.

I did as she said, and for the few moments I ran behind her, and

I wondered if I were following the sexiest being in the universe or *THE* avenging angel of God. We made it to the rail yard, where the battle raged. Four black-uniformed demons ran out from behind a nondescript building and slid to a halt when they saw me.

Truth time: They slid to a halt when they saw Sarah Arias. She glowered at them with the malice of a woman who's discovered the toilet seat in the raised position, and the demons didn't so much melt before her as just crumpled to the mud, where they groveled face down as she stood over them with sword raised.

She said, "It's not your time."

I didn't know whether she meant not their time to die or their time to rule. And yes, I did come up with the demons ruling thought. How could a guy not get Biblical while witnessing history's hottest dominatrix doing her thing over four of the ugliest creatures ever to zip a fly?

"Thank you, white demon," said one of the four in that grating wheeze they used for a voice.

At least I thought he said that. Even with my acute hearing I had difficulty making out words filtered through mud. And the automatic weapons fire didn't help.

Sarah Arias gave them her own version of a Biblical and said, "Be gone."

If I'd been one of that lot? I'd have jumped up and done the Usain Bolt...and that's what I expected. But they didn't get up and run. Rather, they vanished into the mud...probably the quickest way of avoiding nuclear hormones. Don't blame them a bit. And, speaking of Sarah Arias, when she turned those blazing green eyes back onto me, I considered trying to follow those demons.

She said, "Do you know what you've done?"

Never good to hear that from a chick, especially when you've done so many stupid things in your long life. And if you happen to guess the wrong thing-you've-done, the situation goes from deadly to catastrophic. I gave the safest of all bad answers.

"What."

The picture of a male dog canting his head in confusion formed in my mind, and I didn't know if I came up with it myself or if Sarah Arias put it there. I said "What" not as a question, as in "What did I do," but as a statement, as in "What, I'm innocent, and there's no justification for your unseemly behavior."

Sarah Arias stood there for a moment in fiery white perfection. She raised her sword an iota, and despite the sexy green eyes and molded armor around what must be perfect lungs, I diverted all of my focus to that sword. It appeared she understood what I meant by "What." And if she did what I thought her impetuous mind wanted her to do, then I didn't think the rule about having to remove my heart to kill me would apply. I'd simply be dead. And then probably alive within thirty minutes and raining down on some pig pen in hell.

I thought Sarah Arias and I had something going. I mean, we *did* take that trip to Israel and she *did* pretend to be my wife on the flight. We never made it to the hotel, though. So how can a chick go from loving you to wanting to kill you in the blink of an eye? I hadn't come close to solving that nagging question in two thousand years, so I didn't think I'd solve it in the middle of a pitched battle in hell.

Sarah Arias didn't answer my "what" statement when she said, "Maybe it's not too late."

Trust me. It makes you a little more than nervous when your guardian angel isn't sure about something.

"Maybe he will show mercy," she said. "And maybe there's still time for you."

Understood the words—all of them—but none of the meanings.

It may sound strange, but that situation helped calm my thumping heart. Why? Familiar territory for me as far as babes were concerned. And with that sip of calm, my peripheral vision kicked in. I saw armed stripes running for the fence…I also got my first glimpse at the attackers.

I recognized the first face I saw—Bama—dressed in his Confederate uniform. He snipped through the fence with a giant set of bolt cutters while the rest of the boys from the camp laid down covering fire. Each of their shots knocked down a stripe, and I could see chunks explode into the air as the boys' bullets ripped through flesh. The stripes inside the camp returned fire, though I didn't see a single shot find its mark.

The soldier boys from back in the camp had recruited dozens of other men and women to assist in the assault. These new soldiers were dressed in the various uniforms of history—I even saw several fierce-looking Zulu warriors—or as guerillas or partisans from some long-ago war. I zoomed my vampire sight in on Bama and saw, to no surprise, a smile on his face. I mean, who could make this crazy stuff up?

Black-uniformed demons were armed to the teeth, but they stood aside and watched the stripes in their attempts to defend the camp. No luck there, because the defenders could do nothing to stop Bama and his comrades. Once the attackers breached the fence, the battle seemed over. Stripes fell everywhere.

It looked more like a battle reenactment than a real engagement. Except for the stripes. Those poor devils got blown away by the dozens, and I saw close to a hundred either screaming in their own blood or flat out dead. And, if Lumberjack told me the truth, they'd all get back up again to continue suffering death after death after death.

Hell would be a great name for the place.

I didn't understand what was happening or why. I mean yes, the good guys were attacking the bad guys. I got it. But I didn't know if that kind of thing happened all the time or if that day was special. I *did* suspect Sarah Arias didn't always show up in full angelic battle gear.

"You're here to help the demons," Lumberjack had said.

Help the demons, heck. They couldn't even help themselves. Not one of them lifted a finger as Bama and company swept into the camp, and not a single stripe could stand before the wave of good guys.

Not really a wave though, because the stripes far outnumbered the attackers. Thing is, Bama and boys had either better weaponry, body armor, ammunition, or maybe just a better aim. Perhaps all the above. Me help the demons? No way. I stood beside Sarah Arias and watched the cakewalk of a battle wind down. Cakewalk all right. So why did Sarah Arias look so stressed?

I leaned toward her to suggest she relax, and another familiar face caught my eye. Came crashing into focus might be a better way to convey the shock—and renewed fear—that face caused for me. The guy came through the fence low and fast…at the head of a small squad of soldiers also dressed in the crisp uniforms of the World War II German Wehrmacht.

Nazi uniforms, if you want to get technical, but they fought with the good guys. And they wore no Nazi insignia. Once their leader— Helmet—made it through the fence, things happened quickly. The most gargantuan and vaguely human-looking creature I'd ever seen appeared from nowhere and ran for Helmet.

Sarah Arias sprinted after the beast. The creature sported scarred and muscled shoulders as wide as the Grand Canyon. He swung a mace at Helmet that held three spiked balls large enough to drop a herd of rampaging bull elephants.

Sarah Arias deflected his first blow with that gleaming sword. I needed check eBay for one of those things. The clash of weapons emitted an ear-splitting explosion that sent showers of sparks in all directions. I expected to see Sarah Arias lying in her own goo when those sparks cleared. Wrong. She stood with sword upraised to deflect whatever came next…and she didn't look any the worse for wear.

One crazy-dangerous chick.

Good thing Sarah Arias possessed both power and resilience, because if that mace had connected with its intended target, I'm certain my buddy Helmet would have lost a head. Maybe half his upper body.

Helmet. Alive and in his body…in hell and fighting only a dozen yards away. Helmet, who warned me not to step through the portal at the Aachen Cathedral. Helmet, who'd told me not to take the train. He'd shown fear when I spoke about rescuing Sarah Arias. He'd advised me to let it go, to forget her. The demon took another swing and Sarah Arias deflected it with her shield.

He'd been right. Sarah Arias never needed my help. And as I swallowed the truth of what my eyes told me—Helmet fighting his way toward me—the proverbial little birdie in my mind told me Lumberjack might just have been one hundred percent correct.

I was there to help the demons.

TWENTY-EIGHT

GIGANTOSAURUS DEMON TURNED his attention away from Helmet and focused everything on Sarah Arias. No argument from me on that choice. What guy would want to watch another dude when the epitome of feminine perfection stood right in front of him? And as big as Gigantosaurus was, perhaps he had an unobstructed view down the front of Sarah Arias's armor. The big, dumb, lucky pervert.

Sarah Arias parried each of his blows, and so good was she, that it appeared she knew where Gigantosaurus's next strike would land and put up her defense well ahead of his effort. If I had to guess, I'd say the big demon outweighed my guardian angel by six or seven hundred pounds. But that kind of guessing gets a guy in trouble.

I could have watched the fight for hours. Neither of them seemed to tire. Amazing, given my experiences in the numerous edged battles I'd fought through the years. When it's just two people going at each other, one or the other—or both—tends to tire after a couple of minutes. Not with these two. Gigantosaurus attacked, Sarah Arias defended. So yes, I stood mesmerized, and would have remained that way had someone not grabbed my arm.

Helmet said, "We need to go."

"What are you doing here?" I said. "I thought you'd said to avoid the place at all costs."

"I did," he said. "But I knew you'd be too stupid to listen."

Thanks for the vote of confidence, roommate.

"What about Sarah Arias?"

"Leave her."

And yes, it finally dawned on me that leaving Sarah Arias to play with Gigantosaurus might work the best. Despite my strength I saw no way I could be of assistance…unless she wanted me to throw some barbed insults the big demon's way.

I mean, I had the best of those stored in my bag of insults for centuries…waiting to spring them at the right time. But it looked like they'd need languish in that bag. I was pretty sure the bullets flying around couldn't touch Sarah Arias, and it looked like Gigantosaurus would see as much success with her as I experienced with my wandering hand back when Sarah Arias and I snuggled our way to Israel. Some women's defenses are impossible to defeat…even for me.

"Leave her?" I said. "Then why am I here?"

It wasn't Helmet who responded, but rather a familiar wheezy voice from behind me.

No Face said, "I can answer that."

He and the other black-uniformed demons had Helmet and me surrounded.

Perfect.

No Face said, "Grab him," and that's what they did.

But they grabbed Helmet, not me.

My buddy emptied his submachine gun into the first demon to reach for him. It didn't do any good. I expected the demon to crush him, but that didn't happen either. It grabbed him just as ordered.

I thought about weighing in and pummeling that demon's face to cream, but what would be the point? Dozens more of the hideous creatures had appeared. My experience said that although I was more than up to inflicting punishment on a few of them, they were strong enough to overwhelm me with numbers.

Stalemate. Well, kind of. Sarah Arias was winning her struggle with Gigantosaurus, but the rest of the demons pretty much had things as they wanted. And speaking of Sarah Arias, when she saw Helmet surrounded by the black-uniformed demons she let out the most predatory howl I've ever heard, and she used her shield to punch Gigantosaurus in the jaw.

Poor guy went down like the puppet master cut his strings. When he didn't move, I figured he'd be in dreamland for the duration of what was about to go down. I felt a bit sorry for him, but every guy ends up needing to learn his own lessons.

And just like that, the battle died away. Bama may have created the breach in the wire, but he and his buddies only came a few feet into the camp. They held their ground and watched from the periphery. Perhaps they needed to obey some unwritten spiritual rule.

Helmet stood wedged between two demons. He didn't look overly scared but at the same time he didn't look happy. I've described the video Helmet once left running on my computer. The one showing the Americans executing him as a German spy. An American Military Police squad marched him to a sand pit and tied him to a pole. Then they shot him. The look I saw on his face in that video was the same look I saw on his face as he stood between the demons.

I heard weeping to my left and turned to see my warrior angel in tears. Whoa, surprising. Especially given I'd just seen her take out a demon large and mean enough to turn ten great white sharks into sushi. Without a knife. And there she stood crying with her hands over her face.

Freaky.

I reminded myself to walk softly and keep my mouth shut.

She wailed, "Woe to you people of earth."

Do I need to say how frightening that sounded coming from a woman whose entire cast of hormones might just be hanging off the trapeze by a pinkie finger?

"And woe to my precious Gaius of Teutoberg."

Hormones heck. The babe was diggin' me. But then, she resumed the sobbing. I decided I'd better keep an eye on things, just in case I needed to jump off a high cliff into a burning dung pit for a quick escape.

From Sarah Arias, not the demons.

No Face let out a wheezy laugh, and Soyla picked that moment to appear in her sleek black uniform. And darn, if she didn't look just as hot as Sarah Arias...but in an evil, Disney queen sort of way. But I'd had enough of Soyla to last a few years, or at least until she resumed sexting me her portfolio. My sexy Hungarian warrior-woman took a long look at Sarah Arias, and she sneered at the tears.

"She's not for you, my love."

Right.

Like a chick that fakes being my main squeeze while really planning to snuff me would be the one I'd choose to introduce to my parents.

"Sarah," I said, "Can I borrow your sword?"

Sarah Arias didn't respond. And judging by that giant demon unconscious at her feet, perhaps it would end up better of all of us if she kept the sword and used it herself. I mean, I could borrow da Vinci's brushes...but don't expect the Mona Lisa out of me.

"She's defeated," said a calm and friendly voice that belonged to a person that hadn't been there the moment before. Dr. Mengele.

"Defeated?" I said. "Does that mean Gigantosaurus gets the championship belt?" I paused and added, "*After* he wakes up?"

Mengele laughed.

"She's your guardian," he said. "And she's failed."

Yes, but she never really had a chance once I kicked in the stupidity.

But Dr. Mengele—or Helmet—or Bama and his squad—or any of the demons looking on—didn't need to know that.

I said, "This is about me?"

It didn't seem right. Especially since it was Helmet the demons held. And Sarah Arias didn't start her weeping thing until Helmet showed up. As I reasoned it, that could only mean one of two things. Either Helmet's capture would result in some dire consequence for mankind and thus for me...or Sarah Arias was cheating on me.

Well, Sarah Arias and I weren't really a thing, but Helmet had to know that I saw her first. And he needed to remember it...I mean, now that he'd acquired a body that I could choke the life out of. Thoughts of my hands around Helmet's neck vanished when Dr. Mengele laughed again.

"Idiot boy, of course it's not about you," he said, and he held up an arm to point to nowhere in general. "This place is never about one person."

No way to disagree with that. They'd murdered a million and a half in the earth-bound versions. Mengele's masters went after the Jews on my side of the veil. But here, what were they after? What group merited that unwanted attention?

"All of mankind," said Sarah Arias, and she spoke in a voice of such sadness I felt like having a cry with her.

"Wait a second," I said, "are you doing that mind-reading thing again?"

That tickled Mengele's funny bone and he let out another prissy laugh. Glad someone was having fun. Sarah Arias had morphed from a puddle of tears to looking like someone who'd just scraped her flattened puppy up off the pavement.

Strange stuff, but she still had that pile of demon that was once Gigantosaurus laying at her feet, and I noticed No Face kept a nervous eye on her…and on that gleaming sword. Helmet? He looked positively defeated. Despite the Prussian bearing.

Sarah Arias shook her head.

"I can't read your mind."

Right. We'd been through that lie already. But if all this wasn't about me and not *only* about Helmet…

"So, what's this about?" I said. "No need to keep secrets. You've won."

"Indeed," said Mengele. "It's about…"

A scream and a flash. Somebody rocketed past me and into the two demons restraining Helmet. They flew in random directions… like two black-uniformed—and hideous—bowling pins. Only Helmet remained standing. Untouched. Well, only Helmet and the attacker remained standing. Lumberjack.

He'd told me he'd played in the National Football League. A defensive lineman. And he'd just peeled away the blockers and was ready to sack the quarterback. Mengele.

The evil twit said, "I'm untouchable."

Lumberjack decided to help Mengele redefine the word. And sack the quarterback he did. Not only did Mengele's polished shoes go flying, so did one of his socks. Lumberjack rolled over Mengele and he regained his feet. Mengele did not.

Lumberjack did a sack dance, pumped his fists in the air, and then he leaned back his head and roared to the sky. I never got to thank him. Not properly, because as I heard Sarah Arias's "Get moving" order in my head—and yes, I think she planted the words directly into my brain, the little liar—a few of the stripes stitched Lumberjack with a volley from their automatic weapons.

He went down nearly as hard as Gigantosaurus had.

Sarah Arias went from weepy and vulnerable to fierce warrior mode in the blink of an eye. Authentic soccer mom stuff. No Face stepped forward to paw at Helmet, but I could see his heart wasn't in it. He only had eyes for Sarah Arias…and that sword of hers. My angel took a step toward No Face and the demon fell to his knees. It tears at my heart to see a guy realize that nothing he can do or say can save himself from an angry woman.

Lumberjack died without regaining consciousness, so I never will know why he helped us. I knew he'd died at least one time before and probably many times since. That kind of thing happens in hell.

"Get moving!"

This time it was Bama encouraging us from his spot inside the fence. I looked around to determine how many stripes we'd need to bowl over, and I was also more than a little concerned about all that weaponry I'd seen earlier. But I didn't need to worry. Stripped of their leader—Dr. Mengele—and demon protectors, they showed even less appetite for engaging Sarah Arias than the kneeling No Face and his cadre of demons.

The stripes also fell on their faces in front of Sarah Arias, and a few wailed for mercy. I suspected they wanted her to sheath her sword, but as I listened to their pleas, I realized I was wrong. Redemption. That's what they screamed for, and the hopelessness in their pleading chilled me more than anything else had in hell.

Did I say it chilled me? No. It downright terrified me.

I grabbed Helmet and pulled him toward the fence…toward Bama and his buddies standing with weapons held loose and unimportant at their sides. I took a moment to consider how odd it felt to touch Helmet. He'd always been a ghost to me…something with no physical form. So yes, it felt different to lay a hand on him.

Different, but also nice.

For the first time since departing Bama's camp and boarding the train to infinite death I felt something good in my heart. Short-lived though, because right after that that warm feeling I felt something cold...also in my heart.

I'd forgotten about Soyla.

TWENTY-NINE

EVEN ON HER best days, Soyla is not only a self-absorbed, selfish, arrogant, egotist, but she also insists that every man within eyesight make her the center of his attention. Anything short of that and you end up dealing with an irrational and infinitely dangerous Hungarian warrior-women. As luck would have it, most days guys are more than happy to make Soyla the center of their world. That day, I didn't happen to be one of them. I paid for the oversight with cold metal ripping open my skin and piercing my heart.

"You didn't say goodbye, my love."

OK. All those things I said about Soyla? I forgot to add raging lunatic. Though, I think I can be forgiven for omitting that because no man that's ever lived would be brave enough to write down that diagnosis. The knife or sword or whatever Soyla stuck into my back devoured my strength and I sunk to my knees.

A strong arm wrapped around me and pulled me up before my face planted itself into the mud of Auschwitz.

Helmet.

He said, "Move."

Helmet was the third person to tell me to move in less than a minute.

Do people think I'm lazy? He half dragged me as I attempted to put one foot in front of the other. I looked back over my shoulder. Soyla would certainly return for another pass. I didn't know if she'd destroyed my heart to the point I'd finally die—for the first time—but I knew if I waited around, she'd make sure she did just that. Somewhere in the back of my mind I knew there was still a contract out on me, and that Soyla received double compensation if she did the deed herself.

As it turned out, I didn't need to worry. Yes, I did catch sight of Soyla moving toward me for her version of a coup de grace. She never reached me. A flash of light and Soyla flying in the opposite direction. There's something about a cold, edged weapon tearing into a guy's heart that makes the excruciating pain demand most of his concentration, so I had ever-decreasing brain cycles available for considering the ramifications of Sarah Arias knocking Soyla to the moon.

Sarah Arias leaned toward me and whispered one word into my ear. It sounded a lot like "Bitch," but I think angels aren't allowed to use those kinds of words…especially when they're speaking Hebrew. I laughed, and it hurt. I could feel my blood pumping out and over my back…and Helmet's strong arm keeping me moving for the opening in the fence…toward what I felt certain represent safety.

If I didn't die from the wound.

And if I did die? At least I knew they wouldn't leave my dead body inside that hellhole…that I wouldn't need to wake up and die all over again as Dr. Mengele performed one experiment on me after another. I *hoped* so, anyway. As we reached the fence, I forced another glance over my shoulder and saw Soyla lying prone among the demons.

"Goodbye," I said in a shaky, raspy voice. "My love."

I kind of regretted saying that as soon as the words passed my lips, and I can't say what happened after that because all the blood that flowed out of my body left none to power my brain. Either of them. My mind faded into blackness.

I didn't dream.

But I did wake up…in a tent back in Bama's camp. I think it was frying bacon that brought me back to consciousness. Not real meat, as Bama had said before, but something that tasted like it. Because there was no requirement for a death to feed a man there. No need for blood. I glanced around the tent and was half-disappointed to see nobody hovering nearby…wringing their hands over my dying body.

I guess everyone knew I'd live. At least I hoped I'd lived. No telling in this place. My chest ached.

So, no Sarah Arias nearby as my eyes fluttered open, and no possibility of Soyla anywhere close. On the positive side, at least I didn't need to hold in that empty-stomach version of a ten-megaton belch that must have been percolating for however long I'd been out. I let it fly.

"Pig"

Note to self: an empty tent does not mean a soundproof tent.

Sarah Arias walked through the open flap in those blue jeans she used to wear as a bagger and with that oversized, non-descript sweater. The odor of stale tobacco smoke wafted in after her. It made me smile.

I said, "You've been worried about me."

"Why would you think that?"

"Smells like you burned through a couple of packs outside."

"I can't help it if that's the designated smoking area. You're lucky I hung around at all."

"Don't you have to? Being my guardian angel and everything?"

Sarah Arias sat down on the edge of my cot.

"You're lucky about that too," she said.

She absently pulled a fresh pack of cigs from her purse, looked at them with longing, and stowed them for later.

Sarah Arias stared at me for several moments the way chicks do when they want to make sure you will actually hear what they're about to drop on you.

"Goodbye, my love?"

Uh-oh.

I'd forgotten I'd said that to Soyla. Remember when I mentioned how I regretted saying those words as soon as they passed my lips? I thought I was about to find out why.

Time for some misdirection.

"Why are you saying goodbye to me?"

Sarah Arias rolled her eyes.

"I'm not saying anything," she said, "And a *my love* from me?" she'd used a Hungarian accent, "In your dreams."

OK. Compelling evidence existed she could read my mind. Now I had to worry about her nosing through my dreams?

"What's going on here?" I said, still working the misdirection angle.

She said, "It's what *you* said. To that female vampire who stuck the knife in your back."

"Do angels ever lie?"

Sarah Arias shook her head.

"Joke?"

Another shake of the head.

"Then I must have been delirious…that I mistakenly thought I was speaking to you."

"No," replied Sarah Arias, "it appears you were just…you."

Busted.

After all she must have seen me do over the years, all she'd gleaned from my mind, and all that snooping in thousands of dreams I couldn't even remember myself, how could I ever look her in the eye again?

She said, "You'll find a way."

Was she reading my mind right after she'd just claimed she couldn't?

Evidently angels *could* fib. I forgot about all that when she rubbed a hand gently over the sore parts of my chest…which was pretty much all of it. Fireworks careened through my body, everything went numb and my shoulders tingled.

"I'll give you just ten hours to get your hands off me."

Sarah Arias smiled and said, "You wish."

Yes, it felt like heaven all right, but something popped into my mind that ruined it all. I needed an answer and I wanted it immediately.

"Do you also watch over me when I use the bathroom?"

Sarah Arias didn't confirm that. More importantly, she also didn't deny it.

It was crucial to me to always remember two things. First, Sarah Arias was always watching. Wonderful. The second? Never, ever, ever, under any conditions paint a mental picture or fantasize, for even a millisecond, a three-way-date consisting of Sarah Arias, Soyla, and me.

"Pig."

She stopped rubbing my chest and stood up.

"Stew is cooking for you," she said. "You're well enough to take nourishment."

She took a step toward the tent flap.

"Just a second."

She stopped and turned to me; two perfect blonde eyebrows raised in a question mark.

"The woe business," I said. "What was it? Woe to man and woe to me."

When I sat up, I found that Sarah Arias's touch had chased away the pain.

"What was up with that?"

She said, "That?"

"Yeah."

At first, she said nothing more and I worried that my question would end up in the Too-Sensitive-to-Answer folder, though I thought I saw a battle raging in Sarah Arias's mind. "Should I tell him or should I not," and maybe, "How much trouble am I going to get into if I do." Sarah Arias walked back to the cot and sat down beside me. I swung my legs over the edge.

She said, "I was ordered to the camp."

I pretty much understood that part. At least I did by then. No Face told me her side sentenced her to time in the camp, and that it would drive her crazy. He also claimed he'd be going too. Enter that old cliché advising liars to salt everything with a portion of the truth. And boy… did I feel stupid.

"I figured that much out."

Sarah Arias smiled. "And what else do you know?"

I hoped she didn't mean that literally.

"That I got used," I said, and Sarah Arias continued the smile. "Again," I added.

That wiped the condescending grin from her face. Yeah, she'd done the same thing a few months ago. I don't care how noble the cause. I never like it when those I trust turn me into their tool.

But, like I've already said, that's a different story.

"Yes, used," Sarah Arias said. "Darkness understood the omen of my presence."

Say what?

When she spoke that kind of horror movie lingo it reminded me that Sarah Arias wasn't of my world…that she was more alien than most chicks.

"Omen?"

"Yes," she said. "The altar."

Of course. The altar. I should have seen that from the beginning.

"What altar?"

And why did Sarah Arias sit so close? I mean, our thighs were touching, and a couple of times she brushed her foot over mine in a casually-on purpose, accidental way.

"The altar of the martyrs." She sat up straighter and looked hard into my eyes. "You don't know anything about it, do you?"

Ouch.

"You tell me. I mean, you should know, right? Because if I understand this guardian angel thing, if I ever pop a bleeding hemorrhoid, you'll get the 411 before my underwear knows about it."

Had I just mentioned bathroom stuff to a gorgeous babe? Sarah Arias looked at me for a second and shook her head.

"Grow up." And then, "The souls of martyred are gathered under the altar. And from there they constantly cry out for justice."

Right.

How did Bullwinkle put it? "Eenie meenie chili beanie, the spirits are about to speak." Hey, but I was willing to put up with it for as long as she wanted to play footsies.

"So, what does that have to do with me?"

She said, "Nothing," and then added, "At least not directly."

"Then why don't we talk in indirectlies?"

She laughed, and I heard the melodious sound of a thousand songbirds welcoming a cool spring morning. I hope you appreciate how long it took me to come up with that line of bull. Anyway, her answer did a lot to calm the nervous bile rising toward my throat. Being a martyred soul crying out for justice under some altar isn't in my five-year plan.

"The end times," she said. "You have heard of Armageddon?"

"Who hasn't? Big battle. Billions of casualties or something like that."

She nodded and waited for me to say more. I took the opportunity to run my left foot over hers, and she kicked it away without the expression on her face changing. I continued.

"The end of the world."

Sarah Arias shook her head at that. "Not the end of the world," she said. "But a new beginning. The way it was intended."

She let that sink in. Wasted effort on her part, because I didn't see anything good about that kind of new beginning.

"You're right about the casualties," she said. "And horrible as that carnage will be, it pales in comparison to the plagues that will be visited on man."

"Hence the woe?"

She nodded

"And the tears?"

She took my hand in hers and I couldn't imagine how signals could get more mixed. One second she's swatting away my foot, the next she's grabbed my hand. Chicks control the boundaries. Even in heaven.

"We who guard will be withdrawn," she said. "And most of us end up loving those we watch." She let that sink in and added, "Do you need to ask about my tears?"

Great response. I think.

"And No Face lured me to the camp to kick all this off?"

She nodded.

"Wouldn't that also spell the end for him?"

"It does," she said. "But although they can quote scripture, they've never believed it."

I thought about that for a second. Evidently No Face and his crowd had it all laid out in front of them, and still, they didn't believe it. Was there a lesson in that for me?

I didn't think so.

"So, the end of the world," and I held up my hand when she looked like she would interrupt, "beginning of the world," I corrected myself, "*does* have something to do with me."

"Only indirectly."

"I don't understand, because you said No Face lured me to the camp after they read an omen."

"It wasn't Mestephos who lured you into the camp," she said. "It was the other way around."

That stopped my mental elevator between floors. And in the shock, I did something incredibly stupid. I released her hand so that I could wave both of mine in protest.

I said, "I did nothing of the sort."

"But you did. And you're the reason I was there. The omen."

"No," I said. "You must be smoking some heavenly weed."

That got another laugh.

"We don't do that kind of thing."

That's what they all say.

"I didn't know you'd show up at that camp," she said. And then, "But somebody did."

"Predestination?"

"No," she said. "Never that. But knowing what is going to happen in no way influences the decisions that are made."

Crazy chick alert. I decided to try to extricate the conversation from the mire of mumbo-jumbo and return it to something I understood.

"So, you were ordered to the camp because someone on your side knew I'd show up there?"

She nodded.

"And No Face figured if you showed up, then so would I?"

Another nod.

"So, he visited me in Germany to make sure I didn't get cold feet?"

She said, "Keep going."

I tried to keep going, but I couldn't. Brick wall. I mean, if I accepted that Sarah Arias showed up in the camp because someone knew I'd be there, then if I took that thread to the next logical step, I came to… What? Me in the camp.

Hardly the end of the world. And what about the martyrs? What did that have to do with me? Almost nothing, according to my guardian angel. She looked disappointed at my inability to take more than a single baby step before falling on my face.

"Sorry," I said. "But the stuff you're laying on me? *Me* bringing Armageddon."

"It will happen," she said. "But that doesn't mean any of us looks forward to it."

She took my hand again and I noticed she seemed to have moved a bit closer to me.

My seducing angel?

She said, "You wish."

The mind-reading trick. She could make a fortune in a carnival.

"But I thought you said it all wasn't about me."

Another nod, and I stopped just short of asking, "Well then who the heck is it all about." The reason I stopped? An answer popped into my mind.

"Helmet."

She hadn't started the freaky woe malarkey and the ocean of tears until Helmet showed up. I twisted the thought in my mind… examined it at several angles. It made sense. I looked to Sarah Arias for confirmation. She only stared back at me. No smile. No nod.

And it was all the confirmation I needed.

Sarah Arias was ordered to the camp because some entity thought— no, knew—I'd be stupid enough to take the word of a demon and follow my testosterone-infused radar into hell so that I could play the hero and rescue my damsel in distress. And I'd do it despite sane minds trying to beat enough sense into me to stop me before things got out of hand…which usually happens for me as soon as I start something. That same omnipresent entity also understood Helmet would follow—something *even I* didn't know.

As far as the opposing team? If I understood Sarah Arias correctly, they didn't have a clue what was happening when an angel showed up in the middle of their playground…meaning her showing up during their Aachen fiasco last summer. In addition to irritating the heck out of them—and likely scaring the bejeebers of the demon population—Sarah Arias's presence got the red team thinking.

I didn't know for sure, but I'd have been willing to place a large wager against poor odds that angels showing up on the demon's side of the tracks indicates a monumentally important battle is on the way. And the demons knew Sarah Arias belonged to me—or maybe the other way around—and they scratched their collective warty heads to figure out what connection I had with Auschwitz.

No connection at all. I wondered for a moment how long it stumped them and how frustrated they became. Somehow, they got around to noticing Helmet. I didn't know how that happened, though I could smell Soyla somewhere in that. No Face didn't need to remind his superiors that he'd dealt with me before, and it probably wasn't a hard sell to convince them he could lead me into doing something idiotic. He'd done it before.

So, he received authorization to check on things…hence his visit to Bad Homburg, his one-day gig at the commissary, and his insistence on coming home with me and going out with the bagger gang. He needed to get inside my flat to confirm Helmet inhabited the place. I recalled how they'd exchanged glances.

As far as the makeup and the pencil skirt? I suspected it was optional…

his choice. Like, who did he think he was fooling by cramming his hideous bulk into a form-fitting skirt that was at least a dozen sizes too small? I levered my mind away from the sickening memory.

"So why the woe stuff? I mean, you whipped those demons like you caught them stealing chickens."

"The woe," she said, and she reached inside that old leather purse she used to carry back in her grocery bagging days and moved stuff around the way women do when looking for that "one thing" amongst all the mysterious knick-knacks. It didn't surprise me when she pulled out a pack of cigarettes and a red disposable lighter.

"Your bad habits follow you into hell?"

She gave me a distracted glance as she lit one of the sticks.

"Hell?" she said. "Why do you think this is hell?"

"Uh, did you have a chance to look around? I mean, I know making the locals in the death camp miserable must have taken concentration and kicking that giant demon's butt left little time to smell the roses. But still," I said, "didn't you notice the suffering? And who do you think runs the place? You trying to tell me we're really in North Korea?"

"Not who you think," she said, and when I looked blankly back at her she added, "he's the ruler of the earth."

The earth? Talk about an uneasy feeling. I hoped she didn't mean who I thought she meant. But then again, it would explain a few things…like why I never seem to get a second date. In the no-smoking tent or not, Sarah Arias lit up took a long drag on her cigarette and exhaled the prim way some women handle that chore. When you think about it, expelling smoke from your body isn't much different from expelling anything else from your body. Could a chick make a loud belch look as sexy?

"This isn't hell?"

"Do you know what language we're speaking?"

"I'm told it's Hebrew."

"That's what you call it," and by *you* I understood Sarah Arias meant people in general…not me specifically.

"And what do you call it?"

Another drag on her cancer stick and Sarah Arias said, "Nothing. It's just what we speak."

Interesting.

"And the demons speak it too?"

"Yes," she said. "Though we don't call them demons."

"Then what do you call them?"

I half expected to hear some sort of locker-room put-down, but it didn't come. She answered in less than a heartbeat, so I knew she spoke the truth when she said, "Angels."

Angels. Right.

"You trying to tell me they started off just like you and then let themselves go?"

"Something like that."

I tried to imagine No Face before the evil makeover. His Donna version left more to be desired than just his/her hair, nails, and sense of fashion. He couldn't get a ticket to the same universe as Sarah Arias much less the same ballpark. And dredging up the disgusting image of him gave rise to another question.

"Could it still happen to you?"

She must have expected the question because once again, she answered immediately.

It came out sounding petulant when she said, "No."

Like perhaps denying an accusation that contained a half-truth.

"Are they still recruiting."

Sarah Arias stared at me for a second, dropped her cigarette on the ground inside the tent, and stamped it.

"Yes," she said. "Always after us. Always promising." She thought for a second and then, "Always accusing."

A kind of melancholy came over her, so I decided to pull the conversation out of the rabbit hole I'd sent it down. Not being an angel myself and thus unable to lie about my capability for mind reading, I had no clue what she was thinking. Whatever it was, it made her sad enough that I didn't want to know.

I said, "So this isn't hell."

She nodded.

"So where are we then?"

She said, "We don't have time enough to fully explain."

"Above my simple, mortal brain?"

She looked at me like I'd just slapped her.

"How dare you," she said, and her voice began rising as she continued. "You've had every opportunity. Two thousand years and not one moment's concern from you."

"Sarah, I..." She held up her hand.

"Don't play that with me. You don't care about three billion people dead? Fine, you live with it. But don't you ever take that whiney tone with me because I'm not spoon-feeding you something people with half your intelligence already know."

Ouch.

On the bright side, Sarah Arias thought I was twice as smart as *some* people. It almost made me smile. Almost, because how could I smile when she said three billion people will die?

"And when did you say this is kicking off?"

She waited to light another cigarette before answering. Now *there's* the Sarah Arias I remember.

"Nobody knows," she said.

Nobody what?

I felt my own anger rising.

"Perfect, Sarah," I said, "Because for a second there I could have sworn you were blaming it all on me."

"Oh, it will happen," she said. "And it drives great fear into our hearts."

"Why?" I said. "Looked to me like you folks are pretty much bulletproof."

She took my hand in hers.

"Nothing will change for us," she said. And then quickly added, "The white angels."

"And?"

"But it will spell the end of the dark angels," she said. "And their boss."

Ah, the silver lining. What are three billion human deaths against a monopoly in...in wherever we were.

"The end of them? Where are they going?"

"Find out for yourself," she said. And then under her breath she said, "And perhaps you'll not be one of the three billion."

I didn't know what to say...mostly because I didn't know what to think. Sarah Arias grabbed my other hand—she now had them both—and pulled it until our faces were a few inches apart. Sometime during the conversation, her tears had returned. I saw them streaming down her face, each a tiny crystal bottle with a message rolled up inside. Messages for me.

Condemnation? Desperation? Hope?

"Helmut has a position under the altar," she said. "Mestephos hoped to put him there."

"Position?"

She nodded and said, "The end times will not begin until the final martyr cries out for justice."

Was she telling me that Helmet was the final martyr?

Maybe, but that other part didn't make sense. If No Face worked for the red team, and they'd cease to exist after all was said and done… It seemed better to delay things as much as possible. That's how a guy's mind works. Logic. I think Sarah Arias did her mind-reading thing again because she answered the point I didn't ask.

"They think they can win," she said. "But they can't. When all is done, they will be gone."

Speaking of done, I thought she was done with the conversation because she fell silent for a while and sat there holding my hand. A silent, beautiful chick holding my hands in hers.

You'll get no complaint from me.

And, as far as the conversation was concerned, I admit I'd have been A-OK with no more of that. The end of the world is not something I like to think of as a milestone sitting on anyone's schedule.

Sarah Arias stood and walked out of the tent. Just like that. No farewell. No exchange of email addresses. Nothing. I didn't try to stop her because I had some thinking to do. That's a PC way of saying I knew she'd eventually get around to leaving anyway, so I just wanted to sit there and savor the way my hands felt. After her touch.

I waited for several minutes, eyes closed and Sarah Arias fantasy-engine running at full speed. Everything starts with holding hands, right? After that, the sky's the limit. I sensed someone opening the tent flap.

"Excuse me."

Helmet in his Texas twang…the one he picked up when, as a child, he visited his grandfather across the sea.

"Can we talk?"

I stood and walked outside.

THIRTY

SUNLIGHT HIT ME as soon as I passed through the flap. I've read novels where the author writes about bathing in sunlight or some similar overwritten tripe to make the chicks believe he has a romantic mind. This time though, sunlight bathing over me or being awash in sunlight applies. It was that warm thing that doesn't make you sweat…like the best morning you could hope for in late in spring or early in autumn.

The air around me felt so perfect that it was as if my skin had placed the order. I'd like to say Helmet stood there smiling, but that would be a lie. I'd only ever seen him smile at my physical pain—like when Bernard threw me out of my own apartment window a few months ago—or at my emotional distress—like when some chick I've managed to talk over comes to her senses and vamooses. None of that was happening in this land of—what was it? Hell? Sheol? Cleveland?

I said, "How's my martyr?"

It came out sharper than I'd intended. Truth was, he didn't deserve accusations.

"Funny," he said. "Only someone forgot to tell me."

Right.

"I'm just a German spy that got caught and executed."

Just your everyday incompetent spy who didn't take his assigned place under the altar of the martyrs…who happens to be the last of those martyrs who, so if he remains under the altar, he kicks off the destruction and rebirth of the world.

And I'm just a guy who likes my meat a little rarer than most.

"Cut the baloney," I said. "You could have filled me in before I jumped through all the hoops."

"Tried to," he said, "but you've never listened before."

"Maybe that's because you've never said anything before. Three years of silence and you finally speak up a couple hours before I set out to commit an act of gross buffoonery? Thanks, pal."

Helmet didn't look the least put out by my scolding. Typical. Germans think they're justified in doing whatever the heck they end up doing. Anyone who disagrees with them must be crazy.

"Relax," he said. "I've already said I didn't know."

"Nice talking with you, buddy," I said, "But I'm sure you need to get going. Aren't you supposed to be destroying the world or something?"

This time Helmet did react. He stopped walking with me and grabbed my arm. I can report now that his touch didn't feel anything like what I got from Sarah Arias. Nor from Soyla, come to think about it.

I said, "So how'd you get to Bad Homburg anyway?"

"The autobahn," he said. "Like everyone else."

"Funny."

"Sarah," he said.

That one word said everything. Sarah Arias of the guardian angel corps. More specifically, *my* guardian angel. The woe-to-man pinup girl. She said it involved three billion dead…one of them me. Had she helped Helmet escape to give me more time? I didn't know. One thing I did know, though. Old Bama understood all the intricacies of cooking breakfast, because that food smelled like heaven.

I wouldn't let Helmet get away so easily, so I prodded him with, "And?"

"Can't say more," Helmet said. "And give me your word you'll not ask."

I thought about it for a second.

"Answer one thing, and then you have my word."

Even though he looked dubious, Helmet nodded.

"If I can."

"You said Sarah. Did she help you escape?" Not the real question, so I added, "And help you find me?"

Helmet made to open his mouth and then shut it.

"Sorry," he said. "I can't get that specific."

Helmet's answer would have disappointed me except for one thing. He was emphatically nodding his head yes while he was speaking.

Everyone's a comedian. But he'd better remember that only I am allowed to be funny back at the flat. I'll reconsider that rule when he begins paying his share…or when he starts removing Karl's tokens of love.

"We going back together?"

Helmet shook his head.

"We'll have breakfast," he said, "These men will escort you to the portal. I need more substantial help."

Bama heard. He looked up at us as he rearranged the fake meat that passed for bacon. Captain Frog sauntered up to the fire and handed me a note written on vellum.

"For Mademoiselle Bokor."

The immortal body of Captain Frog wanted me to pass French freakin' poetry to the chick who tried to kill me?

"OK," I said, acknowledging the truism that solidarity among guys melts away when you throw a hot babe into the mix. "I'll make sure she gets it."

Not.

Yeah, like I'm going to hunt her down and say "Here, Soyla. From your wannabe squeeze in heaven, hell, Sheol, purgatory...you fill in the blank. There ya go, and have a good time cutting me open and pulling out my internal organs."

Like that's going to happen.

Captain Frog gave me a curt bow and then looked hard into my eyes and added, "It's sealed."

Don't you love it when a person begs you to do them a favor that they don't trust you to accomplish? Helmet caught my eye and rolled both of his. He bent over and whispered something about his willingness to clean one of Karl's steaming piles off the floor if I let him borrow the note.

After all this, my buddy still had the hots for Soyla. But I don't hold it against him, and I don't mind the competition.

The rest of the camp boys showed for breakfast, and soon we were eating and chatting. I had all the same questions about death and afterward that I had when I stepped through the portal, though nobody would speak of those things because, if I read Helmet right, the topic was taboo. And why should they care? These guys were all alive in immortal bodies and out on a perpetual camping trip with their buddies.

Helmet and the German soldier spoke a lot during that breakfast. I didn't mind. Now that I knew he could speak there'd be time to catch up with him at the flat. One interesting thing to note is that the two of them whispered. I suspected they were up to something until they both laughed. I *knew* they were up to something. The German soldier walked away for a few seconds and came back carrying a case of bottles. German beer.

I leaned over to Bama and said, "They allow beer here?"

He said, "Depends on how old you are."

"Two thousand old enough?"

Bama nodded. "'spect so."

"But beer? Here?"

Captain Frog looked at me and said, "Where do you think it was invented?"

"Heaven?"

"No," he said. "France, of course. But we have a reliable importer."

Helmet and the other German soldier handed everyone a bottle, and the caps came off easy enough.

Captain Frog stood and said, "A toast, my comrades. To another battle won."

"Hear, hear," they all said, and each took a long draw on his bottle.

German beer is the gold standard on my side of earth. This stuff? It was like I'd been drinking beaver urine all of my life. My mind lacks the necessary skill in similes to string together the proper words to describe how good that cold beer tasted.

So, I'll leave the fantasizing to you.

I liked seeing Helmet happy and talking. I also liked seeing him in his body. Odd how I always thought you lived the afterlife— if one existed—somewhere over the rainbow and only in spirit. Misconception. Seems life on earth means living in an imperfect body and afterlife on earth puts you in spirit form. Take Helmet, for instance. Why he preferred floating around the flat to hanging out with these guys was beyond me.

Of course, there was that bit about the altar and the three billion casualties. I considered him a friend all right, but it's hard to have that comfortable buddy relationship with a guy who walks through walls. Bottom lining it, afterlife on earth: spirit, afterlife in APOTA (a place other than earth): physical form. Who'd have known?

We ate our breakfast and Bama added a few bonus items when he scooped some yellow mushy stuff on each of our plates.

"Grits," he said.

The taste matched the name, but I kept my mouth shut because beer worked great for washing down anything. And the more grits I ate, the more beer I'd need.

I could tell you how Helmet disappeared after breakfast while I was doing the thing bodies on both sides of the veil need to do after a few beers. I came out of the woods and Helmet was gone. I could also describe how Bama and the boys gathered up their backpacks and took me for a nice stroll to the portal, and how I didn't need to endure the unforgettable site of tortured bodies raining down from the sky. But that would be anticlimactic.

Truth was, I didn't enjoy the hike as much as I could have…as much as I wanted to. Bad things waited for me on the other side. The Seven fragmented and with most of the pygmy crew after my head. There was also Soyla. I'd need to deal with those things, and quickly. Worse though, I needed to face Herr Doktor with rent due within the week. He always gets cranky and suspicious with money time coming on.

I said my goodbyes and stepped through the portal into Aachen. Still night there, and I wondered if any time had passed at all. I scanned for signs of The Seven. No luck. Or maybe good luck, I didn't know which. Just because I couldn't see them didn't mean they weren't there.

Soyla was a different story. She'd find her way back. I mean, she wasn't just a perfect female body with a semi-psychotic mind. She also had a brain. And with my luck, the next time I saw her she'd either kill me right away or ask for her money.

Yes.

Money.

I'd hired her, hadn't I?

Soyla would claim she was playing along with The Seven...that she'd helped me through the portal and assisted me in completing the useless rescue mission. All she had to do was point out I was back and alive...that she was playing a role the whole time and on my side to the bitter end.

Oh, she'd demand millions all right. And after I paid her—I couldn't prove she *wasn't* on my side—she might just go back to trying to complete the hit-for-hire and get a little of The Seven's fortune. Two jobs, two employers, two paychecks. The business side of Soyla. The female side? Well, I'd left the camp with another woman.

The fact that I had no choice because I'd bled out due to a knife Soyla put into my heart? Wouldn't make a bit of difference to her. That's how she thinks. *Women.* And speaking of women, I caught sight of Sister Christian running to me. She threw her arms around me and gave me one of those full body-bind hugs.

She said, "It didn't work?"

That answered the question about the passage a time.

"No," I said. "Couldn't break through."

The lie didn't bother me a bit. How could I tell my friends about what went on and then expect them to keep their sanity? A selfish part of me wanted to unload all of it on Sister Christian, to see if I could find relief from the things I'd experienced by pushing it out of my brain and into hers. But that's not what friends do. I might be a vampire, but I don't use people when I don't *need* to. Says a lot about me, doesn't it?

And when the word vampire flashed through my mind, I realized I had the hunger. Not quite the bloodlust, but not far from it. I needed to disengage from the crowd.

Perhaps I could find that other boar.

"Sorry," said Sister Christian, and then, "I need to tell you something."

She admitted to praying the door wouldn't open for me. *Praying*. That reminded me I needed to think about the people-storms I'd witnessed, and the thing Lumberjack said about a gift. Did I say it reminded me? The truth is, I didn't need reminding at all. All that other stuff—The Seven and Soyla—was just an excuse to put my mind on other things. I left hell with a lot of unanswered questions.

"No worries," I said. "I found out from one of those little cannibal guys that the mission was a fake from the start. Nobody's in danger."

Sister Christian let out a long exhale and hugged me even tighter. If it lasted much longer I could melt. I mentally kicked myself as I released her.

I said, "Let's get home."

"The gang's waiting in the van."

"Good," I said, and I followed Sister Christian to where the rest of them sat waiting.

I scanned for signs of Soyla or The Seven during our walk and I didn't relax until I was sitting among my friends. I half expected to hear "Good evening, my love," as we passed through some of the darker spots. Then there'd be the knife.

It was good to see the bagger gang again. Once more they'd stepped up and risked themselves for me. Nobody knows more than me that I don't deserve their loyalty, but that's the thing about love, isn't it? If you ever think you *deserve* it, then probably you don't.

We rode in silence. Maybe everyone was disappointed at our apparent failure—the boys didn't seem to believe the malarkey about the mission being scrubbed—and I felt a smidgeon of guilt for not coming clean. When I thought about it, I really did fail...just in a different way from how they thought. When the destination ends up the same, does the road you take matter?

We all got out at the Frankfurt train station and went our separate ways. Nobody asked for clarification as to why The Seven and Soyla pulled a prank on me…and that was good. I needed to focus my mind on restraining the growing need for blood.

And I leveraged that need to focus on not attacking my friends to imprison all thoughts of what I'd experienced over the past day and a half to that temporary holding tank we all keep in the back of our minds. The place for the bad stuff we don't want to confront every second of the day.

Truth is, I'd not known a moment of rest since that night my Nellie left me for the other side of the veil. I thought about that and decided that it wasn't quite right. I'd slept well in Bama's camp. Seven hours of forgetfulness, and for that I was grateful.

But Nellie wasn't there when I woke up.

I thought about Helmet and hoped he'd be waiting when I got back to the flat. If he wasn't, I'd give it a day or two before I went out and searched for him. I'd go back to hell for him, if that's what it took. He'd done it for me.

I boarded the S3 for Bad Homburg and got off at Oberursel…my hunting forest. Somewhere out there was an old boar who would not see the dawn.

AUTHOR'S NOTE

I AM THE son of a Holocaust survivor. The horrors of that time hover over my life, as I've discovered it does for other children of survivors. To some extent, it shapes who we become. My father put it behind him for many years, and only began speaking about it beyond the family in his sunset years.

At first, I thought the Holocaust was about a discrete event in history that was perpetrated by a few people. Maybe that's correct, but maybe not. After all, it's not the only example of people enslaving and murdering those with different cultural values, religious beliefs, or political leanings. It's not even the last time it has happened.

"Never again" is the rally cry of survivors like my dad, who actively campaigned against bigotry, hate, and mistrust. He was a champion of free speech and freedom of expression…artistic, political, every aspect. Only with free exchange of ideas and accurate portrayals of history—our successes as a species and our failures—and only with the removal of false barriers that classify humans into anything less than a common race, can "Never again" move from an aspirational goal to a blessed fact.

Ted Minkinow
March, 2021

THANKS AND ACKNOWLEDGMENTS

GARE'S WORLD WOULD have remained only in my head had it not been for the love and support from my wife, Nikki. With love and an expert eye, she manages the children, the household, and encourages me to sit with Gare for many hours on end. She is a blessing in many ways…both to me and to Gare, as she occasionally helps dial back some of his transparency when it comes to dude-thinking.

Once more, and for each of my stories, I thank my starting-to-be-longtime friend in the UK. You might think it odd that I only know his online avatar's name, but hey, it's the 21st Century. Thanks, Baccus, for your spot-on insights, keen eye for story, and helpful suggestions, and for your gargantuan drive to help writers such as me. If Gare is better, it's because of you. If not, well, that's what living 2000 years has done to him.

Thanks, too, to my social media adept children. Their generation will run an awesome world.

THANKS FOR READING the second installment of Gare's autobiography. The next two novels in the Waldlust series are completed and will be published soon.

If you'd like updates, please visit **WWW.TEDMINKINOW.COM**.

I would like to hear from you. Comments, feedback, errors you detected, funny stories, sure-fire stock tips.

You can reach me at **TED@TEDMINKINOW.COM**, or visit my Facebook page (**@TEDMINKINOW**) and leave a comment.

www.ingramcontent.com/pod-product-compliance
Lightning Source LLC
Chambersburg PA
CBHW030546200626
46812CB00022BA/1930